Charlie, Love
and Clichés

Charlie, Love and Clichés

Ella Maise

**SIMON &
SCHUSTER**

London · New York · Sydney · Toronto · New Delhi

First published in Great Britain by Simon and Schuster UK, 2023

1 3 5 7 9 10 8 6 4 2

Simon & Schuster UK Ltd
1st Floor
222 Gray's Inn Road
London WC1X 8HB

Simon & Schuster Australia, Sydney
Simon & Schuster India, New Delhi

www.simonandschuster.co.uk
www.simonandschuster.com.au
www.simonandschuster.co.in

A CIP catalogue record for this book
is available from the British Library

Paperback ISBN: 978-1-3985-2164-3
eBook ISBN: 978-1-3985-2165-0

Printed and Bound in the UK using 100% Renewable
Electricity at CPI Group (UK) Ltd

MIX
Paper | Supporting
responsible forestry
FSC® C171272

To dreamers,
Never let anyone dim your light. You *are*
and always will be the main character of your
own story. So ... what are you waiting for? Go
live your life the way you want to live it and
make sure you enjoy every second of it.

1

Charlie

When I woke up that morning, I didn't think I'd be on my hands and knees, crawling around in the office like an idiot – with *balloons* tied to my wrist, no less. Trying my absolute hardest to make sure *he* – or as he was known among my friends, 'the diner guy' – wouldn't see me.

It bears repeating. With *balloons* attached to my wrist. Professional, right? That's me. Charlie Davis.

It was supposed to be a completely ordinary Monday morning. Nothing more, nothing less. Just as ordinary as the rest of my days, weeks and ... well, life.

Wake up.

Make your bed.

Jump in the shower.

Get out of the shower, realize what time it is and then just start running around, as if finding what to wear for work is a completely new concept rather than something you do every day. And then, of course, rush through the New York streets to work at your dad's crisis management company.

At twenty-five years old, my life had already turned into a boring routine. Go to work, come home, sleep and repeat. Maybe throw in an after-work drink with Rick and Gayle once or twice a week, but even that was too far and between.

I was done with it. Truthfully, I'd been done with it for a while, but I was *done* done with it this time around, and I was determined to do something. Moving away from New York had to be the first thing on the list. It would change my life drastically. I knew it. Everybody knew it. Get away, run away – whatever you want to call it – I needed to move. I was hoping that would be the first step to a better life for myself.

Technically there was no list just yet, but when I did finally write down the things that were on my mind, moving would be the top priority. The only problem was I'd talked about it so much and yet had done nothing, so nobody tended to believe me whenever I said I was going to move. But this time I was serious about it. Being unapologetically honest was going to be the next thing on the list. It was going to be a great beginning. A new start to my life.

The only difference in my schedule for this particular Monday was that instead of heading straight to work, I was supposed to drop by the bakery and pick up a cake for Rob, who was having his last day at the office. And, maybe if I had enough time, some fun balloons. For the cake, we collected money at the office, but the balloons were going to be my little touch to put a smile on Rob's face, because he was one of the few people I actually enjoyed being around at the office and he had a ready smile for everyone. Not to mention he often played referee between me and my dad and was almost like an uncle to me.

And how was I supposed to know what a terrible, horrible idea it was to volunteer to do these things when I woke up that morning?

As the rain started to get more determined to soak me through to my bones, I power-walked the last two blocks from the bakery and, ignoring all the honks and shouts that accentuated New York, ran across the street with my huge box of cake, my umbrella which I used to protect the cake – at least I had my priorities straight – and the balloons. The latter were bound to my wrist, bouncing wildly while I was dripping water from head to toe.

As soon as I was inside the building I worked at, I released a long breath. I successfully fought the urge to shake myself like a dog to get rid of all the water clinging to my skin.

I glanced around and headed straight for the empty reception desk. Holding the cake box with one hand, I did my best to wipe the water from my eyes so I could at least avoid bumping into anyone. A quick glance at my fingers confirmed my suspicions about the fate of my mascara, but I still managed to plaster a smile on my face for all the people giving me strange looks.

Losing the smile when I reached my destination, I put the cake on the reception desk. Catching my reflection in the mirror behind it, I let out a loud groan.

'Jesus', I whispered, having a hard time looking away from the mess that was me. Who would've thought putting on mascara just an hour before could become such a colossal mistake?

Shaking my head in wonder, I pushed away all the hair that was stuck to my face and leaned a little further forward to take a good look at myself. Unsurprisingly, the view didn't get any better. *He is going to kill me,* I thought, thinking of my dad. Giving up on my reflection, I started to wring some of the water out of my hair, then started to furiously rub under my eyes to remove the mascara stains, causing the balloons to dance all over, getting the attention of even more people.

Mental note to myself: Never consider buying balloons for an office party again.

My eyes strayed from my reflection and I noticed Kimberly walking into the building. I didn't dare look in her direction again, and for good measure made sure the balloons were providing some cover. If there was someone else other than my dad who I didn't want to see me, it was my 'pretty perfect' sister, who didn't and couldn't do any wrong in the eyes of my family. Also, as an added bonus, I wasn't exactly on speaking terms with her since she'd thought I was a little too friendly with her husband. We didn't talk if it didn't involve work stuff and after the things said between us I was more than okay with that.

I checked the time and realized I was a few minutes late, so picked up my stuff and headed towards the elevators after I made sure Kimberly had gone upstairs already.

A few steps in, I bumped into someone, and if he hadn't caught me, I would've been sprawled across the floor. His hands left my arms and I quickly apologized, but couldn't actually see who I'd walked into thanks to my hands being so full of cake and balloons.

'No trouble', he muttered through the balloons – which I must have hit him in the face with.

The voice that answered was rich, deep and amused, which sounded slightly familiar, but I shrugged it off. The amusement was for the balloons, I was sure. Who would've thought balloons would be such a surprise to people.

I struggled with the damn cheerful things so I could at least offer an apologetic smile, but the guy was already heading towards the reception desk area in a black suit that fitted him and his broad shoulders pretty perfectly – at least from what I could see. The fit was a very important part of wearing a good suit.

After sighing and giving the guy's rear view one last appreciative look, I turned with my balloons and walked to the elevators. Making sure the cake box was hiding my chest area – which showed off my lilac bra thanks to the rain – I held it up with the hand that was attached to the balloons and tried to do something with my hair. To save time, I took out the elastic that was holding up half of my heavy hair and messed it up some to make it look at least a little intentional – as if I'd just rushed out of the shower. A shower I'd taken essentially with my clothes on.

The doors opened and before I could take a step forward there was a rush of people coming out. Holding onto everything tighter and very close to my body, I waited until the stampede ended. When I looked up from behind the balloons the elevator was already full.

I closed my eyes to hold in a few choice words. I was not looking forward to see my dad at all. A little worry creeping in, I did a full one-eighty so I could check the clock behind the reception desk and then started worrying a little more earnestly. It was twenty past nine. I was officially late. Unable to stand in place, I was hitting the call button repeatedly when I heard a ping from one of the elevators behind me. Rushing towards it before it could leave without me, I hit someone in the shoulder with my goddamn balloons, apologized several times without looking, as I was still moving, and managed to make it into the steel box safely at last.

Relieved, I reached to press the button for the 20th floor that would take me up to my dad's firm and my current workplace, Atlas Communications, where I worked as a public relations specialist, but instead grabbed a real, live, big and hairy hand. Several seconds passed as I stood there holding onto a stranger's finger like an idiot. Someone in the elevator cleared their throat and I let go of the hand.

Leaning forward I met my second victim's eyes and made an apologetic face. 'I'm really sorry. I'm having a bad morning,' I whispered and barely heard the murmur of acceptance.

Grateful for the balloons − for the first time − providing me some privacy and hiding my identity, I tried again, and, seeing the numbers from the corner of my eye, this time successfully hit the right button.

Just when I thought things would look up from that point on, I took a step back. The plan had been to close my eyes, lean my head against the back panel, consider my life choices and just breathe for a minute. The plan did not happen. I walked right into a hard chest and one foot.

Two strong hands clamped onto my waist, I squeaked, my eyes popped open and I did a tiny little jump in place.

'Oh!'

It was *not* my day. Not at all.

The big, strong hands left my body just as quickly as they had tightened on my waist to stop me from moving further. I hastily took a step forward, moving back to my original spot.

'Easy there,' my third victim of the day murmured, pretty close to my ear.

It was the same voice from before. From the guy I'd bumped into in the lobby, not the owner of the hairy hand. A shiver worked its way along my spine and my body warmed, my heart rate slowly picking up speed. Not because of the voice or anything, it was being touched after such a long time that had done it. And yeah, maybe the voice too, just a little.

I do not have a thing for voices.

I do not have a thing for thick, smooth voices.

'You've got to be kidding me,' I whispered, then in a louder and much more embarrassed voice apologized to him for the second time in a few minutes.

I hung my head and hit one of the blue balloons with my forehead. 'You were also in the lobby.' *Kill me now.* 'I'm really sorry.'

There was no manly chuckle, but I could hear a smile in his voice. 'No need to apologize. It's been a . . . different morning.'

'How . . . nice of you to say that. Different can be good sometimes. Still, I'm very sorry.'

'No worries.'

I tried to turn around, talk to his face like a normal person this time, but when I finally managed to save myself from the tangle of balloons, the elevator door was closing and there was suddenly no one standing behind me.

I backed into the corner, cautiously this time, and waited and waited. The doors opened and closed a few more times and I belatedly realized that I'd missed my floor.

When I finally made it to the 20th floor and saw Atlas Communications, Crisis Management in the black elegant font on the marble entrance wall, it was 9.26 a.m. and I knew I was dead. Or pretty close to it.

The front desk was empty, but I put the goodbye cake box on it.

'What the hell Charlie?'

Startled, I whipped around and found a surprised Gayle, my friend and one of the two private investigators that worked in our office, staring at me in horror.

'Don't say anything. I know it looks bad,' I said before she could make a comment about my appearance. 'It's just rain, I'll fix it. Did the meeting start?'

Raising her hands, she tried to hide her amused smile. 'I'm sorry, but I have to. You look both cheery and miserable at the same time while doing a pretty good impression of a drowned raccoon.' There was a big smile stretching across her lips, and her eyes lit up with amusement. 'Very professional of you.'

'You happy?'

'Somewhat. Your skirt seems to be doing fine, but you better do something to your shirt. Unless, that is, you're trying a new look with your purple bra.'

'It's lilac. Are we good now?'

'Yes, thank you. And no, the meeting hasn't started yet. Your dad asked four times if you've arrived though.'

Closing my eyes, I took a deep breath and then listened to the balloons bump each other and squeak when I massaged my temple.

'One more question, because I have to ask. Why are there balloons attached to your wrist?'

'Because I was trying to fly away. Can you do me a favour? Please?'

She raised her brows and rolled her lips, trying her hardest to hold her laughter inside.

I sighed. 'Because the guy at the shop needed to go to the storage area to get one of those weight thingies, and I didn't have the time to wait around. That's not important ... you owe me one, Gayle.'

'Before I circle back to me owing you, let me ask it again. Why are there balloons attached to your wrist?'

'Rob, Gayle,' I answered a little exasperated as I moved my arm and watched the balloons almost hit her in the face. 'These are for Rob. To say goodbye and ... look ... happy ... something. Goodbye party. Remember?'

She leaned back with a frown. 'Rob ... oh, that was today? Are you sure?'

I groaned. 'Yes, that was today. You owe me one.'

She crossed her arms against her chest. 'Excuse me?'

I started to try my best to get the balloons off my wrist, but all I was doing was making the band tighter. 'For the blind double date that went horribly wrong.'

'That was almost a month ago. And I was doing you a favour. You haven't touched a guy in ages. Ever since your breakup with the elusive and hater-of-kissing Craig a year ago, you haven't dated at all.'

Six years of long-distance relationship straight down the drain with that one. 'So what if I haven't dated consistently? I saw what's out there and decided I was better off being alone,' I shrugged. 'Perfectly normal behaviour on my part. I'm happy being on my own.'

'Right.'

'I am,' I insisted, frowning at her smiling face. 'I'd rather be alone than fumble with idiots who can't even ... Never mind. That's not important.'

'Yes, let's not fight about this right now. You want me to help you out in the bathroom?'

'Yes, that. Can you get me a pair of scissors so I can cut these off? Plus my spare shirt from my office. It's in the the third drawer of my desk. That's it. Then we'll be even.'

'Oh, shit. Why didn't you say that right away instead of making small talk?'

'I wasn't making small talk. You were ... what? Why?'

'Your dad is coming.'

'Charlie?'

I froze, only for a moment, when I heard his annoyed voice. Leaving the cake box and Gayle where they were, I swiftly walked towards the bathroom with my balloons flying behind me.

'I'll be right there, Dad, go ahead and start without me,' I shouted over my shoulder while I closed the bathroom door behind me.

Letting out a deep, deep breath, I took a moment to gather myself. There was nothing I could do but go out to the meeting in the same shirt and make sure I stood behind everyone. Which wouldn't be the first time.

'This is as good as it's going to get,' I murmured to myself and ran my fingers through my hair as if it were fixing anything. All I had to do was get to my desk, get my shirt and it'd be fine to explain the rest. Then the balloons were filling my vision and I was cursing myself all over again.

After struggling for quite some time to undo the knot, I gave up and decided to go and find a pair of scissors on my own. As I was passing Blair's – our receptionist's – empty desk, I realized everyone was congregating in the middle of the office, standing around the desks and almost creating a human wall between me and whatever they were looking at.

Noticing Gayle standing behind a desk on the far left, I hid my right arm behind my back, hoping to hell it wouldn't be the first thing people noticed, and made my way towards her.

'Good morning, everyone,' my dad said, causing my steps to slow down. Standing on my tiptoes I looked over some shoulders, only to realize there was some sort of meeting or announcement being held right in the middle of the office instead of the meeting room. Ignoring the looks and apologizing to anyone I had to squeeze past, I quickened my steps and finally made it to Gayle's side in one rough piece.

'Why are we not in the meeting room?' I whispered, as my dad kept going on with some sort of speech about Rob. 'Is this the goodbye for Rob? Is the meeting after? Where is he?'

'You're still wearing the shirt and the balloons,' Gayle added unhelpfully. 'You still look pretty by the way. A little ballsy with the bra showing, but still pretty.'

'Bite me.'

Reluctantly, I pinched the shirt and held it away from my body so my bra wouldn't be visible to everyone. Well, to everyone who hadn't seen it already.

'I tried to get you the shirt, but your dad was standing in front of your room so I couldn't go in. And this isn't about the meeting we're gonna have later. This is a completely different thing. Oh, and apparently Rob isn't coming in today.'

How many meetings were we supposed to have exactly?

'Rob isn't coming in?' I asked a tad bit louder than I'd intended and drew my dad's attention.

'Glad to see you could join us, Charlie,' he drawled, earning me snickers from some of my other colleagues. I ignored them as I always did. I was pretty sure my dad couldn't really see me with how I was standing behind Gayle, so I made sure not to make any sudden movements to draw more of his attention.

'I got the cake and balloons for nothing?' I whispered when he started to talk again.

'He'll be in tomorrow. They'll hold.'

I closed my eyes and took a deep breath to calm myself down.

'What are we doing here then?'

'Meeting the new guy to replace Rob,' Gayle answered. 'William Carter.' She gave me another curious look over her shoulder. 'Your dad didn't tell you about it?'

I ignored her question and asked one of my own. 'I didn't think he'd find someone so soon. Who is he?'

She turned to study me. 'Are you kidding me?'

'Ah, not really.'

'You're telling me you don't know who William Carter is?'

It wasn't really a question, it sounded more like a statement to me, so I opted not to answer.

'Clearly I'm missing out.'

'He is really good at what he does. You should've heard of him. He was based in California. But he is our new managing director now.'

'Okay. I guess we'll meet him eventually. Now can you reach into the drawer next to you and see if you can find any scissors? I need to get these off of my wrist before my dad bites my head off in front of everyone.'

'I like the new guy,' she offered, as she opened the drawer.

'Great,' I mumbled, a little mystified at why we were still talking about him. 'Did you find them?'

'There are no scissors here. Let me try the other one. Oh, I might actually want to be on his team. After you see him, I think you'll feel the same way. No scissors here, Charlie.'

'What are you even talking about?' Frowning, I tried to rise on my tiptoes to look around her to see who they were going on about and got my first look at my new colleague's profile.

Eyes downcast, he smiled at something my dad said, which I could not for the life of me hear, shook his offered hand and then turned to face us.

Tall guy, brown messy hair, broad shoulders, and last but not least, if I wasn't mistaken, brown eyes.

It took me a few seconds – or maybe more than a few, I wasn't exactly sure – to recognize him, and the moment I did, a low hum started in my ears, drowning everything and everyone out. I dropped back down to my soles. I must've let out some sort of a sound, because more than a few faces turned my way. I slapped my hand on my mouth to silence any further objections and hit Gayle's head with the balloons.

Suddenly my heart was having some issues. She turned to peer at me, and after blinking at her for a few seconds, I snapped out of it.

'You have to find me scissors,' I whisper-shouted.

'Let me check and see ...'

I clutched at Gayle's arm. 'For the love of God, get me some scissors!'

'I will, I will. Jesus, calm down, your dad won't see you. What's wrong with you today?'

'Nothing is wrong with me,' I whispered harshly. 'I just need the damn scissors to get rid of the balloons.'

She turned to check another desk so I closed my eyes, took a slow and steady breath to centre myself, and then took another peek at William Carter.

Gayle came back with no scissors.

'It's him,' I mouthed to her before she could tell me.

'What?'

'Him. Him. The one standing next to my dad. It's The Guy. I need my scissors,' I whispered more urgently. When she still looked confused, I kept going with the same description.

'*The* guy. Remember? My Guy. Diner Guy. *The* Guy that I can't shut up about that makes you think I'm so naive? William Carter is my guy. *Was* my guy. And I think I hit him with these goddamn balloons twice already this morning. I think. Same suit. Same shoulders. I can't see his ass, but I think it's his ass. Please find me scissors because I don't think I can move.'

'Okay. Did you lose it? Is it the rain? Are you cold or someth— Wait a minute ... The diner catch?' Frowning at me, Gayle shook her head. 'Don't be ridiculous, Charlie. That was years ago.'

'Why would I ...?'

'Charlie?'

My dad's voice boomed in my ears, and my eyes widened in panic. I might have actually whimpered. Before I could consider what I was doing, I turned away, closed my eyes tightly and faced the windows behind us. I felt Gayle try to pull down the balloons to help me out, but when my dad called my name a second time, I ducked. The third time he called my name I was on the floor on my hands and knees ... one second I was there, the next I was completely out of sight.

Like very bad magic. That was me. Bad magic.

2

Charlie

There was a long moment of stunned silence in the office, during which I wasn't quite sure what would be the next best step for me: get up and act like nothing was wrong, or keep going with the hiding game. There was a very good chance, as in 99% chance, that the diner guy, William, wouldn't recognize me, but ... Then my dad called my name again and things became clear pretty fast. Since I was already closer to the floor, I dropped to my hands and knees and started shuffling around people and desks. If some legs had trouble understanding the emergency of the moment and didn't move, I pushed them out of my way. You could say once I started something I committed to it.

'Charlie!' Gayle hissed.

'Where is she?' I heard my dad ask, and I started crawling faster around more desks and legs. I heard some snickers and whispers I chose to ignore, but didn't stop moving.

For obvious reasons, when you have ten very colourful balloons attached to your wrist flying around, trying to hide isn't really the best option or the smartest idea.

Was I being childish?

Very.

Was I proud of that?

Not at all.

Did I want William to see me in the state I was in after I had such a big crush that even after years had passed, every now and then I still thought about him?

Nope. I didn't think so.

Before I could get to safety, which was anywhere *but* the office at that moment, people parted and my dad's shiny shoes came into view right in front of me. There was no escape whatsoever.

My eyes slowly travelled up.

'My office. Now, Charlie.'

I got up on my own – my face flushed, heart racing, stupid balloons bumping into each other – and moved my hands over my skirt to clean it, as if it would help out my situation. 'Dad, I just need to change befo—'

'Now!' he snapped, and I winced. Turning his back to me, he walked away.

Closing my eyes, I let out a long breath. I knew everyone was staring at me and talking about me, but I was too far gone to care. I was dreading going to his office, but I was dreading coming face to face with *him* even more, so I avoided glancing back to where he had been standing with my dad. I dusted my knees and rubbed on my palms to ease the sting of the carpeted floor. Next thing I knew, Gayle was standing next to me and cutting me free from the balloons.

'I'll take these to the kitchen for you,' she said quietly as I avoided her soft gaze.

'Thanks,' I muttered.

She gave me a small smile and attempted to walk away, but I grabbed her arm.

'Where is he?' I whispered a little desperately. Afraid to look behind me.

She frowned. 'Who? Your dad? He is talking to . . .'

'No. The guy. The new guy.'

'Your dad is talking to "the new guy", as you put it and, oh wait . . .'

Please, oh god, please don't let them come here.

Leaning to my right, she looked over my shoulder. 'Your dad is showing him his new office. Didn't you listen to anything your dad was saying in the meeting?'

I listened to him talk most of the day. Who would blame me if I decided to tune him out every now and then. 'Let's assume I didn't. Fill me in, please.'

Her gaze moved from mine to someone behind me and her frown deepened. 'You're in for a surprise then. You're sure that's the guy you told us about from years ago?'

'Warm brown eyes, slightly curly hair where the ends falls to his forehead just a little. It's messy and not perfect but somehow is really perfect to the point that it makes your hands itch to touch it. And the smile. Also the smile is still the same. A few days' worth of stubble is pretty much the same as well. Yes, I'm pretty sure that's him. Why am I in for a surprise?'

'Huh,' she grunted.

'What?' I asked perplexed.

'Nothing.' She shook her head and met my eyes, a smile curving her lips. 'I like him. For you, I mean.'

'For me?' I sputtered, mortified. 'He is not . . . I'm not still into . . . I only kept talking about him because he was just an example of what I would want in a guy, I don't even remember that much about . . .'

'Charlie!' my dad shouted, and I jumped a little.

'Go,' Gayle urged, pushing me towards my dad's office. 'Your guy just closed his door, you're safe.'

Swallowing the lump in my throat, I turned around, but paused. 'He isn't my guy. Don't call him that,' I announced very quietly to Gayle, then headed straight to my dad. When I was passing by William's office, I made sure to quicken my steps and keep my head down. By the time I reached my dad's door, I was already feeling a little lightheaded and a lot confused.

'Close the door,' he barked the second I stepped in.

Accepting my fate, I sat down on one of the comfy chairs in front of him, my back to the entire office.

'Care to explain yourself?' he started.

Eager to do exactly that, I leaned forward in my seat. When his eyes dropped to my shirt and hardened before he met my gaze again, I swallowed. I had forgotten about my see-through shirt. 'It's raining, Dad,' I explained quietly. Hoping he wouldn't notice, I pinched the shirt's material between my fingers and pulled it away from my skin.

He raised one of his eyebrows, his face completely stoic. 'You've never heard of an umbrella?'

'I was trying to . . . the cake box, I was trying to save the cake,' I finished quickly, knowing that he didn't care one bit.

His stare would've made someone else crumble in front of him, but I was quite used to that disappointed look in his eyes.

After one last look at the state I was in, he shook his head as if I were a complete lost cause he didn't know what to do with and turned his focus to his laptop. He didn't say it out loud, but I could still hear the words he had already voiced more than a few times on different occasions.

Why is she not better than this . . . ?

Or, one of my other favourites . . .

How can my kid be like this . . . ?

'You're smart enough to keep a change of clothes here, so go and change immediately.'

Hoping we were done, I kept my face expressionless and held back my tongue from saying that was exactly what I was trying to do earlier.

'After you're done, go to William Carter's office. He wants to talk to his team alone.'

My heart lurched in my chest. 'He wants to talk to me?' I squeaked out.

My dad gave me a brief glance.

'I said his team. Not just you. If you had listened in the meeting you'd have more information. You're in his team now, I don't want you to handle clients on your own anymore.'

At a loss for words, I just sat there. Eventually, he looked up and met my gaze. 'Anything you want to say?'

Oh, where should I start, Dad?

'Did you say that in front of everyone?'

He let out a short, sharp sigh as if talking to me alone was too much work for him. 'Say what, Charlie?'

'That you didn't want me to handle clients alone anymore?'

'Yes, why?' His focus went back to his laptop screen again as if it weren't important that he'd just broken my heart a little.

'Did I do something wrong, dad?' I could feel the heat rushing to my cheeks. As much as we had our problems, I was still trying to make sure I worked hard and did my job better than anyone so he'd be proud of me. 'Did one of the clients complain?'

He dismissed my questions with a wave of his hand. 'There will be some changes all around so don't be difficult about it. I wanted to talk more about it in the meeting, but you and your antics got in the way.'

My shoulders sagged. 'Who else is in this team?' I asked, feeling defeated. 'Kimberly?'

'Your sister has her hands full already. You'll find out who you'll be working with when you get there. Make sure you change before you join them. I don't want William's first impression of my daughter to be this.'

I knew when I was being dismissed, but I wasn't done yet.

'Can I ask the reason for this specific change? I have my hands full with clients as well.'

Sighing yet again, he leaned back in his seat and studied me. 'You're not working as hard as your sister. And I . . .'

Shocked, I rose from my seat. 'I'm not working as hard as Kimberly? Dad, I'm doing more than my share of work. I'm working longer hours than her. Forget about that, I'm taking on some of her work as well. I barely have any life ...'

'Charlie, do we have to do this now? Please. I have a meeting to prepare for. This is my decision and it's final.'

I squeezed my hands into fists and forced myself to nod. 'What about the clients I'm working with now? Who is going to take them? I've committed hours on ...'

He rubbed the bridge of his nose and cut me off. 'Later, Charlie. We'll talk later. I have work to do. Tell your sister to drop by my office on your way. Unlike you, she is working hard to get somewhere.'

Feeling the familiar annoyance rise in me, I put one step in front of the other and left his room without uttering another word. I had to remind myself how much I otherwise loved my job and my family. Because I was a rebel, I didn't knock on Kimberly's office since we were barely on speaking terms. Keeping my eyes down, I made it to my small office space, walked to my desk and opened the last drawer to take out my extra shirt, only to notice that I didn't have an extra shirt. Only a graphic tee-shirt that had Jack and Rose from *Titanic* on the front. A very fitting tee-shirt for a very tragic day. I was definitely sinking.

Without any other options, I held my chin high – as much as I could – avoided everyone's curious and mocking eyes and headed back to the bathroom to change.

A few minutes later I was wearing my tee-shirt tucked into my black pencil skirt. In my opinion, I actually looked okay – maybe not that professional, but not that bad either. But also, because of whose office I was about to walk into, I couldn't have looked any worse.

I reached William's door and started to pace right to the side of it, which, with the limited space I had from his door to the wall (two steps) wasn't very much of an impressive pacing. That is when Rick showed up and cracked open the door I was very carefully staying away from, gesturing for me to go ahead.

Chivalry. Completely overrated at times.

I heard murmurs from inside, which meant the meeting had already begun. Second one I was going to be late to in a day. A first for me.

Rick and I stared at each other for a long moment, then he broke into a grin. 'Are you having a pleasant day then?' he asked and let the door silently close on its own with us still standing on the wrong side.

'Very,' I agreed and forced my lips to form a smile, but I could tell from his face it didn't look quite right.

He crossed his arms against his chest and leaned against the wall. Rick was one of the good guys, so while I was happy to realize that we would be in the same team (whatever that meant), I was still too nervous to just follow him in there.

'I think I'll join you in a second,' I announced when it didn't look like he would go away. 'You can go ahead. I'm waiting for a phone call, actually.'

'Phone call or some more pacing to do?' he asked, his smile still going on strong.

'Walking is very healthy.'

'I agree. Hence the pacing, I'm guessing.'

His smile got bigger.

Just when I was thinking of something clever to say, the door I was successfully avoiding opened and William peeked his head outside.

Panicking, I dropped to one knee.

I was wearing stilettos. No shoe laces or anything like it in sight.

'Uh,' William started, and I closed my eyes. He must have thought I was an idiot. I certainly did. 'You two must be the last ones in my team, I believe. Why don't you join us so we can get started. I have a few things I need to go over with all of you before you can get back to your day.'

'We'll be right there,' Rick said, at the same time as I mumbled something in a thicker voice than my own, as if that would certainly make me unrecognizable.

When I couldn't see William's black shoes in my eyesight any-more, I slowly rose from my awkward crouch, coming face to face with Rick. He had a shit-eating grin and there was nothing I could say to save face.

'Why do I have a feeling this is going to be loads of fun?' he asked in a low voice as he opened the door for us again.

'Shut up,' I hissed and forced him to go ahead of me while I made sure the door was securely closed behind us.

My heart beating a mile a minute, I closed my eyes and took a deep breath.

What if he recognized me?

What if he had already recognized me?

Was I supposed to say something if he hadn't recognized me?

What was I supposed to say if he *had* recognized me?

What if he didn't recognize me whatsoever?

Ouch.

But maybe not so ouch?

Maybe I should or could say . . . *Hello! How have you been? What a surprise right? The world is so small and you didn't break my heart a little bit at all! I'm so excited to be working with you.*

As more questions assaulted me, I kept my eyes averted from the big desk where I could see him half-sitting, legs crossed, arms crossed, relaxed. I quickly took a look around the room. With him we were five people in total.

Stan, Trisha, Rick, William and me.

William and me.

In the same room after so many years.

I only let that sink in for a second, then I took two steps to my left and chose to stand slightly behind Trisha and Stan. As far away as possible from a still grinning Rick, and a William who was looking at some papers on his desk. With how jittery I felt, I was ready to jump out of my skin.

'Okay. I believe I'll have some chairs later today so I'm sorry for having this meeting standing. Now that we're all here, let's get started. Do you all have clients you're working with right now? And how many?'

'I'm working with one. With two other colleagues, that is,' Rick piped up.

'Actually, Stan and I were about to have a meeting with a potential client today.' Trisha glanced at Stan, then addressed William. 'Also, just in case you weren't told, most of us work in teams. It's very rare that only one person will handle the client.'

William asked Trisha another question, but I didn't hear a single word of it. *I* was busy feeling like that kid who was afraid the maths teacher was going to meet her eyes and ask her something from the multiplication table on the very first day at school. And as soon as they stopped talking, it was going to be my turn to give him an answer. Which meant I was gonna have to come out of my not-so-clever hiding spot behind Stan's back.

While William asked Rick a question, Stan moved. Frowning, I moved with him.

Looking back at me over his shoulder, he frowned too. 'What are you doing?'

'Nothing. Why?' I asked, looking just as puzzled as him. When he didn't face forward again, I improvised and swiped my hand over his shoulder a few times. 'Cat hair,' I muttered.

He didn't own a cat.

His frown got deeper, but he turned away.

I sighed.

'Charlie, right? How about you?' William asked and my heart skipped a beat. The desire to flee was real, but I stood still. I'd faced scarier things than William Carter, I was sure.

I cleared my throat and chanced a peek his way. When I saw that he was reaching for some papers on his desk, I quickly answered. 'Working with three different teams and I have three clients on my own as well.'

'Three? Any reason for that?' he asked as he reached for a pen this time, still not glancing my way.

With my throat feeling so dry, I had to force out the words. 'A reason for what?'

Then he met my gaze over Stan's shoulder, and I didn't know what to do. A slow heat flooded my chest and my heart went into a frantic beat. Also nausea ... that was a problem as well, but I didn't think I'd drop to a new level of low and puke in front of him. Yet, while *I* was feeling all kinds of crazy things all at once, I didn't see even a hint of recognition in his eyes. I forced myself to relax a little.

'Any reason why you're handling so many clients on your own?'

His voice was so deep and I couldn't quite be sure if it was that smooth all those years ago when we had spent hours talking about anything and everything. His voice had been one of the things that made him so irresistible for me back then. Deep and confident. And when he talked he always used to look into your eyes, catching you with more than just his words. Like he cared about you. And the way he talked, the way he just ... talked.

Suddenly it was weird that I knew and remembered a lot of things about him, about his life. Uncomfortable even. I felt like a stranger spying into someone else's world. Privy to their private thoughts.

Like his siblings, and his mom. I even knew about them. How one of his sisters had just gotten married back then and four months in they were already expecting. How their family had struggled when they lost their father to colon cancer when William was only fourteen. How his mom stayed awake some nights worrying about her other daughter who had gone through a rough breakup with an abusive boyfriend, so when William dropped by or stayed over, he always made her her favourite hot cocoa and sat with her in silence into the night. How he knew she had sacrificed a lot of things just so her kids could have a chance at a good life and how hard he worked so he could make sure she was proud of him. How he worked as a delivery guy for a pizzeria during college so he could help out his mom in small ways even though she didn't want his help. And how excited he was to become an uncle and was secretly hoping it was a girl. The life he had hoped to create for himself. I knew details about his world that it seemed like he had only shared with me. A stranger he had met one late night in a forgotten diner.

Me. A complete stranger who had the biggest crush after only a week of talking to him. And now he was here, right in front of me.

'Yes?' he asked, and I realized I'd been just staring at him and now everyone was looking at me.

My voice was a little scratchy when I finally spoke. 'One of them insists on me being their only contact. She doesn't like to let people in on her personal life. The other two . . . I don't have a good answer, my dad, sorry Douglas . . . Mr Davis, I mean . . . wanted me to take them.'

He nodded and broke our brief eye contact to look at the papers in his hand again. 'I need to take a look at all your assignments and determine if there should be changes made. If it's not a crisis situation that requires our involvement, we'll see if you can be spared or not.'

He looked up and met everyone's curious gazes one by one. I took half a step to my left to stand slightly behind Stan again so he could only see a quarter of me. 'After those assignments are done, you'll only work on this team. And don't worry, I'm planning on keeping us busy.'

He straightened up from his desk and walked to stand behind it.

'We'll be spending a lot of time together in the upcoming days, so we might as well get to know each other a little better. If it's all right with you, I'd like to take you all out to lunch and go over a few things while we're at it.'

I could feel the energy change in the room. Rick rubbed his

hands together, a new gleam in his eyes. 'We're taking on a new case, aren't we?' He lived for the rush of the job. 'A big one from the sound of it.'

There was a small, knowing smile on William's lips when he met Rick's gaze. 'I have to talk to the client first to determine whether or not I'm willing to work with him on this, but yes, there is a possibility.'

'A possibility?' Trisha asked with a frown. 'Are we taking him on, or not?'

'We'll talk more at lunch, but ... I have a different work ethic than some others in our field. You'll see this for yourselves in time, but I only agree to work with a client if I believe them and actually think I can help. I don't lie to get out of a tough situation and I'm definitely not going to lie for someone I don't know just to make sure they look good in the public eye. Our reputation is everything in our business, and I don't make sacrifices on this.'

How could someone feel proud of a stranger they didn't quite know anymore?

I forgot that I was nervous about him recognizing me and outright smiled as I studied him.

He hadn't changed all that much in the last six years, yet he looked somehow different to me. His hair was a bit shorter – which I kinda liked, but it was still perfectly messy – the kind of hair that made you want to run your fingers through it. His features looked more defined, his jaw stronger and sharper somehow, but his eyes were the same – that warm and inviting brown. His body looked more filled out, nothing too bulky, but lean and muscular, more so than it had been. Or maybe it was just the suit that was affecting me. The suit and the strong shoulders. There was just something about William Carter that had caught my attention all those years ago, and that same something was still there, but it was more amped up somehow.

And this was a whole new side of him I'd never known about.

I'd never heard him talk about work, since when we met he was just about to graduate. I had absolutely no idea that he was in the same field as my dad. And it made me feel nervous that I was going to work with him.

William looked down at his watch. 'I have a meeting with Mr Ashton at 11 a.m. so we'll know what the situation is by lunch. Then I'll share the details and we can go from there.'

Since at that point I was more than sure that he had no idea who I was, I felt it'd be okay for me to speak up.

'Is my dad, I mean is Mr Davis okay with this?'

Our eyes met for the second time and I swallowed, forcing myself to grow a pair and keep eye contact. It might as well have been just the two of us in the room.

'With?'

'With you, us, rejecting potential clients.' I couldn't see my dad allowing that to happen.

He smiled and it was so beautiful and unexpected that I almost forgot myself and smiled back at him.

'He wanted me enough to overlook that . . . what had he called it? . . . oh, yes, that failing of mine. I'm really good at what I do, Miss Davis. Since we're getting to know each other, I feel okay to share this. I moved back to New York from California only a month ago. I was supposed to teach a class at Colombia and take a little break from the job, but Mr Davis convinced me to do otherwise.'

'Sounds like Mr Davis,' Rick said. And he was right, that sounded like my dad. He was good at convincing people to do things they weren't particularly planning to do. Which was one of the reasons he had become one of the best in the industry.

'Okay. If that's all for now, I'd like to take some time to go over your workload, take the meeting with Mr Ashton and then meet for lunch. Everyone good with the plan?'

We all nodded and gave our approval.

Before I could react or leave, Stan, in his hurry to get back to his work, suddenly turned and walked right into me, causing me to lose my balance and bump my hip hard against the edge of the low bookcase. A few books tumbled down to the floor, breaking the silence.

'Shit,' I cursed, frowning and rubbing my hip. My eyes were already watering from the sharp pain.

Stan helped me straighten up. 'You good?'

Neither Stan nor Trisha were close friends of mine, but we were at least friendly in a professional way.

'Yeah,' I replied. In the time it took me to lean down and pick up the books to place them back where they belonged, Stan and Trisha had already left the room.

Rick waited next to me.

'Turn around so I can look.'

Without thinking, I turned and basically offered my ass to him. Looking over my shoulder, I tried to see what he was looking at. 'Is my skirt okay? Did it rip or something?'

'It'll live.' His hand patted my hip twice in a friendly manner, then he put his hand on the small of my back to guide me out.

I heard someone clear their throat.

William . . . Mr Carter – what was I even supposed to call him – didn't look all that impressed. He opened his mouth to speak, god knows to say what, but I wasn't about to give him the chance.

'Welcome to Atlas Communications, Mr Carter. I'm not with Rick. He is married. I love his wife, she is awesome. Have a good day,' I tossed my hair over my shoulder and quickly escaped from the scene, seeking refuge in my office.

I was an idiot.

A complete idiot.

3

William

My first day at Atlas Communications had been a long one. A productive one, yes, but long nonetheless. The online meeting I had with Michael Ashton before lunch about his electric cars had gone well and, from everything he had told me, we had our work cut out. We had to cut the lunch meeting short, but it too had gone well, and after I got to know everyone a little bit more I was feeling good about the core crisis management team Douglas had handpicked for me.

As the clock hit 7.00 p.m. I sat behind my desk, and while my laptop started up, I took everything in. I could see everyone else who was working late through the glass walls. Since this was a small company, Douglas employed roughly fifty people. There were only around ten or fifteen people left working. You can't exactly predict when a crisis situation will arise, so my job rarely had set hours.

Douglas's assistant, Wilma, was typing away at her computer in front of his office, which was to the right of my room.

Dean, one of the PR specialists working with Douglas's daughter Kimberly, if I was remembering correctly, was talking to her in front of her room, directly across from me.

While the two big conference/meeting rooms were on the

21st floor with a few private spaces for clients to occupy if they needed, our floor housed all the staff offices. Both the east and west sides of the 20th floor were reserved for the personal offices, with two smaller conference rooms that were to be used for the team meetings.

There was a group of three people, huddled together and working on one of the long rectangular desks situated in the middle of the floor that was used as a shared working space. I could almost hear their raised voices as they heatedly argued about something they were working on. I remembered being introduced to the guy that was scowling at the other two, but for the life of me I couldn't remember his name. I'd relearn the next day.

Another duo was standing in front of the office kitchen chatting. There were a few more people scattered around working in their own offices.

Laughter rang out, and I traced the sharp sound to its source: Kimberly. She specialized in risk management and brand consulting, which meant focusing on preventing a crisis by reviewing a company and all its facets, which was quite different from what I did. That said, if I'd read her correctly when Douglas had introduced us, she didn't seem happy about welcoming me to the firm as the new crisis management director. As she headed towards the elevators with Dean she glanced my way and for a brief moment our gazes met. She inclined her head slightly, then continued towards the elevators. Since my role in the firm was quite different from hers, I didn't understand her thinly veiled hostility towards me, but we'd see how things would unfold in time.

A few seconds later, Douglas Davis knocked on my door and let himself in.

'You're still here?'

I relaxed into my seat. 'Just going over a few things to get ready for tomorrow. I'll be leaving soon.'

He nodded approvingly. 'I'd say don't work yourself too hard on the first day, but I have a feeling you won't listen. You sure you're not interested in dinner at my house?'

'Thank you for the offer, Mr Davis, but not tonight.'

'Next week, then.'

'Next week.'

'Call me Douglas, William. I've been meaning to ask, how did the move go? Any problems with the flat that I need to be aware of?'

'Without a hitch. Thank you for offering the place on such short notice.'

'Don't mention it. After the last tenants I'd decided to do some renovation on it, so it was already empty.'

'Good timing on my part then.'

He tapped the glass with his knuckles once and looked over his shoulder when he heard a door close. 'I'll leave you to it. You won't regret deciding to work with us, William. We'll do great things together. See you tomorrow.'

I smiled back at him. 'Bright and early.'

As soon as their boss left, the group of three I'd been watching earlier rose from their seats and dispersed to different parts of the office, likely to gather their things and leave. In mere minutes, there were only a few stragglers left behind, a phone or two ringing every now and then.

I clicked on the light on my desk, picked up the Ashton folder and went through everything again to get ready for tomorrow when he'd fly in to New York to meet the team. By the time I lifted my head, an hour and a half had passed and the blue sky behind me no longer carried its light hue.

I moved my head from side to side, letting the muscles stretch to loosen the tension I'd been feeling these last few hours, and noticed the cleaning crew parking their equipment in front of Douglas's office. My eyes then landed on one specific employee who was also working late hours.

Contemplating for a few more minutes on how I should handle this unexpected situation – as I'd done most of the day, if I was being honest – I got up from my seat, walked around my desk and came to a firm decision by the time it took me to get to the door and open it.

Pushing my hands into my pockets, I watched her from my spot by the door. She was only a few feet away, and after a few more minutes she wrapped up her phone call. With her laptop in front of her, she was seated at one of the long desks in the shared working space, closer to the elevators. I wasn't near enough to follow her conversation smoothly, but I'd heard enough to put two and two together and waited for her to finish her call with the B-list celebrity I knew she was working with.

I took her in. Something I had done more than just once in the last few hours.

Charlie Davis.

One of my new – for lack of a better word – teammates who also happened to be Douglas's other daughter.

'Jesus,' she growled loudly.

Then she dropped the phone onto the desk and rested her forehead in her hands. I couldn't see her expression since I could only watch her profile, but she looked tired. Tired and done with the day. Which was understandable since she'd spent most of her time either actively trying to stay away from me or trying her very best to hide in plain sight.

'She's giving you trouble, isn't she?' I asked.

Her head snapped up, eyes rounding as she met my gaze. She muttered something I couldn't quite hear and looked up at the ceiling.

'Excuse me?' I asked.

She swivelled in her chair to face me. 'You scared me, Wil . . . Mr Carter!'

'William is enough, and I apologize. I didn't mean to.'

'I didn't think there was anyone else left here!' she lied, still talking unnecessarily loudly. I'd caught her more than a few times giving my office sideways glances and quickly looking away. She knew I was here. Once or twice I even caught her suddenly power-walking when she was passing my office or noticing my eyes on her. Though I was pretty sure she thought she was being discreet.

'How about instead of shouting across the room, you come to my office so we can have a quick talk and let other people work?' I asked in a normal voice.

Some colour rushed into her cheeks as she noticed the cleaning crew and the few other employees now staring at us. If I was being honest, I half-expected her to get up and run straight to the elevators. It was a toss-up after how our morning had started.

'I should call Laurel back and smooth things out. She is not good with change. Then I have to do ... the other things.'

'The other things. Like what?'

'Like ... other things that you don't know about, Mr Carter.'

'Just William.'

I'd repeated the same line close to ten times since we had sat down for the lunch meeting. While the others had no problem calling me by my name, every time Charlie Davis had to speak directly to me, she couldn't quite decide which one to go for. If she called me William once, she called me Mr Carter five times.

I wasn't sure whether I should end her misery or let it go on for a little longer, since it was undeniably fun for me.

'Let's call her together and see how that goes. If she is adamant about working with you that much, we'll handle her account together,' I offered with a straight face.

One of the guys from the cleaning crew started up a loud vacuum, causing me to have trouble hearing her answer.

'Ah, teamwork ...' she started, then began yelling '... isn't really required with this one. I can handle it myself.'

'I'm sure you can, but ...' I started shouting, but then stopped, sighed and rubbed my face. Now *I* was starting to raise my voice to be heard over the racket. 'Can we talk about this in here, please? Or your office if you'd prefer that.'

Her face fell. 'I'm going to leave soon.'

Jesus. She made me feel like a school principal.

'That's okay, this won't take long.'

She slowly pushed her chair back and rose, then rifled through the papers on the desk, picked up her phone and looked around as if she was hoping to find something to distract herself so she could get far away from me.

It took her some time to make it to my room. After she grabbed her laptop and everything else, she started looking over her shoulder. I assumed she was looking for an easy out.

She might have sent longing looks towards her own office and the elevators, but she still walked through my open door. I called it a win. I closed it behind her and she just stood in the middle, hugging some papers, her laptop and her phone to her chest, ready to bolt at any moment.

Unsure how I was going to keep a straight face in front of her misery, I sat down in one of the chairs in front of my desk and gestured for her to do the same. 'Please.'

'I'm okay,' she responded, but leaned down to drop the papers and the laptop to the seat instead. 'I'll call Laurel so we can deal with that. I already explained that there are some changes going on in the company. If you could just explain to her that I won't be available for . . .'

Eyes on her phone, her fingers moved over the screen.

'I'll call her in a second,' I interrupted her. 'First I'd like to talk about something else.'

Her fingers stopped moving and she slowly lifted her head up to meet my gaze.

'Something else? Like?'

'Is there a reason you're trying to avoid me? Did I perhaps do something to you?'

'Ah . . . I . . . I wasn't trying to avoid you. I just have a lot of things I need to get through and I have to get back home and . . .'

'If you don't want to work with me, we can talk to Douglas and maybe find a different solution. I don't work well when there is animosity inside my team.'

'Animosity? I ...' She opened her mouth and then closed it. Started to say something, but gave up on that as well. Since she didn't know how to respond I thought I'd end her suffering.

'You look good, Charlie,' I said, unable to hold back my smile any longer. 'Great actually. You haven't changed at all.'

Which was almost true. She looked the same as she did six years ago, but also not quite, if that made sense. All those years had been kind to her. More than kind actually.

She had gained a few pounds and it had obviously worked in her favour. The black skirt did a great job at hugging her new-to-me curves, the tee-shirt she had on was a far cry from professional, yet she still looked great in it, which was why I tried to avoid looking at that specific area for too long. She shifted in place, so I quit studying her from head to toe and forced my eyes up and away from the length of her body. When I reached her eyes, I found her looking at me with a funny and slightly hopeful expression.

'I look ... You remember me?' she breathed out quietly.

I laughed. 'Of course. I still haven't met any other girl named Charlie since you.'

A big smile lit up her face and she sat down on the chair she'd refused just moments ago. Right on the papers and the laptop. Her smile dimmed, her cheeks colouring a little. She lifted one side of her hip and pulled on the items, placing them in her lap instead. 'Sorry.'

I shook my head, still smiling. 'It's been what? Six years, *Hazel*?'

The smile came back in full force and she leaned forward in her seat. 'You called me Hazel? I called you *the diner guy*!'

She laughed and I couldn't help it, I laughed back, my eyes on her smiling hazel ones.

'You didn't say anything,' she continued. 'I was almost having a nervous breakdown this morning trying to stay away from you.'

'I noticed,' I admitted. 'I didn't recognize you when you were crawling around with the balloons or when you crashed into me in the lobby or the elevator for that matter . . .'

She scrunched up her nose. 'Don't remind me, please.'

'I only recognized you when you came into my office for the meeting. Though I have to give it to you, you did try your best to hide behind Stan.'

Groaning, she buried her face in her hands.

'It was that obvious, huh?'

'Unfortunately.' She would be hard to ignore wherever she went. 'Then there was the lunch meeting.'

She lifted her hand. 'Okay, you can stop there. Let's never talk about the lunch meeting. I was nervous. That's not how I normally act. I didn't know whether I should tell you I knew you or not. Did you see the looks Stan gave me?' She glanced towards the ceiling and groaned again. 'He thinks I've lost it.'

I leaned back in my seat. 'I'm afraid he does. And you didn't help the situation.' There was a moment of silence where she avoided my eyes. 'Why didn't you say something?' I asked.

'Because you clearly didn't recognize me – at least that's what I thought – and that kinda hurt a little if I'm being honest. I know we just talked to each other for one week, but it was kind of . . . a big week to me . . . does that make sense? Well, maybe not a big week, but let's say it left an impression on me.'

I noticed her fingers tightening around the papers and the laptop: she was still nervous around me, and probably nervous about admitting that the week we met was important for her.

And what she said made sense because I'd felt the same.

'It does,' I admitted. I kept my eyes on her as she quietly released a long breath. I gave her a small smile. 'It left an impression on me, too, Charlie.' How could it have not.

'We pretty much showed up at the same diner for a week and bumped into each other day after day. That doesn't happen all that very often, does it? At least to me. It doesn't make much sense I know, but I felt this weird connection. At least that's what I thought back then.' She winced a little as if she was already regretting sharing all of this. 'I probably shouldn't tell you this.'

I shook my head. 'No, you can. You should.'

She grimaced a little, but kept going. 'To go back to my explanation: I told you so many things about myself and just things in general. So what if I told you that we'd met before in front of everyone and you still couldn't remember me? I'd rather die, which is too dramatic, I know, but it's just an expression. Basically, too much anxiety all around. So I thought I should just forget about the whole thing and be normal – which somehow didn't work in my favour at all. And now I'm just blabbering. I'll shut up.'

'Don't shut up. Perhaps it didn't work out in your favour because you acted the opposite of normal?'

'I did do that,' she admitted then smiled at me. 'Enough about my stupidity and weirdness. Let's pretend I acted a like normal human being the entire day. Why didn't *you* tell me anything then?'

'I was planning to, I tried for the entire day to catch you alone just so I could tell you, but you are kind of slippery.'

She gave me a mischievous smile while biting her lip. 'I was busy.'

I nodded. 'Right. You're gonna stick to that, I see.'

'Anyway, how are you?' She changed the subject. 'How have you been these last six years?'

Since she didn't say it out loud, I decided to ignore the elephant in the room about why those diner meetings had ended so abruptly. Instead, I leaned forward and smiled at her.

'I've been fine. I was working in California. Took my first job there actually. Got married. Got . . .'

'Oh, congratulations,' she interrupted before I could finish.

'Thanks. Got divorced.'

'Oh no . . .' She winced again. 'I'm sorry.'

'Nothing to be sorry for. Didn't work out, that's all. It's been a little over six months since we signed the papers. Just recently decided to come back here and teach at Colombia for a little while, but obviously changed my mind about that. I also want to be close to my family after being away for six years.'

'Does your family still live here? Was it ... Montauk? Do I remember correct?'

'Yes they still live in Montauk. Did you ever end up visiting? I remember you wanted to after you saw all the photos.'

She shook her head with a rueful smile. 'Still haven't. But they're all good? I think your sister was having a rough pregnancy, right?'

'You remember.'

'Of course I do.'

There was a whole lot of smiling going on, on both of our faces.

'She had a healthy baby girl, who has each and every one of us dancing to her tune. She is the best.'

She bit her lip, hesitating. 'And you're an uncle. You were really excited about that, I think.'

She knew how excited I'd been – she'd listened to me talk about it for hours.

'I'm the best uncle in the whole wide world.'

She laughed out loud. 'You heard that from the source, I think.'

I heard more people leaving the office as their voices slowly faded. I watched as Charlie's eyes tracked people over my shoulder then let her gaze connect with mine again. I relaxed further back into my seat. 'Every time we talk on the phone she reminds me. Then she gives me a list of things she wants me to bring her. She is very specific and bossy for a six-year-old, too. You'd be surprised what a hard job it is to be her uncle.'

'I'd believe you. She sounds adorable. Do you have kids of your own?' she asked hesitantly.

'No. What about you?'

She offered a small and shy smile as she shook her head. 'Not married. And no kids.'

'You did want kids though, right? That's what I remember. I think you wanted two.'

'You do remember.' She paused. 'Yes, I do want two kids. One or two, I'll take either.'

'I think I remember pretty much everything we talked about as if it were just yesterday. Strangely enough.'

'Kinda strange, maybe. A little.'

'You think so? I remember because it was important to me.'

She narrowed her eyes a little, thinking. 'I'm curious, what kind of things do you remember exactly?'

'I remember you hated people who talked loudly and disrespected our favourite seventy-year-old waitress. Doris, was that her name?'

She glanced at the floor for a second, then back to me. 'Yes! Doris – I remember her. She was the sweetest.'

'She was. Then I remember how your cheeks would hurt from smiling at me and you'd have to hold your cheeks to relax a little. And you'd avoid my gaze when I complimented you.' This time, listening to me, she didn't avoid my gaze. She was fully interested in hearing what I was saying. I found myself wanting to keep going. 'I remember talking about your mom who left when you were little. Then I remember coming to the diner before you and you coming in and your eyes searching the place. Then you'd see me and just smile. And I remember both of us asking whoever was there first: "Is this seat taken?" As if that was our keyword. I remember staying and talking to you till closing time.'

We stared at each other for a long while. Suddenly the tension in the room thick.

'I seem to remember a lot of things,' I admitted out loud. Both to her and myself. And I remembered more.

'I guess we both do.'

Then there was a moment of silence; she avoided my eyes and looked over my shoulder again. 'I think pretty much everyone left,' she said and slid forward in her seat a little. 'I don't want to hold you. Ah, I mean hold you up, not hug you or anything.'

'You're not holding me up, Charlie. How have you been? How is everything?'

'Not much has changed really,' she started and rose up so I slowly got up to my feet as well. Maybe I was the one who was holding her when she had plans.

'Still single,' she continued. I thought I saw her wince a little, but then she quickly covered it up with a smile. 'Been in the same city since you last saw me. And . . . nothing new really. Nothing too exciting at least. I do date of course, but yeah. Nothing serious. Had a long-distance relationship for a few years, but it didn't work out. And considering it's been six years, the fact that nothing new has happened to me is slightly pathetic, so on that note I think I'll leave.'

'Charlie,' I started and waited until she looked at me. 'You're not pathetic. I'm sure a lot of things happened in your life. I know you had a million things you wanted to do.'

'Plans change, unfortunately.' Avoiding my eyes, she took a few steps forward, then spun around and walked backwards until she reached the door. 'Is it okay if we call Laurel tomorrow? She'll feel like we're ganging up on her after my call.'

'You know your clients best. If you say she'll react better after cooling off for a little, we'll do that.'

Her hand reached for the doorknob behind her, and she squeezed herself in through the little opening she created.

As I watched her trying to get away from me – again – I felt something in my chest that I hadn't felt in a long while, but I wasn't that surprised. If I thought back on it, Charlie Davis had had that same effect on me six years ago as well – and I remember being startled by it back then. Startled by the fact that I'd ended up at that diner at the same time, every single day for a whole week, just on the offchance she'd be there as well. We never told each other whether we'd be there the next day or not. We never made a date. We never gave each other our numbers, I knew nothing but her name. We always ended our late-night conversations as if it were the last time we'd see each other. I remember her saying the same thing for seven nights straight as we said our goodbyes right outside the door of the diner.

It was so nice meeting you, William. Thank you so much, it's been a great night.

And I also remember laughing at her and her smiling back at me, her cheeks slightly flushed, eyes sparkling under the dimming lights of the diner – as if I was the highlight of her day, just as she was mine. She somehow, completely unknowingly, made me feel happy to be around her. Whether it was because of how warm and sincere she was, or something else, I had no idea.

There had been a different kind of connection. One that I hadn't come across before her.

I pushed my hands into my pockets and followed her to stand near the door. I also stopped staring at her face so intently to try to read her thoughts.

'Looks like you were right. Only the cleaning crew is left behind,' I commented after glancing around the office space.

Still holding onto the door, she looked over her shoulder before glancing back at me.

'Looks like it,' she agreed. There was another quick glance around, then she released a long sigh. 'Okay then. It was nice seeing you again, William. And I'm excited that we'll be working together. Welcome, again. Did I say that before? Welcome, I mean.'

I nodded and had to work on holding my smile back. 'I think so. I think at the lunch meeting you said it twice and then once before that.'

'Oh well. Since we'll never mention the lunch meeting again . . .' She moved her hand – the one that wasn't hugging the laptop, the papers and the phone – in a wide arc, I believe to give the gesture *there you go*, but hit the back of her hand against the glass instead, rattling the thin walls.

I winced and took a step forward. 'You okay?'

'Oh, I'm fine.' She held the laptop and the rest of her stuff tighter to her body with both hands and kept the door open with her hip instead, allowing her to speak through just the small opening.

The smile she gave me showed a lot of teeth and maybe a little bit of forced cheer as well. 'Goodnight then.'

'Goodnight, Charlie.'

When she heard her name, the smile softened and she let go of the door, sending me one last quick wave.

I was still watching her as she took a few steps towards her office – which could be seen from mine – then hesitated for a moment or two before she squared her shoulders and came right back to my door with determination on her face, pushing it open with her body.

'Hi. Hey. Me again,' she started. The only part of her body that was in my room was her head.

'Hi, Charlie. I can see that,' I replied as I waited.

'So . . . I want to . . . no it's more like I *need* to say something, but before that, I'm actually very surprised that you remember me.'

'You seem to remember me just fine. And in detail, too. Why shouldn't I remember you?'

'You know why. But that's not what I wanted to say. I was a little bit more . . .' she paused and winced, looking anywhere but me.

I frowned at her. 'A little bit more, what?'

'Never mind.'

She hesitated and started to turn. I thought she was leaving, so I took a step forward and grabbed the doorknob, planning on following her out there.

'No, no, no,' she protested when I started to open the door and closed it shut. 'I'll tell you. You can just stand there.'

I was both amused and intrigued at the same time, so I let it go and waited for her to go on.

After taking a deep breath she finally started to speak through the glass door.

'Okay. I'm gonna ramble for just a little bit. I'm doing this thing for myself . . . there is a list. I didn't finish writing it yet, but I'm writing a list, rules to live a good life . . . or just rules – I'm not one hundred percent happy with the title yet, but anyway that's not important. I have this newly developed thing about being honest. At least *trying* to be honest as much as I can instead of keeping things in and driving myself insane and basically hurting myself in the process.

'I had this huge crush on you back then, which I'm pretty sure you were aware of, so that in itself is not that important. But I just want you to know, I don't right now. Have a crush on you, that is. You still look great – don't get me wrong, anyone would be happy to have a crush on you and if I looked too closely you probably look even better now. We, women I mean, almost all women like more mature guys, but I'm better now. And just to add that stubble does look great on you. I'm only mentioning it because it didn't look this good on you back then.'

Taken aback by her admission, it took me a few seconds to process everything that she was saying and speak again. I wasn't sure which end of the conversation to start on. 'You . . . are better now? You made me sound like an illness.'

'No, I didn't mean it like that. I just don't feel that way towards you anymore, that's all. Just wanted you to know so you don't feel awkward about working with me or anything. If you don't want me on your core team I'll understand it completely. And about the crush; I'll be moving soon anyway so it wouldn't make sense to have a crush on you even if I had one – which I don't.' She paused, stood a little straighter. 'That's all. I just wanted to let you know so it's not that awkward between us. Okay then. Bye.'

My frown got deeper as I had trouble following her one-sided conversation and digesting everything she was saying at the same time. 'Slow down. You're moving? When? Where?'

She nodded. 'Yeah. Long story. I need to move, so I'll move.

Simple. And soon. I don't have a set date. I need to find a job first. And there is a big chance I'll move to Los Angeles or Oregon. Nobody here, my dad included, knows yet, so I'd appreciate it if you could keep that to yourself.'

'I understand. I won't tell anyone.'

She nodded again. 'Okay then. We're good?'

I nodded back.

'Goodnight, William.' As she turned around and let the door close, I grabbed it and opened it again before she could get too far away.

'Charlie?'

She turned when she heard my voice, but instead of stopping she kept walking backwards. I looked around, but the cleaning crew were nowhere to be seen even though their cart was still in the same spot.

'Yes?' she asked when I didn't go on, already halfway to her office.

'I won't feel awkward working with you, you don't have to worry about that. I have a rule where I never get involved with colleagues, so we're safe. And last but not least, I think we both know back then I had a crush on you as well.'

She stopped moving for what seemed like a full ten seconds, but was probably just a few, and we stared at each other. 'You don't have to say that, but you did and that's fine. I don't quite believe you, I think, since we both know how that went, but still it's nice to hear.' Then slowly she lifted her chin and gave me a warm, wide and beautiful smile. 'It's good to know. Great. Okay, then, I'll just leave now. See you soon.'

She started with her backwards steps again and gave me a small wave right before bumping into her office door.

Hours later I was still smiling whenever she came to my mind. And she came to my mind more than once or twice. All in all, even with all the awkwardness and avoidance, I figured it was a good first day. It was actually a great one.

4

Charlie

After one of the most disastrous days of my life, I made it home in one piece. Barely, but still, it counted. I walked in to my dark apartment on the Upper East Side, as I did every single night, closed and locked the door. I flicked the lights on and rested my back against the door as I took a deep breath.

The weirdest and most awkward day you've had in a long time, Charlie . . .

When I finally opened my eyes I saw the clock on the wall had hit 9.30 p.m. I groaned loudly and dumped my handbag on my very comfy and deep couch that I was planning to get lost in as soon as I had something to eat in my hands.

As much as I had heard from my dad that maybe I should consider not eating after a certain time, there was no force on earth that would stop me from having dinner. Skipping a meal wasn't something I ever did. And after the day I'd had, the least I owed myself was food.

Dashing into my bedroom, I took off my skirt and walked away from it. Letting the *Titanic* shirt drop to the tops of my thighs, because I wasn't about to cook naked, I headed straight to my small but modern kitchen and considered my limited options. A salad sounded good, but I knew it wouldn't sate me after the day I'd had. Pasta might not have been the best and healthiest idea, but it was the easiest.

After rummaging in my bag, I opened Spotify on my phone and hit play on my On Repeat playlist. As soon as I heard JP Saxe and Julia Michaels, I set it down and started on dinner. It took me twenty minutes to toss together a weird, but hopefully tasty dish that contained pasta, tuna, some lemon juice, parsley, salt and pepper and quite a lot of parmesan. I would have preferred a bolognese sauce, but time was a problem. As it always seem to be with me.

As much as cooking was helping me avoid thinking about William, I couldn't stop my brain from conjuring him up every ten seconds.

Who would've thought I'd meet him again? I still couldn't believe it. It was wild.

William Carter.

We'd never asked our last names all those years ago so I hadn't been able to stalk him on social media. I'd always considered him as my *once-in-a-lifetime thing* and someone that was pretty much unattainable. Figuratively and literally. I knew this. He had been this stranger who I'd look forward to meeting at the end of every day even though I wasn't even sure if he'd show up. I'd get all the butterflies as I sat there at the diner hoping he'd be the next one to walk in the door. Every time the bell over that door rang, my heart would lurch with an extra thud. It was one week of hoping and dreaming, and even though I pretty much knew nothing would come out of it, the hope I'd felt every time he showed up and walked straight to my table had been something else.

And even after he stopped coming, every now and then when I felt alone or hopeless I'd remember our short time together and think about what could've been or *if* it could've been. Daydreaming had always been kinder than reality to me. And wasn't it said that the best things are the ones that haven't happened yet? Like the best words are the ones that haven't been spoken yet? I think that was what William had been to me. Maybe it wasn't the crush I had on him that was important, maybe it was just the idea of him being mine that gave me that butterflies in my stomach. Maybe if something had happened between us, it would've been the worst relationship in the world.

Maybe his feet smelled.

Maybe he was terrible in bed.

Maybe he hated kissing as well.

Maybe . . .

Sighing, because I was overthinking unnecessarily, I grabbed a plate and hurriedly served everything up.

For the time being, I was living in a one-bedroom brownstone which was owned by my dad. If it weren't for him, I couldn't afford it. I still paid rent, but only a third of what he could've gotten from someone else. It wasn't as small as some other NY apartments and my kitchen still looked like a kitchen with limited counter space and everything, but no matter how beautiful the building was, sometimes it still made me feel like I was trapped and there was no escape in sight.

The beautiful arched windows I had in the living room somewhat made up for everything else because they were my favourite part of the building. I loved sitting on the window seat and reading a good book during sunset – not that I was ever home during a sunset – or early morning. Or just staring at the sky when it rained or snowed as I listened to my playlist in the background when I was too tired to do anything else. In the chaos of the city and my mind, those moments were my calm.

Also, I couldn't argue with the fact that the rows of brownstone townhouses and the colourful tree leaves in the fall made for romantic scenery. I just had the feeling that it wasn't enough to keep me there anymore.

I grated some more parmesan, because why not? Nobody was around to judge me. I sprinkled the remaining parsley on top of my pasta and grabbed myself the bottle of prosecco I'd left from a

few nights ago. As I pulled my legs up and got settled on the corner
of my couch, I considered turning on the TV, but gave up on the
idea pretty quickly. Reaching for my phone, I grabbed it from the
coffee table, paused Dermot Kennedy mid-song and called Valerie,
my best friend since high school, who was currently three thousand
miles away. She picked up on the fourth ring.

'Hi! Are you home? I need to hear everything, tell me! Did you
take a photo of him like I told you to at lunch?'

Smiling, I put my plate down next to me and reached for the prosecco bottle. 'Hello. How are you? How was your day? I'm so tired.'

I heard some shuffling sounds in the background then she huffed.
'Oh, shut up. Tell me you took a photo. This William guy is like
the yeti of our lives. I won't believe he exists until I see a photo.'

Shaking my head, I took a sip of my drink. A big sip straight from
the bottle because I was classy. 'Unfortunately, I was too busy trying
to avoid him the entire day. So no photos.'

'No, you didn't.'

'Yep, I did.'

'Ed,' she called out, and I had to turn down the volume and put
her on speaker to save my eardrums. 'She doesn't have a photo and
apparently she didn't tell him who she was either.'

'I didn't say that,' I corrected her.

'Ed, she says – oh wait, I'll just put you on speaker.'

'Sure, let's share my embarrassment with the whole world.'

'Just my fiancé will do for now. Come on, don't keep us waiting
any longer,' Valerie begged.

'Hi, babe,' Ed greeted me. 'Val couldn't stop talking about it.
Rough day, huh?'

'Exactly!' I said, nodding my head and throwing my hand up and
almost sloshing my prosecco on my shirt.

Valerie groaned. 'I've been waiting for you to call ever since you
texted me this morning. What else do you want from me?'

'He remembers me,' I said, looking up at the ceiling. It was impossible to hold my giddy smile back. I knew it didn't mean anything, but since all I'd felt was heartbreak when I assumed he didn't in fact remember me, I was taking it as a win.

Valerie squealed, making me wince. I heard Ed murmur to her to take it easy, but my best friend's voice only got louder.

'You know what this means, right?' she asked excitedly.

I rested my head on the back of the couch and closed my eyes for a second. In another reality, it could've meant that I'd have a tiny chance of having another shot at someone I had a huge crush on, but in this reality where everything wasn't so easy or romantic, it meant nothing.

'Nothing,' I mumbled, opening my eyes again. 'It means nothing. But it was nice talking to . . .'

'Charlie . . .'

'Okay, fine, it was really really nice to hear that he recognized me.'

'Charlie what are you talking about? It could mean . . .'

'I'm going to move, you know this, so him being here means nothing. He looks amazing, Val. Insanely amazing. So he's still a little out of my league, if not even more, and there is the fact that I'm going to mo—'

'Charlie . . .' This time it was Ed, sweetly murmuring my name. 'You're beautiful.'

I smiled, warmth spreading throughout my body, and put down my bottle. 'Thank you for saying that, Ed. I'm not saying I'm the ugliest person in the world, I like myself just fine, but he is a little too much for me. Not that he wants me in that way right now, but even if he were mine I wouldn't know what to do with him. Let me repeat it again, I like myself. And anyway,' I continued before Val could interrupt again. 'I can't stay here, you know how it is with dad and grandma and even Kim. I'll lose my mind if I stay here another year. I want a new start. A fresh one. Somewhere that isn't New York. I'll date anyone you deem worthy when I come to California. I solemnly promise.'

There was a stretch of silence on the other end of the line.

'Sounds like a good plan, Charlie,' Ed said when Val didn't comment. 'I didn't see the guy so I have no idea what your concept of insanely good is, but he'd be lucky to have you if you wanted him as well. Valerie said you'll be working with the guy, so I'd say dating him might be a bad move anyway.'

'No,' Val whisper-shouted. 'Don't say that to her! Why would you say that to her?'

Ed murmured something I couldn't hear.

'Thanks, Ed,' I agreed, cutting Val off before she could start on him. 'It was just a shock seeing him, you know. We met so many years ago and now he is here and I'm going to be working with him. I can't wrap my mind around it. It's a very … pleasant surprise, but it doesn't necessarily mean something.'

I took a long long sip of prosecco.

'Fine. Then just fuck his brains out,' Valerie contributed.

I started coughing loudly, the bubbles going down the wrong tube.

'What?' Val protested, and I figured Ed must've said something while I was busy choking. 'It's been way too long since she had some. I don't even count Craig the small snake.' My eyes bulged out and I kept coughing. 'Fuck him, kiss him. Do *something*. It'll be like your vengeance,' she continued unaware.

'What kind of vengeance is that?' I asked in a raspy voice, leaning forward and putting down my bottle.

'He stood you up. You can fuck his brains out and show him what he's missed all those years ago. It's a win–win in my book.'

'I love your logic. Since I haven't had sex in years, I'd be so good at it now that for sure his mind will be blown and he'll realize what a mistake he's made. And thanks for telling Ed I haven't had sex in years. Always wanted him to know.'

'Okay, I don't want to be here for this conversation. Babe, we need to head out anyway. We have plans with friends, Charlie.'

'But, Ed . . .' Valerie protested, then there were murmurings too quiet for me to hear.

There was an awkward moment of silence. 'Okay, guys. You go have fun. I'll talk to you soon.' I would've been lying if I'd said there wasn't this tiny little bloom of jealousy in my chest that disappeared as soon as it appeared.

'I'm sorry, Charlie,' Val muttered. 'I would've cancelled, but . . .'

'Don't be crazy. Why would you cancel plans for this? This is just a blip in the ordinary. Nothing more. We'll talk later.'

'Give me a second, I'll take you off the speaker. Okay. Done. You go, Ed, I'll be right there. Okay, Charlie I'm walking away from Ed, he can't hear me. You were half in love with the guy. You talked about him for months even after he stood you up. This is me you're talking to, so don't act like *him* being right there doesn't mean anything. If it didn't you wouldn't have literally run away from him.'

'I didn't run away from him,' I grumbled, picking a ghost lint from my leggings.

'Oh, sorry. *Crawled* away from him. How could we forget about that.'

'Val, it's been years. Of course him being here doesn't mean anything. It was just a shock to see him at the office all of a sudden. He was married, did I say that? Apparently he got a divorce recently, but still what I'm trying to say is, we're not the same people. I don't even know him anymore. I've had crushes on a lot of people. Take Chris Evans the insanely good-looking movie star for instance: just because I've had an ongoing crush on him for years doesn't mean I'll start stalking him forever or won't ever be with anyone else.'

'That was a weak example and you know it. You already stalk Chris Evans.'

I admitted to nothing.

'We'll talk about this when I get back,' she began in an unimpressed voice. 'You're not off the hook. You need to start dating again.'

'Jesus. I dated. Every now and then. When you get back, I'll be asleep. It's the weekend, I'm going to sleep for twelve hours. And you know I want to be with someone too. I miss being with someone, being an important part of someone's life. But we saw how the online dating and blind dates went. I'm okay like this too. I like my own company. I'm happy. I'm not going to settle just to tell other people I'm dating. I'll find someone when it's time. We'll talk later, go. Ed is waiting.'

She sighed. 'You're staying in tonight?'

'Yup.' I stayed in every night. 'Got stuff to do around the house anyway,' I lied. Kinda.

'Okay. We'll talk tomorrow then. Text me when you wake up, okay? Especially if you guys talk again. And . . . you never know, Charlie, right this minute he might be thinking about you too.'

'O—okay. Bye now. Give Ed a hug from me.'

I ended the call and sat back for a minute, my dinner already forgotten. I should've made French fries, I would've never given up on French fries. The more time passed, the worse I started to feel. I was so tired of feeling lonely. So tired of being by myself. I wasn't lying, I did enjoy being alone, but being lonely was a whole other thing when you thought about it.

Even when I had Craig, I didn't actually have him. What brand of an idiot was I that I'd spent almost six years of my life in a long-distance relationship that was clearly going nowhere? Just because I was scared to lose one more person in my life and because it was easier to deal with. Not all of it had been bad, since he was good to me the times that he actually paid attention, but more than that he was really good at manipulating me into staying and telling me everything would be great. It just wasn't the right time yet.

I had a few close friends who were scattered all around the country. Sure, I had a family, but sometimes dealing with them broke my soul in the worst way.

A grandma who didn't even accept hugs, let alone a simple kiss on the cheek. Forget about feeling loved by her; love was weakness and even if you loved someone you should never show it – her words, not mine. Since her husband left her with a four-year-old (my dad) for someone else, she'd become bitter and closed off. I didn't want to become like her.

A dad who didn't know me, didn't even *care* to get to know me, who judged me constantly, who made fun of people I loved by calling them names, who was so set in his own ways that he didn't listen to what I had to say about any subject. A dad who didn't respect me, but whom I still loved.

A sister I barely talked to anymore and had nothing in common with.

Not to mention a mom who chose someone else, a man she barely knew, and left her kids and her marriage, only to never even call them again.

When you thought about it, it was high time I made some real changes and a real list would be a good place to start. The written word always had more power. Downing the rest of my prosecco, I picked up my half-eaten plate and the now empty bottle and left them in the sink.

Heading to the corner in the living room where my narrow desk lived, I picked up a legal pad and a pen and settled down on the window seat, trying to think of new rules to live by. I rested the side of my head on the windowpane and glanced at the pear tree right outside the townhouse. Then, after thinking for a little while, I started on my list.

Make sure you don't die alone.

How I was gonna actually make sure that I didn't die alone I had no idea, since I sucked at dating or finding a decent person, but even admitting that I didn't want to die alone felt as good a start as any. After some more thinking I added:

But also please don't settle just because you're afraid of dying alone.

I'd rather spend years alone than settle down and make myself even more miserable. I wanted to be head over heels in love, not *kind of* in love.

Biting the end of the pen and chewing it between my lips, I thought about the second item that would have to be on my list. It didn't take long.

Move. Move. MOVE.

Once I started writing, the rest came easily and I had my checklist of life rules in no time:

- Make sure you don't die alone. But also please don't settle just because you're afraid of dying alone.
- Move. Move. MOVE.
- Romanticize your life a little. We only live once and if you want to make your Sunday breakfast special, or if you just want to watch the stars one night instead of watching TV, or if you want to light all the candles and just read – do it. Make sure you enjoy your life, make sure you're happy; nobody else is gonna think about you as much as you think about yourself. Main character energy is what you'll strive for.
- Experience love at first sight. Highly unlikely to happen, but you never know.
- Move.
- Laugh more. This is a necessity. You have to do it. Don't become like your grandma.
- Be honest as much as you can. (If you feel something, you have to talk about it. It causes nothing but hurt when you bottle it all inside.)
- It's okay to be selfish sometimes. You're important. You need to be your number one.
- Do NOT, I repeat do NOT postpone your life anymore.
- MOVE.

- Flirt. Flirting is fun and you're surprisingly not the worst flirt in the world. Try it a few times.
- Kiss a lot. It makes you happy and smiley and all gooey inside. You went without it long enough. Find someone who is a good kisser and KISS for days. Enough is enough.
- Fall for a stranger again. Even it's for only the night. At least once more, because you know how that feels in your heart. (Very important as well.)
- But really fall in love with someone who deserves to have you in their life. Somebody who won't make you wonder if you matter or not. Otherwise forget about it. (I really want you to fall in love.)
- A puppy. You need a puppy in your life. A rescue. A cute little good boy maybe?
- Surround yourself with people who knows how to hug the right way. A good hug can fix a lot of things.
- You know how much words hurt. Be kind to the ones around you.
- Find your happy every day. No matter what. No matter who. You need to have a smile on your face every night when you go to bed.
- And LIVE. You've only got this one life, don't waste it. Like a good book, make every chapter of your life something you're proud of. You don't want to look back and only see everything you've missed out on.
- Sex. It's all I'm going to say. S.E.X. Find someone who knows all the positions. Or at least more than one. And it wouldn't be that bad if you actually orgasmed every once in a while – with an actual live penis, that is. And it needs to be longer than two minutes. Please.
- Don't ever change your life around for a guy. Or wait around for them.

God save me, but I was gonna have to give online dating another go. If I felt completely hopeless, maybe even a blind date.

When I fell asleep on the couch that night with my notebook in my lap, I felt lighter and somehow a bit more positive about things. And if I had a smile on my face it was not because I was thinking of William Carter right before sleep took me. Not at all. Because I'd never do that.

5

Charlie

The next day Michael Ashton was flying in from California and we were to have a discreet meeting as the core team to get all the details.

While being around William wasn't as nerve-racking as the day before – and I managed not to embarrass myself in front of the whole office – somehow having him in my space was still a bit mystifying and alien. I kept catching myself studying him as he worked in his office and still avoided him in general. I also learned that he was a pacer. I watched him walk up and down in his office as he was on phone call after phone call.

As we kept waiting for the client to show up, we heard news that his flight had been cancelled and the meeting had to be pushed back a day.

My dad wanted William in on two other meetings, so for hours they were away from the office, but from what I'd heard from Gayle, we weren't getting those potential new clients because William wasn't convinced they had problems we wanted to work on.

The only time I spent more than a few minutes by his side was in the afternoon when he came back to the office and we were calling Laurel Nielson, the celebrity I was working with, to get me off the hook. I watched him talk to her for less than five minutes and, when he hung up, I couldn't hold it in and started laughing.

'You just said yes to her!' I accused him, forgetting to be nervous and smiling widely.

'I didn't . . .' he started, his brows drawing together. 'What the hell just happened?'

'She got you,' I replied, quieting my laughter. 'You should see your face.'

His brows drew even closer and his forehead creased as he looked at me. Slowly, I stopped laughing, the big grin still intact, but I wasn't sure what he was thinking. Was he pissed at me? I wouldn't think so, but . . .

Sure, I knew details of his old life, his family and his favourite colour – if it was still green, that is – so, yes, I knew back then. But now? I wasn't sure.

'What did she say to you?' I asked as I got up from my chair, keeping my smile to a minimum.

'I actually have no idea. I also have no idea what her situation is,' she rambled some, but I didn't understand a word. She was trying to negotiate with me for you.'

'And you still said yes?'

His scowl got worse.

'So you basically gave me to her. Did you even get anything out of the negotiation?'

'I . . . she confused me. I'm going to call her again tomorrow and fix this.'

'Instead of doing that, would it be okay if I kept working with her? She is a handful, but I actually want to work with her. Help her.'

He sighed and rubbed the bridge of his nose. 'Tell me a little about her situation then.'

Looking up, he motioned for me to sit again, but I shook my head.

'I have a thing I need to get to. I'm already late as it is.'

He checked his watch. 'I understand. Okay, Laurel Nielson? Do you have time to give me a quick rundown at least? I don't believe this is a crisis situation that is happening at the moment, am I wrong?'

'You're right. She was at this talk show last month and the host came onto her backstage. He visited her room to say welcome and good luck, which he does for every guest, so nobody thought anything of it, and then when she started talking publicly about what happened in the room – he got a little handsy or tried to get a little handsy, that part is a mystery – on social media way after everything happened, somehow they turned it on her. The guy is married and old enough to be her father so nobody believes her. In return he accused her of coming onto *him* and Laurel lost it. She kind of made a mess of everything, got drunk and got on camera and eventually lost her role for a new TV show. Her agent was fuming and they hired the wrong company initially, which made a complete mess of the situation. She fled to Spain to take a few weeks off. She isn't big yet, but she was on her way there and all of this happening is killing her career before it even started.'

William leaned back in his seat, carefully studying me. I squirmed in my place and broke our eye contact.

'And you believe she is telling the truth.'

I nodded, meeting his eyes again. 'I'm a little like you. I had Gayle look into it and I think this host tried to pull the same thing on a few more B-list celebrities, but they didn't take it to the press so it never got out like this. But Laurel is . . . a firecracker is a good word to describe her, I think, and she isn't good at controlling her emotions that well. I'm okay with her sharing what happened on social media, but she handled it the wrong way and now she is the one who looks guilty. Which pisses me off. I don't know what she was thinking, but she thought she could handle it herself and it just didn't work out in her favour.'

'Okay.'

'Okay?' I asked sceptically. He had just spent five minutes trying to get her to work with someone else and now it was just okay?

'Yeah. If you believe her and if Gayle looked into the whole thing and thinks it's legit, we'll work with her together. Tell me why does she want you this badly again? Do you two know each other?'

'I worked with one of her friends last year. She saw me around and liked how I handled the situation, I think. That's what she told me when she got in touch with me anyway.'

'I'm guessing it'll be an ongoing thing and you were considering your long-term strategy? Does she have a problem with alcohol or was this a one-time thing? Does she actually listen when you're talking?'

A little flustered, I cleared my throat. We were gonna work on this together? In close quarters? Just the two of us? 'Yes, I mean no. Yes to the first thing, no to the second, yes to the last. She just got drunk when she was out with her friends for a bachelorette party and they pushed a camera in her face. And William, I heard that you prefer not to work with celebrities, it's okay for me to handle her myself.'

'It's fine,' he said after hesitating for a second. 'I don't want anyone in the team to work alone on something. I need your focus on the team as a whole. We'll have a meeting with her when she gets back from . . . Spain?'

'Yes. She has family there, she was ready to come back but I wanted her to lay low and get away for at least a few weeks just so she wouldn't be hounded by the paparazzi. She is bound to say something that'll end up hurting our work. She agreed, so she'll be there for another week I think.'

'That's good. Something else will happen in the celebrity world by the time she's back and the focus won't be on her as much. We'll have a meeting outside the office just in case she is seen coming in here. I don't want everybody to see she is getting help before we actually talk to her. This is good. You and I will sit down and talk about what we can do a day or two before she gets here. You're okay with that?'

Nodding, I smiled. He smiled. It was smiles all around. And maybe for the first time in two days it wasn't so bad. Or at least so weird.

Eyeing the door, I started moving towards it while still facing William. 'Okay, now that we decided on that, I'm going to head out then. Anything else I can help you with?'

'No, I'm fine. We have the meeting with Michael Ashton at ten tomorrow, don't for—'

'I won't forget.'

Before he could finish his words I was already out the door, half-running to my own office to pick up my stuff. Excited and nervous as never before.

6

William

It was finally the morning of the meeting we had scheduled with
Michael Ashton. Ending my call with him, I walked into the conference room and found that Stan was already seated and busy working
on his laptop, and Rick was hovering around the coffee station that
was set up at the far end of the room against the windows. Our client
had landed in New York without a problem, but he was stuck in
traffic and would be late by ten or twenty minutes. I looked around,
but couldn't spot Trisha or Charlie anywhere.

'Morning,' I greeted the guys as their eyes landed on me and
got two distracted chin lifts. 'Charlie and Trisha are on their way,
I assume?'

Without waiting for an answer, I headed straight for Rick and the
coffee station, hoping it was a fresh brew. Rick mumbled his good
mornings and moved out of my way.

'Any reason why we needed to be here an hour early? I thought
the meeting was at ten.'

I gave him an amused look. 'Couldn't get your beauty sleep?'

He grumbled something under his breath and took a big gulp
of his coffee before answering my question. 'Trisha was grabbing
Gayle. You asked Gayle to be here, right?'

I nodded.

'They should be here in a few. Ashton guy landed this time?'

I grabbed a mug and started pouring the black liquid, deeply inhaling the rich scent and enjoying the quiet. Nodding, I put the thermos back down. 'He is on his way, he'll be here in fifteen. He needs to take the next flight back, that's why we changed the time.'

Turning my back to the busy city view, I closed my eyes and took a big sip. Savouring the taste, I casually glanced at Rick and found him eyeing the croissant and fruit plate that was probably made ready for Ashton.

'And Charlie?' I asked nonchalantly, even though I wasn't quite sure why I was trying to appear as if I wasn't curious.

'I didn't see her yet,' Rick answered, eyes still on the plate as his hand reached for a slice of apple that was on the very edge of the carefully constructed arrangement.

I turned to Stan when he spoke up from his seat. 'I think I saw her in Douglas's office before I came up here.'

Having given up on the fruit and croissants, Rick sighed next to me. 'I came up right after Stan, but I didn't see anyone in Douglas's office.'

'Considering we were having trouble finding her yesterday as well . . . Is she always so hard to pin down?'

'She does work a lot,' Rick said defensively.

'Didn't say she wasn't working.' Not sure what to say, I took another sip of my coffee. 'Can one of you call her? I don't have her number yet. I need everyone in the room so we don't have to go over everything with the client again.'

'I'll give her a call,' Rick announced and, taking his coffee mug with him, headed towards the chair that was already pulled out next to Stan. 'I'm sure she'll be here before Ashton.' He reached for his phone.

I focused on my coffee and checked the time again.

'She isn't answering,' Rick commented, already raising the phone back to his ear.

We heard the elevator doors ping and a few seconds later Trisha and Gayle walked in and greeted everyone. No time left to wait for Charlie; we were roughly going over things I already knew when I received a text from Ashton saying he was coming up.

I checked my watch. Five minutes past the planned meeting time and there was still no sign of Charlie. I cleared my throat, trying not to show my annoyance. 'Ashton is coming up. Any news from Charlie? I need everyone to be present when we're talking to a client.' I glanced at Rick again since he had been the one to call her.

He checked his phone and shook his head before meeting my gaze. 'I can run downstairs and try to . . .'

'No,' I cut him off, sharper than I had intended. 'We're going to start without her. I'll talk to Douglas – maybe she'll be better off in another team.' I knew I was being harsh, but I took my job very seriously and if she didn't have a good reason for not showing up I wouldn't tolerate it. When we deal with crisis situations I need to know I can depend on my colleagues. That's the only way we could work well together.

I caught Gayle's questioning gaze, but had to ignore it when we heard the elevator doors open again. I rose to greet Michael Ashton at the door.

'Hello, William. Good to see you again.'

We shook hands as I smiled at him. 'Good to see you too. Come on, I'll introduce you to your team.'

Looking nervous, he released a big breath, let go of my hand and turned to the room. 'I hope I didn't make you wait for too long.'

In under a minute, I could see that he was a hit with everyone. It could be his boyish looks, or simply how sincere and awkwardly nervous he was when he was talking to people. When everyone introduced themselves and was done with the niceties, I started the meeting properly.

'If you're ready to start, Michael?' I gestured for him to sit.

He gave me a timid smile, ran his hands over his pants and then took a seat.

'I need you to go over everything you told me in our phone call yesterday for the rest of the team, but go into more details so we know all aspects of what we're dealing with and can work towards fixing the situation.'

He nodded a few times. 'Yes. Yes, of course.'

Everyone was scattered around the table and Gayle had chosen to stand against the coffee cart, arms crossed against her chest. As I rounded the table to take a seat, I watched her take out a small notebook and pen from her pants pocket. After giving me a small distracted smile, she focused on Michael again.

'We started our company EVA with Isaac right after college and we've been working on a new ...'

There was a distant ping and then a loud crash and an audible curse that cut off Michael's words mid-sentence. Everybody, including Michael, glanced towards the door right as Charlie barged in with a shoe in her hand and then froze halfway into the room.

Her eyes found mine first. Then she quickly stood a bit straighter and forced a smile on her lips as she focused on Michael. Her cheeks were blushing.

Closing the few steps between them, she limped towards him – seeing as she wasn't wearing one of her shoes – and thrust him her free hand.

Already feeling a headache coming on, I started rubbing my temples.

I glanced up to see Michael looking at her with uncertainty.

Finally they shook hands. 'I'm so sorry for being late and ... well for the shoe. I was trying to run, but the elevator wasn't having it so I just broke my heel and now you're looking at me as if I've lost it. I didn't, I'm just rambling, I'm sorry. You must be Michael Ashton.' Right at the tail of her words, she turned herself into an impromptu pretzel to put her broken-heeled shoe back on with her free hand.

'Yes, uh, I am. And you are ...'

Michael gave me a quick look before addressing Charlie again. Charlie just kept smiling at him as I watched them in shock and bewilderment.

I stood up. 'Michael, Miss Davis was about to leave ...' I started, but Charlie interrupted me.

'I'm in Mr Carter's team. Charlie Davis. I was held downstairs by something unexpected, but I ran up here as fast as I could.' Pausing to take a breath, she pushed her hair behind her ear, somehow warmed up her smile even more and kept going. 'I'll just take this seat,' she continued, tiptoeing her way over to a seat. She took the one that was two chairs left of Michael and sat down. She angled it so her whole body was facing towards him. 'I hope I didn't miss too much, but I'm all ears now, Mr Ashton. You keep going and I'll catch up.'

The smile still stuck on her face, she turned to us, the rest of her speechless team, and lost the spark of her smile a little when our eyes met. 'I'm really sorry for interrupting. It won't happen again.'

Begrudgingly I sat down. 'Thank you, Miss Davis.'

'I ... had just started,' Michael commented.

Charlie's smile got bigger and she turned her attention to Michael from me while starting up her laptop.

'Really? That's great. Okay, Mr Ashton, how can we help with your problem?'

Feeling like I'd already lost control of the situation, I cleared my throat. 'Please, continue Michael.' After a quick and meaningful look at Charlie, I started studying the documents that were in front of me as Michael began again.

'As I was saying, we started EVA right after college and it took us over ten years to develop the technology we're using in our electric cars today. We are – or I should say we were – really close to ... No, actually, Isaac suddenly left the company, I bought his shares only a month ago. So my people and I were rushing to get ready for the launch when everything went south.'

'Why did Mr Isaac leave the company so close to the launch?' Gayle asked, finally taking a seat right next to me. I settled back in my seat, satisfied because she was asking the right question. Even though I'd gone over the work of every single person in the room before I accepted them into my team, this was still the first time I was going to handle a case with them. It was going to take a while to trust my colleagues completely to do their jobs.

'We were having problems. Personal ones and some other disagreements about our work. I never would've thought he'd leave because of some minor difference of opinion, but he wanted out.'

'You're still in contact?' Gayle continued.

Michael rubbed the back of his neck. 'That would be a no.'

Gayle scribbled some notes on her notepad as she kept asking more questions about what kind of difference of opinion they had and then nodded for him to keep going when she was satisfied.

'Anyway,' Michael continued. 'We used a technology nobody was giving a chance and we knew it'd take us a long time, but we managed to get where we wanted. We developed this prototype of functional city cars. We already started working on our marketing campaign a year ago. People are sceptical because the technology we're using is so innovative, and we're going against well-established automobile manufacturers. We made a huge impact with publicity. I'm the face of our social media campaigns because we thought that'd be the best way to show people what we're doing and what we're hoping to achieve.'

'That was a great idea, you have a very sincere and warm personality. You must have a good marketing team,' Charlie cut in with a smile.

Michael turned to her and responded with a smile of his own. 'Thank you.'

'Tell us about this specific marketing campaign that started the problem, please,' I cut in before they could derail the subject again.

Michael faced my side of the room and clasped his hands on the table. To my annoyance his body was still slightly facing towards Charlie.

'So, with our marketing team we made a plan for publicity and marketing to send one of our prototype cars to a few hand-picked people and give them access to it for twelve hours. The first two people had no problems and everything was great. The third person, a reporter, Kylie Combs, received the car next. Three hours into it she has an accident. She was driving the prototype and the car showed over fifty percent battery left when it was actually almost out of juice. She was stranded at night and while she was trying to figure out what was wrong, another car hit her.

'She got hit when she was still in the car?' Trisha asked.

'No. No, she was outside. The prototype is fine. She got hit when she decided to stand in the middle of the road to stop someone for help. The whole thing was recorded because she was going to use it on her website to talk about her experience with our car. I saw the video and the cockpit clearly shows the fifty percent battery left.'

'The police are involved, I'm guessing?'

'Yes. They haven't found who hit her yet, the video only shows her getting hit. They have the car model, but no news as of today.'

'You brought the video with you, right?' I asked.

'Yes, I brought it with me.' He searched in his pocket for something, then slid a thumb drive towards me. 'This is a huge opportunity for our competitors to run a smear campaign against EVA and I have no idea how to handle the situation.'

'How is Kylie Combs doing?' Charlie piped up.

Michael shook his head. 'Sorry, I should've mentioned it. She is ... not fine of course, but it could've been worse considering the whole situation. She injured her leg, broke her ankle. And she has bruises and cuts. She is suing us.'

'Let's talk about the battery,' Stan said. 'Did you see the proto-type? Do you know why it malfunctioned?'

Michael started to talk about how they had designed their own batteries and were working with a third-party battery developer. It was their design that was going to set them apart from others.

'EVA has a set of code, a set of data we put into the car's computer. It is unique and only for our car batteries. This is what we programmed. So, a simple answer to your question is, yes, it is our fault that this has happened. But the problem here is that it shouldn't have happened. I went over everything myself and I found something in the software, I don't know how to explain it without giving you a headache, but the codes were wrong.'

'So, this *was* completely EVA's fault.' Trisha commented matter-of-factly, putting a pause in the conversation.

I was thinking, but I felt eyes on me, so I looked up. My eyes caught Charlie's and she gave me a barely-there smile before quickly looking away and taking some more notes.

I frowned.

Michael sighed and ran his hands over his face. 'Yes and no.'

We spent another hour discussing every little detail, everyone taking turns asking their questions to Michael to try and cover the missing parts. When a worn-out Michael left to catch his flight back to California, it was just the five of us left in the room. I couldn't exactly say why it bothered me that Michael had lingered over Charlie when he was taking his leave and they had both laughed at something Charlie said, plus they had shaken hands longer than anybody else in the room. That wasn't exactly what bothered me, but I wasn't a fan of getting too close to the clients. Specifically, romantically involved. Maybe that was something else I'd have to talk to the entire team about.

'Gayle, I need you to look into the software company. And try to get in touch with the ex-best friend and now ex-partner too while you're at it,' I suggested. Her eyes still on her notes, she gave me a nod and left the room. I realized I was going to like working with the no-nonsense Gayle, because every question she had asked in the meeting was smart. The whole team had done very well.

'Stan, Trisha. I need you two to try and get ahead of this. All of this, Mrs Comb's accident, happened only a few days ago. Somehow they managed to keep this between them, but I don't think that's how it's going to stay, so prepare the statements we need and show me what you're thinking in terms of media relations. I'll get you in contact with a few people.'

After they left, Rick and Charlie got up from their seats, and I started to gather all the documents about the EVA.

'Charlie, you and I will get more details about what went wrong with their software and . . .'

'Maybe you could do that with Rick?' she interrupted, causing me to lift my head so I could look at her. 'I was thinking maybe I should stay in contact with Michael and talk to their marketing team about . . .'

'Any specific reason you can't work with me?' I asked, stopping her mid-sentence. Maybe I'd have to talk to Charlie and only Charlie about getting romantically involved with clients.

All three of us were standing around the desk. Charlie was avoiding meeting my eyes while she paused before she could turn off her laptop, and Rick was looking from me to Charlie.

'No. No. It's nothing like that,' she managed to say, eyes on the papers that were still in my hands. I put them on the table and glanced at our spectator and slowly sat down.

'Rick? I want you to start talking to employees. Try to get a feel for the company and how things used to work before one of their partners left. And do you mind giving Charlie and me . . .'

He nodded before I could finish my sentence. 'I'll head downstairs and get things started.'

I kept my eyes on Charlie as she squirmed in place. 'Yes, please.'

Before Rick could leave the room, I watched Charlie quickly pick up her laptop and take a few wobbling steps back.

'I'll go with him and s—'

'No, I think you'll stay.'

She closed her eyes and let out a sigh, still hugging her laptop to her chest. Rick whispered something to Charlie that I couldn't hear and then disappeared out of sight.

'Okay. Let's talk this out,' I said when I heard the elevator ping and knew we were alone. 'I thought we'd decided we weren't going to be awkward around each other and that you had no problems working with me in this team. First you're late to the meeting and now this?' I paused, trying to read her face so I could figure out what the problem was. 'Did you change your mind about staying in the team?'

She studied me for a brief moment, then sighed and put her laptop back on the desk. 'I didn't. I mean I didn't change my mind. I can be in this team. But . . .'

'But?' I prompted when she didn't go on.

'It *is* a bit awkward still.' She winced a little. 'It kind of isn't, but also is? It doesn't make sense, I know.'

I leaned back in my seat. 'Did you come late to the meeting just to avoid me then?'

Her eyes rounded a little and she shook her head. 'Oh, no. Not at all. I would never do that when it comes to work. Trust me. I might act all weird around you, but I care about what I do too much to do that.'

'Then?'

'My dad was meeting with a new client and he wanted me there. Sometimes he wants me to be there when he is meeting with someone new. I tried to tell him I had a meeting with you, but he said he just needed me for a few minutes, then those few minutes turned into half an hour and then I was late. Trust me, I wasn't trying to avoid the meeting because of you at all.'

I let the silence fill the space between us as we studied each other. She didn't really look into my eyes, but it was close enough.

'Okay then,' I said, choosing to believe her that she wouldn't avoid a meeting knowingly.

'Okay?'

I nodded, standing up. 'Yes, okay, Charlie. But one last thing. I don't condone getting romantically involved with clients, so let's be very clear on that.'

'Excuse me?'

'If that's a problem for you ...'

I watched her as she stood straighter. 'That's not a problem because I have never done that, and I don't plan on doing it anytime soon either.'

'That's good. Let's go downstairs and get started on things.'

Another slight wince as she took a step away from the desk. 'Actually, I promised my dad I'd take care of a few things for him after the meeting. Which is why I said maybe I should just be in contact with Michael and his team. But if you need me to work with you, I'm okay with that too. Is it still okay if I get to my dad first and then join you guys?'

Using the time to carefully think about my answer, I picked up the documents, grabbed my phone and rounded the table towards the door.

'Do I need to talk to Douglas about ...' I stopped moving and stared at Charlie as she took off her shoe, the one with the heel still intact, and started bending it this way and that way. 'What are you doing?'

'Huh?'

I raised my brows and pointedly looked at the shoe in her hand. She glanced down, then looked up at me and I watched as heat rushed to her cheeks.

A sudden grin threatened to form on my lips, but I managed to hold it back.

She straightened up, put her shoe back on and cleared her throat. 'Oh. Nothing. Let's go downstairs and start working.'

Before I could say anything, she picked up her laptop and started walking – no, it was more like limping – ahead of me and out the door. I followed her simply because I didn't know what else to do.

We stood side by side as we waited for the elevator.

'And no, you don't have to talk to my dad. I did talk to him this morning and he still wants me to work outside of your team too,' she said, breaking the silence.

I frowned and looked at her profile, but she was staring straight ahead, waiting for the doors to open. 'That wasn't my deal with your father. I'm supposed to have a core team and they're supposed to focus on whatever I . . .'

She gave me a quick look. 'I know. That's what he said, but he still needs me to handle a few things here and there. With Stan, Trisha and Rick there he doesn't think you'll need me that much. He mostly wants me to learn from you apparently. You really got the best people in the office in your team. I think you'll do great things together whether I'm there or not.'

I didn't like what she was saying at all. 'That's for me to decide. And if he thinks you need to learn stuff from me, why does it look like he needs you more than anybody else in this firm?'

She gave me a surprised look and scoffed. 'He doesn't need me more than anybody else in the firm.'

I had only spent a couple of days at the firm, yet had already seen that Douglas had invited Charlie to almost every meeting he was having. I chose to let it go. It wasn't my problem unless Douglas made it my problem. 'That's not what I've seen or heard. You won't have time to work on other things. I can't have you or anyone in the team distracted.'

The elevator doors finally opened and we stepped inside. You could faintly hear the piano solo coming through the speakers.

'It's okay. I'm used to working on a few things at once. I won't be distracted, don't worry.'

The doors closed and before I could think to hit any buttons, instead of going down to our floor, the elevator headed up.

'I really like Michael,' Charlie continued. 'He seems genuine. And as much as my dad thinks I need to learn more to be more cut-throat or whatever, I'm a hard worker. I won't slow you guys up or let you down.' She gave me a quick look. 'If you still want me on the team, of course.'

That wasn't what I'd been thinking, but I decided to stay quiet and give it a day or two to see how things shaped up. Then if I needed to talk to Douglas I would. Not because it was Charlie, but because I needed every member of my team to actually be on my team.

The doors opened on the 32nd floor, but there was nobody waiting. In the quiet, just as the doors started to close on us again, I pressed the button for our floor and watched as she bent down to deal with her shoe.

'Is there anything I can help with?' I asked out of courtesy.

Letting out a big breath, she straightened up with her shoe in her hand.

She thrust her laptop into my arms. 'Could you hold this for a minute?'

With her laptop in hand, I looked down to her now naked foot and noticed her toes were painted in lilac. For some reason, I kept watching as she stood on her toes and and turned her back to me. Curiosity won over, and I managed to force my gaze away from her small feet. I glanced over her shoulder as she raised her hand and brought down the heel of her shoe on the holding bar. It cracked with a loud noise and the broken piece clattered on the ground.

She was hopping on one foot as she tried to put the now heel-less shoe back on when she lost her balance and kind of fell against my chest, rocking me back a step. I wrapped my right arm – the one that wasn't holding her laptop – around her small waist. We stood like that for a few seconds longer than necessary. Both of us were a little surprised, I think. Then, still holding her laptop, I managed to set her back on her feet and she quickly moved away from me.

'I'm sorry,' she whispered to the elevator doors, then bending down, picked up the heel from the corner of the elevator.

The whole thing lasted for ten, fifteen seconds and then both of her shoes were without heels.

Without looking at me, she held her hand open and I wordlessly handed back her laptop.

'Thank you,' she mumbled in a small voice.

'Okay then,' I said and pushed my hands into my pockets. I was stuck between amusement and some other emotion I couldn't quite put my finger on. Attraction? Maybe.

After a few seconds of heavy silence, Charlie sighed. 'You think I'm weird, don't you?' she asked into the quiet.

I smiled – she sounded so heartbroken about it. But because she was very focused on the elevator doors she didn't see it. 'Charlie, I think you're . . .'

Before I could finish my sentence the doors opened and without a word she practically ran away from me.

I saw Charlie twice that day. We were all working on Michael Ashton's complicated and – as we realized as we dug deeper – sticky situation. And Charlie did join both meetings I'd called in my room, and did everything I asked her to do. She talked to Michael Ashton and got all the missing information we needed and I realized she was very good at her job. Much better than the rest of the team. When we'd gathered everything we could for the day, she fled to her own room, then shuffled back and forth between her dad's office and her own.

Whenever I looked up from my desk she was always busy and running around. She didn't look in my direction the entire day. Not even once. Which was why when I called both meetings I had to leave a note on her desk to give her enough time to get there on top of sending her a meeting request through her email. Maybe trying to make sure whether she got my notes was why my eyes were always following her around. Because there couldn't and shouldn't be another reason.

It was around 7.30 p.m. when I got off the subway and started my walk back to my temporary apartment courtesy of Douglas Davis. Because my mind was still filled with work and things I needed to go over when I got home, I didn't hear the shouts or the quiet curses.

It was a miracle that I didn't fall on my ass when first a dog ran right past me, its body a hair's breadth away from my leg, and then a human barrelled into me from my left side.

'Please hold me!'

I grabbed the lamp post at the last minute so neither one of us would have to fall onto our faces and then tried to soften the blow by slightly turning so the girl could hit my chest. If I had missed it we would've for sure ended up at the hospital with the speed she ran into me.

I grabbed her shoulder and arm as she tried her best to hold onto the end of the leash as the dog tried his best to drag her behind him.

'I'm so sorry,' she gasped out, her body straining forward. She slightly turned her face towards me, but had kept her eyes on the dog. 'You have to stop,' she panted, pulling on the leash. The dog looked back at her and then down the street again. 'You lost her,' she continued, pulling a little harder. 'She is gone, buddy. You scared her to death and saved us. What a good boy. Time to leave the stranger and go home now.'

I recognized who I was holding onto the moment she spoke.

The dog looked back at her over his shoulder, whined a little, body shaking to keep following whatever monster he had been following, but another tug from Charlie had him strutting back to her with his tongue lolling out.

Charlie let out a long sigh, her body relaxing a little bit. 'I'm so sorry,' she repeated as I relaxed my hold. 'He saw the cat – and I didn't know he would . . .'

I let her go and she finally glanced back and up at me.

'I don't k— no . . . no. No! Are you serious?' she asked, her voice rising.

I chuckled at the genuine disappointment on her face.

'I'm afraid so,' I answered, still smiling down at her shocked and unhappy face.

The dog made it to her side and with his body pushed her a step forward – into me.

She immediately took a few steps backward for good measure.

'Where did you come from? Are you . . . were you following me or something?'

I chuckled and glanced down at the dog when he barked at me once. 'The subway. And yes, Charlie,' I replied, chuckling. 'That's what I was doing, following you, when you ran into me from behind.'

'But . . . Okay, that was a stupid question. What are you doing here?'

'I could ask you the same question,' I retorted with a raised eyebrow.

Holding the leash in a death grip, she ran her hand up and down her arm. 'I live here.' She pointed across the street a few houses down, then looked back at me waiting for her answer.

'Well,' I said, a little surprised, 'I live right across from you, it would seem.'

Understanding dawned on her face. 'My dad's place,' she concluded.

I nodded. Half-hiding behind Charlie, the dog barked again, grabbing my attention. I squatted down in front of them. Immediately he backed off, trying to fuse himself to Charlie, his tail tucked between his legs.

'Oh, it's okay, baby,' Charlie cooed at him, her tone completely different. 'He is not that bad, Pepp.'

I looked up at her from my spot. Scrunching up her nose with a little smile, she shrugged.

'What's his name?' I said quietly.

'They called him Duke, but we decided to change it to Pepperoni. He really loves them. I ordered pizza last night, and I wanted to give him a piece to celebrate the fact that we found each other and he just picked all the pepperoni slices and left the rest.'

Pepperoni bumped his head against her thigh, so Charlie squatted down next to him, petting his head.

'You just got him?' I asked, smiling.

She smiled back. A genuine and ... beautiful smile. 'Two days. Love at first sight. Actually he was the reason why I had to run off that day at the office.'

My eyes got stuck on her lips. 'I can see that.'

Our knees weren't quite touching, but it was close enough. Pepperoni burrowed his head under her arm, earning a chuckle from her.

A car sped by, honking at someone. Both the dog and the owner looked at me.

'This nice man who managed to stop you from dragging me around is William, Pepperoni,' she said, introducing us. 'He is also my colleague.' Hugging the dog a little closer and running her hand over his head and his floppy ears, she glanced at me. 'And this good boy is Pepperoni. I call him Pepp.'

I chuckled as Pepperoni started wagging his tail and licked her cheek once. Holding out my hand, I waited as he gathered up the courage to take a step forward and sniff me. He kept throwing glances at me as he got closer, his body alert the entire time. Once he realized I wasn't going to hurt him, he took another step forward and let me scratch behind his ears.

'Rescue?' I asked, my voice a little rough.

Charlie sighed. 'Yeah. Two different families brought him back. And he was bullied by the other dogs too.'

I shook my head as Pepp bumped his head against my arm, expecting more pets.

'He is beautiful,' I said, holding his face between my hands. 'Great Dane, right?'

She nodded as she smiled at Pepp.

'How old is he?'

'Nine months.'

'He is going to be a monster, you know that, right?' I tilted my head to glance at Charlie when nothing but silence answered me.

'I don't think he'll get bigger than this.'

'Prepared to be surprised then.'

Feeling safe enough, Pepp decided to give me a thorough sniff and walked behind my back, pulling on the leash a little, mostly pulling on Charlie. Before she could tumble on me, she straightened up and walked around me to follow Pepp.

'Well,' she said when they had completed the tour and she was standing in front of me again. 'I'm sorry for holding you up for so long. And I'm sorry for barrelling into you like that. At the shelter they said that he naps all day. I wasn't expecting this level of . . . excitement. Also sorry for questioning your motives on being here.'

She made me laugh again, and I was awarded with another one of her smiles.

'Glad to hear you don't think I was stalking you.'

'It's just . . .' Pepperoni pulled at the leash, his nose on the ground. Charlie looked at me over her shoulder. 'I wasn't expecting to see you here, you know.'

When she started walking because her dog couldn't be contained, I fell into step beside them.

'I was surprised to see you too. Douglas didn't mention you lived on the same street as me.'

'It's his apartment too. The one I'm living in, I mean. I had my own place, but I needed to stay with my grandma for a while when she got sick and then when I was looking I couldn't find ... anyway, I'm just rambling. I guess we're neighbours too as well as colleagues now.'

'You don't have to sound that disappointed, but it looks that way.'

Her gaze jumped to me. 'I'm not disappointed. Just surprised.'

We stopped in front of my place. Pepperoni sniffing at the plant next to the stairs.

Charlie looked up at the stairs and then, avoiding my gaze again, started to back up. 'Well, this is you. You're probably tired from work. It was nice bumping into you, William. Goodnight.' Pulling at Pepperoni, she turned around and walked to the edge of the sidewalk.

I took a step towards them, hands in my pocket. 'Since I'm new to town, I don't know the area well, I haven't had anything to eat yet. You know a good pizza place or something around?'

Standing between two parked cars, she turned around to face me. 'You've lived in New York, William.'

'Not this area.'

We stared at each other, then both of us smiled. I just watched her. 'And?'

'Oh. Yes. Ah, there is an Italian pizzeria down the street to the left. Johnie's. It's very small, but they make the best pizza around here. You won't be disappointed.'

'Would you like to join me?' I didn't think too much on whether it'd be a good idea or not to have dinner with someone on my team before I asked. But after the words got out, I decided it wouldn't be the worst thing to have a casual dinner together to maybe ease the tension between us and become friendly again. I realized I would actually like that.

She took her time before answering. I wasn't sure if it was because she was considering my offer or trying to find a way out of it.

'I can't,' she said eventually. 'I kind of have a date.'

I raised an eyebrow. 'A date?' It wasn't my business. 'Kind of? How does that work?'

When Pepp started pulling at her, she checked the street before she started walking backwards with Pepp's guidance.

'I have no idea. It's kind of like an online thing so I'm not sure if it counts as a date. I'm giving it a try so that should count for something, I guess.'

I nodded. 'Ah, got it. The wonders of online dating.'

'Oh yes, the wonders ... I would go with horrors, but let's be positive like you. Okay then, have a good night. Oh, and thank you for the save.' Raising her hand, she gave me a wave.

'You're welcome.' I took a few steps as if I were going to follow her until I caught myself and stopped. I was standing on the edge of the sidewalk like she was on the other side of the road. 'Rain check on the pizza?' I asked. I had to raise my voice a little so she could hear.

She stopped moving towards her stairs. 'Ah ... sure. Maybe another night? We'll all go out together with the team.'

The team, yes. That was probably the right answer as well.

7

Charlie

'I need someone to kiss me. You know this. Are you one hundred percent sure he is an okay guy?' I asked Gayle as she hovered in front of my office door. After my online date had turned up drunk and looked absolutely nothing like his profile pic – which I could've ignored if he was apologetic about it instead of being drunk and shouting my name across the bar in an effort to find me – I was willing to take drastic measures. And it didn't get any worse than blind dates. I knew that much. Had learned it the hard way this last year after my breakup with Craig.

'What is it with the kissing? I told you he is one of Kevin's friends, he is an orthodontist. I've only met him twice ...'

'Yes, yes, I know. Your husband is great so his friend can't be that bad. What was his name again?'

Gayle sighed and, crossing her arms, leaned against the doorframe. 'His name is Ralph.'

'Ralph.' I tried his name a few more times and made a face. 'I've never dated or kissed a Ralph before. Not sure how I feel about it.' When I saw Gayle straighten a little and open her mouth – her fighting stance – I raised my hand, palm out, stopping her before she could start on me. 'I know. I know. I'm being annoying. I just ...

we know how bad I am with blind dates or dates in general. I'm nervous, that's all.'

She cocked an eyebrow. 'You've only been on what? Two blind dates? The one that Rick's wife set you up with, and the other one I can't remember. Was it the guy from the 13th floor?'

I shivered. 'Yes, it was. The IT guy. He looked so sweet, but . . .' I shivered again and Gayle chuckled. 'He single-handedly ruined blind dates for me. Wouldn't you agree?'

After considering it for a second or two, she finally nodded. 'Yeah, I'll give you that much. That part when he tried to lick your feet at the restaurant . . . yeah, that was maybe pushing it a little.'

'You think so?' Feeling a little nauseous at the reminder, I shook myself out of the nightmare that was my blind date a few months ago. No wonder I didn't want to go out with anyone.

'Ralph is a good guy,' she continued. 'I'm pretty sure he won't try and get under the table to lick your feet. He is pretty mellow compared to Kevin's other friends. I like talking to him when he is around. And you saw his Facebook, he is a good-looking guy.'

'Very nice smile,' I admitted. A good smile was always very attractive.

'If nothing else comes out of it, you'll have a nice meal and a good conversation and it'll be a practice run for you. You've only been on, what, three, four dates after Craig?'

Since I was planning on moving, which Gayle didn't know yet, I wasn't looking for anything serious. I just wanted to try and see how it went . . . in general. Kinda like practice runs. I sighed and tipped my head back so I was staring at the ceiling when I embarrassingly admitted, 'Yeah, just four dates. And I kissed none of them. Or none of them kissed me. And it's been five or six years since I've been *kissed*.' The second the words left my mouth I wanted to stuff them all back in. Slowly I closed my eyes and hoped Gayle hadn't heard what I'd just blurted out.

There was silence for quite a few heartbeats, then I heard Gayle close the door to my office and walk towards my desk. I didn't look at her – the ceiling was, interestingly enough, more . . . interesting.

'I think your math is wrong there, Charlie. You broke up with Craig a year ago.'

I groaned and used my arm to hide my face.

She sat down in the chair in front of my desk. 'Explain.'

I groaned again. 'I don't want to talk about this.'

'Tough shit, we're talking about it.'

There was a knock at the door and I peeked under my arm, only to see Rick opening the door.

'Hi Gayle. Charlie, we have a new case, William wants a meeting . . .'

I'd already jumped up the second I heard the words 'a new case' and by the time Rick finished his sentence I was standing right next to him.

'That was quick.'

'Ah, I'm sorry, Gayle. Work calls,' I apologized, made her an exaggerated sad face, then before she could utter a word, grabbed Rick's arm and pulled him away from my office.

'How are you today, Rick?'

'Do I even want to know what's going on?'

'You would love to know actually, but I'm not telling you anything. Do we know what the new case is?'

'A shopping app is having problems with the customers. We're taking them on. Although not sure where William stands on that yet, so maybe we won't take them on? His exact words were: *we'll see.*'

Linking my arm through his, we headed straight to William's office. 'The electric car problem is taking a lot of our time. How many cases do you think we'll take on at one time?'

'I have no idea. I'm still trying to figure out how William works and where we stand.'

I hummed, but stayed quiet.

'Did you hear about the new app?' he asked.

'What app?'

'You know, the new app everyone is talking about. Maybe it's better than your app. Maybe you should look it up.'

I cocked my head, squinting at him. 'You kinda lost me. My app? What are you talking about?'

'We know you're giving dating another try.'

My steps faltered, I let go of his arm and stopped walking altogether. Rick paused long enough to look back.

I felt heat creeping up to my face.

'Define we,' I pressed as an awful feeling swarmed me.

He gave me a smile that I translated as a sad one. 'Well, sweetheart . . . a lot of people in here know you haven't dated in a long time so . . . they have been taking bets . . .'

A little mortified at the thought of people talking about my non-existent love life let alone *betting* on it, I pushed down all the feelings that threatened to come up to the surface and shook my head. 'Did you . . . ? Okay, no, I don't want to hear about this. How did you even know?'

'Someone heard you talking with Gayle the other day.'

'Just so you know,' I started, raising my voice a little so more people could eavesdrop. Again. 'It's my choice that I don't want to date anyone. It's not like there are a sea of great choices when it comes to men, and I failed to choose one of them. I'm choosing not to settle, and if that means I won't date every single loser I come across and I'm lonely for a while, not that I'm even lonely, so be it. Let's go.'

Before he could open his mouth and respond, I took his arm yet again and quickly dragged him towards William's office.

It was 9 p.m., and I was still stuck at the bar. There hadn't been a sighting of a Ralph as far as I knew. And considering we were supposed to meet up for dinner at 8 p.m. at a restaurant halfway

across the town and he hadn't showed, I figured I had been officially stood up.

Blind dates, my luck and life and all. Pretty fun combo.

Since I was already there and the bartender seemed nice enough,
I stuck with him and decided to make a night out of it. I was already
kind of dressed up anyway. I was sipping on my second drink. The
bartender, whose name I didn't know, wasn't aware that he was my
date for the night, but he didn't really need to know that anyway.

My upstairs neighbours Antonio and Josh were babysitting Pepp.
Not so surprisingly, their five-year-old dog Daisy loved Pepp and
my timid Pepp loved Daisy too, so I didn't want to cut short their
playtime by showing up early.

> **Valerie:** How is the date? Do I need to save you by starting
> a fire in your house? Or something more clever?

> **Charlie:** No need. He stood me up.

> **Valerie:** Well . . . screw him. Onwards and upwards.

My elbow was resting on the bar top, my fingers playing with the
stem of my margarita glass. Just for a quick second I closed my eyes
and hummed to the mellow song playing in the restaurant. I didn't
know who it was by, but it was a piano solo and it was lovely.

I heard a stool being pulled and the sound it made against the
floor somewhere far away made me wince slightly, but it didn't ruin
the moment for me, so I kept my eyes closed.

'Are you sleeping?' someone asked right next to me, and I jumped
up from my stool, splashing some of my drink all over my hand as
if they had just shouted in my ear.

'Shit,' I mumbled, wiping my hand with the napkin as I straightened a little and glanced to my left, only to come face to face with
William as he took the seat right next to mine.

He gave me a quick look, eyes roaming my body from head to toe, making me squirm in my seat, then faced the bar as if he hadn't just shocked the hell out of me by showing up out of nowhere.

'I can hardly sleep in a bar,' I answered, trying my best to look unruffled. 'Who would fall asleep at a bar?' Still a little disoriented, I frowned at him as I furtively pulled down the hem of my dress and looked around the restaurant. Everyone seemed to be where I'd left them.

'I assumed you were. I apologize. Your eyes have been closed for quite some time so I reached the wrong conclusion.'

'What are you doing here?' I asked, only to hear how scratchy my voice sounded. I cleared my throat, casually glanced towards the mirror behind the rows of alcohol bottles to check if my hair looked okay. Had I seriously fallen asleep? It'd be a new low for sure.

'An old friend of mine was in New York for a day. We had dinner.'

He lifted his hand and my eyes caught on the movement as he somehow in a sexy way gestured to the bartender to get his attention. I frowned at myself and looked away from his attractive hand. Who even found a hand attractive?

'Here? You had dinner with him here?' If he had, he must've seen me sit at the same spot for an hour. I groaned inwardly.

My question earned me another look from him, but I managed to hold his stare.

'Yeah, here. Why?'

'No reason. Perfect. Out of all the places in New York, of course you'd have dinner here,' I mumbled to myself, slightly turning my head away and taking a sip of my sloshed margarita.

'Excuse me?' he asked, and I could clearly hear the amusement in his voice.

I gave him a forced smile. 'Nothing.'

The bartender came over with a smile and took his drink order: scotch on the rocks.

'Another one for you?' he asked me. I'm pretty sure I wasn't imagining how his smile got just a tiny little bit warmer when he was talking to me.

I looked down at my drink, then looked at William and found him looking back at me, waiting for my response.

This wasn't a great idea. I had no issues, or not that many issues, working with him, but spending extra time with him could become dangerous if you considered the past. Not to mention the fact that I had been stood up and he'd had a front row seat to it didn't really help. I was shaking my head as I started to slide off of my seat so I could leave, but William put his hand on my arm, causing me to pause my movement. He leaned towards me and my heart had a little trouble deciding how to react to his sudden closeness.

'Keep me company a little?' he asked quietly as he caught my startled gaze.

I swallowed the lump in my throat as his touch burned through my skin, sending tingles all over my arm.

'Sure,' I answered, finally managing to look away from his warm brown eyes. I was being ridiculous. Clearly it was the alcohol's fault. I cleared my throat. He let go of my arm after gently squeezing it. I had to flex my hand to shake off the electricity running through it. I focused on the bartender and smiled back at him. Safer sight. 'Sure, I'll take another one.' Then I kept my eyes on the bottles lining up the mirrored shelves.

'Rough night?' William asked after a few seconds of uncomfortable silence. I wondered if it'd been a little weird between us the first time we'd met as well. It wasn't how I remembered it, but maybe I was embellishing the past. I didn't know how I felt about that.

Having lost my filter on my second drink at least half an hour ago, I decided I didn't want to tiptoe around it. Especially considering we'd have to be around each other every day. And that aside, I had promised myself that I was going to stick with my list, so this was the perfect moment to be more honest.

'Doesn't this feel a little too familiar to you too?' I asked back, instead of answering his question. 'I mean what are the odds of you ending up at the same restaurant as me? Especially when we both live halfway across town.'

The bartender came back with my drink, and after a quick thank you, I immediately reached for it, taking a small sip of my fresh and very delicious margarita. Not everybody got it right, but my bartender was talented.

William thanked him when he slid his drink towards him, and my drink still clutched in my hand, I stared yet again as he took a long sip and turned halfway in his seat to look at me. I was finally feeling okay enough to take in what he was wearing: a dark grey sweater with the sleeves pulled up covered his fit, broad shoulders and the black slacks that covered the lower half of his body fitted perfectly. It was such a simple outfit, but as it was with some guys, he made it work for him. It must have only taken him a few minutes to get ready and he looked like a model. Whereas I'd taken almost an hour, fussing in front of the mirror, and I just looked . . . *not that bad*.

'It does feel familiar, you're right,' William said after a lengthy pause.

I mentally shook myself out of my thoughts and focused on our conversation. 'I know I've been saying this for days now, but it's so strange.'

'What? Me being here?'

'Not specifically here, but in New York, maybe. Or in general *us* being here. Again. After all this time.'

He nodded. 'It is strange, I'd never imagined I'd see you again.'

I chose to keep quiet and played with my glass. Had he thought about seeing me again? After?

'You are waiting for someone, I assume?' William asked, filling the silence between us.

My date. Right. I refrained from groaning and sat just a little bit straighter. 'I was, yes. But I think he's a no-show at this point, so I thought I'd just enjoy the company of the bartender and make the best of it.' And wasn't it funny or ironic or whatever you'd want to call it that the guy I had waited over two hours for all those years back, the guy who had stood me up as well, was just now sitting right next to me asking about another guy who had stood me up?

The joys of life.

'Your friend got busy?'

A little lost in my own thoughts, I shrugged and faced towards the bar. 'Not my friend. My blind date got busy. I guess,' I murmured.

William leaned towards me just a little, and I leaned away to protect myself . . . from what, I wasn't sure.

'I'm sorry, I couldn't hear you.'

'I just said, my blind date got busy.'

'A blind date, huh? Is this the same one from when I bumped into you the other day?'

I gave William a sideways glance and smiled when I saw he was smiling back at me. It was hard not to when he smiled at you. It was that exact smile and a few other things about him that had kept me going back to that diner every night all those years ago. So, whatever I thought I was feeling just because of his proximity, I tried to shake off. We were colleagues, I couldn't act like a blushing schoolgirl around him – which was probably how I was back then. Now? I couldn't be like that. At least not constantly. And maybe it wouldn't have been that bad if we'd become friends. Tentative friends with a limited number of smiles shared in between. I could very well handle that.

'Ah, no, that was an online date. This was another one – a blind date. They're the worst, I know,' I admitted, forcing myself to relax a bit more. 'But I'm trying to put myself out there a little and just see how I do at it. Flirting and everything. Not looking for anything serious at all, but just dipping my toe in, I guess. Are you dating anyone?' When I realized how that sounded, I decided to backtrack. 'You don't have to answer, of course. It's not my business. It's just that you said you got a divorce and . . . I guess I'm just asking because I'm curious if it's just terrible for me or if it's an all-round thing.'

He took another sip of his scotch, the smile still strong on his lips. 'You can ask, Charlie. It's okay. I haven't dated since my divorce, but when has dating ever not been terrible?'

'Right?' I asked enthusiastically, turning my body towards him a bit more. Tentative friends could be good. 'That's always what I thought, but trust me, blind dates *and* online dates are a completely different category.'

'I'll have to take your word for it. It's been a long while since I've dated in any shape or form.'

'No online dates?' I asked a little surprised.

'Not yet. Not ever.'

'Oh, you're like a baby. The innocence!' I clasped my hands together and gave him my sweetest smile. 'You're missing out on so many things.'

His smile got bigger as he took me in, his eyes lingering on my lips. 'Yeah?'

I smiled back. 'You have no idea. You'll have to let me know how the first one goes. It'll be fun, probably the best time you've ever had.'

'Why do I have a feeling you'll be the only one enjoying that date?'

'I would never enjoy someone else's misery.'

He laughed, the warm sound making me grin.

'Deal,' he agreed. 'If I start online dating, you'll be the first one to hear about my experience.'

The curiosity got the better of me and I couldn't keep my mouth shut. 'So, you're not dating because you're not over your ex?' As soon as the words were out of my mouth I regretted them.

He gave me an interesting sideways look, complete with an eyebrow raise, and I had the decency to look away. I wiped the condensation on my glass to avoid looking at him.

'That was a little personal, sorry. But now that I asked you something personal, you get the chance to ask me one, in return. If you don't want to answer that's okay too, of course.'

He chuckled and shook his head. 'I'm over Lindsey. My ex. Trust me. Just don't have time to date right now. It'll happen when it happens, but it's not gonna happen for a while. I'm not interested in dating at the moment. I'm not worried over it.'

I cleared my throat and nodded. 'I can understand that.' *Lindsey* had no idea what she had lost. I took a few more sips of my drink in the silence before I spoke again. 'I find that relationships are hard. I've been thinking about this a little more than usual lately and sometimes I think it's not worth going through the heartache to find someone decent to spend your life with. If you're happy by yourself why bother, right? But sometimes I think we're not wired to be alone and loving someone and being loved is … not a necessity, I don't want to say necessity, but maybe one of the important things we're looking for in life?'

In the aftermath of my words, he was quiet next to me. And the people in the restaurant went on with their nights, completely unaware of William and me. Was that too deep for a random conversation? Was he thinking why he even bothered to come and sit next to me? Which he had probably done because he felt sorry for me waiting on my own for an hour. There was lots of chatter, clinking noises and loud voices around me. In the grand scheme of things, I guess sitting with the guy I'd had the biggest crush on in my life after so many years and having a deep word vomit didn't affect them much.

'Sometimes it can be worth the trouble,' William said eventually. 'With the right person for you.'

'Is there even a right person? *The* one? Or a perfect one?'

'Depends on how you look at things. I don't believe there is somebody perfect out there, but there could be someone perfect for you. Who complements you, who fits you, who is flawed – because we're all flawed – but is perfect for you.'

'Sounds nice.'

I cleared my throat, trying to ignore how vulnerable I'd just sounded even to my own ears.

'Okay, your turn to ask me something very personal.'

'Do I get to use it later?'

I relaxed. 'Of course.' After my comments, I didn't want to get even more personal. 'This is strange. I don't feel drunk,' I said casually. I never claimed I was good at changing a subject.

'That's usually what drunk people say.'

I raised my full glass, inspecting it thoroughly. 'I know, but I really don't think I am. This is my . . .' I frowned trying to figure out my number '. . . third? I usually have a two-drink limit when I'm out, but I don't feel bad. And I did slosh more than half of my second drink when you showed up so . . .' When I felt his eyes on me, I glanced at him. 'Okay, don't tell anyone, but I'm not a big drinker. I'd never tried a martini before. I tried tonight. It was my first drink.' I shook my head vehemently and put my glass down. 'I didn't like it. I took two sips. I guess that one doesn't count and the second one got sloshed and this . . .' I said, lifting my margarita glass between us, 'is my first official drink.'

His eyes warmed as he smiled. 'I think you're a little tipsy, Charlie.'

'I promise you, I'm not,' I said with feeling. I wasn't quite sure if the warmth I was feeling all over my body was because of William's existence in my space or because of my one-and-a-half margaritas, but I knew I was cold sober. 'You probably forgot, but I have this superpower that makes me ramble on endlessly if there is too much quiet. I'm making up for it. And . . .' I kept going under his watchful gaze, 'as fun as that is, I'm sure, I should probably leave soon. I should get Pepp from my neighbours. They're looking after him until I get back.'

'Let me finish my drink and we'll share a cab. Is that okay with you?'

Normally, it wouldn't be, but as we lived on the same street, going separately would've looked weirder on my part. Acting as if I weren't affected by him all that much would make me not as weird, so I decided to go with that.

'Of course it's okay. We live on the same street.'

There was another long pause, and I watched as William kept turning his glass this way and that way instead of drinking it so we could leave. He had recently divorced, maybe he didn't want to go to an empty home? Maybe he wanted to stay out late? Meet new people? He was new in the city after all.

'If you want to stay, I can get a cab or an Uber on my own. I'm not drunk, I'm serious.'

He gave me a sideways glance. 'No, I need to get back too. It's been a long day.'

After another nod, I took one last sip of my unfinished margarita and pushed it away from me. Neither one of us said anything for a full minute. I wasn't drunk, that was a fact, but it didn't mean I wouldn't put my hands on the bar top, palms down and close my eyes. The music, the chatter and all the sound around us blended perfectly together.

I took a deep, quiet breath and got a whiff of William's heady cologne. I remembered it from the day before when I was in his office. It was subtle, fresh and a little woodsy – nothing that would give you a headache. The cologne just took me somewhere completely different and I sat there, right next to William and imagined myself with a boyfriend. Someone who was flawed, but someone I could trust and share a life with.

'What are you doing now?' William asked with an amused voice.

'I'm . . . trying to dream a little,' I answered honestly.

'Don't make me wait now.'

'Are you using your personal question?'

'Looks like I am.'

'Okay.' I cracked one eye open and looked at him for a quick second, only to find his gaze on me. I closed it again. 'I'm thinking of my dream boyfriend. How it would be.'

'Let's hear it, then.'

I hummed. 'If I say it out loud it probably won't happen.'

'It works like a birthday wish?'

I could still hear the amusement in his voice, so I fully opened my eyes and looked at him.

I was supposed to answer his question, I knew that, but instead I found myself blurting out things he absolutely did *not* need to know. 'I think first I should admit that it's been quite a while since I've *dated* dated someone. So I've had quite some time to think about what I want.' Needing to busy myself with something, I hauled the margarita glass back and started playing with the stem.

'Dated dated? How does that work, exactly?'

I thought about it and realized maybe I *was* a little tipsy. Especially if I was sitting here and talking about my lack of love life to William just to distract myself from staring at him.

'I feel like I should maybe warn you, I might be a little tipsy.'

'Does that mean I'm gonna get a good answer?'

I thought about it. 'It might.'

I looked at him as he gestured to the bartender.

As soon as the bartender showed up, William asked for a glass of water for me.

'Thank you,' I said.

William's eyes found mine, and I couldn't look away. 'You're welcome. Now don't leave me hanging. Tell me about this dream guy. Do you have a description? What does he look like?'

I tried my best to break eye contact, but couldn't quite find the strength to do it. He was the first one to look away when our bartender showed up with my water.

William turned to me with his drink in his hand, settling in his new position. One elbow on the back of his seat, one on the bar top.

'Or maybe you should explain the dated dated part first though, so I get the whole picture.'

I drank half of the water. 'I just meant I went out with a few people, three to be exact. Three relationships in total, I mean. I've dated, but I haven't been in a relationship in the last year. Going out on dates with the same person more than once, that kinda thing.'

'How long has it been then? Spill the beans, already.'

I laughed. 'Spill the beans?' Facing him, I took a few more sips of my water as I watched him smile at me. Had his hair been this good back then?

'You spill it first. How long has it been since *you* dated?'

'Hmmm.' He took his time, thinking about it. 'Six years, I'd say. Before I got married.'

'Okay, well. At least you were married. A living, breathing human being right next to you. You're already ahead of me with just that. I was in a long-distance relationship for five years so even though I was considered to be in a relationship, I actually wasn't because we were barely speaking. And it's been a year since I broke up with Craig. But even before the breakup I hadn't seen him face-to-face for two years.'

'Okay, you win. Long-distance, huh?'

'Yeah, because I love dating so much, I decided that trying all the versions I can while I have the chance is a good idea.' I shook my head, then resting my elbow on the bar top, leaned my head against my hand. 'The worst idea I ever had. Ten months into our relationship, it turned into long-distance when he moved to London for a work opportunity and we maybe saw each other three or four times in all those years.'

'Why did you break up? The distance?'

I shrugged. 'The distance and he cheated. Probably more than once.'

'I see.'

The second William finished his scotch, I straightened up and got the attention of the bartender and asked for my bill. It was time to go home before I made a fool of myself by talking more than I already had.

I glanced at William apologetically. 'I really should get back to Pepp. If you're done, I'm gonna call an Uber, is that okay? If not, I can go by myself.'

He shook his head. 'I'm done. We can go.'

We both paid for our drinks. I arranged the Uber and then I led the way all through the restaurant as William followed me silently.

8

William

Outside, I stood next to Charlie as we waited for the Uber on the sidewalk. Either the different location had melted the subtle tension between us, or it was the drinks she had had, but I felt like we were in a better place.

A group of five exited the restaurant laughing loudly, looking and sounding drunk. After a quick peek over her shoulder, Charlie took a step towards me as the guys ended their short walk when they reached our side.

'Let's move a little,' I suggested quietly, when one of them got too close and Charlie looked uncomfortable with their proximity as their voices started to get the attention of people walking by.

She nodded, and instinctively I put my hand on the small of her back, surprising both her and myself. Frowning, I dropped my hand.

She was doing better with meeting my eyes, but I guessed that we weren't quite friends yet. Touching each other randomly was not wise. She pushed both her hands in her coat pockets and kept her eyes averted as I took a step back to put some healthy distance between us.

'Our ride should be here in a few minutes.'

Because I'd been so intrigued with our conversation back at the bar, I couldn't keep myself from asking, 'You were gonna tell me about this dream guy.'

She gave me a sideways look, then looked at the loud idiots who were making a ruckus.

I watched as she made a decision and then released a breath.

'I'm going to be honest with you, so you better appreciate that and no laughing.'

Trying my hardest not to smile, I cleared my throat and nodded. 'I wouldn't dream of it.'

She sighed and shook her head at me. 'You're gonna laugh, but anyway. I want a lot of things obviously, as all women want. But, first of all, I want him to have stars in his eyes when he looks at me,' she admitted quietly just for me as I stared at her profile. She tipped up her chin, gazing at the sky. 'I want the "you're mine and I'm yours line". I want the cheese.'

I was still staring at her profile when she gave me a quick look – I'm assuming to check if I was laughing at her – then turned back to watch the street for the Uber.

'You want him to give you his cheese?' I asked to make her relax.

'I . . . what? No.' She gave me a surprised look and laughed. She had a beautiful laugh. Soft. Not too loud. Not too quiet to the point that it was weird. It was just the right amount of sound to grab your attention and hold it. And I'd always thought she had a beautiful smile. She was still smiling when she met my gaze.

My eyes on her lips, I smiled back.

'No, I mean I want all the cheesy lines. They make me happy when I hear them in the movies or in books. When they really mean it, that cheesiness make me happy. A cliché is a cliché for a reason. It works on those who have a romantic heart and even on some who don't.'

'Now you have to give me an example. Just how much cheesiness are we talking about here?'

She considered my question seriously as she furrowed her brows and focused on her feet.

'Ah,' she exclaimed with a satisfied gleam in her eyes. 'A favourite. *When you realize you want to spend the rest of your life with somebody, you want the rest of your life to start as soon as possible.*'

'Which movie is that from? It sounds slightly familiar.'

'*When Harry Met Sally.* A classic. If my dream guy said that to me . . . my romantic little heart would be over the moon.'

'Ah, okay. Got it.'

She gave me an unsure look as if she were pretty sure I hadn't gotten it.

She turned her body towards me and stared into my eyes almost as if she were challenging me. 'I'll give you another one. *Kiss me. Kiss me as if it were the last time.*'

Did she realize that her voice had dropped and had gotten softer?

'I know that one. *Casablanca,*' I guessed gruffly; it had been one of Lindsey's favourite movies. 'Good movie.'

'Great movie,' Charlie agreed, and nodding once, broke our eye contact. 'Of course, I want the passion too. I want him to say: there you are, I found you. I've been looking and waiting for you for quite some time and I'm so happy that you're here now.'

Right at the end of her enthusiastic words, one of the guys in the group bumped into her and she was forced to get closer to me. The guy apologized, but I was already annoyed with them. I reached for Charlie's arm and pulled her closer to my side. She gave me a small smile.

'Are you lost, Charlie?' I asked seriously, after a moment of silence in our little corner of the night where we were standing maybe a little too close to each other.

She looked straight into my eyes, lost her smile a little, then after a few seconds blinked and looked away. I shifted in place and decided to shut the hell up.

'Am I lost?' she started when I was ready to let go of the conversation and change the subject altogether. 'The honesty thing again. Okay, I'm gonna be honest. You ready?'

'Hit me.'

'I'm not sure. I think – I'm not sure anymore. I think I might be lost. A new guy won't suddenly complete me, I know that. I don't mean being lost in that sense. I don't *need* a guy. I like being alone, I make myself happy. I just mean that I'd like to have someone I can lean on from time to time. Someone I can come home to and talk to, share some laughs, some conversation. Share a life. Build a life together. I think I'm a little tired of doing things on my own even if it's a small decision like what to have for dinner. Sometimes it feels like I'm so lonely that I might start to lose my mind. And I don't want to find someone just because I feel lonely. I just feel like I'm ready to have that special thing in my life some people are lucky to have. I want that for myself. Does that even make sense?'

Something tightened in my chest, and I remembered why Charlie had been so dangerous for me all those years ago.

'Passion, you said,' I prompted, instead of telling her I understood what she meant all too well and that there was nothing wrong whatsoever about what she wanted from life.

Picking up on my effort to lighten the mood, she continued as if she hadn't given me one of the most honest answers I had heard in a long time. 'Oh, yes. You gotta have passion. Nothing crazy necessarily, although it's always good if that exists, but you have to have at least that electricity run through you when you touch, that . . .' she glanced down at her shoes then looked away '. . . that I-can't-wait-to-be-alone-with-you look on your face when you're in a crowded room. I'm not going to go into too much detail here, but I don't want to have a boring relationship where we are perfectly content about not touching each other for a long period of time. Nothing wrong with that. I had a friend who only had sex with her husband once a month. And even that only happened because the husband reminded her that it'd been a month since the last time they did it. I just don't want that for myself, that's all. If I wanted that I'd find a roommate. I want to love someone as if my heart will never break.'

Before I could gather my thoughts and open my mouth to say something, make a small comment, tell her that I knew ... she moved from my side.

'Oh, look. I think that's our ride.'

And then she moved away from me.

We were in the car and almost at our street when she leaned closer again. Thinking she was going to say something important, I leaned in as well.

'I still don't have a crush on you,' she whispered, eyes on the driver.

Amused, I kept my eyes on her. She pulled back from me.

'I think you made that pretty clear the last time we spoke about this,' I reminded her.

She nodded. 'Okay, just wanted to mention it again.'

I laughed quietly. 'You're good. We've established that you don't have a crush on me.'

9

Charlie

After a somewhat quiet weekend lovingly spent with Pepperoni where we bonded enough that he felt comfortable to snuggle up and fall asleep in my arms, Monday was a rush at work. The woman who had gotten injured while using Michael Ashton's car, Kylie Combs, had finally spoken about the whole situation on a vlog and as if that wasn't enough damage on its own, she had also written an article on it for one of the biggest technology websites, bashing Michael's company. After getting a short and to-the-point text from William, I'd jumped out of bed, taken care of Pepperoni in record time and basically ran to work. William was already there at 7.30 a.m., and I was glad to see I was *not* the last.

The meeting lasted for longer than any of us expected, but we knew from the start that the whole deal would keep us busy. Trying to figure what went wrong was one of my favourite things about our job.

As I took notes, I discreetly watched William out of the corner of my eye. My eyes just naturally managed to land on him. Did I feel guilty about it? Not really. Not at all. But he caught me staring more than a few times and like deer caught in headlights, I tried to act innocent. Twice he put his hand over mine to stop me clicking my pen. He didn't say anything. It felt so intimate.

When we wrapped up the meeting and everyone left to get to their tasks, it was just me and William. Suddenly the room seemed to be too small for two people.

'We're together then?' I asked and then immediately backtracked. 'On this, I mean. We're together on this specific thing.'

His mouth curved into a smile. The first one of its kind since we first crammed in this room. With some hesitation, I smiled back.

'You get nervous around me when we're alone, don't you?'

Pffff. Why would I do such a thing?

I forced myself to smile more and shook my head as if he were being ridiculous. 'Not really. Why would I?'

He chuckled. 'I agree. Why would you? Especially since you already told me you don't have a crush on me anymore.'

I tried my very best to not make a weird sound, and I was successful, thankfully. I kept the smile intact on my lips. 'Exactly. To be honest, you're not very crushable anymore. You got old, I think. That might be it.' I wanted to take the words back the moment I heard myself say them because it sounded a lot like I was flirting with him, and I didn't think it was my best idea to date.

He raised his eyebrow. 'I'm not crushable, you say?'

We'd been staring at each other's eyes for at least a few seconds – which felt like minutes rather than seconds – when William sighed and slowly shook his head. 'I'm sorry, Charlie. That was inappropriate for work.'

I made another noncommittal sound and gave him a dismissive wave, then changed my mind about not commenting. *Be honest and go for it. Remember the list.* 'What do you say we keep it professional when we're around the team, but when we're alone we can be friends like we were the other night? Otherwise I'm pretty sure I'll make it awkward every single time we interact with each other, and I really don't want to do that. Plus, we're neighbours too, so it's not like we'll only see each other at work. I feel like that would be a good arrangement, but what do you think? Would you like to be friends with me?'

'Okay.' He nodded to himself. 'Yeah, let's do that. Friends, then?'

He had beautiful eyes that looked at me in a way that was hard for me to put into words. His smile was even more beautiful and he was my friend. After thinking about him every now and then for years and wanting to be with him or someone very much like him, we had officially friend-zoned each other.

I wasn't sure whether I should cry or be relieved. I felt the need to offer my hand to seal the deal on our fate of just being friends, but I held it together. 'I think we'll be good friends. I can see our potential,' I said, almost believing my own words. 'At least until I move.'

Another smile danced on his lips and I moved my eyes away from the sight.

My phone pinged with a new message.

Valerie: Updates, please. Updates. You're hogging information.

Charlie: We officially friend-zoned each other a minute ago. You can calm down.

'Something important?' William asked, and I put my phone down.
'Nope.'

'Anyway, we need to prepare his statement together,' he continued. 'He's never had media training so you're gonna have to walk him through it since he is more comfortable with you. I need him to look confident and like someone who knows what they're doing in front of the camera while also looking apologetic. We can't have him breaking apart from the stress.'

'I can do that.' I reached for my notepad and opened my laptop. 'Where should we start . . .'

He stood up. 'Let's get out of here.'

'We're not working here?' I asked.

He shook his head. 'Let's take ten first though. I need to clear my head and make a call to another contact.'

He was right – taking ten sounded like the best idea since I'd been sitting on my ass for the last two hours, and as padded as it was, it was starting to hurt. After leaving William to his phone call, I dropped my laptop in my office, then took that ten to go and find Gayle to talk about Ralph the no-show. It turns out he had had a family emergency and was apparently extremely upset that he had stood me up.

'He wants to make it up to you,' she said. 'He also wanted your number to call and apologize in person, but I didn't want to give it without your permission. I really think you should go on a date with him, Charlie, it'll be good for you. It's my fault that I didn't pick up his call and let you know he wasn't gonna make it. Go on another date with him.'

Sitting on the edge of her desk, I winced, because I couldn't tell her about my plans for moving yet. 'You're not pushy at all. I don't know about another date. Let me think about it for a while, and I'll let you know.'

Seeing as my ten minutes were up, and Gayle was heading out for a short lunch date with her husband – which I wasn't jealous of at all – I was on my way back to my room when I spotted my dad talking to Wilma, his assistant, right in front of Kimberly's office. I ducked my head and hoped that he wouldn't notice me passing them, but I wasn't lucky.

'Charlie, wait a minute.'

I met his eyes and nodded. I could already tell from his flat tone and disapproving look that he wasn't happy with me about something and it wasn't about work. He had a completely different tone of voice when he wanted to talk to me about work-related stuff. Standing to the side and waiting for them to finish their conversation, I glanced towards William's office, but he wasn't there. Done with their talk, Wilma walked past me, offering a small smile. Preparing myself for whatever he was about to say, I turned to my dad.

'How is it going with William?'

Oh. Maybe I'd misread the tone after all. I relaxed. 'It's good. I like his style. And you picked a good team to work with him. It's going pretty smooth, I think he'll be good for the firm.'

He nodded. 'Of course he will. The others are good with working with him too, then?'

I shrugged. 'So far it looks like they are. They like the case and Michael Ashton. It's a little messy and there's a lot to fix. Someone in his team talked to the media so we're trying to get ahead of that and today Mrs Combs called Michael and basically asked for a bribe, threatening him ...'

'Good. Good. William will give me a report on that. I need you to call the manager of that singer we worked with a few months back.'

I quickly glanced over my shoulder to check William's office, then faced my dad again. 'I was about to go into a meeting with William. We need to work on the statement for tomorrow and I'll coach Michael through ...'

'Charlie, call the manager. I think William can handle things without you just fine.'

Swallowing a bitter response, I just nodded. I didn't have the time to argue with him. 'Anything else you want from me?'

One of the interns, whose name I didn't know, walked past just as my dad asked, 'How is your diet going?'

I felt eyes on me, but instead of looking at the stranger who had heard and would probably tell it to the entire office, I swallowed again. This time it wasn't that easy, but I managed. If my voice was quieter than before when I answered my dad, I couldn't help that. 'It's going great,' I answered, even though I wasn't dieting. He'd been asking me that same question ever since I was a teenager. For some reason my weight had always been a big issue for him and even though I *knew* it was my natural body shape, his words always affected me. More so when I was younger, but still I was dealing with the lingering effects of his questions.

'Are you sure?' my dad asked, completely unaware of my internal struggle with his words. 'Charlie, I know you're sensitive about these things, but I think you need to be a little more careful about what you eat if you want to lose weight.' Taking a half-step back, he gave me a thorough look as I tried not to squirm under his scrutiny. With my right hand I grasped the elbow of my left arm. My fingers slightly biting into my flesh over my shirt, my shoulders slumped forward. After shaking his head in disappointment, he leaned forward and gave my cheek a kiss as my whole body tightened. 'Your skirt is already too tight. I'm just thinking about your health, that's all. Don't get mad at me,' he whispered.

My eyes watering, I tilted my head up just a little and chose not to say anything, since this was a conversation we regularly had and no matter what I said, he neither heard nor understood. Another shake of his head and then he sighed and moved on. I stood there for a few more seconds, then headed straight towards the bathroom so I could pull myself together. There was one thing I was not going to do at the firm and that was cry.

I made eye contact with Kimberly, who was standing in the doorway of her office, only for a short moment, then quickly looked away. Did I need to lose weight? I wouldn't look awful if I lost ten pounds. Did I not like myself the way I was? I very much did. I liked my butt, I liked my curves, my waist, my boobs. I also loved food. But because it was my dad who was commenting and criticizing how I looked when he was supposed to be the *one* person who was supposed to love me just the way I was, it hurt more. It could be because I hadn't grown up with a mom who could teach me to love my body and myself no matter what at an early age, but instead had my dad make me feel ashamed of myself on and off throughout my entire life. Even though I was smart enough to know I shouldn't have let what others thought get to me, what he thought still mattered.

After I took a minute in the bathroom to shake off his comments, I headed back to my room and saw a note on my desk.

Would you like to have a quick and friendly lunch meeting with me at the park while we work on the statement? I'll order you something with cheese.

Reading the last line made me laugh, and I looked up from my note to see if I could spot him, but he wasn't in his room. Oddly happy about a lunch meeting with William – friendly or not – I was smiling embarrassingly as I gathered up my things to leave, my dad's comments already forgotten. I grabbed the note and put it in one of my drawers for safe keeping and then straightened, only to find William waiting for me by my office door.

My smile got even bigger and I felt my body just light up.

'Hi.'

'What do you say, Charlie?' he asked.

'One thing you should probably know about me if we're friends now: you can get me to say yes to a lot of things with food.' I paused. 'Wait, when I say a lot of things, I didn't mean it to sound like I meant . . .'

William just chuckled, cutting me off. 'Don't worry, Charlie. I won't use that confession against you.'

It was probably the best lunch meeting I'd had in a very, very long time – if not *the* best. It was both fun and strangely professional. It was, I think, one of the first moments when I realized how much I enjoyed working with William and wouldn't mind actually being his friend.

When the clock hit 9.30 p.m. our entire team was all dead on its feet, but we had done everything we could've for the day and it was time to finally leave the office. Everyone else in the firm had already left by that point and our team was the last to finish things up. Considering we thought we'd have to stay in until 10.30, we counted ourselves lucky.

I gathered my things, closed my laptop, turned off my desk light and was about to shut my office door when I saw William heading my way. His hair looked dishevelled and I knew it looked that way because he worked his hand through it whenever he was frustrated. I was starting to get to know him all over again. Other than his hair, he looked unfairly perfect.

Yet, I still didn't have a crush on him. Thankfully. I liked him, but I wasn't really salivating after him. A soft crush maybe, but that was kinda, sorta normal.

He was holding his jacket in his hand. His white shirt was still clinging to his broad shoulders in a way that distracted you way too much, and his pants ... there wasn't much I could say about those that wasn't indecent. I was embarrassed to admit to myself – also maybe not – that I might have caught sight of some bulge earlier that night while we were working with everyone in the meeting room, and ever since then I was having a hard time stopping my eyes from trying to catch another sighting. Some things just couldn't be hidden. Not my fault.

'Hey, Charlie. You're ready to leave?'

I gestured towards the elevators. 'I just finished. Heading home. You?'

His brows drew together. 'You're not coming?'

'Coming? Where?'

'Stan and Rick invited me to this bar you all frequent, apparently. Just to have a beer. They said a group of you head there a few times a week.'

I felt a bit awkward since nobody had invited me, but that wasn't a big deal. Sometimes Rick or Gayle forced me to go with them, but mostly I was excluded. Maybe because I was the boss's daughter, or maybe because I was just plain boring. Most of the time though I just had to work late. I started walking towards the elevators and he fell in step next to me. 'Oh, yes. They do. Gayle joins them too. You'll have fun.'

'How about you?'

It felt weird to admit to him that I wasn't invited every time they met, plus I didn't want him to think I was too dull to be included, so

I chose not to mention it. 'Occasionally I tag along too, but mostly I'm too tired to enjoy the crowd and noise. I tend to be the last one to leave the office so that doesn't help either'

The elevator doors opened. There were three guys already in there, heatedly discussing football. I moved into the left corner, William took the spot to my left and to my relief there was some space between us.

Eyes up, Charlie. Eyes up.

I was studying the ceiling – just to make sure my eyes didn't betray me – ignoring the soft chatter around us when William spoke up.

'So?' he asked, slightly leaning towards me, his arm touching my shoulder. I managed not to move or lean towards him.

Success!

'Are you coming tonight or not?'

I glanced at him. 'To the bar? It's pretty late, I should probably head back home to Pepperoni.'

'He's alone?'

'No, I called my neighbours earlier when I thought we'd finish around 10.30, 11 p.m. They took him up to their place so he can spend some time with their lab, Daisy.'

'Sounds like you have good neighbours.'

I gave him a small smile, thinking of sweet Antonio and Josh. 'They're amazing. Josh is an author. He writes crime novels. They offered to help with Pepp whenever I need it, especially when I'm at work since he doesn't seem to be a fan of me leaving, but I kinda don't want to overdo it. I know Josh needs his quiet time when he is working, but Pepp and Daisy get along so well. We have keys to each other's apartments in case of an emergency. Josh takes Pepperoni with them too when he is taking Daisy out for a walk.' My smile got bigger, just thinking about Pepperoni's reaction to me coming home. 'You should see how happy he looks when he sees me at the end of the day. He acts like we're long-lost lovers.'

William chuckled. 'He is taken care of for another hour then.' He stopped near the doors, so I stopped too. 'Come on. Let's grab one beer then we'll leave together. I couldn't say no since this was the second time they invited me already. Not to mention I hate getting the subway alone.'

Fascinated, I watched as he started putting on his jacket and his waistband pulled at the crisp white shirt.

Look. Away. Charlie.

'I really don't look good enough to be out in public, I should head home.' Unconsciously, I checked my ponytail and pushed a few strands of hair behind my ear.

William tilted his head and gave me a confused look. 'Try a better excuse. Maybe something that has some truth in it this time?'

As he stood before me waiting for my answer, it took me a moment to realize I needed to stick to my list and go with him. As dramatic as it sounded, this was the only life I'd have and I had to stop thinking there would be a better moment to say yes to things.

I nodded, reaching for my handbag. 'Okay, then. Let's have a beer.'

His eyebrows rose and I watched as his lips tipped up.

'Yeah?'

'Sure. We're kinda good at this friendship thing, right? So what's one beer among friends. Why not?'

There was no way I'd make a fool of myself if I had just one beer with him.

Famous last words.

10

Charlie

The walk to the bar hadn't taken us long and Parker&Quinn was already crowded exactly like I'd assumed. The others — there were around seven of them, including Gayle — had taken ownership of two booths with high tables. We said a quick hi to Rick, Gayle and everyone else and thankfully they tried not to act too shocked to see me there. William sat next to a girl from accounting, and I took the only remaining seat right across from him. I was a little removed from the others since I was on the very end, but that wasn't news to me, and I was actually more comfortable like that. I took off my jacket, draped it over the back of my chair and put my handbag on my legs, slightly hugging it to my stomach like a safety blanket.

I looked up and Gayle winked at me. I smiled back, relaxing my shoulders. I was fine. I would just have a beer or two then head back home to Pepp. As a bonus I'd get to spend time with William and not look like a hermit. This is how you lived your life and followed the steps on your list. Spending time with others. Mingling.

One of my arms around my bag, one elbow on the table, my chin was resting against my palm while I was taking in my surroundings as our group laughed and chattered when William spoke to me.

'Are you comfortable?'

Did I look uncomfortable? 'Yeah, sure. You?'

His lips stretched out and he smiled at me as if I had said something funny. Unsure, I smiled back. He leaned across the table and my heartbeat slightly picked up its rhythm. Just stuff that hearts do. Completely normal.

'I'm comfortable, Charlie.' His eyes dipped to my lap, then back up to my eyes. 'You're hugging your bag.'

I looked down to my lap, then back up at him. 'Yes, it seems like I'm doing that. I like it. It's comforting.'

His smile softened, and he put some distance between us again by moving back. 'Okay.'

'I'm not being weird, if that's what you're thinking. It's a comfort thing.'

'Not what I was thinking at all.'

I didn't have a comeback for that. 'Oh, okay then.'

'And just so you know I happen to like weird.'

I averted my eyes from his inquisitive gaze when I felt arms around my shoulder.

'Charlie, you know I didn't invite you because I didn't think you'd come, right?' Gayle whispered into my ear.

I relaxed in my seat and put my hands on Gayle's arms as she rested her chin on my head.

'I never come, why would you keep asking me?' It was almost true. She still asked me to go out after work every now and then, but since I always felt dead at the end of the day, or some days I had to deal with family stuff, all I'd want to do was go home and relax. Of course, when I was home and relaxing I'd always regret not going out.

'Apparently I wasn't the right person to do the asking,' she remarked.

There was a pause, and I noticed William staring at us. As soon as we caught each other's eyes, someone on the other side of the table asked him a question and he gave them his attention.

'I'm here only for one beer,' I quietly answered Gayle. 'It has nothing to do with that.'

Twisting my neck, I looked up at her, but before I could say anything else a waitress stopped by the table, planting a martini in front of me.

'Oh, I didn't order anything yet,' I blurted out, but Gayle let go of me and reached for the drink.

'Mine, babe.'

The girl turned to me with a small smile. 'I'm Lola. Can I get you anything?'

'Can we have two beers?' William asked, grabbing my attention again. Then there was a commotion and two more people joined our group.

'Charlie?'

I turned my head to meet William's gaze. 'Ah, yes?'

He smiled, his eyes sparkling. 'I asked if whatever is on tap was okay with you?'

I cleared my throat and met Lola's gaze. 'Sure. Whatever is on tap is great.'

After a bright smile Lola left us to ourselves.

'Charlie, can you move?' Gayle asked.

I looked up at her in confusion. 'Move? Where?'

Taking a sip of her martini, she motioned towards William with her chin. Or more like to the tiny spot next to William. 'My spot is taken. You sit across, I'll sit here. My feet hurt.'

I frowned. 'Why don't *you* go and sit there? I'm already sitting here.'

'I want to talk to William, and I can't do that sitting next to him. Do you have something to say to him?'

'I …' I glanced at an amused William as he scooted to his right a little.

'Does he bite or something?' Gayle asked, making me go all bright red. I looked at our table, but realized no one had heard her.

My face fell. 'Gayle,' I said simply.

She raised her hand. 'Okay, sorry.'

Flustered, I got up.

'Did you hear back from your contact yet?' William asked Gayle as I sat my ass down next to him and settled my bag on my lap again.

Shaking her head, Gayle took her stolen seat and put her martini on the table. 'Tomorrow is the day, I think.'

Lola returned with our drinks and put them on the edge of the table before leaving. Suddenly before I knew what was happening, William was all in my personal space as he leaned over me to get the beers. His chest was against my shoulder, his arm almost brushing my boobs and god help me . . . his face, that stubbled cheek was just inches away.

And his cologne . . .

His cologne.

Extremely too close.

Extremely too much.

Gayle had completely disappeared from my view, and all I could see, all that I could smell, was lots of William. If I leaned a few inches forward I'd touch his cheek with my lips, and the idea fascinated me. I felt myself sway a little, my chin tipping up to get a deeper sniff of his cologne, and I thought how cool I would look if I could rest my forehead on his neck and just stay there for a second or two. Sounded very rational at that moment.

Essentially it was like dangling a big, sweet, juicy carrot in front of a bunny. Too much closeness, too much touching, and I knew myself enough to know that I'd start acting like an idiot and my heart would decide to take the carrot and just run with it.

Remembering where I was and what I was doing, I looked up at the ceiling and released a long breath. Being this close to him was clearly not the best idea. Especially when I could feel his body heat searing the right side of my body.

As a bonus, William's thigh pressed against mine and I closed my eyes.

Game over.

Thankfully he stopped the torture and as soon as he got our beers – which I could've easily reached for – he pulled back, and I was able to take a normal breath again.

'Here you go,' he said softly, completely unruffled and unaware of the battle I had just faced. As I was trying to find the right words to say, my eyes met Gayle's across from me. I didn't like the gleam in them.

'Thanks,' I muttered and watched as he laughed at something Rick said and drank almost half of his beer at one go. My hearing wasn't working at full speed so I had no idea what the hell was going on around me.

After I gained my equilibrium, I took a long sip from my beer and enjoyed the cold drink sliding down my throat, until Gayle put her arms on the table, leaned forward and opened her mouth.

'So, William, six years ago, why did you stand Charlie up?'

I started coughing uncontrollably, hitting my chest with my palm. 'Gayle!' I choked out. I already knew my face was as red as a tomato as I gasped for air. I felt William's hand on my back as he tried to make sure I was okay. When I calmed down he handed me a bottle of water out of nowhere, and I managed to drink without killing myself in the process. Our eyes met, and I couldn't tell if he was angry or not.

'Where did that come from?' I asked, turning back to Gayle, my voice still scratchy.

'What?' she asked as if she hadn't just dropped a bomb. 'I was just trying to ...'

'I'm assuming from that question, Charlie told you we met a few years back,' William interrupted quietly.

'I told her ages ago. She knew from way before,' I rushed to explain.

Her gaze turned to William and she nodded. I held my breath. I hadn't asked that question myself at the end of that first day at the office because I actually *did not* want to hear the answer to it. Self-preservation and all that.

'I think that's private between me and Charlie,' he said.

I let out a breath – too early.

He turned to me. 'Do you want to hear why? Now, Charlie?'

'No. No, I really don't. Not here or anywhere,' I rushed out, shaking my head. 'It doesn't matter anyway. Come on, it was years ago. It doesn't matter,' I repeated myself for good measure.

'It matters.' He gave me a long look, then nodded before turning to Gayle. 'I don't like to talk about my personal life to colleagues. I'd appreciate it if you didn't open this subject again. Not with me.'

Gayle gave a half-shrug. 'Fair enough.'

If looks could kill, Gayle would've been six feet under already.

And that was it. The mystery remained a mystery. Which was good.

Then Gayle asked something about William's old job in California and the conversation turned to safer things. Because it was my superpower to blend in, and I was still somewhat removed from the group, I didn't participate much. Gayle's phone rang and she had to take it outside. I was almost done with my beer and taking in my surroundings again, when I felt William's eyes on me. It was impossible not to notice his attention.

'Have you decided on a date?' he asked quietly and I frowned at him.

'What date?'

His body moved towards me, slightly, and there was his thigh pressing against mine again. My body hummed.

'You said you were going to move soon. Do you have a set date?'

'Oh, I don't. I need to save up a bit more and if possible find a new job first. That would be the best plan. Two, three months, maybe? Hopefully not more than six.'

He gestured towards where Gayle had disappeared to with his chin. 'She doesn't know, does she?'

Feeling a rush of guilt, I sighed and shook my head. 'No I haven't told her. Not just yet. She knows I want to move, but she doesn't know it'll be so soon. I've been talking about moving for so long that I think she doesn't believe me anymore. I want to make sure I have everything set up before I tell anyone. Also she kind of doesn't want me to move.'

'She doesn't want to let you go.'

He drank from his beer, so I did the same and let my eyes wander around the room again.

'Been on any more dates?' he asked, right as I spotted Gayle in her red top and black jeans heading back to our table with a troubled look on her face.

Distractedly, I focused back on William. 'Sorry?'

He tilted his head a little, searching my gaze for something.

'I'm heading out,' Gayle said as soon as she reached our side, saving me from William's scrutiny. She picked up her coat that was hanging on the back of another chair and quickly put it on.

'What's going on?' I asked, sensing her annoyance from the way her lips were pressed into a thin line.

'Nothing important, don't worry about it. I'm gonna check on something then head home.' She exhaled loudly and pulled out her ponytail from the back of her coat.

'I can come with you if you need me,' I offered, knowing she wouldn't take the help.

'It's fine, trust me. Kevin, my husband, is having some problems at his work, he just needs to talk to me, that's all.' Then she met William's gaze. 'I'll call you as soon as I get the info we've been waiting for, boss.'

William nodded as I glanced from one to the other.

Gayle raised her hand in goodbye to everyone as she came to my side and leaned down suspiciously to whisper in my ear. 'You two look great together. I approve. Go for it.'

I sputtered something unintelligible, but she was already

weaving between tables. There was absolutely nothing to go for and she knew it.

'I'm not going for anything,' I yelled after her, because I wanted to have the last word on this subject once and for all. All I got was a distracted wave as an answer and some weird looks from strangers.

'Not going for what?' William asked, and I closed my eyes in defeat before turning to him.

'Nothing important.'

'So I'm not that important then?'

For a second I froze, then I groaned. 'You heard that, didn't you?'

He tapped his ear. 'I have pretty good hearing.'

'I'm gonna keep that in mind.' I shook my head and drank from my beer. 'She doesn't know what she is talking about. We don't look great together at all, and I wouldn't go for you.'

His eyebrow rose. 'You wouldn't go for me, huh?'

'Not at all. You're not my type anymore.' Lying had never hurt anybody.

Distracted, I heard how the rest of our table was heatedly discussing an old case of the firm's. It would've looked weird if I ignored William by shouting a random comment from my seat to be included in the conversation. So that was out. William shifted in his seat, facing me almost completely and ignoring the rest of the group. I managed not to move.

'Who is your type these days?'

'That sounds like a personal question to me.'

'Are we gonna keep a tally on personal questions?'

'Just trying to be fair.'

'You'll get your turn.' He leaned a little closer to keep the conversation private and said in a lower voice, 'If I'm not your type, who is? I have an idea of what you want from the other night, but physically? I've heard some women say I'm everybody's type before.'

I chuckled and somehow managed to lean closer. 'That sounded a little cocky, don't you think?'

I watched as his eyes dropped to my lips for a quick second, then he was smiling back at me. 'You did have a crush on me at one time. Which should prove my point.'

I leaned back a little, feeling happy that there was no awkwardness left between us. At least not in that moment. 'I'd go easy there. The key phrase being: at one time. And my crush these days is Chris Evans. I will never get over him like I got over you.'

He frowned. 'I look nothing like him.'

I laughed. 'There you go. Which is why I'm not going for you.'

He shook his head. 'When we were last out together, we were talking about dates, I think,' he continued.

I grinned. 'I'm hopeless when it comes to dates.'

'Why?'

I shrugged. 'I genuinely have no idea. The long-distance one . . .'

'What was his name?'

'Craig. He did a number on me, so my self-confidence isn't what it should be.' It wasn't what it should be thanks to my family in the first place, but that was a whole other conversation that I wasn't willing to share with him.

'If things weren't going great with him why didn't you break up with him?'

'To be completely honest, I think I was just afraid to lose someone else. Plus, it's really hard to find someone decent online. You have to have really good luck. And that's not me. I had one experience with an online date and that was quite enough.'

'And you need good luck with blind dates.'

I nodded, reaching for my beer. 'And those. The blind date from the other night was more so Gayle would stop badgering me about it. She set me up on two other dates in the last year. None of them worked out.'

'Yeah? And the guy from the other night – what was his name?'

'Ralph.'

'I don't think I like it.'

'His name?'

I watched as he sipped from his beer. 'Yeah.'

'Well. Okay. When I saw his photo I liked his smile. I really like a good smile.'

His eyes dropped to my mouth again, then he looked away. 'I can't argue with that.'

William's own lips curled up and, lo and behold, Ralph had nothing on him. 'What if the dates turn into something serious? Will you postpone the move or not even move at all?'

'With my botched dating experiment? Or with Ralph?'

'Any of the future dates, I guess. I thought Ralph would be over since he stood you up. He still in the running?'

'Apparently he had an emergency that night, and he does want to meet with me again. He didn't have my phone number, and couldn't reach Gayle so she could call me.' I sipped my beer and noticed it was almost done, and so was his.

William angled his head and gave me a long look.

'What?' I asked, feeling trapped under his gaze.

'Do we believe him?'

I laughed. 'Don't know about you, but I do, I guess. And about the move . . . I'm moving. I won't let another guy control my life again. I waited for Craig for so long, I'm not gonna do that again. I come first.'

William opened his mouth, but Lola cut into our conversation. 'Another round?'

We both looked up at our waitress, almost surprised to see her there.

William glanced at me. 'One more?'

I checked my watch and realized I was enjoying just chatting.

'Okay. I can do another fifteen minutes.'

Lola nodded and left us.

'Why are you dating if it's not gonna go anywhere? Correct me if I'm wrong, but I thought the whole idea of dating was to get to know someone to see if they were a good match for you.'

Playing with my glass, I avoided William's gaze. '*That* is usually the idea, but I'm not interested in something serious. At least not now that I decided on the move.' I peered up and he was still looking at me expectantly. To tell or not. I sighed and looked behind him to see if anyone was focusing on us. They were not. It didn't even look like we were a part of their group. I crooked my finger between us so he'd come closer. And that's when I realized the beer was getting to me.

A smile dancing on his lips, he leaned towards me, and I leaned close to his ear. To anyone around us it would look like we were lost in our own bubble, but that wasn't the case. I was just trying to make sure none of our colleagues would hear us. Especially Rick, because he was one of the worse gossips at the firm. It wasn't because I secretly enjoyed being this close to him or anything like that.

'I'm going to be honest again, are you ready for it? And you can't make fun,' I whispered a little loudly.

He pulled his head back and looked into my eyes. I managed to hold his gaze until he gave me a brief nod. Then I leaned forward again, closed my eyes and took a deep breath, inhaling his amazing scent.

'I haven't kissed a guy in five or six years,' I blurted out.

When we pulled back from each other, his brows were drawn together.

'Here you are.' And there was Lola again.

I looked at up at her. She had brilliant timing. 'Thanks.' As soon as she put the beer down, I grabbed it and took a few swallows.

William was still staring at me.

'You're joking,' he managed to get out, his face completely serious.

I shook my head. 'I'm afraid not.'

'How? When did you break up with this Craig?'

'It's been a year.'

'You just said six . . .'

'Five and a half, six. Tomato, Tomato.'

I drank some more from my beer as he reached for his, brows still furrowed. It looked like he was trying to do heavy math. The way he was looking at me made me laugh, drawing the attention of the group. I made eye contact with the girl from accounting and we smiled at each other.

Meeting William's gaze, I moved towards him just a little as I responded in a quiet voice.

'He didn't like kissing. We kissed a handful times, but it was mostly little pecks.'

'He didn't like kissing,' he repeated, pulling back to look into my eyes.

'Would you like to hear his reason for not liking it? Because that's the cherry on top.'

He shifted in his seat and drank his beer, eyes boring into me.

I cleared my throat, waited for dramatic pause and whispered, 'He had a short tongue.'

'He . . . what?'

I chuckled. 'He was afraid to kiss because he had a short tongue. You know . . .' not knowing how to say it, I randomly waved my hand around my face '. . . how it works. When there was stuff happening, he got scared. I think it's kinda like a phobia. I'd say he was afraid I was gonna suck down his tongue.'

'Are you sure you know how to kiss, Charlie?'

My eyes grew big. 'Of course I do! I did.'

At that his brows rose high. 'You did?'

'You would forget how to kiss after six years too.'

'I don't think so.'

I didn't know if it was because I was hungry that the two beers had hit me that strongly or if it was because I felt so tired, but at the end of my second beer I was feeling all kinds of happy and tipsy. Not to the point I wouldn't remember what I had said or done by the next day, but enough that my tongue had – unfortunately for me – loosened and I would end up very much regretting my new-found *honesty is the best policy* kick.

'Anyway,' I rushed out, not wanting go into detail about kissing. 'Come on, admit something personal to me, quick. It has to be something good too.'

He took his eyes away from me, his hand tapping on the table. 'Something personal ... I'm still a little shocked, that's the first time I've heard something like that. Give me a second. Okay. I think you'll like this. I'm not going to date for a while. Because of everything that went on in my marriage, I don't think I trust women at the moment.'

The chatter and low music filled the quiet around us.

'Wow,' I managed to say after a few seconds. That was not what I was expecting to hear.

He finished his beer and looked away from me. 'You said to make it good.'

'That was good. True.'

Wow, I repeated to myself in my head. It sounded like Lindsey had really hurt him. And to be honest, I hated her for that.

'If it makes you feel any better, I don't think I have a lot of trust in men either at the moment. Which is probably why I haven't had any interest in dating recently. I know how to make myself happy so why risk that with a guy?'

'We're a pair, aren't we?'

I nodded with a smile. We were still staring at each other when my phone started ringing. I checked the screen. It was my grandma. I let it go to voicemail because I knew she was calling me to complain about the fact that I'd gotten Pepp. I'd made the mistake of taking him to her place so he could meet the family, but it didn't go so well. She'd called the last few nights. I silenced my phone and put it in my bag.

'Something important?' William asked, getting my attention.

I shook my head. 'Nope. This is random, but if it's not too much can I see your ex-wife's photo?'

His brows rose. 'Why?'

'I wanted to see what she looks like after everything you told me, but it's completely okay if you don't want to share, of course. I'm just very curious by nature. I'm wondering what your type is.'

He thought about it for a second or two. 'Why not. Give me a sec.'

Reaching for his phone, he scrolled through until he was holding a photo with him and his ex-wife in front of me.

'Wow. She is beautiful.' I focused on William's face in the photo. He was smiling, but it didn't feel right. Her smile was bigger, but hers didn't look right either, somehow.

'That's it?'

I shrugged and gave him a small smile.

'Your turn. Let's see your short-tongued ex.'

My grin got bigger, and I lifted a finger. I found a picture of us together and showed William.

His fingers touched mine as he took the phone from me and our eyes met, briefly. Then I had my hand on my lap, and he was looking at the photo.

'Huh.'

'What?'

'Nothing.'

He looked at it some more then put my phone down.

'And . . . ?'

'I don't like him.'

I laughed. 'Okay, I guess.'

'Yes, I don't like him for you.'

Weirdly, hearing that from him made me happy.

His eyes dropped to the almost empty beer glass I was moving on the table. 'Want to get out of here?'

I didn't have to think about that. 'Sure.'

In just a few minutes we had said goodbye to everyone at the table, whom we had completely ignored the whole time we were there, and then we were back out on the crowded New York streets.

I did my best not to fill the silence with mindless chatter. But I did keep stealing glances at him as we weaved around people and ended up walking side by side each time. I'd seen more than a few women trying to catch his attention as they were walking past, but I don't think he noticed any of them.

He was extremely good-looking, that was unquestionable – even more so than he was years back. But more than his looks, I was drawn to his personality, the way he talked to me, the way he'd smiled when he was looking into my eyes, and just the way he'd given all of his attention to me tonight.

We caught the next train and as we stepped out on our stop, William surprised me.

'I have a personal question to ask you, so ask me something personal first.'

I glanced at him in confusion.

'Go for it,' he encouraged.

I looked up at the starless sky as we walked up the stairs. Okay, I could do that. 'Can I ask what went wrong with your ex-wife? You know a lot of details about my non-dating life now so I feel like it's only fair if I know more about yours.'

I watched him as he focused on the sidewalk as we slowed our steps. 'We had our differences even from the beginning. Essentially, I'd say we didn't want the same things out of a marriage. She told me some lies, changed her mind about a lot of stuff after we got married. Long story short, we tried to work on it, but grew apart. It was a mutual decision to end it.'

'Is she still in California? Is that why you moved?'

'Not just because of that, no, and yes she still lives there. As much as I liked the firm I was working at, we were starting to accept all kinds of cases I wasn't comfortable taking on, and I think after the marriage failed so miserably, I thought coming back here didn't sound so bad. Being closer to my family felt right too. Plus the university offer came through at a perfect time so I put things in motion and gave my resignation. Then right before I got here . . .'

'My dad got in touch,' I finished for him.

He nodded.

Feeling a little chilly, I pushed my hands deeper into my pockets.

'Are you cold?' William asked.

'Nope. I'm good.'

Instead of listening to me, he started to take off his dark grey jacket and, despite all my protests, draped it over my shoulders.

As his scent surrounded me, making me feel all kinds of things at once, I ignored each and every one of the goosebumps across my skin and quietly thanked him.

'What was your question?' I asked.

'My question is,' William started as he turned his head to me. 'If you haven't kissed anyone in six years . . . does that mean you haven't had . . .'

I raised my brows and waited for him to go on with a small smile on my lips. 'If you want to ask me, you're gonna have to say the whole thing.' Then I couldn't hold it in and chuckled, and like two idiots we smiled at each other. 'I'm not gonna answer unless you can say it out loud.'

'I'm not shy, Charlie,' he warned in a low and rumbling voice.

I scoffed, ignoring what the tone of his voice did to me. 'You can ask then.'

'Okay. Does that mean you haven't had sex in six years?'

My lips twitching, I faced forward again. Because I actually was shy, even though he probably couldn't tell from the things I'd blurted out this evening. But I'd be lying if I said I wasn't enjoying being completely honest with him. 'Five years. Give or take a few months.'

'Okay. Got it. But you met with him after he moved away, didn't you? You didn't even have sex?'

'You're really interested in this, aren't you?'

'Shocked, more like it.'

'Yes, we did meet, but I didn't want to do anything. I was sensing that things were wrong so I wasn't really up for it and he didn't say anything either. I think we loved each other, but not romantically after a certain point.' I shrugged. 'It's hard to explain.'

'I get it. Wow. Five years, huh . . .'

I laughed and shook my head in wonder. 'Why are guys always so intrigued when it comes to sex?' I quickly raised my hand. 'Don't answer. Listen, I'm happy by myself. Ninety percent of the time at least. But I want a man who will hold my hand because he can't help himself. No one has to see it, but if we're watching TV or just walking down the street, I want him to reach for me. I want him to do all that, but I want him to want it on his own as well.'

We stopped in front of my apartment and William was still listening to me carefully.

He gave me one of his soft smiles. Barely there and gone. And I remembered this exact smile from so long ago. It was a good memory. I shrugged off his jacket, handing it back to him. The buzz of the beer was disappearing and just like Cinderella, the time to flee had come.

'Thank you for . . .'

'You could keep the jacket I . . .'

We stopped, laughing.

He shook his head a little, rubbed the back of his neck with his palm and looked down the street.

'Charlie!'

At the loud and familiar voice, I jolted, and both William and I glanced up and saw three faces staring down at us. My neighbour Josh, Daisy and Pepperoni. The biggest smile stretched across my face.

'He's been crying and whining ever since we heard your voice,' Josh said.

'He has?'

Josh laughed. 'Yeah, his tail is going a mile a minute, sweetheart. He missed you.'

I gave William a quick glance and saw his lips curl up in a smile as he stared up towards my neighbour's window.

'Pepp missed me,' I told him, my excitement colouring my voice.

Then there was a sweet and impatient bark. When William looked down, I was still staring at his lips. Maybe I had talked about kissing a little too much.

'I love him,' I said, as my heart filled with love, and met William's gaze again. 'It's only been a few days, I know, but he has already made everything so much better.'

Then came another high-pitched, impatient bark, followed by a sweet whine, and feeling nothing but joy, I laughed.

'I should go. I've been summoned.'

'Yes, don't make him wait for you.' The words caused another series of goosebumps on my arms, so I rubbed my hands up and down to get rid of them, only to realize I was still holding onto his jacket.

'Oh, here. Thank you.'

He took it from me. 'Have a good night Charlie. I'll see you tomorrow.'

'You too. Goodnight William.' Halfway up the stairs, I paused and turned around. 'Quick question. I remember a lot of the stuff from back then, but was it like this then too? Did we talk this easily to each other?'

His mouth curved into a smile. 'Yeah. That's why we kept coming back every day. And that's why we sat across from each other for hours, talking about anything and everything.'

I nodded, feeling happy that his thoughts matched mine from all those years ago. His words still swirling in my mind, I went up the rest of the stairs, took out my key, opened the heavy door and then looked back for one last time before stepping inside while keeping the door open behind me. Hands in his pockets, he was still standing there, waiting for me to get in. I took a few seconds to burn him into my memory. He was someone I wanted, but wouldn't have. We studied each other. I smiled and his smile got bigger.

'Ready for another honesty thing?' I asked.

'Yes. Hit me.'

'I don't think I'll ever forget about you, and I think I like that.'

His smile was slowly disappearing, but I didn't give him a chance to respond.

I raised a hand in goodbye, then heard the telling pitter-patter of paws running down the stairs. The last image William saw of me that night was me with the biggest smile on my face, ready to say hi to the goodest boy.

11

William

Things got very busy at the office and we spent a little over three weeks handling nothing but Michael's faulty electric car case. As soon as we found out that Michael's best friend and partner for years, Isaac, had sabotaged their work – thanks to Gayle and her skills – we started working on a different plan. Michael shared another video of him explaining the situation with all the proof, but still taking the blame since it was his responsibility and his brand, no matter what had happened behind the scenes. His apology had been sincere and effective.

Michael still wanted to keep us working with him so his company could have a successful launch. The negativity towards the company hadn't disappeared completely, but as a team we were all happy with how public opinion had changed. And because of that we had finally stopped working such late hours. I couldn't be happier with the work we had done, especially considering it was such a big case and it was our first one together.

And because the team had been working so well together, Charlie and I could fit in Laurel Nielson for a meeting. Even though she had returned from Spain just hours ago, she had been calling Charlie non-stop for the last two days asking for a plan. The truth was that we didn't have one. Until I could actually talk to her face to face, I wouldn't know how she would feel about any plans I made for her.

It also didn't help that her situation was no longer a crisis moment by definition. The actual crisis had already passed over two months ago. The PR department in the company would've been the better choice for her, but because of her insistence on working with Charlie, here I was away from the office and stuck at a coffee shop on the Upper East Side.

The line I'd been waiting in finally moved an inch, and I watched as two people walked past me with their hands full of coffee cups and pastry bags.

I tried to ignore the heated conversation the couple in front of me were having about party hats and balloons, and checked my phone for new emails. Surprisingly there was nothing urgent that needed my attention. There was one email from Lindsey, my ex-wife, I was assuming about the house, but I chose to ignore it. I saw the time and realized there was still over half an hour before the meeting at Laurel's Park Avenue townhouse. I'd considered sending Charlie a text to see if she wanted to meet up for coffee beforehand, but gave up on the idea since it was probably good to limit our interactions outside the office. The memory of walking home together had played on my mind for a good while and I didn't think it was smart for me to spend too much time with her. She was dangerous to my peace of mind.

'William?'

I frowned, thinking I'd conjured Charlie's voice in my imagination, but when I heard my name called again, I turned around and there she was. My eyes briefly passed over her, taking her in. She held the door for a teenager who was heading out, then made her way towards me.

'Hi! What are you doing here?' she asked, her smile entirely too big and enticing for the hour of the day.

'Hey. Getting coffee.'

Her smile got bigger, her eyes warming for some reason. 'I'd assumed that much. I meant what are you doing at *this* exact coffee shop?'

I looked around. 'Why? What's wrong with it? Does everyone hate it because of the lines? Because I'd understand that.'

She shook her head. 'No. No. Are you kidding me? Nothing's wrong with it. I just thought it's odd we bumped into each other when there are literally at least fifteen more coffee shops around here. Anyway, don't mind me, you made the right choice, they have the best coffee. And some of their pastries . . .' Her eyes rolled to the back of her head and she licked her pink lips, catching my attention. I was starting to learn that Charlie loved lipstick. Almost every day it was a subtly different colour. Always on the natural side, but different tones of pinks and nudes. On some days where she was feeling especially happy there might be light red tones. Every single colour looked beautiful on her. And then I realized how much time I was spending looking at her lips and focused on her complicated hazel eyes instead. In this light they looked almost green. I needed to stop looking at her face. Period. And I needed to have my morning coffee.

'They're the best around here. Trust me, you're gonna love it.'

'If I can taste their coffee in this century, I'll let you know my thoughts. The coffee machine I've ordered hasn't arrived yet, so I imagined I'd be able to get one from a cafe before the meeting. Look how wrong I was.'

Another smile formed on her lips, this one smaller but somehow warmer.

'Is someone grumpy without their morning coffee?'

'No. But someone, just like everyone, doesn't like to wait in line,' I countered, checking the line yet again. How was it that it hadn't moved?

Charlie patted my arm for a quick moment, distracting me from my thoughts as she moved this way and that way to see the food display. 'It's worth it. Trust me. I love their stuff. I love their decor and how simple and relaxing and beautiful it is with the flowers and everything. Oh, the name? Do you know where the name came from? Tell me you know.'

'What even is it?' I looked around. 'Around the Corner Coffee Shop? Because it's around the corner?'

'William, you're disappointing me. It's from the movie. *You've Got Mail.*'

'Ahh,' I drawled.

'And it's not just . . .' she leaned in close, and I listened to her carefully. 'Ah, never mind.'

Charlie moved away again. 'Tell me. It's not just what?'

She sighed. 'It's not just why I come here. I love reading books, okay?'

Confused and intrigued I stared at her. 'Yes?'

'So, I love reading romance books. I read a lot of genres but I love reading romance books because they give me hope of something beautiful. It gives me a fix, so to say. A romance fix. My happy fix. I get that same fix by coming here.'

I knew this, because whenever I had to leave a note in her office she had a different book on her desk almost every time. 'Please don't tell me you get your cheese from here, too.'

'I get my what?'

I gave her a flat look. 'Cheese? What you were looking for in a relationship?'

Understanding what I was talking about, she started laughing. Causing my own lips to twitch.

'Oh, William.'

Thank God, another trio finished giving their orders and moved to a table with their chosen sandwiches and muffins and coffees. Who ate that much so early? I glanced over and saw four teenage girls reading the menu out loud and asking each other what they were getting. I sighed and rubbed my hand over my face. If the next couple in line did the same thing I was going to leave. Coffee be damned.

'I'm enjoying this grumpy side of you immensely right now.'

I cast a glance at Charlie and saw she was grinning at me. 'Glad one of us is having a good time, but I'm going to leave if I have to wait another twenty minutes.'

'Oh come on. Don't exaggerate.'

I stared at Charlie with an unimpressed face. 'I've been waiting for the last ten minutes, Charlie.' I gestured behind me. 'Entertain me so the wait is more bearable.'

Charlie beamed up at me. 'I find you fascinating right now, William. Gayle, Rick and I all find you fascinating when you're grumpy in the mornings, but this is kinda like a special show for me and I'm here for it.'

'Glad I'm the entertainment for the office,' I grumbled. I opened my mouth to say something else, but Charlie was leaning closer, her eyes on something outside the cafe, and then she grabbed my arm as if she needed my help to stay upright. 'Oh, look. It's Monday! I forgot about that!' she whispered.

Distracted by the feel of her small hand still clutching my wrist, I looked over my shoulder to see what she was talking about, but all I could see was a guy walking in through the door with a big bouquet of roses in his hands. 'And?' I asked, still trying to find something outside. 'What exactly am I looking at?'

She had been holding onto my wrist with one hand, but when the guy with the flowers passed us, she grabbed my arm right above my elbow with the other, almost plastering her body to my side. 'Watch,' she whispered. 'You're gonna get a demonstration of what any woman would consider swoon-worthy.'

Surprised, I forgot what I was supposed to look at and glanced down at Charlie instead. She must've felt my stillness, because she looked up and our eyes met. Then she realized how close we were to each other and the fact that her hands were still on me. Her lips parted and she let go of my wrist first, then my arm.

'Sorry, I got excited,' she mumbled, taking a healthy step back.

I cleared my throat and she shook her head.

'You're not looking, William,' she repeated in a strange voice. She gestured with her head to the counter where the guy with the flowers was talking to one of the baristas.

I tried to see what she was talking about.

The barista called out a name and a woman walked out of what looked to be a kitchen at the back.

The beautiful woman said a few words to the guy with a big smile on her face and then lifted the flip-up counter top to get to him.

'What are we watching right now?' I asked, still unsure of what was going on. Did she know the couple?

'She is his wife,' Charlie whispered, with something close to envy in her voice. 'He brings her flowers every Monday.'

'Are you friends with her or something?'

'No, of course not.'

'Of course not,' I repeated, suddenly not so surprised. 'I don't know how I could've thought that.'

She looked up at me with a small smile on her lips. 'I asked one of the baristas one day. Apparently he's done it every single week ever since they opened. It's their thing. I want to have my own thing with someone. Something that we do. That's the kinda cheese I want. Did you have a thing like that with your ex-wife?'

'No. I don't think we did,' I answered, distracted as I stared at Charlie.

Her smile warmed up. 'I'm sorry, I wish you'd had that.'

I noticed the couple in front of us had gone quiet and the girl was watching the scene with the same rapt attention as Charlie while trying to look like she wasn't watching at all. I looked around the cafe and everyone else was minding their own business. I couldn't help but smile as I heard Charlie sigh; the guy was giving his wife a kiss as he cupped her face with his hand. The woman was stand-ing on her toes, clutching the flowers to her chest and was slightly flushed when he let go of her, only to lean down and whisper something in her ear. She laughed and gave her husband a kiss on his cheek.

'This is highly inappropriate to watch,' I whispered to Charlie, but she shushed me.

'Don't make me sound like a creeper, I'm not watching them. I'm just an observer observing.' She finally turned to me when the wife started fixing the guy's tie. 'That's the cheese and cliché I was talking about that I want. Can you imagine the amount of trust that goes into a relationship like that? The love. And just knowing that you have each other?' She released another sigh and faced forward. 'That's the reason why I won't settle with just anyone.'

A cute couple who were waiting in line ahead of us started to argue in a low voice; we couldn't tell what they were saying since they were talking in German. He turned and looked at the girl, then gently dropped a kiss on the top of her head. From the corner of my eye, I could see Charlie already melting at the scene. The girl wrapped her arms around him and they gave each other a quick hug and another kiss. Charlie sighed next to me and the girl looked over her shoulder.

'Hi. Sorry were we too loud?'

Charlie shook her head with a smile on her face.

'Not at all. Don't worry about it.'

Thank God, the teenagers moved away with their order, bringing me one step closer to my coffee.

'William this is what I'm talking about. Wouldn't you want this?'

'Want what?'

'The banter is such a cliché in the best way possible—' Charlie started whispering, leaning towards me a little, but immediately stopped when the girl in front of us turned to us again.

'Hi, I'm Melinda.' She smiled brightly. Too bright for the hour. 'Quick question, do you think I should go to my friend's wedding alone, just because this one doesn't get along with my friend?'

Charlie didn't even hesitate before answering. 'Oh, no he has to come. That's not even a question.'

The guy gave Charlie a quick look. 'Great, there's another one of you.' Then he grunted and looked away.

'Please ignore him,' the woman apologized. 'He knows I'm right so it's annoying him.' She turned to her boyfriend. 'We're going together. It's gonna be great.'

The guy sighed and shook his head.

'I love this,' Charlie exclaimed, giving me a big smile. 'I want this.' She faced Melinda. 'You guys are lucky to have each other.'

'We are,' the guy murmured with a soft look on his face.

Charlie turned to me expectantly.

'How should I know,' I muttered unenthusiastically.

Charlie rolled her eyes and put her hand on my arm again, pulling it back the last minute. 'His answer doesn't count, he is just grumpy because he hasn't had his morning coffee. You should see him when he gets right out of bed. It's a sight to see.'

There was a loud pause. I couldn't help but lean down to meet Charlie's fleeting gaze. 'And do you see me first thing when I get out of bed every day?'

She stuttered, trying to avoid my gaze while also trying not to smile too widely.

'Yeah,' I murmured, straightening and crossing my arms against my chest. 'That's what I thought too.'

'You guys just got together?' Melinda asked.

Charlie nodded, looking unsure.

I didn't look at my new girlfriend, but gestured towards her with my head. 'A whole two weeks of rainbows and sunshine with this one.'

Charlie laughed and looked up at me with a big smile. 'I fell in love with him on sight,' she said, causing me to raise my eyebrow. 'Couldn't spend another minute without him. It was the most romantic thing to ever happen to me.'

'Grumpy men are so sexy, I know what you mean,' Melinda put in.

I sighed and looked up at the ceiling. I was starting to question the sanity of thinking I should get coffee in the morning.

Charlie was nodding excitedly. 'Oh yes. You should see him when he's lost in thought and just a little frustrated. I secretly watch him when he is working and he runs his hand through his hair in this way that ... ah ...'

Probably remembering who was standing right next to her and what she was actually saying, she bit her lip, met my startled gaze then turned back to Melinda again.

'Umm, anyway,' she mumbled waving her hand aimlessly as if she could just brush away what she had just said.

'Charlie?' I called, softly and waited until she met my gaze with uncertain eyes. Even I wasn't sure if I was just following her steps and acting as if we were a couple to these strangers, but I was too curious not to ask. 'You watch me?'

She laughed, started coughing in the middle of it, patted my arm then stopped. 'What kind of question is this? I always watch you, you know this ... dude.'

Breaking character, I threw my head back and laughed. Couldn't hold it in anymore. 'Did you just call me dude?'

She shifted in place, giving it a thought for moment. 'My man?'

I held back my smile, raised an eyebrow and thoroughly enjoyed watching her get flustered. 'Try again.'

'Love? Babe? Baby?' When I didn't give her a quick enough answer, her voice slightly rose. 'Pick one already!'

I stared at her eyes for a few seconds, making her wait. Then I lowered my voice and said, 'I like it when you call me baby, love, babe, sweetheart ... I like everything you do or say, Charlie. And I definitely like it when you tell me I'm your man, too.'

Charlie just stared at me with a slightly parted mouth.

Melinda chuckled, helping Charlie out of her bewilderment, and hugged her boyfriend.

The line moved forward again, getting me one step closer to

freedom. Not thinking about it I put my hand at the small of Charlie's back, helping her move along since she was still stuck in place and too quiet.

'Finally,' Melinda's boyfriend murmured and I nodded in agreement.

Somebody must have heard us because the next person in line ordered a simple black coffee and was gone in a moment.

'You think we should share a table and have a quick morning coffee?' Melinda asked.

Charlie was nodding when both the guy and I said *no* at the same time. They looked at us in surprise.

'We have a meeting . . .' I checked my watch. '. . . in fifteen. Does that ring any bells my dear love?' I said as Charlie's eyes bored into me thoughtfully.

The couple placed their order, we said a quick goodbye and finally it was our turn.

Charlie turned to me.

She was slightly flushed, her hair falling in big waves around her face, her eyes happy.

'That was fun, wasn't it? We should do that again.'

'You mean it was fun pretending we were a couple when we are not?'

'Yes! And do you get now what I mean about clichés. It's the best thing. I'm up for scoops.'

I waited for an explanation with interest, but it never came.

I chanced a guess. 'Are we talking about ice cream? Because of the cheese and passion fruit, is this ice cream and I'm missing it? Are you the ice cream? Or do you want him to buy you ice cream?'

She thought about it. 'I don't think I'm the ice cream, but maybe I am? I want to be scooped up as in I want someone to come along and just scoop me up. I'm up for scoops.'

I narrowed my eyes. It was too early, period. 'You want him to carry you?'

'No!' She laughed and I just watched. 'I'm just ready to have someone notice me for who I am. And to have that someone wanna take me off the market, scoop me up. Makes sense now?'

'Just as much as the cheese and passion fruit. Thank you.'

Before I could open my mouth and make another comment, she continued. 'Okay. Enough dilly-dallying. How do you want to handle the meeting? Let's share our thoughts on how we want to handle her.'

Her face was full of smiles through the entire meeting and I found that I couldn't stop staring even for a second.

Later that night, after I had wrapped up some work I had brought home, I decided to head out and take a quick walk towards the little pizzeria Charlie had mentioned. With my hands in my pockets, my mind going in all different directions, I tried to remember Charlie's directions to the shop and enjoyed my late-night walk in the crisp April weather.

I sent a quick text to Lindsey, since I had ignored her emails and latest calls, but then quickly forgot about her.

I walked for ten minutes till I spotted the pizzeria's blue and yellow sign over the door that said Johnie's. I went inside and realized I was one of the only customers, apart from one couple who were sitting in the very small corner. I met and chatted with Johnie and his wife, Emilia, as he worked on my pizza dough in front of me and placed the toppings very generously. When my mind had finally cleared from work thanks to Johnie's and Emilia's engaging conversation and my pizza had cooked, I paid and said my thanks and was putting my credit card back in my pocket when someone opened the door and started yelling for their order.

Recognizing her voice, I chuckled and turned around to see Charlie, trying her hardest to contain a very exuberant and strong puppy from rushing inside.

'I'm so sorry,' she yelled with one hand holding the door open while the other held on to Pepperoni for dear life.

I heard Johnie chuckle behind me as his wife yelled, 'No worries, Charlie. You hold onto the beast and we'll get your order for you.'

Charlie sighed and there was an excited bark from Pepperoni. 'Thank you.' Then she finally saw me standing just a few feet away from her and her eyes rounded. 'William?'

I strolled towards her and closed the gap between us. 'Second time in a day, Charlie?'

'I'm not following you if that's what you're thinking.'

The pizza box in my hand, I got down to Pepperoni's level. 'Hello, Pepperoni.' He did his thing again, hiding behind Charlie's leg, but his tail was thumping very hard and this time it didn't take him too long to say hi. He nosed my palm, and I gave him a scratch behind his ear while looking up at Charlie. 'Didn't even cross my mind. What are you doing out here this late?'

She smiled as she watched Pepperoni try to get his nose into my dinner. 'We were doing our last walk of the day and realized we forgot to have dinner.' She met my eyes and I rose from my crouch. 'I don't like going to bed hungry so here we are. You?'

'Basically the same thing.'

'I guess it's inevitable that we bump into each other when we live so close.'

'I'd say you're right.'

We smiled at each other, and Charlie pushed a loose strand of her hair behind one ear, looking away from me for a moment.

'Excuse us.'

The couple in the pizzeria had to walk between us since we were still standing in the entrance, and I took the time to take in Charlie. She gave the couple an apologetic smile as Pepperoni pulled her back a few steps in his hurry to get away from the strangers. She was wearing sport leggings and, under her thin jacket, a light blue tee-shirt that said Only Love in colourful letters. The light blue suited her very well. There was still a slight flush to her cheeks that could be from the short walk or from Pepperoni's effort to drag her along. Either way it added to her allure.

Which I had no reason to notice. She had no allure for me. No matter how easy it felt to talk to her, or to be around her – that was all it was. Yet I still took note that her hair was half-up and half-down and she looked beautiful. Relaxed, natural and just . . . beautiful. She had looked beautiful earlier in the day too when she had first walked into the coffee shop and acted as if we were a couple – and she looked beautiful now. And I needed to stop.

I joined her outside and she closed the distance between us.

'Your pizza is getting cold, I don't want to keep you,' she said, relaxing her hold on the lead as Pepperoni decided to plop down right in front of me. I guessed he was hoping to work me over for a slice.

'That's okay. I'd like to walk with you guys if that's okay.'

She smiled. 'Thanks. We'd like that.'

Pepperoni gave me a little bark, and the moment I looked down his tail started going again. While we began to negotiate for a slice of pizza with a small bark here and there, I enjoyed listening to Charlie's laughter as she took in our ridiculous back and forth. Every time I said 'No' or 'I don't think so', Pepperoni would give a small bark and shift his feet as if he were tapping on the concrete ground.

When Charlie's pizza was ready and paid for, I decided to carry it for her so she could focus on Pepperoni and we started on our short walk back.

'I don't really want to talk about work outside of work, but I'll only ask this. What did you think about Laurel? I couldn't guess at the meeting.'

'I think she's telling the truth. I think I'd like to help her out of this mess even though it isn't exactly a crisis anymore.'

She released a long breath as Pepperoni walked a little bit in front of us, sniffing at everything. 'Okay, that makes me happy. I know you're picky with the cases you want to work on, but I'm glad you didn't want someone else to handle her.'

'You like her.'

She gave me a quick look. 'Yeah. She is a little all over the place, but I do.'

Her phone chimed with a new message and she quickly looked at it.

'A possible date?' I asked, all of a sudden not sure where the question had come from.

'Yeah,' Charlie murmured, putting her phone back into her pocket without sending a reply.

I don't know if her reply surprised me or what, but I didn't know what to say. After a moment, I asked, 'The one who made you wait or a new one?'

She stole another glance at me and gave me a small smile. 'I'm not that good at saying no. It's the one who didn't show up. Gayle gave him my number and we texted a little. It wouldn't hurt to go out once, right? It'd be good for me. A change.'

We had reached our street and we stopped in front of Charlie's place. The ten-minute walk back with Charlie next to me felt like only a minute or two.

'Sure,' I agreed, not actually sure if I agreed or not. 'Change can be good.'

'Yeah, I guess.' We stared at each other for a beat, and she gave me a small smile. 'It was nice bumping into you again, William. Thank you for keeping us company.'

'Anytime, Charlie.' I handed her her pizza and scratched Pepperoni's head one last time as he gave me a quick lick.

'You're such a good boy,' Charlie said. 'Let's go home.'

The pup listened and pranced around her.

'Goodnight, William.'

'Goodnight.' I stopped her before she could go into the building. 'Charlie.' She turned around with a smile on her face, her key in her hand. 'When is the date?'

'He has an out-of-town thing for two weeks. Maybe when he comes back. Maybe. I'm not sure. Why?'

'Just curious.' I had no legitimate reason to ask. None whatsoever. 'You guys are keeping in touch then?'

'Texting. A little. Sometimes.'

That was a lot of maybes and sometimes. 'Hope it works out this time.'

After one last goodbye, I watched as she walked into the building with a still excited pup beside her. I crossed the street and walked into an empty home – not all that hungry anymore.

12

Charlie

The day after the meeting with Laurel, which took us almost the entire day, things didn't start off so well for me. After taking Pepp out for his morning walk, I said a pretty long goodbye to him and rushed to the office so I could start on the proposal my dad wanted me to work on. Since I was in William's team, it wasn't my job to woo my dad's clients anymore, but that was only one of my other skills my dad and Kimberly didn't like to acknowledge but used plenty of times. When I reached our floor only two other people were there, drinking their coffee and just turning on their laptops.

I popped into the kitchen area, poured myself a cup of coffee. Sitting down at my desk, I turned on my laptop, pulled up the file my dad had emailed me the night before and started to work on it.

Before I noticed, an hour and a half had passed and when I finished preparing the proposal I started working on some research on Laurel Nielson that William had asked me to do.

There was a knock on my door, and I looked up from my laptop. Gayle and Rick burst in before I could utter a word.

'Meeting,' they said at the same time, Gayle almost shouldering Rick away.

Gayle looked at Rick and scowled. 'I said I'll get her. You get Stan.'

Rick huffed and left – Gayle was scary when she wanted to be so I didn't blame him. I saved my Laurel Nielson file and picked up my laptop as I rose from my seat. 'New case?'

'Yes,' Gayle answered, watching my movements. I stretched my back and winced. 'When did you come in?' she asked.

'Early. I needed to prepare something for my dad.' I made it to her side and we started heading towards the small meeting room where I could already see William and Trisha talking. 'What's the case about?'

'Did you text Ralph?'

'No,' I huffed out and gave her a quick look. 'Like I said, we texted a little last night, but that was it. He wants me to give him another chance.'

'Will you?'

'Not sure yet. The case?'

'A private company data breach. On top of that, it looks like some of their execs sold their shares before the word got out. They're scrambling. He asked me about you again.'

William? I thought for some stupid reason. 'Who?'

'Ralph. This is the last time I'm asking you about him, promise. Just wanted you to know he wants to hear back.'

'Okay, I'll text him.'

'Yeah?'

I nodded and we walked into the meeting room. I was about to follow Gayle and walk around the desk to take a seat while we waited for Rick and Stan, but William was standing at the head of the table and as soon as he looked my way, he pulled out the seat next to him, gesturing for me to sit down.

'Morning, Charlie,' he said absent-mindedly.

'Good morning, William,' I said with a smile.

I studied him for a few seconds, but he didn't look grumpy so he must have had his morning coffee.

Gayle gave me a questioning look as she took her seat across from me, next to Trisha. I shrugged at her.

After the others showed up, William took his seat and started to give us all the information he had on the new case and what was happening.

We were right in the middle of the meeting, talking to the CEO of the company, explaining the steps we needed to take, when there was a knock on the door and my dad popped in.

'Charlie?'

'Yes?' I whispered. He was wearing his dark navy blue suit and there was not one single hair out of place.

'The proposal?' he asked, his eyes focused on me.

I held back my sigh and after giving William a quick look, quietly excused myself, stepping out of the room to talk to my dad.

My hand still on the handle, I tried to keep it short.

'I emailed it to you this morning.'

'It's not in my inbox, Charlie.'

Closing my eyes, I rubbed my temples. 'I sent it over two hours ago, dad.'

'Send it again. Did you make sure to add the info?'

Glancing over my shoulder, I got caught in William's gaze. His lips were moving, but his eyes were on us. I turned back to my dad. 'Yes, I added everything you asked me to. Is it okay if I resend it to you after I'm done here? It shouldn't take us long before we take a break.'

'I need it before four.'

'No problem.'

'Good.'

'Okay. I'll talk to you . . .' I pushed on the handle and was about to go back in when my dad's hands on me caused me to freeze.

'Dad,' I hissed, mortified as he buttoned up one more button on my shirt. 'What are you doing?'

'I can see your bra,' he said, as if it were completely normal for him to button my shirt in the middle of the office where everyone could see us. Not to mention he could *not* see my bra at all. 'What's happening with your skin? Your face is different.'

Someone walking behind my dad stared at me, then averted their eyes.

I tried so hard not to let his words get to me, but it was next to impossible to ignore them lately. I felt goosebumps on my skin and they were not the good, happy kind. I was starting to reach the threshold of my patience when it came to my family and things were starting to bubble up.

Closing my eyes, I took a deep breath. When I opened them my dad was staring at me. 'Nothing is wrong with my skin,' I answered, my voice small and tired. 'I didn't have time to do my makeup today.' I could already feel my face heating up.

He shook his head, forever unhappy with me. 'It's the dog, isn't it? I told you it was a mistake to get one when you have so much to do.'

My heckles rose. 'It was the best decision I've ever made,' I retorted. 'I'll resend the email. If there is nothing else, I need to go back in.'

As if I was being too much, his mouth pressed into a thin line. 'I can't say anything to you lately.'

'I have work to do.'

I would've loved to get into it, but I gave him a curt nod and opened the door instead. The phone conversation with the CEO was already over and I'd missed it. Everyone but William was busy either on their laptops or on their phones. Gayle stood up and was coming my way.

'I'll get in touch with the execs who sold their shares,' she announced into the room and offered me a small smile on her way out. I didn't have one in me to offer back.

My face still heated, I took my seat. I was hoping William hadn't seen my dad buttoning my shirt, but with my luck I was pretty sure he had been watching us the entire time.

'Everything okay, Charlie?' he asked softly and something in me melted at his voice.

I swallowed and, keeping my eyes down, decided to just nod so I wouldn't react. I lifted my laptop, trying to look busy while also trying to listen to Stan, Rick and Trisha talking so I could catch up on the plan.

Then I felt a warm hand on my wrist and lifted my eyes to William's. He raised his brow, insisting on an answer.

A little flustered under his gaze and his warm touch, I hastily looked at our co-workers and noticed they were all busy and unaware. We were supposed to act like professionals when we were at work, not like friends. I looked back at William and forced a small smile on my lips while my heart thundered in my chest.

'Everything's okay,' I whispered, trying to sound reassuring.

He kept his eyes on mine, binding me to him for a few more seconds, then he pulled his hand back and I could breathe a little more easily. I rested my hand on my lap and rubbed the spot he had touched to get rid of the stupid tingles.

William's phone rang so I took the opportunity to lean towards Stan, who was sitting next to me and writing something on his notepad.

'What did I miss?' I whispered.

He didn't glance at me. 'You're good. You're still on the statements and we're heading to their offices tomorrow.'

I nodded. 'Okay, thanks Stan.'

'Charlie.' William said, and I turned back to him. 'You're not working on something outside of the team, are you?'

My anger and frustration almost gone; I shook my head. 'Oh, no, I'm just yours.' Then the words reached back to my own ears, and I was blushing for a completely different reason. And I'm afraid this time I had everybody's attention. I looked around and, yup, all eyes were on me. 'Oh, come on. You guys know what I mean,' I spluttered.

My gaze jumped back to William. 'I'm committed to this team. My dad asked me to do something, and I took care of it outside of work hours. That's all I meant,' I added the last sentence for the sake of everyone else.

I could see a small twitch starting on William's lips so I heaved a sigh and ignored everyone in the room, focusing on the work I needed to do. 'I'm gonna prepare the statement that will go out in their emails,' I said to no one in particular and got down to business.

We took a late team lunch break around three. Or, I should say, *they* took a late lunch break, but I had to resend the proposal email to my dad so I stayed in my office instead. I was heading back to my office with my cup of tea in my hand when I decided to drop by my dad's office just to make sure he got the email this time.

I knocked on his door and entered. I was standing halfway inside and halfway outside to make a quick escape.

My dad looked up from his phone.

'Everything okay with the file I've sent?' I asked.

'Yes, yes. Thank you for taking care of it so quickly, Charlie.'

'You're welcome. I'll see you later, Dad.' I was already closing the door when he stopped me.

'Oh, wait. Come inside for a minute.'

I pushed the door open and stepped inside, choosing to stand in the middle of his room instead of taking a seat. 'I still haven't had lunch, Dad, and we have another meeting soon. It'll have to be quick.'

His eyes moved on my body. It was a quick motion, but I caught it anyway. And I could tell what he was thinking, but trying not to say: you can afford to skip a lunch. I ground my teeth.

He called someone on his phone.

'Charlie is here, you can come.'

I frowned. Holding my mug in between my hands I took a sip, wondering what he was gonna ask me to do now.

'Who is coming?' I asked when he hung up.

'I'm starting to get tired of this thing between you two. You work together, you need to . . .'

Before he could finish his sentence, Kimberly walked in with her red pant suit and the temperature in the room dropped a few degrees.

'Hi Dad. Hey, Charlie.'

I stood a little bit taller and gave her a nod, taking another sip of my drink. I wasn't a vindictive person. Not necessarily. But after the whole situation with her husband, things had never gone back to normal between us and to be honest I was fine with that. Because our normal had never been great either. It wasn't like we hated each other, but we'd never had a close sibling relationship.

'I'm in the middle of something, so I have to be quick,' she explained as if she were the only busy one. She looked at Dad, then at me. I just raised my brows, waiting.

Dad sighed. 'Charlie, in a week or two I need Kimberly in Michigan for a few days, but she has a dinner meeting with a client here. The timing isn't working, I need you to handle the dinner meeting.'

I lowered my mug and addressed Kimberly. 'Can't someone from your team handle it? I mean, wouldn't they know more about your client?'

She shook her head from side to side. 'No, Charlie. He is an old client of mine. This is more like a babysitting job to appease him. I'll be here for our meeting the next day. And my team are working on other things. I can't pull them out for this.'

Right. But Charlie could leave whatever she was doing and dance to their tunes. Not so much anymore.

'I'm sorry,' I said, trying to look apologetic. 'I have plans for that week, and a lot of work. I'd have loved to help out, but I can't.'

'Charlie,' my dad sighed, massaging the bridge of his nose as if I were being particularly difficult. He looked up at me while Kimberly stood next to his desk.

I could already feel the walls closing in one me, and I realized it didn't matter what plans I did or didn't have.

'What plans do you have?' he asked. 'Work-related?'

'No. I have a date.' I didn't, but Gayle had said that Ralph was waiting to hear back from me, so just to get out of the babysitting thing I could very well go out on a date. So I had a date.

He raised his brows, disbelief apparent in his eyes. 'You're dating again?'

'Yes,' I replied. 'Is there a problem with that?'

He lifted his hands up. 'No. No. Just surprised, that's all. Is it new? Or did you start talking to Craig again?'

He had liked Craig. I bit my tongue so I wouldn't snap. 'Craig cheated on me, Dad. You know this. Why would I talk to him? It's someone new.'

'I'm just asking, you don't need to get defensive.'

'If that's all, I need to get back to work,' I continued, ignoring his words, trying not to let it get to me. I took a few steps forward to leave, but I wasn't that lucky.

'Reschedule your date to another week, Charlie,' he ordered and this time it was my turn to raise my brows.

'Don't look at me like that. This is important for the company. What does it matter if you go out with someone on a different day?'

'Dad . . .'

Kimberly's phone started to ring and after she glanced at the screen, she looked at Dad. 'Dad, I need to take this. Can I go? You got this, right?'

'Yes. Go, go.'

Kimberly left the room, and I stared after her in astonishment.

'Charlie,' he sighed. 'I know you're still pissed at her and you have every right, but this is work.'

'I'm not pissed at anyone,' I muttered, but we both knew it was a lie. 'She is back to being okay with her husband, right? That's all that matters.'

'We both know you don't feel that way.' He stood up and came to my side, fixing the collar of my shirt when it didn't need to be fixed.

I closed my eyes, tried not to fidget and took a deep breath.

'You need to make up with your sister. She feels bad about everything that happened.'

Not so surprisingly, she had never told me she felt bad. Suddenly I couldn't breathe in his office anymore. Just so I could get out, I gave in. 'I'll change my date to a Saturday and meet her client on Friday. I can't promise on the babysitting. I don't work in her team.'

He pressed his lips into a thin line. 'You can be so stubborn sometimes.'

'Can't change who I am,' I muttered, tilted my chin up higher. I had no problems with myself.

'Okay,' he commented, letting out a breath. 'Okay. Let it be your way.' He gave me a hug and I tried not to stiffen in his arms while I hugged him back. I loved my dad, but sometimes he made it hard to like him. 'I'm glad you started to see someone again. Hope you'll make a good choice with this one. You're still making your lasagne for dinner at your grandma's place tonight, right?'

I barely held back my groan. I'd completely forgotten about the monthly dinner at Grandma's place. So that explained why I had so many missed calls on my phone from her.

'Dad,' I started, pulling back from his hug. 'I have a lot of things to do with the new case we got today and Laurel Nielson as well.'

'It's okay. I'll talk to William and you'll leave a little early. He and his team can handle things without you.'

His phone started ringing at the same time someone from accounting knocked on his door.

'Mr Davis, I have these ready for you to look over.'

And just like that I'd missed my opportunity to weasel out of tonight's dinner.

When I was finally out of his office and in my own again. I closed my eyes, took a deep breath and tried to let out all the bad energy that was clinging to me. I repeated it a few times to calm myself down. Then I took out my phone to text Val, but my eyes landed on the book I was reading. I couldn't help but smile when I picked it up and found a note between the pages.

Why didn't you have lunch Charlie? I'm willing to share my sandwich this time around. I might also have a brownie for you. And some extra fries if you're interested.

The smile grew into a fully fledged grin and I immediately looked towards William's office. There were people walking around in the shared working space so I couldn't see him immediately at first, but then he was right there. Leaning against his desk and staring right back at me.

I laughed, and he smiled back. I sent him a small wave and lifted one finger to indicate I'd be right there and mouthed it too for good measure.

I didn't want him to think I was a lunatic, so I turned around with my grin and took a quick photo of the note and sent it to Val before putting it next to the other ones in the drawer.

Charlie: This is his third note. I think it's a thing. Tell me if it's a thing. I think it is.

Valerie: Is that from Willy? Tell me that's from Willy.

I chuckled. William was most definitely not a Willy.

Charlie: It's from *William*, yes.

Valerie: Charlie!

Valerie: He is into you. Sandwich, fries and a brownie? Are you kidding me? Marry him or I will.

I shook my head.

> **Charlie:** He isn't into me. We're friends. But the notes do make me happy.

> **Valerie:** No comment, but know that you're being stupid. What is he wearing?

> **Charlie:** A black suit. He took off his jacket in the middle of the meeting. It was a sight to behold.

> **Valerie:** Eeep!! Take a video next time.

> **Charlie:** How about I call him to my apartment and ask for a private undressing?

> **Valerie:** Oh! Good idea! We'll do a video call.

Still laughing, I stopped texting and headed to William's office. I opened the door and walked in, closing it behind me.

We stared at each other for a second too long.

'Hi, friend,' I said simply with a smile as something inside me shifted. I was so screwed.

William stood up and smiled at me in his black pants and crisp white shirt. 'Hello, Charlie. I believe you're here for the fries.'

'Fries are very hard to say no to.'

I beamed at him, feeling happy.

Oh, how I wish that had been the last time I'd seen him that day.

13

William

I'd left the office around 7.00 p.m. and soon enough made it to the address Douglas had sent me. Since I had to turn down his dinner invitation twice before due to all the things I needed to handle – new place, new team and cases – I'd said yes this time around.

Home didn't exactly feel like home either yet, so I had accepted the invitation. He had mentioned his mother and Kimberly would be there, but not Charlie.

Which is why I was so surprised when I knocked on the door of the luxurious townhouse, only a few blocks away from my place, and Charlie answered the door.

She was still wearing the same black skirt and lilac shirt she had been wearing earlier that day but where her hair had been loose and wavy, now she had it up in a bun with only a few errant pieces framing her face. The curve of her neck caught my attention as my eyes followed the V of her shirt down to the buttons. I snapped my eyes up.

'William?' she asked, the surprise on her face echoing in her words. 'What are you doing here?'

'Douglas invited me over to dinner.'

'Oh,' she muttered, her face falling a little. Still holding the door, she looked over her shoulder. 'I . . .'

I frowned. 'Is that okay?'

Her head jerked back towards me, but she was avoiding my gaze.

Confused, I just waited on the threshold with the wine I'd purchased on my way.

'If this is a bad time . . .' I trailed off.

'No,' she rushed to say. 'No. Of course not. Dad didn't tell me.' She sighed, opened the door wider and gestured inside with her hand. 'I'm being an idiot. I'm sorry, please come in.'

I stepped inside and handed her the wine after she closed the door.

'Is that William?' I heard Douglas ask from somewhere in the house.

'Yes, Dad,' Charlie called.

I couldn't put my finger on it, but she looked stressed – something was not right.

'Charlie,' I muttered and leaned closer to her. 'I'm not sure what's wrong, but if you're not comfortable with me being here, you can tell me.' I looked into her eyes and she finally met my gaze. Standing this close, I also noticed the slight flush high on her cheeks. 'I can find an excuse and leave.'

Her face softened and finally a smile made its way onto her lips. A small one, but I'd take that too.

'Don't be ridiculous. Come on. My dad is in the living room. Dinner is almost ready.'

Still a little uncertain, I followed her through the hallway and came face to face with Douglas.

'Welcome, William,' he greeted me.

I shook his hand, but my eyes were on Charlie. Holding the wine bottle I had given her, she gave me one last look and then exited through another door. Douglas took me into the living room where I met his mother Susan, Kimberly and her husband Scott. It looked like I was barging into a family dinner. Maybe that was why Charlie had been acting weird? After some small talk, Charlie came in to let everyone know the dinner was ready.

In the dining room, I sat next to Douglas and Kimberly sat across from me. When her husband reached for the seat next to me, I lost hope of sitting next to Charlie. Shaking off the unexpected disappointment, I watched as Charlie and her grandma brought in food that smelled amazing. Charlie started cutting into a lasagne and like an idiot I couldn't take my eyes from her. Had she cooked? I waited to see if she'd look at me, but it didn't happen. Not even once.

The table was set beautifully, the conversation flowed and in a few minutes almost everybody had a plate full of food in front of them, but Charlie still didn't look like herself at all. No easy smiles. No stolen glances my way. No intriguing conversation as she at last served herself. Somehow it was as if I was watching a watered-down version of the Charlie I'd come to know again these last few weeks and it bothered me enormously. It bothered me to the point that I could barely stop looking at her because I was trying to catch her gaze so badly.

'Charlie.' Her dad called her attention as she was about to sit down with her plate. 'Isn't that a little too much for you? Get some of the green bean salad instead maybe?'

Confused I glanced between Charlie and Douglas. Charlie froze in place. Then without saying a single word, she cut almost half of her lasagne and put it back in the casserole dish and sat down in her seat. Not having a good feeling about what had just happened, I shifted in my seat and tried not to frown too hard, but I couldn't help it. We made small talk as we started eating, but I still couldn't help but steal glances at Charlie.

If someone asked something, she answered with a distracted smile, but she wasn't exactly *in* the conversation somehow.

'William?' Kimberly called, and I stopped trying to catch Charlie's gaze and focused on her sister whom I hadn't had time to have many conversations with at the office with the workload we had. 'I have to admit, I already knew about you before you came to our firm, but I didn't expect you to handle the Michael Ashton electric car case as well as you did. I heard you helped the marketing team as well. Their new ads are really catching the eye of . . .'

'Kimberly,' Douglas interrupted. 'Let's skip work talk for tonight.'

'Of course, Dad.'

I smiled at Kimberly. 'I'll say this much. The team Douglas picked out for me was perfect. It was definitely a team effort, we all worked on it day and night.' I glanced at Charlie and saw the corner of her mouth quirk up. Such a small gesture, but it put a smile on my face and I tried to relax. 'We make a good team,' I added. Nothing was wrong. Maybe she just had been surprised to see me in her family's home.

I turned to Charlie's grandma, who was sitting at the head of the table opposite Douglas. 'The lasagne is really good, Susan. Thank you for having me over for dinner.'

She was taking a sip of her wine and gestured towards Charlie. 'Oh, it's all Charlie. We were supposed to have salmon, but I was craving Charlie's lasagne so I asked her to leave work early so she could come and cook. For some reason I can never get it right.'

So that's why she had disappeared from the office. I was looking at Charlie as Susan spoke and was just about to make a comment when Douglas got there first.

'Isn't it a little watery this time, Charlie?' he asked. 'Maybe the ragu?'

I glanced between Douglas and Charlie and then down to my plate as I frowned. Had he fucking lost his mind? It wasn't watery in any shape or form. It was the best lasagne I had ever tasted.

'Watery or not, Douglas,' Susan chimed in, 'it still tastes okay.'

I watched as Charlie swallowed her food. 'It needed some time to rest, Dad. When you cut into it too early sometimes it doesn't stay in shape. Is the salt okay this time?'

'Maybe a little less would've been better.'

My frown deepened. The lasagne tasted perfect. What the hell were they talking about? Before I could cut in and tell Charlie how incredible it tasted, Douglas spoke up again.

'I know I've just said no work talk for the night, but William, how is working with Charlie going?'

I looked at Charlie in case she wanted to be the one to answer, but she was still silent and barely eating anything that was on her plate. 'She is great. As I said, I'm really happy with the whole team.'

Kimberly nodded at me. 'I wanted to have Charlie with me, but she doesn't do that well in teams. I'm glad to hear it worked out for you.'

I watched as Charlie stiffened in her seat. I wasn't exactly sure what was going on, but I knew I didn't like any of it.

'She is actually great with the clients,' Douglas continued. 'Sometimes I call her in for a meeting if I need to calm someone down since Charlie seems to be great at that.' From what I'd seen he called her in more than a few times, but I thought I'd stay out of it, for now. 'But for some reason she is mostly a loner. She barely has any friends.' I stiffened in my seat and slowly put the knife and fork down. The food was leaving a bitter taste in my mouth.

We all turned to Charlie when she spoke up.

'Not that I need to explain myself, you know I have friends. But when would I have the time to go out with those friends? I spend most of my time at the office.'

'You had time for a dog, which I'm still not happy about.'

'You don't need to be happy about it. And having time for a dog is very different from going out with a different friend every night. Just because you guys don't like to spend time alone with yourselves, doesn't mean I have to be a social butterfly either. I'm happy with who I am and the amount of friends I have.' I watched as she cut a piece of her lasagne and angrily put it in her mouth.

'Charlie,' Kimberly sighed. 'No one is saying anything about who you are. We're just saying sometimes you're maybe a little antisocial.'

'And that doesn't sound like a bad thing to your ears? Anyway, if you want to call me antisocial so be it. I'm happier when I'm spending time on my own or with my very limited friends. You can worry about yourselves.'

The tension in the room spiked up, and I was too shocked and uncomfortable to say or do anything.

Douglas sighed and shook his head while he reached for the wine I'd brought in and poured himself a second glass. 'No one is judging you, Charlie. We just think it'd be better for you if you went out a little more maybe. Meet some new people.'

Charlie put her fork down and picked up her water glass. 'Well, Dad, I'll keep that in mind when you ask me to stay after work hours. You might be right after all.'

'Charlie, Douglas, this is not the time for this talk when we have company,' Susan cut in and focused her attention on me. 'I heard that your family lives in Montauk, is that true?'

'Yes,' I answered, still a little unsure of what was happening and pretty pissed off as well. 'Yes, they do. Me and my sisters were born there. One of my sisters lives in Pittsburg, but my parents and the other sister are still there.' I tried my best to be respectful as I focused on Susan. The respect I had for Douglas was already gone.

'They must be happy you moved closer to them. Maybe they'll visit soon?'

'I'm planning on making a trip when I have a free weekend maybe. It'll be easier for me.'

I studied Charlie as she took a few swallows from her water glass – she had barely touched her food when everyone was happily eating what she had cooked. And this was how they were treating her?

'I'm not the biggest fan of green beans, but they taste amazing. Is it the dressing, Kimberly?' I asked just to be annoying. She met my eyes and I saw the small line of confusion between her brows.

'Oh, I'm sorry, I assumed you had prepared it. Charlie made the lasagne and I thought the rest was from you.'

'I'm afraid not. I don't enjoy cooking as much as Charlie does, as you can tell from her figure. Plus, I had a lot of things I had to deal with at the office. Between the two of us, she is the better cook. She has more time. I'm extremely busy with the cases at the moment.'

Even I knew that Charlie barely had time to breathe at the office.

'Even I'm a better cook than Kimberly,' Scott added, speaking maybe for the first time since we had sat down. I had almost forgotten that he was even there.

Kimberly smiled at her husband and he returned it.

'That's true,' she agreed easily. 'Scott is good with pasta and eggs.'

'We learned it was better if I handled the kitchen early on in our marriage,' Scott affirmed.

I forced myself to take another bite of my lasagne and tried to not to follow every move Charlie made. 'How long have you two been married?' I asked Scott. He was blond with dark green eyes and in my opinion too quiet and passive for someone like Kimberly. I didn't think anything was wrong with her necessarily before this dinner, but she reminded me of someone I'd worked with a couple of years back, and I wasn't too surprised to see that she wasn't a close sister to Charlie since they were polar opposites, character-wise.

'Four years,' Scott replied, pulling me out of my thoughts.

'Congratulations.'

'Thank you,' Kimberly said. 'I heard that you have just gone through a divorce yourself. I'm sorry.'

I stiffened in my seat a little, but thought I hid the reaction well. I took a sip from my wine and nodded. 'Yes, that's true. Are you in the PR business as well, Scott?'

Chewing his food, he shook his head. 'That's the Davis family thing. I'm actually a high school teacher.'

'That's great,' I commented, only half-listening to him as my gaze kept going back to Charlie. She was half out of her seat, reaching forward to get the salt shaker, which is when I noticed Susan gesturing at Charlie to pull up her shirt at the front so she wouldn't show cleavage. Then for some reason she looked at Scott and then at Kimberly.

I watched as Charlie quickly plopped her ass back in her chair, looked down at herself, then met my eyes. I kept watching as a little colour reached her cheeks, then she quietly fixed her shirt and sat up straight. I kept the conversation with Scott going and asked a few random questions about being a teacher to steer the attention away from Charlie.

It was a little into the dinner and Douglas had already asked for another piece of lasagne from Charlie. Watery and salty, my ass. The more minutes passed the angrier I got on Charlie's behalf. It was a little comment here and a little comment there in passing and it was really starting to get on my nerves. Sometimes she just ignored them, but even when she tried to respond it almost looked as if nobody actually heard her.

I rubbed my temples and tried to get rid of the headache I could feel coming in. 'I'm very uncomfortable with the way you're treating Charlie right now.'

Douglas laughed off my comment as if I hadn't just spoken.

'Oh, she is fine. It's great you're dating again, Charlie,' Kimberly said, offhandedly as she kept eating. 'I'm glad for you. You took a long time after Craig, even though he wasn't even that into you, but I hope at least this time you'll find someone who'll stick around and someone who is *available*, of course.'

Charlie must have had enough, because she finally dropped her fork down and it made a loud clinking sound against her plate.

'Kimberly,' Scott said softly and his wife frowned at him.

'Are you kidding me?' Charlie blew up. 'Do you honestly think this is something you should speak of in front of my colleague? Somebody I'm working with? Your colleague? Should I just start asking you about your marriage problems? Because I can definitely do that.'

'Charlie, enough,' Douglas cut in in a firm voice.

'Enough?'

When her voice broke a little, I looked up from my plate and noticed that her eyes were filling with tears. I made fists of my hands under the table and barely held myself back from going to her side and taking her away from her family, just leaving everybody behind.

'That's nothing to be ashamed of, Charlie,' Susan cut in. 'You're who you are, like you said, and you're set in your own ways. So maybe you won't find someone you want to be with for the rest of your life like Kimberly did so early. I've been alone for what? More than twenty years? I'm perfectly happy.' She reached and put her long, thin fingers over Charlie's hand. 'You don't have Kimberly's looks so it's hard.'

Kimberly smiled, probably thinking it would go unnoticed, and I watched in shock.

'And if you don't want to live alone anymore, you can always come back and live with me. I don't even know why you wanted to move away when you didn't really have to.'

I couldn't take my eyes away from her and watched as a single tear finally fell from her eyes and trailed down her cheek. I'd never turned over a table in my fucking life, but that's exactly what I wanted to do in that moment. I was about to get up, punch someone and physically get Charlie away from here, but she beat me to it. She slowly pushed her chair back and stood up as everyone including me watched her.

She looked over at her dad. 'I'm sorry, Dad. I have some things I need to work on since I left the office early to come here and cook. I think it's best if I leave now.'

'Charlie, don't be ridiculous.'

'Please, enjoy your dinner. Goodnight.'

And then she just walked out of the dining room. A few seconds later I heard the front door quietly open and close.

Kimberly's sigh drew my attention first. 'I didn't mean anything by my comment. I was happy she was putting herself out there again. I don't know what I said wrong.'

Douglas put his fork and knife down. 'Charlie can be . . . a little too sensitive sometimes,' he explained to me. 'I hope you won't think badly of her. She is great at her work. I'll have a talk with her tomorrow.'

Then as if nothing had happened, everybody picked up the conversation and kept eating. Still a little shocked, I sat there and listened to them talk.

Not even ten seconds had passed when I pushed my chair back just as Charlie had done and put my napkin down. 'I think I'm done for the night too.' Even though I knew I had all their eyes on me, I fixed my focus on Douglas. 'I'd like to thank you for inviting me into your home, but I'm sad to say that would be a lie. Just like Charlie, I'd like to be anywhere but here, so I'm going to leave and catch up with your daughter and properly thank her for the dinner she cooked, since none of you thought to do that.'

Douglas stood up.

'No need,' I said, not giving him time to speak because if he said the wrong thing, I wasn't sure how I'd react and I didn't want to deck my new boss – at least not just yet. 'I'll see myself out. I think after what I've seen tonight we should only interact professionally.' I turned to Charlie's grandma and inclined my head. 'I'd say it was nice meeting you ma'm, but I'm having trouble forming the words. Have a good evening.' I ignored both Kimberly and her husband.

And just like that I left their home, knowing I wouldn't come back again. As soon as I was out I started jogging towards our street hoping Charlie wouldn't have called an Uber for herself and I could catch up with her. I saw her hunched-up form two blocks ahead and slowed down to a walk so I wouldn't scare her.

'We need to stop bumping into each other at random places like this,' I commented softly when I reached her side.

She avoided my gaze. Emotions I couldn't quite describe when it came to Charlie stabbed at my chest.

'Charlie,' I murmured and she wiped the tears under her eyes with the back of her hand. 'Remember your honesty thing? I would like to hear what you're thinking.'

'I feel embarrassed,' she whispered. 'I don't think I want to do the honesty thing right now.'

My forehead creased. 'Why would you feel embarrassed? You did nothing. In fact you handled that a whole lot better than how I would've handled it.'

'Nevertheless, I would've preferred if you hadn't seen it.'

'Is that why you were a little distant after seeing me at the door?'

She wiped at her face and sniffled once, before giving me a small nod.

I just wanted to walk her home, I wasn't after rehashing the dinner disaster, so I pushed my hands into my pockets and silently walked beside her for the next five minutes.

'I wrote a list, you know.'

I stayed silent so her eyes briefly passed over me.

'I wrote a list the day I saw you at the office. When I came home that night, I mean. It didn't really have anything to do with seeing you again after so many years, I've wanted to write it for a while now.'

'What is it about?'

'It's called The Pursuit of Charlie. I'm still working on the name. I need to change some things in my life. And the first thing on the list is *move*. I wrote it multiple times. I love my family. I love them. Trust me, I do, they aren't like this all the time, but lately I feel like they have lost it completely and I don't think I can handle it anymore. Everything they do or say bothers me, and it just seems to get worse, somehow. I think it'll be so much better if we don't see each other as often as we do.'

'Trust me, I get the why after tonight.'

'Yeah.'

'Can I ask one thing?'

'Sure. How much worse can it get from what just happened. Go ahead.'

'You don't have to answer. Not that I understand why your dad or grandma said any of the things they said, but is there something more with Kimberly? She seemed to push you more.'

She took a deep breath and let it out slowly. Crossing her arms over her chest, she gazed up at the night sky. 'I hate that we can't see the stars because of light pollution. I always wanted to live somewhere where I can spend hours just watching them. They're beautiful.'

She was silent for another moment, but then kept going. 'Kimberly and I had a big fight last year. Which is when I started to consider moving more seriously. She thinks I flirted with her husband. Genuinely believes that I was ... or who knows, maybe still thinks I'm interested in Scott. Her reasonings were: because he is quiet and you're quiet too, and he smiles at you and you smile at him when you think I'm not looking. I guess we texted every now and then? I don't even remember what it was, but I promise you I never saw him as more than a brother. Why in the hell would I? When she first accused me of it, I was quiet because I was shocked. She took that as affirmation and ran with it. Thankfully Scott doesn't know about it because clearly I was to blame. Considering the guy might have been the problem – not that he was, he loves my sister with all his heart – never crossed her mind. And she took the fact that I hadn't dated in years as proof of my unrequited love for her husband.'

We walked in silence for at least a few minutes before she continued.

'Neither my dad nor my grandma was on my side. They didn't believe that I actually had feelings for Scott, not that, but they didn't stop Kimberly from saying all the things she said to me either. They thought I was being ridiculous. I don't know how to get over it. Any of it. They keep saying I'm too sensitive or I'm making a big deal out of nothing, but I'm pretty much done being quiet.'

'How did she let it go?'

'Kimberly?'

I nodded.

'I have no idea. I guess she believed me after all because she came to my office a few days later and said that she'd just gotten jealous.'

'But she didn't apologize?'

'Nope. Even if she had apologized, the fact that she actually believed I could even think something like that . . .'

'It's hard to gain back trust. I understand.'

'I'm still sorry for how I acted tonight. I didn't want you to see that.'

'Why?' I pushed. 'I'm just some random guy you bump into every now and then.'

'You're not though.' I felt her eyes on me so I met her gaze. 'Not really. I had a big thing for you,' she admitted with a small and sad smile that didn't make me happy to look at. 'It's embarrassing for me.'

'Let me repeat it. You have nothing to be embarrassed about – tonight didn't change what I think about you as a person in any way. But if it's gonna make you feel better we can forget about it.'

She nodded. 'I'd really appreciate that.'

It took us another ten minutes to reach our street and we found ourselves yet again standing in front of her building.

Charlie glanced up to her apartment window and I followed her gaze.

'You think he'll hear you again?' I whispered.

She shook her head. 'He is home tonight. He usually just sleeps when I'm gone.'

I didn't want to let go of her just yet, so I asked something that'd been on my mind. 'How is the job hunting going?'

'I had an online interview yesterday. After work. I don't think we were a good fit. I'll keep looking.'

'I can help you,' I offered. 'If you'd like.'

Her eyebrow rose. 'Help me how?'

I gestured towards the stairs leading up to her building door and sat down. She followed suit.

'I can call a friend, Nora, she just started a new PR company in California. I think they need to hire a few more people. They'd be lucky to have you.'

Linking my hands, I let my forearms rest on my thighs.

'You think they'll be okay with an online interview since I can't leave work right now to go to California. For an interview I mean.'

'Sure, why not?'

A teenager and his dad walked past with their labrador and we paused our conversation as we watched them running in circles around the dad.

'I can also talk to someone from the company I just left, but I don't think it'd be a good choice for you. Nora might be a better option.'

'I'm gonna accept the help because it doesn't look like I'm making any progress on my own. I keep pushing things back and delaying my life, it feels like. I'd really appreciate that, William. Thank you so much.'

I smiled and inclined my head.

There was a comfortable silence between us, and I think neither one of us wanted to break it, or leave it behind. Not just yet.

I stared straight ahead. 'This list you wrote. What else is on it? Do I get to ask?'

'What else . . .' she hummed and then chuckled a little. 'The kissing is there, I'm afraid. Pretty high on the list too.' She hid her face in her hands and groaned. 'I'm pretty focused on the kissing.'

I laughed quietly. 'You really miss it, huh?'

'I think so. I miss the easy part of the relationship, I guess. Waking up and just being happy to have someone you love next to you and just kissing. The first few months before Craig left felt really good. He was different. The kissing thing sucked, but everything else was good.'

'Always the kissing,'

She nodded with a big grin on her face. 'How about you? You miss it?'

'I don't think it's been long enough for me, yet.' But I thought about it. Maybe. Maybe I had missed the easy parts of being in a relationship. The happy parts. Lindsey and I hadn't experienced those parts all that much towards the end. 'What else is on there?' I asked, trying to distract myself from relationships and kissing and Charlie's lips which were bare and yet still somehow a dark pink.

Charlie brought her knees together, put her elbows on her thighs and rested her face in her hands.

'I have the honesty thing in there. I try to say whatever I'm feeling or thinking – most of the time – so I don't have a buildup of emotions.' She gave me a quick look then focused forward again. 'It's not exactly a bucket list kinda thing. It's more like a list of how I should live my life. I have flirting on there.'

'Flirting?'

'Yeah. Just for fun, you know. It makes me smile. And I like smiling.'

'You're good at it.'

'What, flirting?' She looked at me with a little frown on her face.

'I wouldn't know.' I kept my eyes across the street. 'You're good at smiling. It looks good on you.'

From the corner of my eye I saw a smile bloom across her face.

'Thank you, William.'

'Are you good at flirting?'

'I'd say so. Why? You think I'd be bad at it?'

'I don't know. You want to try it on me one day?' I was a glutton for punishment. My question proved it.

'Flirt with you?'

'Not the best idea, maybe, huh?'

'I don't know. Just for fun, right?' she asked slowly.

'Sure.'

'Yeah. I'll show you what I got, I guess. Good practice.'

I chuckled.

She gave me a thoughtful side eye. 'You're not considering offering to work on my kissing as well, right?'

I let out a laugh. 'Don't worry. That's more than I can handle, I'm afraid.'

'Pfff. You wish I'd want to kiss you.'

I chuckled – she was right. I'd probably wish that. 'How are you feeling?' I asked instead, studying her profile.

She took a deep breath and slowly let it out. 'Better.' She met my eyes. 'Thanks to you. So, thank you, William. I appreciate it.'

'I didn't do anything, Charlie.'

'Just listening to me. And being here for me. That's more than enough, not everybody gets that.'

'Anytime. I'm thinking of getting some quick breakfast before work tomorrow, you want to bump into me around 7.30?'

'Bump into you where exactly?'

'You pick. You'll have a better idea of where to go.'

'Okay. Then let's bump into each other around 7.30 in the middle of the street, then we'll go have a quick breakfast before the day starts.'

'Deal,' I agreed.

Slowly she stood up, so I had to stand up as well, but I could've used another few minutes talking to her. Maybe just another half an hour.

We studied each other for a few seconds, and I tried not to think too much.

'Thank you again,' she repeated.

'I didn't do anything.'

A smile danced on her lips.

'You know you did.'

Then she took a step forward and, surprising me, gave me a hug.

'And I appreciate it,' she whispered. 'I should go in.'

'Is there something I can say that would make you feel better, Charlie?'

'You said all the best things.'

My body relaxed against hers and instinctively I wrapped my arms around her back and smiled. We should've let go of each other, but . . . we didn't.

Slowly the seconds ticked away as we stood under the dim lights of the night, and I was surprised to admit or realize that I was losing my head a little over her perfume. Soft, slightly flowery, maybe roses or something, but definitely fresh. And then there was the feel of *her* in my arms. I closed my eyes for a second.

'I always wanted to do this, you know,' she whispered.

'Hmmm,' I murmured like an idiot, because I couldn't think of anything else to say. I didn't even know what she was talking about.

'I'm making this slightly awkward, aren't I?'

I let out my breath, my arms still around her. 'Not so much.'

A moment passed.

And in that little moment I made the mistake of realizing how well her body fitted against mine.

'William?' She turned in my arms and rested her temple against my shoulder.

'Yeah, Charlie,' I answered gruffly.

'You wanna know something else from my list?'

'Tell me.'

She pulled back a little, her arms still around my shoulders and mine still around her back, and we studied each other.

'Hugging. I think it was something like: find people who give good hugs.'

Then she took a step away from me, and I had to let her. Our arms dropped to our sides.

'Do I make the cut?' I asked, trying to sound as normal as possible.

She looked straight into my eyes and gave me a big happy smile.

'You do.' She shook her head. 'Even your hugs are good.'

Then she leaned forward, cupped my cheek with her palm, got on her tiptoes and planted a soft kiss on my other cheek. She was staring into my eyes when she spoke, and I couldn't look away.

'And the best hugs are the ones you didn't ask for.'

'You have to ask for hugs?'

She shrugged, and I felt her look too deep into me.

'I think I like being your friend, William. Thank you.'

Just like that, she left me standing there and disappeared into her building. It wasn't the first time I'd felt what I'd just felt when I was around her, and I didn't think it'd be the last time either. I just hoped she'd move away before either one of us fell into it. It seemed like we'd never meet at the right time. Because there was no way something, anything between us could happen.

14

Charlie

We had just wrapped up another crisis situation that had taken us ten days to work through. We had worked late almost every night except the night before. Since today was Saturday, I had done nothing but lounge around in my apartment and spend time with Pepperoni. We were both in heaven.

And I had to admit it was nice to be in William's team, working with him, Trisha, Stan, and Rick. I realized I was happier sharing the load with them than running around the office trying to get to everything my dad was throwing my way. He was still doing that, but not to the same extent. And if I was not mistaken, he was still a little embarrassed about what had happened at the dinner. Not because of the way they treated me, because none of them saw anything wrong with it whatsoever, but because William had witnessed it. I had no idea what words they had shared between them or *if* they had shared any, but I could see just from body language that William was being distant in general when they were both in the same room. Or more professional in a sense.

Needless to say I didn't think he'd accept a dinner invitation from our family anytime soon, if ever again.

Maybe after I left.

It was around 7 p.m. and I was enjoying shopping in the grocery store when I saw him pop up in the bread aisle. I saw him before he noticed me, and I was already smiling, something in my chest fluttering. I'd learned really well to ignore that fluttering in the last few weeks, but regardless of that fact it hadn't disappeared yet.

My eyes slowly took in what he was wearing – a thin, black sweater and jeans, and he was taking off his black sunglasses. The image of him caused my heart to lurch with an extra thud.

My smile got bigger when our eyes met and he beelined straight towards me with a smile of his own. My fingers closed around the pack of bagels I was holding a little too hard, so I had to force myself to relax. He was shaking his head when he stopped in front of me.

'Are we even surprised?' I asked.

'I can't go anywhere without bumping into you,' he returned.

I laughed. 'You're just gonna have to admit that you can't get enough of me. The more you think about me, the more the universe will give me to you.'

He raised one of his eyebrows and a slow burning heat flooded my chest. 'Is that so?'

I tried to backtrack. 'When I say give me to you, I meant as in show me to you.'

His lips parted with a smile. 'I know what you mean, Charlie.'
Phew.

His eyes and the way he looked so deep into me as if he were trying to understand me just by looking at me always got to me and I melted a little. On the inside, of course. I think I was very good at hiding that I had a crush on him again. As much as I was loving the being honest thing from my list, this was one of those things that I didn't think would do any good to admit out loud. Under different circumstances, sure, maybe.

At the moment. No. It would do no good and only make things awkward.

'Okay. Good. Because ... you know what? I'm not even gonna try because I'm pretty sure I'll just dig myself deeper.'

'I'll help you change the subject,' he said, with humour dancing in his eyes.

'Not that I needed any help, but please go ahead.' I dropped the bagels into the basket in my hand and we started walking together.

'I'm glad we ran into each other, because just an hour ago I heard back from my friend in California. I'd mentioned her to you. Nora, remember? She'd been out of state, but she's back and she'd like to have a Zoom call with you this week whenever you're free. They're looking for someone and I think you'd like working with them.'

I stopped and faced William. 'Are you serious?'

'Yeah. I told her about you a little and she is excited to meet you. The position is still available.'

'I could kiss you right now, Mr Carter,' I blurted out softly, without thinking what the hell I was saying. My heart went into a fast, frantic beat.

There was a pause as I wondered if I could take back what I'd said or just laugh it away, but he spoke first.

'Far be it from me to keep you from ...'

'Excuse me,' someone said in a light voice and both William and I turned towards the owner of it. A teenager, looking awkward and wary. 'If you could ... I just need to get some bread?'

'Oh, so sorry,' I muttered and started walking again. I was an idiot. A second later I felt William following me. I closed my eyes and took a deep breath.

Get it together, Charlie.

No kissing.

'No hot dates tonight?' William asked when I turned around a corner.

'I was on a date the entire day,' I replied distractedly. 'He tired me out and now I need food.' William was quiet so I looked over my shoulder. 'You coming? I need cheese.'

'What was his name?' he asked when he caught up with me. 'Was it Randy the runaway?'

'Randy who?' I frowned. 'You mean Ralph? And the runaway? Really?'

'Fugitive, deserter, escapee. All the same, isn't it?'

'Isn't that a little harsh? I haven't even met the guy yet.'

'So you decided to see him then. Last time we spoke you weren't sure.'

'Yeah. I think. We texted a little bit, the other day. We'll just go out for dinner. For the fun of it. Nothing serious.'

'Sounds good. So who was today's date?'

'Pepp. I'd promised a day to him and we made the most of it.' I glanced at him on my way to the cheese section and saw his soft look. It looked good on him. I sighed. He looked good in every way. 'So, what are you doing here?'

'What do you mean?'

I looked around us and raised my brows. 'In the grocery store.'

'Oh, right. I need coffee and some olives.'

'Nice combination.'

'You don't like olives?'

'I love olives.'

'Good.'

I chuckled. 'Good. What's wrong with you?' He looked a little confused and grumpy. 'It's evening so you can't have gone without coffee for this long. Why so grumpy?'

He gave me a long look then, shaking his head, sighed. 'Just tired, I guess. And I feel a little unbalanced around you sometimes. I declined another case today. A family feud. One of those reality families. The producer got in touch.'

I chose my favourite cheddar and grabbed some Swiss cheese while I was at it to go with the bagels.

'Thank you for that,' I said, glancing at him over my shoulder. 'I was looking forward to spending some time at home this weekend.'

'I have nothing to do. Would you like to . . .' he said, but his phone started ringing, so he apologized and answered on the third ring.

'William Carter. Yes. I understand. Can you give me some information?'

As William kept talking to whoever was on the other end of the line, I spotted a kid no more than seven years old who was running towards us with his mom rushing after him.

'What steps did you take so far?' William asked.

I gently put my hand on William's forearm and pulled him away to the side so we wouldn't get bulldozed by the kid. William's gaze dropped to my hand on his arm, then still talking on the phone, he lifted his gaze up to me. I gave him a small smile and pulled my hand away.

He was still staring into my eyes when he ended his call.

'I'm afraid I'm about to ruin your plans for tonight, Charlie.'

My face fell, but I tried not to show it. I was looking forward to just being with Pepp, cooking and watching romantic comedies.

'What happened?'

'We have a crisis with a dating app. It's been hacked and some information has been stolen.'

'We're heading to the office?'

He stared at me for a few seconds. Calculating something.

'I'm a little sick of seeing the office walls this week. How about we start the work at my place for tonight and head to the office tomorrow? You think everyone else can come?'

A smile broke out on my face. 'That sounds great. I'm sure they'll prefer that too.' Then I remembered Pepp and the fact that my neighbours were gone for a little romantic weekend trip. He was perfectly fine with staying home all by himself now, but that didn't mean I wanted to be apart from him, especially on the weekend.

William started to walk away. 'I'm running low on coffee so I'm gonna get that, then we can leave. Can you call the others? We don't need Gayle to come over for now.'

'William,' I called out and he stopped to look at me. 'I don't want to leave Pepp alone tonight. Can I bring him too? He'll be good, promise.'

The way he kept looking at me ... A girl could get used to that, I thought.

He tilted his head, a small smile on his lips. 'Charlie, you never have to ask.'

Did it make me a little upset that our *never* would be too short since I would be leaving New York? Maybe. Maybe it did a little.

An hour later, everyone was at William's place. Trisha had taken a spot on one end of the L-shaped couch, Stan on the other. Rick was standing in front of the windows overlooking my place, talking to the IT department of the dating app. I was sitting on the desk eating the last slice of pizza we had gotten for the team from Johnie's. Pepp was sleeping right next to my chair, softly snoring after he had tired himself begging food from everyone. I had no idea where William was.

Because of the heat in the apartment, I had already secured my hair in a bun at the nape of my neck, but it started to feel hotter as the minutes passed. Wiping my hands on a napkin, I took off my thick sweater and released a sigh at the coolness of my tank top. I looked down at myself and pulled up the front a little bit. Since Trisha had come straight from a dinner date with her husband, her dress had more cleavage than my tank top, so I felt okay showing more skin. Nobody was interested or looking anyway. It was either that or sweat to death.

I got up and dumped the pizza box in the kitchen and turned on the tap to wash my hands. Still feeling a little hot, I rubbed the cold water on my neck and then ran my hand over my shoulders and my throat. As much as I had gotten used to being around William, being in his home felt like a new intimacy. I discreetly looked around. He cooked for himself in this kitchen – which was definitely bigger than mine – and spent time on the couch where Stan and Trisha were working. He probably . . .

'Charlie.'

I jumped, splashing water everywhere. 'You scared the shit out of me,' I hissed, holding my hand over my heart as I turned to look at him. 'What?' I asked when he just stared at me from the table.

There was something in his eyes I couldn't pinpoint. His gaze bore into mine.

'What are you doing?'

'William, the CEO isn't sure about informing their users before they figure out what happened or exactly how it happened,' Trisha called out, breaking our eye contact.

William went to her side, and I followed suit. Pepp woke up and lifted his head. I stopped at his side, leaned down and ran my still wet hands over his face. 'Hi,' I whispered. 'Hi, handsome boy. Are you sleeping?' I leaned down further and pressed a kiss on his nose and got one back myself. 'I love you, too,' I whispered, as he put his head back down and stretched his arms and legs.

I straightened up and got caught in William's gaze again. He was talking into his phone, but all his attention was on me. I don't know what came over me, but all of a sudden all I could think was walking straight towards him and kissing him. Everybody in the room could've just disappeared for all I cared. My breathing quickened, and I felt slightly lightheaded, lost in his gaze. I had no idea what he was thinking looking at me like that, but I felt that strong pull towards him.

Then he looked away and I could breathe normally again. I sat my ass down on the chair, next to Pepp again, and reached for my laptop and phone.

Charlie: Distract me.

Valerie: From what?

Charlie: The whole team is working in William's apartment. We keep making eye contact and I'm struggling just a little.

Valerie: Are you insane? Keep the eye contact! Don't look away. This is good news.

Charlie: This isn't distracting me.

Valerie: Shhh. Go look at him a little, I'm busy.

I looked at him. Every now and then. We worked non-stop for three hours.

It was around 11 p.m. when both Trisha and William were standing over my shoulder pointing out what else I needed to add to the initial statement for the CEO. Before a journalist could hear about the story and create panic among the users, we had advised that it was important to keep their customers updated every step of the way.

'I think this is good,' Trisha said from my right. 'It's not a generic response, it expresses concern, it's sincere, and it shows they're working on the problem. It also lets them know their credit card information has not been stolen since it's on a different system. I think we've done all we can do for tonight.'

'I think you're right. Okay.' William took off his glasses, rubbed his eyes, then put them back on again. And I just kept staring at the new object that looked absolutely perfect on him. 'Okay, I'm calling it a night. We'll meet at the office tomorrow and go through the rest of the list.'

Trisha walked away, but William was still standing on my right and was absent-mindedly petting Pepp as his tail thumped against the table's leg. Then Rick called Pepp to his side to say goodbye – they had become fast friends in under an hour – and he ran over with an excited butt wiggle.

I was still smiling when I noticed William looking at me.

'Something wrong?' I asked. His eyes dipped to my lips then back up to my eyes then back to my laptop.

'Would you mind staying another twenty or so? I think we need to add to this.'

'Ahh . . .' I checked the time on my laptop before half-turning to him again. 'Sure,' I mumbled. I pulled back a little as our eyes met. I cleared my throat. 'Of course.'

I focused back on my laptop, shifted in place and tried not to fidget too much.

'This one, Charlie,' he said quietly right next to my ear, tapping the screen with a finger. 'Something is missing. Try first person maybe. Then I want to add something else.'

This was the fourth time he'd leaned down to point something out to me. The first time it had happened I hadn't reacted at all. It was good. We were all good. Rick had done the same after all, and I'd been just fine. The second time it'd happened his warm breath had hit my neck and my eyes had slightly fluttered. The third time I'd lost my voice for at least a few minutes and had just nodded and hummed my answer to whatever he was telling me.

His chest was against my shoulder and I could feel the softness of his sweater against my bare skin. I tensed. Goosebumps covered the skin on my arms, and I closed my eyes. I didn't move. Didn't start on working on the paragraph either.

'Charlie,' William whispered this time.

Had he noticed that I was struggling with having him so close? I held my breath.

Because of the way our backs were turned to the others, I don't think anybody could tell there was something going on with me. While I could still hear them talking and getting ready to leave, to me William's quiet voice was the loudest in the room. I was stuck between moving forward so his sweater wouldn't caress my skin and just leaning back and living the moment to the fullest. I did neither. Torture being fun and everything.

Rick thankfully chose that moment to ask William something so I could start breathing normally again, but my heart hadn't gotten the memo and was determined to keep up its fast and frantic beat. I waved at myself with my hand to cool down at least a little. Why wasn't anyone opening a window?

The others said their goodbyes as they left, one by one. 'Bye, guys,' I yelled as I planted a small kiss on Pepp's not so little nose. He was getting bigger by the day. 'You're such a good boy,' I whispered, holding his face in my hands. He bumped his nose against mine and I smiled.

While William was letting Rick and Stan out, I grabbed my laptop and headed straight towards the couch, Pepp following after me. I sat down and quietly groaned. My butt had plenty of cushion to it, but after three hours straight on a chair it still hurt. I closed my eyes and sighed. Pepp jumped up onto the couch and curled into a big ball, his back resting against my thigh. My right hand on the keyboard, I trailed the fingers of my left hand between Pepp's eyes – his favourite spot. His eyes slowly closed and just like that he fell into sleep.

I heard the door close.

'I hope you don't mind finishing on the couch because my back and my neck hurt like crazy,' I said to William as I deleted a paragraph and started rewriting with both hands.

And then suddenly there was a hand on my neck. I slid forward in record time as a shiver worked down my spine and put the laptop on the coffee table. I glanced at Pepp; his eyes were still closed and he hadn't even moved from his spot. I rested my back against the back of the couch and tilted my head up to meet William's eyes as he gently kept his hand on the base of my neck. 'To what do I owe the pleasure, Will?'

'William. Do I call you Charriot? And you worked more than anyone tonight, no wonder your neck hurts.'

I let out a big laugh and finally woke up Pepp. He turned his head to look at me. 'I'm sorry, baby,' I murmured and ran my hand along his body until he relaxed back. 'Charriot?' I asked, tilting my head up again, still smiling. 'What does that have to do with Charlie? I shortened your name to Will. There was a logic.' His fingers squeezed my shoulders and I jumped forward again so I could look over my shoulder. 'Are you flirting with me, William? Because I'm very good at flirting. I told you this before. I'll see it from a mile away.'

William laughed and then sighed. I bit on my lip. 'You did tell me before. Do you want me to loosen your muscles, or not?'

Grinning, I leaned back again. 'Thank you. I'll take that. Would you like me to show you my flirting skills? You can be my training wheels for my date this week.'

Why was I suddenly playing with fire?

'Finally going out with Rupert?'

I looked over my shoulder. 'Are you doing that on purpose?'

He grinned at me. 'What am I doing exactly?'

I shook my head and faced forward again. 'Don't know who Rupert is, but with Ralph, yes. Depending on how work goes, maybe Thursday.'

'Good luck.'

'Thanks. How about the flirting?'

'Relax your shoulders,' William muttered as his hands made contact with my skin again and it was music to my ears. I was nothing but putty under his fingers. My body was slowly melting, I could feel it. Not just because of his hands on me, but also because of his voice.

I had to force myself to keep my eyes open when he started to knead my muscles.

A few moments passed in silence and then he hit a particular spot and my eyes closed all on their own. 'That feels really good,' I whispered, and when William hummed back I had to fight off the goosebumps on my skin. It was no use. The shiver raced down my arms and all over my body. 'Could you talk to me? I really like your voice.' I tilted my neck to one side and quietly moaned. A girl could really get used to having him around. And not just because of his massage skills.

Just like that, the big, skilful hands were gone from my skin and a moment later the couch dipped. I slowly opened my eyes to find William sitting right next to me.

He cleared his throat. 'Let's look at this so we can send it out.'

I kept my grin as small as possible. 'I told you I was good at flirting.' I got a pillow so I could put the laptop on my lap so we could both see the screen. My back wasn't into that idea whatsoever.

'You didn't even say anything. What are you talking about?'

'I'm that good. I don't even need words to flirt,' I said in a serious tone and smiled when I heard his laughter. 'You can lie to yourself, of course. I know the truth and that's what matters. Okay,' I started, turning my eyes back to the screen. 'Since you don't want to flirt with your friend, let's finish this so I can take my baby home.' I brought the cursor to the paragraph he wanted to go over.

'Okay, let's do this.' He leaned towards me so he could get a better look at the screen, but I leaned back. 'What's wrong?' he asked, eyes on me as he tilted his head.

'The glasses.'

'So?' He took them off, and we stared at them for a second, then he put them back on. 'Sometimes I need to wear them if I'm working late.'

'William . . .' He met my gaze. Did I really want to say what I was about to say out loud? I probably didn't, but also kinda did. The honesty thing. I could always blame the honesty thing. 'You never wore them at the office. Tonight is the first time I'm seeing them. I'm trying really hard not to crush on you right now. And just so you know, it's a real struggle.'

He gave me a long look and stayed quiet for a few more seconds after I'd ended my confession.

'I'm trying to understand if you're flirting with me to prepare for your date or if you're being honest.'

I gave him a small smile. 'If I tell you something it's because I'm being honest. Flirting or no flirting. Your glasses are really throwing me off.'

His eyes didn't let me look away. 'You like how I look,' he guessed.

It wasn't a question, because he already knew I liked how he looked. I had this sudden urge to reach up and touch his messy hair, but I balled my hand into a fist at my side to stop myself.

Since he wasn't looking away, my heart started to beat a mile a minute again, and I had to force myself to glance away. 'You already know,' I murmured, shifting in my seat to reach for the laptop. Closing my eyes, I took a deep breath and then slowly let it out to balance myself, because it was fine. I was just fine. I slowly opened my eyes to focus on the statement, since we had to send it to the CEO tonight. It was still too hot in the room and suddenly too bright as well. I didn't look at him, but I could feel the weight of his eyes on my skin all the same.

Flirting with William was not sensible, 'Okay, that might have been a mistake on my part. No more flirting, I think.' Clearing my throat, I started changing the paragraph to first person as fast as possible.

'Why did you change your mind? I thought you wanted to practice?'

I ignored him.

'Okay, how about this?' I turned the laptop so he could see the screen better, but he scooted closer until our shoulders were almost touching. First, I couldn't put space between us because Pepp was a heavy weight settled right against my thigh. Second, it would look weird. I sat up straighter and tried to act like his closeness wasn't affecting me at all.

'Charlie, I believe that's the wrong paragraph.'

I was looking away from the screen, but as soon as he spoke up,

I realized my mistake. 'Ah, I'm so sorry. I'll change that back to what it was. One sec.' I clicked 'undo' and then started on the actual paragraph he wanted me to change.

'That's not first person. What are you doing, Charlie?' William whispered against my ear, and I had to stop typing altogether. 'Are you affected by me?' A slow shiver worked its way down my spine, and I curled my fingers around the edge of the laptop.

We were working. We had a time limit. The company was waiting to hear back from us. I wasn't supposed to get lost in what I was feeling. What he was making me feel.

'Just a second,' I whispered and closed my eyes to get myself together. It wasn't just his eyes, his hair, his arms, his chest or even his glasses, his closeness, his voice that was throwing me off, it was his cologne too. 'I think I should go...'

'Charlie,' William said softly, and I stopped speaking. I turned my head and looked straight into his eyes.

I didn't say anything. William lifted his right hand and my eyes followed it. When his fingers gently touched my temple and swiped my hair away to tuck it behind my ear, I froze. My skin grew warm, the path his finger took leaving behind a tingling sensation as my heart lost its steady pace. Time slowed down as I looked into William's eyes and I was taken back to that one week I had spent rushing to that diner to see him. *That* Charlie would've been ecstatic right about now if she saw the look in William's eyes. This Charlie was ... she wasn't sure what she was exactly, but if anything she was overwhelmed.

'You're beautiful, Charlie,' he said simply.

'But ...'

'No buts. No buts with you.'

I swallowed and tried to think. 'Ah. Okay then. Um ... yes, the document.' I cleared my throat and frowned at the open document on my lap. 'You wanted me to change it to first person. Then you wanted to read it again and do something else about it. Okay. Yes, I'm going to ...'

'Charlie,' William murmured, then to my surprise slowly closed the laptop.

I opened it up again. 'Nope. I'm not gonna flirt with you. You're not playing fair.'

He chuckled next to me. 'Charlie, I'm not flirting with you. Well, I am, but I'm not trying to be ... as you put it ... your "training wheels" for your date.'

'I still have a crush on you,' I blurted out, then physically covered my mouth with my hands and slowly turned my head to William.

He gave me a long look as the silence stretched between us, and I slowly lowered my hands from my face. This time I closed the laptop.

'Can we act like I didn't say that?' I asked.

Instead of giving me an answer, he sighed and reached for my hand, surprising the shit out of me, and linked our fingers together, resting the backs of our hands on his thigh. I couldn't look away. Why did it feel so natural? Why did it feel like my heart had released a long sigh as if this was it? As if William, and William's hand around mine, was it.

'I feel the same way I felt for you all those years back, Charlie.'

I let his words simmer under my skin. Boiling my blood. Seducing my heart.

We were sitting next to each other. Shoulder to shoulder. Thigh to thigh on a relatively big sectional couch facing the window. My hand was resting slack in his hand. From shock, I believe, but after hearing his words, I squeezed his fingers. Holding on harder, because this was too big to just float alone. I needed him as my anchor.

'Why would I believe that, William? You didn't come. I asked you. I worked up the courage and asked you. *If you feel like this could go somewhere I'll be waiting here for you again tomorrow.*' I admitted, feeling beyond vulnerable. I still remembered my words. 'I believed you'd come. So you saying this now doesn't mean a lot.'

His fingers tightened around mine. 'I had a crush on you back then and I have a crush on you now. If you're ready to hear it, I can tell you why I stood you up.'

I thought about it for a second, but realized I didn't want to learn. Simply because I was too scared of the answer he was going to give. I didn't want him to break my heart for the second time. I didn't even care if that made me a chicken. 'I don't think I am.'

We sat there, holding each other's hands for minutes. At least it felt that way. I'd wanted nothing but to get out of this city for so long. And now he was right here.

'I . . . William . . .'

'Charlie, I have a confession to make.'

I listened in silence.

'The best part of my day is when I catch you staring at me in office meetings. I lift my eyes to find you in the room and you're right there staring back at me. I guess I should say *one* of the best parts of my day is looking up and seeing you being so close to me.'

I could feel the heat spread across my cheeks. I could hear the beat of my heart slamming against my chest, begging to be let loose. The butterflies in my stomach. And the goosebumps on my arm.

Then William turned and faced me, meeting my wild eyes.

'What is the other?' I asked in nothing but a whisper. Afraid that it would all disappear before my eyes.

He sighed. And again, lifted his free hand and tucked another piece of hair behind my ear. This time his fingers taking their time.

My lips parted. My chest rising and falling.

'The other is when I catch you staring back at me. Then you panic and act like I didn't just catch you. The best part of my day is just when I get to see you.'

I dropped my gaze to our hands and watched as William gave it another squeeze.

'Remind me why this wouldn't work,' he said quietly. 'Why we shouldn't start something. Because I've been struggling with that lately.'

The words were on the tip of my tongue, but I couldn't speak right away. At that moment I wanted nothing but to give this thing between us a try. Absolutely nothing. But I had promised myself that I wouldn't change my life so drastically for another guy. I owed it to myself.

'I have to move,' I said eventually. I didn't think I had to give an explanation on that. 'I have to and you just moved here.'

William nodded, rubbing the bridge of his nose with his free hand. 'I got a divorce – what, seven, eight months ago. I wasn't planning on dating. Just focusing on work.'

'You don't trust women,' I added.

He grunted in answer.

'We work together,' he pointed out. 'I know you're going to leave, but for the time being we work together. In the same team.'

'Yes. That would be difficult to navigate, I think.'

'You don't trust men wholeheartedly either,' he stated, then let go of my hand and got up from his seat. He stood next to the window and ran his hand through his hair like he always did when he was stressed or thinking.

He was right about me not trusting men all that much. I probably didn't.

William's phone rang and he moved back towards me to pick it up from the coffee table.

'The CEO,' he said, but didn't answer.

I cleared my throat and got up from my seat as well, being careful not to wake Pepp up, although I'd have to do that anyway in a few minutes. I ignored the way my hand was tingling and picked up my laptop.

'Where are you going?' William asked, his eyes on me.

I headed for the table. 'This spot is safer, I think. We need to send this ASAP. Come and help me so the CEO doesn't call my dad when you don't answer a second time.'

We finished the statement and then went over everything with the CEO on the phone. It was past midnight when I got up, woke Pepp and headed for the door.

I saw William grabbing his keys and following us out the door. 'You don't have to come.'

'I do.'

Despite my objections he followed me up to my door and I watched as he squatted in front of Pepp and petted him. I thought I heard him whisper *take care of her for me* to Pepp, but I couldn't be sure. When he stood up and met my gaze I was confused.

'No flirting for us, William.'

His smile was small, but he smiled nonetheless, his eyes touching every inch of my skin as if he were trying to memorize every part of me.

We watched each other for a few seconds, and I thought maybe ... he ...

'No flirting,' he whispered, his eyes piercing my heart. 'You make it dangerous.'

15

William

It was already Wednesday and I had no idea where Monday and Tuesday had gone. The dating app fiasco had blown up in the media, but because we had responded so quickly they hadn't lost an alarming amount of users. It still wasn't entirely wrapped up since they were trying to figure out exactly what had been hacked, but we were doing our part, and the response was amazing. I couldn't have been happier with my team.

I turned off my laptop, done for the day, and looked across the office to see if Charlie was done too. I was trying to ignore the fact that this was the fifth . . . or maybe the eight time I had looked her way. She had been in her room around 5.00 p.m., the third time I had looked, but not after that.

Suddenly, a head popped up in my view and Gayle walked through my door.

'Looking for someone?'

I kept my face straight. 'No. What can I do for you Gayle?'

'Would you like to ask me something?'

I frowned at her. 'Ask you what?'

She gripped the back of one of the chairs that was right in front of my desk.

'Like where Charlie is.'

I tried not to look interested, and sighed instead.

She straightened and tilted her head to give me a long look. 'You're into her.'

I kept my mouth shut and leaned back against my seat, waiting to see what she'd say next.

'Maybe I haven't been to all the team meetings, but I've been to enough of them to catch some longing looks on both sides.'

And that was all I could take. I rose from my seat and started to roll down the sleeves of my shirt so I could put on my jacket and leave. Then I couldn't keep my mouth shut. 'I told you this before, but I'll repeat myself. I don't like to talk about my personal life with my colleagues. You're pushing it, Gayle.'

'So you're admitting it. You're interested in Charlie.'

I stopped working down my shirt and levelled my gaze at her. 'Charlie and I are friends. I don't date coworkers. This is the first and last time I'll indulge you on this. There is nothing going on between Charlie and me.'

'Okay. Got it.'

She gave me a thoughtful look and a quick nod before heading towards the door.

Releasing a long breath, I reached for my jacket and put it on as I watched Gayle leave. My eyes strayed and I glanced around: half of the office had already left.

'Charlie actually texted me ten minutes ago,' Gayle added in a light tone, standing next to the open glass door. 'But I guess that wouldn't interest you.'

I watched as she held her phone up. 'So?' I muttered. If I wasn't being more harsh with her that was only because I knew she was close with Charlie, and I could understand her trying to protect her or whatever she was currently trying to do. I reached for my own phone across the desk. I, on the other hand, had not received any texts or calls from Charlie. Not that I did before. Nor was I waiting for one.

I mentally shook myself. 'Do you have a point, Gayle? Or can I leave?'

She gestured outside my office with her hand. 'Of course you can. It's just that Charlie needs my help with something, but I thought you'd be a better choice under the circumstances. Plus I'm waiting to hear back from someone so I need to stay here. But if you don't want to, I understand. I'll help her and come back here.'

I put my phone in my pocket and tried to act nonchalantly when I wasn't exactly feeling it. 'Is it related to work?'

'You wouldn't help her if it wasn't?'

I kept staring at her until she gave up.

'Fine. Yes, it's work-related. I'll text you the address.' She started typing on her phone. 'She is babysitting a client for Kimberly since she is out of town, I think she ran into some trouble.'

My phone pinged in my pocket.

'I'll go, of course. If you can't, that is, but Charlie is more than capable of taking care of a client.'

Gayle smiled, and I narrowed my eyes at her as her smile only got wider.

'Yeah, well, I'd agree with you, but maybe not this one. I'll give you that much, that's why Douglas wants her in as many meetings as possible. She is great at interacting and convincing them to work with us. But, yes, maybe not this one.'

When the clock hit 9 p.m., I was standing in front of a fairly simple building. It had taken me over half an hour to get there with an Uber, and I'd already called Charlie five times, but each call had gone to her voicemail. I tried one last time, but heard the same recording. Hoping Gayle hadn't sent me out to the wrong address or on a wild goose chase, I headed inside what looked like a bar or club. They asked me for the word of the night, but Gayle had already helpfully sent me that in another text. The second they opened the door and I walked in, the heavy, loud music surrounded me. The interior of the space wasn't as dark as you'd expect a club to be, but the lights were dimmed. People were dancing in the middle in a big circle and the giant space was edged with tables. I could see some people dancing right in front of their tables instead of getting onto the dance floor.

I looked over to my right to see if I could spot Charlie, but instead my eyes got caught on a couple enthusiastically going at it at their table as the guy's hand slowly sneaked under the girl's dress.

Thinking I might actually consider killing Gayle if I found Charlie in a similar situation, I spotted the bar on the other side of the writhing bodies. I decided to cut through the crowd to get on higher ground and try to spot Charlie and the client that way.

It took me quite some time to make it to the short stairs that led up to the bar that ran the length of the entire space. Feeling the heat, either from the the place or the bodies that I had to get a little too close to, I ran a hand through my hair and loosened my tie a little before starting to walk up the steps.

I had no idea what Charlie was thinking bringing a client here, but I couldn't wait to find out.

A tall blonde girl was at the top of the steps, looking down at the dance floor; when our eyes met she slowly smiled at me. Next thing I know she had her hand on my shoulder and then my tie in her hand. In one hand she was holding a drink — what looked like a martini with olives at the bottom of the glass — and the other was currently pulling me forward a little by my tie. When she reached the end she let it drop and leaned towards me.

I raised an eyebrow at her boldness, but she didn't seem to mind that I wasn't quite responding to her. She kept her eyes on me as her pink shiny lips curved up in a smile. Her lips didn't really interest me.

'Are you here with someone?' she asked into my ear, her hand gripping my tie again.

I pulled away from her and smoothed out my tie, gently tugging it out of her hands. 'Yes, I'm with my friend.'

'Too bad.' She pouted a little, but let me walk around her. 'Find me if you want another friend. I wouldn't mind joining you.'

I watched her leave with a frown on my face. I didn't remember the last time I'd been to a club, but it was probably before I'd gotten married. In college maybe? I wasn't too into it back then and I didn't like it any better now.

I studied the dancing crowd and let my eyes wander over the tables. Couldn't see Charlie anywhere. I took out my phone and tried her again. No luck.

Sighing, I turned to my left and, just like that, she was right there. At the other end of the bar, talking to someone. Smiling. It took a me a moment to take her in with her red lips and black dress. Her brown hair took me another moment to get over. It was falling in big waves below her shoulders. It was a little messy, as if she had just gotten out of bed and didn't have time to do much but mess it even more. It was a contrast to how careful and professional she was at work. She still wore it loose and in waves, but not like this. Not like she had just had sex.

Did she have sex?

I found myself rushing to her side, and while it had looked like she was smiling and chatting with someone from afar, as I got closer to her I could tell she was a little uncomfortable and stressed. I have no idea when I'd started to read her tells, but even with the way she was smiling without showing her teeth, or the way her eyes weren't smiling back, or the way she was . . . I stopped thinking about how she looked when she was standing in front of *me*, talking to *me*, and just focused on getting to her.

Just as I was getting closer, the guy she was talking to nodded and left her side. She looked up at the ceiling and, rubbing the bridge of her nose, muttered something to herself before taking a step forward. Then she looked around as if she was searching for somebody, her gaze stopped on me and her eyes widened.

'William?'

I couldn't hear her, but I watched as her lips formed my name, then I strolled to her side.

Her eyes got bigger the closer I got, and she shouted, 'What . . . what are you doing here?'

I put my hand lightly on her arm and leaned down so I wouldn't have to shout back. 'Gayle asked if I could . . .'

She groaned and gripped my wrist before I could finish my sentence.

'Okay. Gayle sent you. Great.' Leaning forward, she rested her forehead on my chest then, letting go of my wrist, gripped the edge of my suit jacket instead. 'I'm just gonna breathe for a second then I'll tell you what's going on.'

At first I was surprised and didn't know what to do, mostly because I had no idea what was happening, but I stupidly assumed that she had lost the client and was panicking. So I found myself running my hand up and down her arm to make her relax. She took another deep breath, let go of her grip on my jacket, then looked up at me without taking a step back. Putting her hand on my shoulder, she leaned up to speak to my ear while the music changed and slowed, affecting the mood in the club. It looked like things were taking a different turn.

'Kimberly's client. Celebrity,' Charlie explained. 'They have a PR thing, but no one told me what. Last week they asked me to babysit him because Kimberly is out of town. She returns tomorrow and has a meeting with the guy, but she was supposed to take him out for dinner and keep an eye on him. The manager asked her to do that. Her schedule changed so they asked me. I did take him to dinner, but he brought us here after instead of going to his hotel. I had no idea until he parked his car in the parking lot. Hell, I still had no idea when I stepped in here.'

I sighed and shook my head to myself. *This family*, I thought.

She pulled back and met my gaze, probably expecting me to say something, but I was too struck by the feeling of her small and delicate hand on my shoulder and the way her chest was practically pressed against mine. I swallowed and tried to focus on her face, but her red lips kept catching my attention. Why did she wear red lipstick to babysit? And there was the hair too. The way it was framing her face, making her eyes appear bigger with the makeup. Her heels were sexy as hell, and now she was closer in height to me, it'd be so easy for me to kiss her. And her smell, the softness against me. She was . . .

'William?' she asked, her brows drawing together.

I closed my eyes for a second and took a deep breath, hoping that would help. It didn't – all I could smell and see was Charlie.

'I'm listening,' I muttered, angry at myself.

The confusion didn't clear from her face, but she kept going. 'After I realized where he brought me, I tried to get him to leave, but he slipped away from me.'

'You can't find him, that's why you called Gayle?' I asked, still trying to focus on the subject.

'My dad can't know I let him come here.'

'Why?'

'Charlie?' someone shouted and Charlie looked over her shoulder, but kept her body against mine.

I had to get a grip of myself.

I looked up and saw the waiter talking to her.

'That way?' Charlie asked, raising her voice, both of them looking at some spot over my shoulder.

The guy nodded, and I felt her slightly relax next to me.

'Thank you so much,' Charlie said, and then the next thing I knew the guy put his hand on her waist and said something in her ear and she shook her head, then he let his hand slide off as he walked away. Charlie had practically pushed herself against me, I assumed to avoid his touch, and I had to wrap my arm around her waist to hold both of us still.

When she looked up at me, her cheeks were flushed.

A girl on her way down to the dance floor bumped into her and Charlie put her left hand on my chest and awareness jolted through me. We might as well have plastered our bodies together while we were at it. If I had never thought about kissing her before, the way we were standing would have put an end to that very quickly. But I already had so many times. Looking straight into my eyes and without even realizing her effect on me, she licked her lips. I could feel her heartbeat quicken against me because her chest was falling and rising faster.

'Fuck,' I muttered and closed my eyes for a moment.

I had to stop looking at her lips – and thinking how she hadn't kissed anyone in years and that I'd love to be the one she kissed for the first time again – just for my sanity, if nothing else.

My jaw tightened. I opened my eyes and cleared my throat at the exact same time she looked away and took a small step back, lowering her hands from my chest. We both chose to ignore the moment.

'A friend of yours?' I asked, but couldn't exactly find the strength in me to drop my hand from her waist.

She looked at me again. 'Who?'

'The waiter.'

'Oh, yes. No, I mean, I don't know him, but he saw who I was with when we first came in, so he knew who I was looking for.'

I knew I had no right to ask, but I had to ... 'But the way he touched you ...'

'Oh, that.' She took another step back from me, and I had to let her go. 'That is probably because this is a ...'

I couldn't understand what she said, so I leaned a little down and asked her to repeat it.

Her response didn't come quick. 'I don't want to shout.'

Frowning a little, I leaned down until her face was next to mine, and I could feel her hair against my cheek. I closed my eyes, waiting for her answer.

She tilted her head up until her mouth was right next to my ear and put her hand on my shoulder to hold on again.

'You're going to kill me,' she whispered into my ear and my eyes opened waiting to hear the rest. She was practically killing me too. 'Apparently this is a sex club for the rich. Welcome!'

I opened my mouth to say something, but couldn't think of anything particularly helpful. I drew back a little and met Charlie's eyes, then my gaze dropped to the small smile dancing on her lips and my frown deepened.

Leaning down again, I spoke into her ear. 'Did you say sex club?'

When I looked at her face, another grin was tugging at her lips and she was nodding at me. She got on her tiptoes and pulled me down with her hand that was still on my shoulder to whisper back to me. 'We really need to find him though. We can't risk anyone recognizing him. I called Gayle because I didn't think I could handle him by myself. You being here is better.'

I took a moment to take in our surroundings. Nobody was actually having sex right in the open, but I could see that it wasn't just another bar.

Curiosity won. 'What did the waiter say in your ear?' I asked this time.

Her mouth curved into a big beautiful smile. 'He asked if I was interested.'

I opened my mouth and closed it.

Charlie laughed. Then as if we had done it a million times before, she grabbed my hand and started dragging me behind her. We were walking through the gyrating bodies when she looked over her shoulder, the smile still going strong on her face, and I realized I would have to try harder to stay away from her. If I *was* going to stay away.

We made it to the back of the club where a narrow hallway greeted us. The music wasn't as loud as it had been on the dance floor so it was easier to hear her when she spoke.

'Apparently he was heading to one of the private rooms. How do you want to do this?'

I lifted an eyebrow. 'You plan on telling me who it is we're looking for exactly before we discuss how we're going to do this?'

'Oh, sorry. Do you know Hugo Oak?'

'No. Who is he?'

'Twenty-one years old. One of the members of the music group everyone is talking about? The Oaks? Three brothers.'

'I have no idea who you're talking about.'

'Oh, William. You really need to stop working so hard. Come on, you're not gonna recognize him anyway, it looks like.' She went to grab my wrist, but I held onto her hand and wrapped mine around hers. She paused and glanced at our connection.

When we reached the first closed door, we realized we didn't have any other option but to open it and check who was inside.

'I've seen other people have sex. I watch porn too. This is not a problem,' Charlie said to the door and just barged in. As she just stood there watching a group of people going at it very loudly, I had to be the one to pull her out.

'Needless to say, watching porn and actually watching people have sex right in front of you are two very different things,' I said, as she flushed crimson and purposely avoided my gaze after we walked away. She did try to let go of my hand, but for some reason I didn't want to let go of her and held on and just moved to the next door down.

The client wasn't behind the next five doors we checked, but plenty of other people were. Nothing I'd seen affected me as much as seeing Charlie get affected by it all. When we reached the sixth door, her pupils were dilated and her breathing was ragged. And it was taking her a little too long to close the doors we kept opening.

Her little hand was gripping mine with all her strength. I paused and ducked down to meet her gaze. Her big eyes met mine, and I watched as she studied my lips as her chest rose and fell faster.

I opened my mouth, but she got there before me.

'Give me a break,' she started a little breathless and looked away from me. 'It's been over five years for me, remember? No kissing, no sex? Obviously it's gonna affect me. It's live porn. And then you're holding my hand and looking like you do . . .'

I tried, but I couldn't hold back my smile. 'Charlie, I was gonna ask you what he looked like. Google him and show me a photo. I don't think you should look into any more doors.'

'Oh.' She took a deep breath and then let it out. 'Ignore what I just said, okay?'

'Okay, no I haven't heard anything. Tell me what the client looks like.'

'Blond.' She looked at me again, taking me in. 'His hair is similar to yours, but yours is better. His looks weird. Tall and thin, I think.'

'You think?'

'Well, he isn't as big as you. Doesn't have your shoulders. Doesn't have your arms, you know. He looks more like a kid than a man. Don't make me spell it out for you.' She took out her phone and showed me his photo.

'Spell out that you like my shoulders and my arms?' I asked, my voice dropping lower.

A couple holding hands eyed us and stopped right next to Charlie. She took a step towards to me and wrapped her free hand around my forearm.

'Want to play?' the young, bald guy asked as the girl rested her head against his back and gave us a soft smile.

'Thanks, but not tonight,' I said and nodding to us, they moved down the hallway.

Charlie lightly hit my arm. 'Not tonight? As in we'll come and have sex with them tomorrow night?'

'I thought you wanted to have fun and kiss someone,' I replied distractedly as I checked lucky door number six. No blond guys. We moved down to another door.

'Yes. You maybe. Not them.'

I stopped walking and Charlie walked straight into me.

'Oomph.'

'Me? What? Maybe?'

'Just giving examples. I'd rather kiss you than a stranger, I guess.'

'You guess?'

Forcing my gaze away from her eyes, her lips, her dress and everything that was Charlie, I tried door number seven and saw a blond guy kissing two women and getting undressed.

'This him?' I asked and let Charlie walk in front of me so she could check him out.

'Yup,' she said and closed the door. 'That was him and his penis.'

I laughed. 'You want to come in and help me with him or . . .'

'How about I'll wait here and you bring him out. I think I've seen enough cocks and pussies for tonight.'

'Charlie . . .' I groaned. Even the words coming from her mouth were having an effect on me. My dick was unexpectedly having a very rough night. 'I think you're gonna have to be more careful with words around me.'

Without looking at her again, because I wasn't sure how many more times I could make myself look away, I dropped her hand and went inside the room.

It took me several minutes to convince the guy to leave. I didn't exactly know who he was or his music group for that matter, but the mention of a media frenzy was enough to leave the club behind.

We went outside without the girls as they kept going without Hugo. Taking one look at an anxious Charlie, Hugo sighed and dramatically said, 'Oh my Charlie, we were meant to be.'

'Yeah, yeah,' Charlie muttered before I could cut in. She grabbed Hugo by his arm and started walking away. 'I think I've heard enough from you tonight.'

She looked at me over her shoulder. 'Back door is over here. I asked when you went inside. Come on. You're gonna have to drive his car. I didn't have anything to drink, but I don't think it'd be best if I drove right now.'

I followed them all the way to one of the SUVs parked outside in the back. I'd be lying if I said I didn't thoroughly enjoy Charlie turning down the guy repeatedly.

'Charlie. Come to my room tonight,' Hugo insisted. 'We won't tell anyone.'

'How about this one who is standing right next to us? He already heard so it's too late. Plus, you're drunk,' she said for the fifth time.

Producing a key, she unlocked the back door.

'But you like my voice. I can sing to you.'

'So? I like his voice too.' She pointed at me over her shoulder. 'Do I jump on him just because I like his voice? I don't.'

The guy gave me a long once-over as I chuckled at Charlie's words, then shook his head as he held on to the back door Charlie had just opened.

'So you two are together?'

Charlie huffed. 'Do you even hear what I'm saying? Get in. My dad will kill me if they learn what you did tonight.'

The guy sighed, but followed her instruction and climbed inside, closing his eyes the second he was seated. 'Killjoy.'

'Thanks, I try,' Charlie deadpanned.

I moved forward to close the door, but Charlie still had half her body in the car, trying to put the guy's seatbelt on. She started to move back, but before I could do anything the guy pulled Charlie forward onto the back seat and I heard her gasp my name.

My smile disappeared pretty quickly as I rushed forward and held her by her waist with both my hands to pull her out. As soon as I had her up on her feet I leaned inside the car, getting into his face. 'Touch her again and I'll break your hand.'

He grinned and shut his bloodshot eyes. No doubt he'd be asleep in ten seconds.

I slammed the door shut and started trying to calm myself down.

This was one of the many reasons why I never liked working with celebrities. They thought the world revolved around them.

Luckily Charlie was fine. But I had her trapped between the car and me, so now I was the one mauling her. She was gripping my arm, the one that was still holding onto her waist. Finding myself a little too close to her, I looked down and into her eyes as she watched me silently.

Everything around us disappeared and dropped. 'Charlie,' I murmured.

'I'm not doing anything,' she whispered.

'You know you are.'

'You're the one who is touching me.'

'I was trying to help you out of the car before he pulled you onto his lap.'

'I wouldn't let him do that.'

We silently stared at each other for a few more moments. Then the wind blew in and a strand of her hair covered one of her eyes and she blinked. She was reaching up to get it away from her face, but I couldn't help myself and acted before her. My knuckles caressed her face as I gently tucked it behind her ear, the simple act making my heartbeat accelerate. I relaxed my hold around her waist and her body gave a slow jerk, a barely there movement. I met her eyes as I slowly released my breath.

'What do you think I'm doing?' she asked, quietly. 'Exactly.'

'You're tempting me,' I responded, having trouble hiding a small smile.

'Okay. But what am I doing exactly to tempt you? Not that I'll use it as a weapon against you – just asking for research purposes.'

'Because you want to tempt future dates?' And why did that bother me so much? Why did I want her to tempt me every day with every look she sent my way no matter where we were?

She tilted her head up a little and my gaze dropped to her lips for a brief moment. From this close, she was even more beautiful. Her eyes. The hazel mixed with the brown. And even more than the eyes . . . She was saying I was looking at her in a certain way, but she had no idea how expressive her eyes were. She was stunning. Top to bottom, she was just stunning. Slowly she shook her head from side to side and licked her lips.

'No,' she whispered. 'Just so maybe I can have them look at me the way you're looking at me right now.'

I sighed.

She tilted her chin a little more, her eyes studying me.

I found myself lowering my head down, my focus on her lips. Maybe just one kiss wouldn't hurt that bad. It wasn't like we would get addicted to each other. It wasn't like I'd want her more after just one kiss. I wondered for a second who was suffering more from this attraction between us. I didn't think there was a winner.

'Where are we going?' I whispered, resting my hand against the car so I could stop myself from touching her.

'Where do you want to go?'

I chuckled and took a deep breath. Closing my eyes, I rested my forehead against hers instead of tasting her lips.

'You need to focus here. One of us has to.'

She released her breath and gently nudged her nose to mine.

'Why does it have to be me? I think you'd be better at focusing.'

I huffed out a breath and smiled. Not being able to stop myself, I cupped her cheek with my palm and lifted my forehead from hers, but stayed close. Her eyes slowly closed the second my hand touched her skin. Her lips were almost just a breath away.

Lifting her hand, she rested it against my chest, warming my body with just that small contact. 'Do you think it's just the sex and the music, or is it us?'

She asked her question so quietly, so sweetly, that I didn't know what to do with myself. My dick hardened in my pants. 'Both,' I answered, uncertain of my own answer. 'Mostly us, I think. I want to touch you so fucking bad right now, Charlie.'

'I wouldn't say no to that,' she whispered. 'Remind me why we couldn't do this again?'

I sighed. It was a good question. A reminder would help us both. 'You're moving.'

'Yes, I'm doing that, aren't I?'

'Yes.'

'What else?' she whispered. Her fingers gently crumpling the material of my shirt against my chest as if she needed an anchor. 'William?'

Hearing my name out of her mouth almost destroyed me. 'I can't remember,' I whispered back, my head slowly inching closer to hers again.

She opened her eyes and our gazes met. Her fingers still gripping my shirt, she went up on her toes, her chest touching mine and I . . .

There was a loud thump against the window right next to where we were standing and the shithead ruined everything. 'Hey! What about me!'

Both Charlie and I snapped out of it, having completely forgotten about Hugo or whatever his name was. It took a moment, but I dropped my hand from her face and stepped away.

'We should drop him off,' I muttered.

Charlie cleared her throat. Once. Twice. 'Yes. Yes.'

'The key?'

'The car key. Yes. I . . . One sec.' She opened the back door, ignored Hugo – who already had his eyes closed and head dropped to the back of his seat – and bending, she grabbed something from the floor and shut the door again.

'Here.' She offered me the keys, her voice coming out a little breathless. 'Let's go.'

As soon as I had them, she turned and got into the passenger seat. I took a few deep breaths and had to discreetly adjust myself as I rounded the car and got myself in the driver's seat.

'Where to?'

16

William

It didn't take us nearly as long as I thought it would to get to our destination. Hugo had snored all the way to the hotel, and Charlie and I had decided to stay quiet. I couldn't help but steal glances at her every now and then, but I had no idea what she was thinking. Was she thinking maybe it was stupid to stay away from each other when there was clearly a connection or attraction or whatever you'd call it? I was starting to think so.

I was about to pull into a spot in front of the hotel when Charlie noticed a group of people waiting at the doors.

'You think they're here for him?'

'Could be.'

She sighed and let out a groan. 'We should take him through the back door. Just in case. I don't want all of our faces plastered on some tabloid for my dad to see.'

I decided not to make a comment about her dad, but it was hard to swallow down the questions I had.

'You're the boss,' I said lightly and manoeuvred the car away from the curb. It took us a few minutes to locate the secret entrance to the hotel – and a phone call to the hotel concierge made by Charlie. As soon as we got there, we both jumped out of the car, but this time I didn't let the idiot's hands get anywhere near Charlie as she followed us at a healthy distance.

The concierge met us at the door and showed us the way to a small elevator meant for employees. The idiot finally came to as we stumbled in through the door of his room. Charlie thanked the concierge and closed the door, leaning her back against it.

Hugo ignored both of us and headed for the bathroom, slamming the door closed. Seconds later came the telltale sound of a hard night. Served him right. I ran my hand up and down my face and walked back to where Charlie was. My shoulder brushing against hers, I rested my back against the wall as well.

'You think we should leave?' she asked quietly.

'Yes, I think we should. But let's wait until he is done.'

There was a heavy thud next to me as Charlie rested her head against the door not so gently and let out a long breath. 'I'm so tired.'

I gave her a sideways glance and took in her features. Now that she was in a better light, I could see how pale she looked. Who knew how the guy treated her before the sex club fiasco.

'Before the club . . .' She turned her head, waiting for me to finish my sentence. 'He didn't try anything, or do anything, did he?'

Her lips puckered up, then she squinted and covered her mouth with her hand and yawned, looking away from me again.

'What was that smile for?'

She didn't answer, but her smile grew even more and soon she was full-on smiling.

I was looking at her lips when she looked my way again and our eyes met.

'Tell me something else from your list,' I asked her to distract myself.

She cast her gaze downward for a moment. 'You met my grandma. I don't know whether you noticed or not, but did you see her smile?'

I thought about it, but wasn't sure. Whether her grandma smiled or not wasn't what had my attention at that dinner. 'Maybe. Once or twice. Sorry, I wasn't paying attention really.'

Her expression unreadable, she looked away from me. We could hear the sound of dry heaves coming from the bathroom, but both of us ignored it.

'She turns eighty years old this year, and she has these permanent lines around her mouth. Downward.' I watched as she raised her hand and traced an invisible line around my mouth with her fingertips. Her touch softer than feathers. I struggled to hold myself back, but she was already pulling away. 'She rarely laughs. It's like she enjoys others being miserable around her. Everything is always bad. Don't trust anyone. Men suck. Life sucks. No one is how she wants them to be. And if you're actually enjoying life, she genuinely tries to upset you so you're not that happy. Then acts like she has no idea what you're talking about. And she could never be wrong about anything. She knows the best because she is the best.'

She met my eyes again and gave me a small smile. 'Long story short. It's: laugh more. That's on the list. It's a necessity. I don't want to have those lines around my mouth if I'm lucky enough to get to that age. I don't want to become like her. I want to laugh more.'

Before I could make any comment, Hugo walked out of the bathroom, water dripping from his hair and a towel wrapped around his waist. He stopped when his eyes landed on us and I straightened up.

'If you're done, we're leaving.'

With his bloodshot eyes he nodded and scratched the back of his head with his hand. 'I'm sorry, Charlie,' he mumbled. 'I didn't mean to let the night get so out of hand.'

Charlie gave him a barely there nod, straightened from her spot and opened the door. 'Goodnight.'

I followed her outside and pulled the door closed behind me.

We waited in front of the elevator in silence. When the doors opened we stepped inside.

17

Charlie

'Thank you for coming,' I said, offering William a smile. Then had to cover another yawn.

'Don't worry about it.' From the corner of my eye I saw him push his hands into his pockets and it made his shoulders look amazing. He glanced up, and I just stood there, leaning against the back of the elevator taking all his features in. His jawline, the stubble on his cheeks that suited him perfectly, even his throat looked sexy.

'Does this kinda thing happen often?' he asked as we descended.

I nodded and rubbed my eyes. 'I mean, not always, but yes, sometimes I do have to cover for . . .'

Before we could reach the lobby, the doors opened on the eighth floor and a group of five women filed in, chatting and laughing.

Instinctively, I took a step closer to William at the same time as he came to my side and my back bumped into his chest. I looked up and over my shoulder in surprise and met his eyes. His beautiful eyes that got me every single time we made eye contact. It made me forget things.

'Sorry,' I whispered, but I didn't move away. He didn't move away either.

I have no idea whether I was so-tired-that-you-act-stupid kinda tired, but even though there was still some space in the elevator, I shifted on my feet and got half a step closer to him, my back firmly resting against his chest. I closed my eyes and savoured the feel.

Then he put his hand on my waist, and my heart lost it. It wasn't just butterflies that I got when I was close to him, it was more than that.

The women were clearly a group of friends because they were laughing and chatting loudly while I was having a small heart attack in the corner of the elevator. I tried to breathe like a normal person and not make a big deal out of a very tiny situation, but I realized I was holding my breath to see how long he would keep his hand on my body. I didn't know what to do with my hands or arms.

A slow heat flooded my chest as the laughter got louder and my heart started thudding heavily. For the second time in the same night, I was starting to feel lightheaded by just being around him and the possibility of us. Unable to stop myself, I looked up at him. His eyes were already on me. I gave him a weak smile then looked away again.

The elevator doors opened, and I cursed under my breath. The girls started exiting, but William and I didn't move a muscle. For a few seconds we let everyone else leave, then I felt him give my waist a slow and gentle squeeze that radiated throughout my entire body and I had to force myself to put one step in front of the other.

I cleared my throat as we started walking across the lobby. 'What are we gonna do? Get an Uber or . . . ?' My hand automatically went for my handbag so I could check the time, but I realized I wasn't holding it.

I stopped walking and turned to William. 'Oh. My things are back in the car. I dropped them when he pulled me in.'

He looked around, then headed towards the reception desk, towards the concierge who had helped us sneak into the hotel. A few minutes later we had the car keys and we were heading out to get my things.

William unlocked it, and I reached for the back door and leaned inside. Before I could bend down and get my stuff from the floor where it had fallen, William's hand on my waist stopped me. The spot tingling, I looked over my shoulder.

He sighed. 'Maybe you shouldn't do that in front of me again.'

I straightened up. 'Do what?'

'Bend down like that. Let me.'

A little confused, I moved to the side and watched him lean inside and get my things. Then as my eyeballs landed on his ass – that ass that had gotten my attention the first day I'd seen him in the lobby – I understood why he didn't want me to get my stuff myself.

Feeling giddy, I bit down on my lip and tried my very best to hide my grin and not say anything.

Unfortunately it didn't take him long to come back up.

'Your phone,' he started, holding it out to me and looking a little uncomfortable. 'You missed some messages.'

Frowning, I took it from him and checked who had texted me.

One was from Valerie, the other three were from Ralph.

After reading them, I glanced up at William and opened my mouth, but this time his phone started ringing. His eyes still on mine, he took it out of his pocket and checked who was calling. Instead of answering, he lowered his phone, but it kept ringing.

'Who is it?' I asked, thinking we could have another late night working. To be honest, I wouldn't be complaining.

'My ex,' he answered.

'Oh.' I tried to think of something to say, but couldn't come up with any words. I looked away.

'What was Erasmus saying?'

'Erasmus . . .' I shook my head. 'We have a date tomorrow. He wants to know where I wanted to go.'

He nodded. 'That's good.'

It was? It was good that I was going out for a date with another guy? I didn't see the good in it. Not anymore.

Finally his phone stopped ringing and we both looked at it.

'You're not gonna call her back?'

'No need. You ready to go home?'

I nodded after a moment of quiet. Home. Coming from William that sounded a little too perfect.

18

William

It was the day after the sex club fiasco, and I was in my office trying to get hold of a journalist about the dating app situation. The CEO was happy with us because instead of losing users they had brought in new ones. But that was not what was on my mind. My head had been all over the place the entire day. Not like me at all. Almost every single thought somehow had Charlie in it.

'What's wrong with you today?' Rick asked as we stood right outside my office. I turned to him.

'What do you mean?'

His brows rose. 'I've asked you the same question for the last minute and you didn't even hear me.'

I sighed and started rubbing my temples. 'I'm a little distracted. Sorry, Rick. What did you want to know again?'

Keeping my eyes on him and only him, I managed to focus this time and answered his questions.

'You're heading out?' he asked when we were done.

My eyes flitted to where Charlie was standing, around one of the rectangular tables in the shared work space, and I watched as she laughed at something a guy was saying. 'Not yet,' I answered distractedly. I should've known I would pique Rick's interest, but I hadn't been thinking straight the entire day. Why start now.

The guy, who must be a client since I hadn't seen him at the office before, touched Charlie's back, his touch lingering before he pulled it away. Charlie looked up at him and gave him a warm smile.

'William?'

'Yes,' I responded, but kept my eyes on Charlie.

Douglas passed the duo and paused next to them for a second. I watched as Charlie stiffened for a moment, but then her dad must have said something normal because she relaxed and offered him a smile as the three of them started chatting. Then Douglas moved on and it was just Charlie and the guy again. He took one step closer and leaned down to say something into her ear. Charlie's smile widened.

I took a step forward then stopped myself.

Someone cleared their throat next to me.

I clenched my fist and then forced myself to relax.

'They're friends,' Rick offered simply, his voice quiet.

I took my eyes off of Charlie and looked at him. 'Thank you, Rick, but I don't see how that's my business.'

He cocked an eyebrow at me. I sighed and gave my back to Charlie and her *friend*. Which I wasn't sure if I believed.

'We work together. I don't like office romances between colleagues.' Not colleagues for too long, I thought to myself, but didn't voice it. 'Not to mention I'm not looking for any type of relationship at the moment.'

'I get that, but the way you looked just now says otherwise.'

I gave Rick a long look, then headed back into my office. He followed me in as I sat behind my desk and tried my best to look busy. I'm not sure I was successful, because he just stood there waiting for my attention.

'How did I look?' I asked in a bored voice, avoiding his gaze.

Slowly his lips stretched. 'Exactly how you've looked since your first few weeks.' He turned around and headed out, but paused in the doorway. 'You're interested in her. I was sure you two would've started something by now. She's great.'

I grumbled something under my breath and started separating some papers that were on my desk. I would have to check and see what the hell they were later. Of course I was fucking interested. Who wouldn't be interested in Charlie. And anyone who thought she was anything but amazing was an idiot. Of course none of that meant I was going to act on it. Not when we had so many things working against us.

'You're not gonna ask who she's talking with?' Rick challenged.

'She can talk to whomever she wants to, Rick. If you don't have any other questions for me . . .'

'She was talking to Liam. He had a family emergency so he was on leave, but he's back today.'

With that parting remark he left my office.

Had the two of them once dated? No they couldn't have. Maybe in the last year? I didn't think so. But she was ready now . . .

I leaned back in my seat and closed my eyes for a second. Got up, walked around, then sat back down. I massaged the bridge of my nose, but nothing was helping. I didn't even try to work. My gaze darted around the office and when I couldn't find them around the desks, I stood up and spotted them walking into her office. He held the door open for her and then followed her inside.

I hurried across my office and I was going to . . .

My phone started ringing, breaking my focus. I answered on the third ring without checking who was calling, my eyes following Charlie and this Liam's every move as I stopped before I opened my door.

'Yes?'

'Yes? That's how you answer the phone?'

I let out a long breath and, dropping my head, closed my eyes. My sister. 'Beth. Sorry. I was in the middle of something. Can I call you back when I'm done?'

'It's okay, you don't have to get back to me. Ivy wanted to make sure I called ...' There was a rustle and then I heard a sweeter voice come on the line. 'Uncle Willie, you're coming, right? Mom said we should maybe call in the evening, but sometimes I fall asleep and sometimes she forgets to call even though she says she will so I wanted to make sure you'd come. You'll come because you promised, right?'

The stress I was experiencing over Charlie melted right off of me and I smiled. 'Yes Ivy, I'll be there.'

'See, Mom, I told you he'd come. Hello Uncle Willie. Did I forget to say hello?'

'You did. Hello back to you, little monster.'

There was a giggle that warmed my heart.

'I'm not a monster. I missed you, Uncle Willie.'

'You missed me? Am I hearing that right? Is this the same girl who left me all alone to go play with her new friend across the street when I was last there?'

'Yeah, I missed you very much. And I don't like him anymore. He is stupid.'

I heard Beth's sigh and soft voice in the background saying: *Ivy you can't call him stupid.*

Ivy ignored her mom.

'Boys can be stupid sometimes. But I love the sound of you missing me. Can you say it again, please?'

More giggling came through, then her sweet voice got quiet. 'I missed you so much, Uncle Willie.'

'I missed you too, beautiful. And I'm heartbroken that you'd think I'd miss your birthday. No way. Of course I'll be there.'

'But you missed three birthdays so far – what if you miss this one too.'

I walked back, went around my desk and sat down. 'Not a chance in the world. Who would bring your present then? I'm gonna be there the whole weekend.'

'But you promise, right?'

'I promise, baby.'

'Okay. I believe you. And no crisis okay? I don't want any crisises.'

I laughed. 'Thank you for believing me.'

'But no crisis,' she repeated, her voice going low. 'Say it.'

I had to hold back my laughter. 'No crisis.'

'No Lindsey?'

That pretty much wiped off my smile. Ivy did not like Lindsey. At all. I could hear Beth murmuring to her in the background as well. 'No Lindsey. Just me.'

'Okay. Don't forget my present. Here, you can talk to my mom now, but not too much. No doodling.'

I chuckled to myself. 'No dawdling. Okay. Thank you, little monkey.'

I was still smiling when Beth came back on the line. 'Sorry about that, William. She has all of us dancing to her tune.'

'No worries. I'm glad you guys called.'

'Why? Is something wrong?'

'No. Nothing's wrong.' Although it had been exactly the right timing before to stop me doing something stupid. 'Just a hectic day. Anything you guys need from here?'

'Just you. William, we didn't get to talk much these last few weeks. You're doing good, right? With Lindsey . . .'

'Yes, Beth. I'm good. Everything is better now.'

'Okay. We'll talk more when you get here. Mom says hi. We're all excited to see you.'

'I was just there a few weeks ago.'

'We miss you, what can you do. Okay, I need to go, Ivy is climbing the tree again. Ivy! No! You aren't allowed . . .'

Before I could say goodbye the line went dead.

'William?'

I looked up and saw Gayle standing at my door.

'Yes.'

'Douglas wants to see both of us in his office about a new case.'

I stood up and walked to her side. 'You know what it's about?'

'I think it's an airline. That's all I know, he just got a call when we were in another meeting.'

As I closed the door, I couldn't stop myself from looking towards Charlie's office. 'Charlie left already?' I asked Gayle when I couldn't see her in there. No sign of her or that Liam. 'If we're starting something new tonight we'll need her to come back.'

'I hope not. She is finally on a date.'

I stopped walking. She was already out on a date with Liam?

'With Liam?' I asked surprised, forgetting myself.

Gayle stopped as well and turned to look at me in confusion. 'Liam? Liam from the office? No, she's out with Ralph.' She tilted her head and studied me a little too closely.

I cleared my throat, pushed my hands into my pockets and started moving again. Thankfully she didn't question me and fell into step beside me. Ralph. Our little deserter. Shithead. I'd completely forgotten about that one.

'Hope it goes well. She was going to the bar we all went for beer at the other night, right?' I asked nonchalantly, as if I knew anything about where she was.

'No, not the bar. They wanted to meet somewhere quieter.'

'That sounds ... logical, I guess.' I was hoping she'd mention where Charlie was, but she didn't take the bait.

'If we have a new case, this isn't the right time to go out on a blind date. We should call her ...' I started, but didn't continue as we stopped in front of Douglas's office.

Gayle opened the door before meeting my gaze and responding quietly. 'Stop worrying, she is only four blocks away. Plus, we can do without her for one night. Let her have some fun. Rick is still around.'

I opened my mouth, but she stopped me with a shake of her head as if I was exasperating.

'She'll be here if she is needed.'

*

It took me over half an hour to find the restaurant she was at . . . after looking in a handful of wrong places. Four blocks didn't actually narrow things down all that much. I didn't leave the office thinking: here's my chance to go stalk her and then ruin her date. No. That wasn't it. I just wanted to make sure she was okay and that runaway Ralph hadn't left her waiting one more time. The plan was just to make sure she wasn't alone and that this Ralph guy wasn't an axe murderer or anything, then go home.

When I finally spotted her, I didn't quite know what to do or what the hell I was thinking. Showing up unannounced didn't seem like the best idea after all. Neither did leaving.

I stood there considering the lack of my options. Ralph the Runaway had showed up after all. So as soon as I saw that, I should've turned around and left, which was the rough plan in the first place, but I didn't. I stood there like an absolute idiot and watched her with another man. Just as I had done all those years ago. Dread and disappointment filled my chest, and I couldn't move. She looked just as beautiful as she had then, even more so really. Because I knew her better now.

She wasn't a stranger I had been attracted to and curious to learn more about. She was more now. Sweet, kind, beautiful, smart, thoughtful . . . beautiful. I knew more about her. More of *her*. Of who she was. How she was. What she wanted from life. What her motivations were. What pushed her, what made her smile. And I wanted her even more for it. But I was stuck in place, on the other side of the window yet again as she smiled. The only difference now was that she wasn't sitting alone waiting for me. This time around she was sitting across from someone.

A date.

Not me.

This time around, I couldn't find the strength in me to walk away. Not that I had planned on walking away back then either. But just as I stood on the other side of the window of that diner that night, about to walk in so we could maybe give our newly and unexpectedly found friendship a try outside of that bubble, I had gotten a phone call from Lindsey after not seeing her or hearing from her for weeks after the breakup. I still remembered Charlie's shy words from the night before that day.

If we happen to be here tomorrow evening, again, maybe we can go somewhere else. Maybe try?

I remembered smiling at her.

'*You mean like a date?*'

'*Yeah. Maybe. If you're interested, of course.*'

And then the next night, as I was about to walk in, I hadn't been able to. Lindsey had been my girlfriend for three years, and I had asked her to marry me only a month before I had met Charlie at that diner. When Charlie came into my life, I wasn't looking for anyone At all. But she had just been there as if she had always been waiting for me. She was different from everyone else. Something about her. The fact that I'd ended up at that diner, night after night, just on the offchance that I'd see her again and we'd just talk, had been unexplainable. And when I was right across the street from the diner, watching Charlie, a sudden phone call had changed everything.

Lindsey was ready to marry me now. She thought she was pregnant, and not only that, she had realized that she didn't want to spend her life without me. She was the one who had said no to my proposal. But this was her wake-up call.

I didn't go to her that night because I was still insanely in love with her – something had shifted in me when she had said no so easily. But the possibility of a pregnancy ...

A kid.

My kid.

I had to choose Lindsey over someone I had just met at a random diner. It didn't matter that I had been more excited to see Charlie that night than I was over seeing Lindsey again.

I still went back. The next night. But she wasn't there. I'm not sure what I would have said if she had been or what I'd have done. Whether it would have changed anything or not. But she wasn't there. And then things got a little better with Lindsey even after we learned that she hadn't been pregnant and we got married and Charlie became a good memory that made me smile from time to time.

Someone walking on the sidewalk bumped into my shoulder and I shook myself out of the memories. I let out a long breath, looked at Charlie's smiling face again and I couldn't, *wouldn't* walk away. Not this time. As selfish as I acted, I didn't know how to leave her with him. Maybe if I watched them for a little, maybe I could convince myself that I didn't have a right to disrupt her plans.

I sneaked in, hiding behind people so I could get to the bar area without being seen by Charlie. I bumped into a waiter but somehow we righted each other without him dropping any plates and moved on in our respective directions.

Once I was sitting at the bar, it was too late to leave. Since I was already here, I could just get a drink and *then* leave. I chanced a look over my shoulder and watched as she smiled at her date and whatever-his-name nodded enthusiastically. She reached for her drink and took a small sip, still smiling at him. Ralph kept on talking and I leaned back, straining my ear to hear what they were talking about, mainly to hear what he was saying that was making her smile, but it didn't work. There were too many people around. And I was too far away.

'What can I get you?' the bartender asked, and I jerked in my seat as if I'd been caught. I felt like a complete idiot. Rubbing the back of my neck, I tried to think. I had no right to be there, that was for sure, but I wasn't going to leave. Not yet.

'Whisky, please,' I said after a sigh.

I decided to have my drink, maybe half of it, make sure she was having a good time – because she deserved a good date – and then just leave. The last thing I wanted to watch was Charlie on a date.

Or Charlie at the end of a date. Kissing the said date. But clearly I was acting like a jealous fool, and I didn't think I had the strength to move away from my seat, unless it was towards her.

I chanced another look over my shoulder after the bartender left. Ralph, this blond and blue-eyed guy, was grinning at Charlie happily, his eyes not straying from her, and Charlie was leaning forward as if she were about to tell him a secret. Since she was wearing a black dress and showing some serious cleavage that lifted her boobs, I watched as his eyes strayed. Charlie's face fell momentarily as she noticed where he was looking. My shoulders stiffened.

'Your whisky, sir.'

Sighing, I turned around. 'Thank you.'

Raising my glass, I shook my head and took a healthy swallow. I had officially lost my mind. My gaze darted around, taking in all the other customers enjoying their dinner and drinks. Then I glanced at the reason I was sitting in a restaurant. She looked amazing. As always. And almost happy. I knew her smiles by now and this one wasn't one of my favourites. I took another long swallow from my drink, my throat burning from the smooth liquid. I managed to spend a few minutes without glancing over my shoulder as I played with the glass. I checked my phone. Twice. I massaged my temples. I did everything but leave.

Letting out a long breath. I looked their way again. They were eating their dinner in silence. Then Charlie looked up and offered him another one of her smiles. Seeing her smile caused a jolt of excitement to shoot through me, but it died pretty quickly. Ralph must have said something fucking funny because her smile widened and she laughed. The soft and somehow pretty sound reaching my ears. Or maybe I had gotten so used to it that I could already hear it in my head. Then what's-his-name reached for his phone instead of joining her and started texting somone. It was the second time he disrespected her and I didn't like it.

Pretty much disgusted with myself, I order another glass of

whisky. My last one. When I put my hand on my bouncing knee to stop it since it had started annoying even me, I decided it was time for me to go as soon as I finished my drink. She didn't look ecstatic to be there, but she must have been enjoying herself. She didn't need me to come and save her.

My phone vibrated with a new text message next to my glass and the screen lit up. I picked it up and saw a whole range of emojis, from mermaids to birthday cake to balloons. Smiling, I sent a quick message back to Beth so she could show it to Ivy. I was about to put my phone down, but I held onto it. I took another sip of my drink.

Then decided I was going to text Charlie. If she ... texted me, maybe she wasn't enjoying her date as much as it seemed. If she didn't write back or even read my text, I needed to leave immediately.

My fingers hovered over the screen, but I wasn't sure what I wanted to write.

William: Hello again.

I groaned quietly, but couldn't find it in me to delete the text. I wasn't sure if she'd remember, but that's how I'd greeted her for a week when we'd met at the diner years ago. It wasn't original or even interesting, but who knew if she'd even check her phone. I hit send and waited without turning around to see if she'd notice.

Charlie: Hello William.

She texted me back.

William: You okay? I barely saw you at the office today.

Charlie: Didn't we have a meeting today?

William: Yes. I barely saw you. Also I don't count meetings.

Charlie: Did you ... by a small chance miss me? Maybe?

I turned my head and looked at their table yet again. Charlie had her phone on her lap and was staring at the screen, but I couldn't tell whether she was smiling or not. Then her date said something and she looked up at him. I kept my eyes on her, and a corner of her mouth lifted, but it didn't look like one of the smiles she gave me. She didn't brighten up for him. I turned back around and focused on my phone.

William: Would that make you happy? Me missing you.
Would you like me to be right next to you, right now?

I glanced back at Charlie again

And this time ... This time she couldn't even try to hide how my text made her feel even if she wanted to. She brightened up. For me. But then the guy touched her hand that was still on the table next to her water glass, and Charlie looked up at him with *my* smile still on her lips. The lips I seemed to be so fascinated with.

That pretty much called it for me. I left some bills next to my drink and headed towards their table without stopping to think about what I was doing.

I stopped next to Charlie, my eyes on her date. He looked up at me and his brows drew together in confusion.

'Can I help you with something?' he asked.

I pulled out a third chair at their table and sat down without a word. Charlie was staring at me with an open mouth, her eyes flitting from me to her date.

'Ah ... I ... What are you ...'

Completely ignoring the good-looking Ralphy, I faced Charlie and pulled my chair closer to her.

'Why are you doing this to me?' I countered, loud enough so her date could hear what I was saying.

She glanced at her date, then stared at me with a frown.

'I'm . . . what?'

I closed my eyes and shook my head, trying my best to look upset. 'You're breaking my heart. How could you do this to us, Charlie?' I met her confused eyes and waited for her answer.

'What is going on here?' Ralphy asked, putting down his wine glass and looking from Charlie to me. 'Do you know this man?'

I paid him no attention. Reaching out, I grabbed Charlie's hand and held onto it. 'Do you remember the day you told me you fell in love with me on sight?' The second I grabbed her hand, she tried to pull it out of my grasp. She was still looking very much bewildered. If I wasn't trying to look and sound so serious, just the look on her face would've set me off. And it wasn't as if I was lying, she had actually said those things before. Almost. 'How can you forget what we have so quickly? You always said you couldn't spend another minute without me.'

The more words spilled out of my mouth, the bigger her eyes got. Then she leaned forward, stopped trying to pull her hand out of my grasp and touched my forehead with the back of her right hand.

'Do you have a fever or something?'

'Do you know him, Charlie?'

'Rowan, stay out of this,' I ordered without glancing back at him.

The edge of Charlie's lips just slightly tipped up as she looked into my eyes. 'His name is Ralph, William.' Then she turned to meet Ralph's gaze. 'I do know him. He is my . . .'

Still holding onto Charlie's hand, I looked at a comically confused Ralphy and finished her sentence before she could. 'Boyfriend.'

'He is not my boyfriend,' Charlie corrected me quickly, but I looked down at her hand and she was *not* trying to pull away at all anymore. I allowed myself a small smile, then focused back on the beautiful girl in front of me.

'We were on a break, Charlie. I'm still your boyfriend. Didn't you say you used to watch me, secretly, when I was working and lost in thought? You still do. I always know when your eyes are on me. And you like the way I run my fingers through my hair when I'm frustrated. Was that all a lie?'

Hand in hand, she stared at me for a good long moment. 'Sounds like I said a lot of things.'

'I think I should ...' Ralph mumbled, but I cut him off mid-sentence.

'Charlie, what are you doing here with him?'

'I'm on a date?'

'But you're still mine.'

'I am?'

'Aren't you?'

'Am I?' she asked, leaning towards me as she squinted her eyes. I barely held back my laughter. 'Are you leaving me for him?'

'Okay, I think we should ...' Ralph tried to interrupt.

I moved to the edge of my chair, getting closer to Charlie. 'Would you like me to tell you a few of your favourite things? Just to show you how much I care?'

'I'm all ears. This should be good.'

'You don't think I know your heart by now?'

'Sounds like we spent years together, I guess you must.'

'You love lunch dates, you love French fries, you don't like carrots and love putting them on my plate. You love it when I hold your hand, doesn't matter when or where. You love it when I leave you notes in your office – especially the ones I leave in your books. You love my hands on you ...'

'You work together?' Ralphy asked after clearing his throat.

Charlie turned her face to him, but kept her suspicious eyes on me. I struggled to keep my face straight.

'We do. We're in the same team.'

'I don't want you to leave me for him, Charlie.'

'But we're on a break, like you said,' she answered. 'Sounds to me like you already gave up on me, so why shouldn't I go on a date?'

'Charlie, you didn't tell me you were in a relationship,' Ralph butted in.

'One second, Ralph,' she grumbled, turning all her focus on me. 'You were saying?'

'Are you doing this because I didn't like the cake you got me on my birthday?'

'Please. That was the perfect cake. Not my fault you didn't appreciate the gesture. There was nothing wrong with that cake.'

'Will you come back to me if I agree with you?'

She tilted her head and smiled at me a little. 'Why do you want me back, William? Why are you here?'

I leaned forward in my seat and focused on her and just her. I did play pretend because I knew she enjoyed it before, but I was dead serious when I opened my mouth. 'Because you are you. You're so rare. So beautiful. Kind. Self-aware. Hard-working. Fun. Sweet. And because I know what you want from a relationship. I know you now. And I think you deserve to have the kind of relationship you've always dreamed of having.'

'What kind of relationship do I dream of having?' she asked quietly, her smile slowly disappearing.

I know I was going a little too far maybe, but I couldn't shut my mouth. Not when she was looking at me the way she was. It was all true anyway. I gave her hand a squeeze.

'You don't just want someone to share your time with. You want to love someone just as fiercely as you want to be loved. You want to matter to him. You want to be important. You want to always be the first to someone. You're not an option. You're the choice. The only choice, and you want to be able to feel that. And you want to laugh. You want to smile. You don't want to waste your time anymore. You want to be happy about your every day. You don't want to be alone anymore. You don't want someone to break your heart. You want to grow old with someone. Have that someone you can laugh with and cry with.

You want to be their best friend. You want to trust someone without a second thought.'

For me the restaurant quieted, and I forgot about Ralph and everyone else around us. I reached out and rested my palm against Charlie's face. 'You're . . . sometimes I can't take my eyes off of you,' I whispered.

'It sounds like I want too many things,' she whispered back.

'And why shouldn't you have all of it?'

'Does anyone even get to have all of the things you've said?'

I caressed her face with my thumb. 'I don't know about other people, but I know you will.'

One corner of her lip curled up. 'You came here to tell me all of this?'

'That's not good enough?'

The smile I'd come to anticipate so much widened, and I couldn't take my eyes away from her.

'It is. It is more than good enough,' she said, her eyes smiling back at me. 'Wow, you really want to be my boyfriend again, huh?'

Ralph noisily cleared his throat, breaking the connection between me and Charlie. I dropped my hand from her face and she pulled her hand out of mine. I leaned back in my chair and enjoyed Charlie getting all flustered.

'I'm sorry, Ralph,' she apologized in a low voice, shifting in her seat. 'I . . .' She gave me a quick look that clearly said, *save me, say something* then her eyes went back to her date. 'I don't know what to say.'

I knew what to say, so I thought I'd make things easier for both of them. It wouldn't have worked out between them anyway. 'We should leave.' I stood up and offered my hand to Charlie. She looked at it for two full seconds with wonder in her eyes, then she took it and rose up. I entangled our fingers and turned to Ralph.

'I'm sorry, but I couldn't give her up, man. No hard feelings?'

He looked up at me with a confused frown etched onto his brows, then his eyes moved to Charlie, who was holding onto me just as tightly as I was holding onto her. Game or not. Ralph rubbed the back of his neck, his eyes still on Charlie. I glanced back at her, our intertwined hands in between us. She wasn't returning Ralph's gaze, but when she felt my eyes on her, she looked up at me and gave me a small smile. I gently squeezed her hand and turned back to Ralph so we could leave.

'Yeah,' he croaked out, then cleared his throat again. Then he smiled at us and nodded. 'Good luck to both of you.'

'Thank you, Ralph. It was a lovely evening,' Charlie said softly.

I gave him a nod back and pulled Charlie with me. Before leaving the restaurant, I paid their bill. It was the least I could do after interrupting them. When we were leaving, I had a quick look at Ralph again and he was still sitting at their table. I felt sorry for him, because I knew *exactly* how it felt.

The second we were outside Charlie started chuckling, her eyes bright and happy. Her hand was still in mine.

'That was ... something. But it was also so much fun! You should've been an actor!'

I quirked an eyebrow at her as I slowly pulled her closer to me, under the disguise of pulling her out of the way of other people.

'You did say we should do this again sometime. I aim to please you as your fake boyfriend.'

Her smile was larger than ever. 'I did say that and I couldn't have asked for a better fake boyfriend. You made my night, Willy.'

I scoffed. 'Willy?'

'If we do this again, I want to have a nickname for you.'

'We're not doing this again.' I pulled her even closer. We wouldn't need to pretend.

She raised her eyebrows, her voice turning calculative. 'We should do it at least once more before I leave.'

I stared into her eyes. 'Not Willy,' I said simply.

She beamed up at me. 'Will?'

'No.'

'Willie? With an i and e?'

'No.'

'How about Liam?'

I frowned at her. 'Fuck no.'

'Just William? That's it?'

'You don't like my name?'

'I love your name.' She paused. 'As in it's a good, strong name. I like it as a name of its own.'

'Got you. Then we're settled. You'll call me William.'

'You're no fun whatsoever.' She sighed. 'But I can't say that, because you are. Tonight proved it. You're just really sneaky about it. I can only imagine how I looked when I saw you standing over us.'

Shaking her head, she looked away, but she was still smiling.

'Can you imagine,' she started, before I could get in a word, 'someone tracking you down like that, saying all those romantic things to get you back? One day, you know. Hopefully.' She let out a long breath, looked up at the sky, then into my eyes.

'You want two guys going after you?'

Her eyes widened. 'What? No! I'm talking about just being so necessary to someone that they can't be without you.' She scrunched up her nose a little. 'It doesn't sound so healthy when I say it out loud like that, but do you know what I mean? I mean you making the choice of not giving them up. Every day. Because loving someone is an everyday choice.'

I didn't say a word, but I couldn't help myself and reached up with my free hand to tuck a loose strand of hair behind her ear. It was becoming one of my favourite things to do.

My eyes still caught in hers.

My hand still wrapped all around hers.

I wondered for a quick second if she'd noticed that I was still holding her hand or, just like me, it felt so natural that she didn't even give it a second thought.

A moment passed as New York kept moving all around us at full speed. I'm not sure whether it was because I wasn't saying much or something completely different, but I found myself drawn to her. Until that day I had never dated a collegue, but tonight had made me realize that it was pointless to try and stick to that idea. It was pointless because it was Charlie I was interested in. She was the exception and as unsettling as it was, I had realized that I was grappling with my own feelings and I didn't want to anymore.

'William,' she whispered, her voice an intimate caress in the air between us as her eyes jumped from my lips to my eyes. 'I forgot to ask. How did you even know I was here? Why did you really come? Do we have a new case?'

'Charlie?'

We were standing hand in hand and so close to each other that at first the fact that someone familiar was calling Charlie's name escaped us.

It came again. 'Charlie.'

The second time the tone was firmer and there was no mistaking who the voice belonged to. Both Charlie and I sobered up and she was the first one to look away. Then she slipped her hand out of mine before I could do anything about it.

'Kimberly,' she said simply, as she turned her back to me. Her shoulders were rigid, her chin held high.

Kimberly and her husband looked at Charlie first, then to me with a questioning look in their eyes. I inclined my head to both.

'Good evening, Kimberly. Scott.'

'What are you two doing here?' Kimberly asked.

I opened my mouth to speak, but Charlie was faster.

'Not what you think,' she said, her tone stiff. 'I was on a bad date and when I saw William walking into the restaurant I texted him and he got me out of it. He wasn't holding my hand because he wanted to, don't worry. No office romance.'

Kimberly chuckled a little as she shook her head. 'I have no problems with office romance, Charlie. Dad, however, as you know, isn't a fan of dating within the office. But still ... if you guys are together, I'll keep it between us.' She looked at me and then back at Charlie, waiting for either one of us to respond to her.

I followed Charlie's cue. 'No need. I just helped her out. We're working in the same team. A relationship wouldn't be smart.' I let go of Kimberly's gaze and turned my focus on Scott. 'Going out for a date?'

'Kim is meeting with a client,' he replied, wrapping his arm around his wife's waist. 'Would you two like to join us? It'd be more fun. What do you think, Kimberly?' He looked at his wife, and Kimberly, after watching Charlie and me very carefully, shook her head at him.

'I'm pretty tired, Scott,' Charlie cut in. 'I came here right after work so I'm going to head home. Thanks for the invite anyway.'

Ignoring Kimberly and her prying eyes, I discreetly put my hand on Charlie's lower back. She did stiffen a little, but she didn't move away from my touch. 'I'm ready to head home as well. We were planning on sharing a cab.'

'Oh, right. You guys live across from each other. I forgot about that.'

'How about we get together another night?' Scott asked.

'I'm sorry, I'm very busy with work at the moment. Have a good night, both of you.'

And with those words, Charlie just walked away. Kimberly was smiling at me, but Scott was looking after Charlie with a scowl on his face.

'Is she okay?' he asked.

'I believe so.' I managed to smile at them both. 'I better catch up with her. Have a good evening.'

In a few strides, I caught up with Charlie, leaving Kimberly and Scott behind.

'I don't want to ...'

I cut her off before she could finish her sentence. 'Do I have something to apologize for, Charlie?'

She stuttered at the sudden change of subject and frowned at me as we walked side by side. 'What? Apologize?'

'You were on a date. And it looked like an okay one, but I didn't like a few things he did. That being said, what I did in there, should I apologize for it?'

'Are you sorry about it?'

'Not at all,' I answered easily.

She looked forward again. 'Then no, you don't have anything to apologize for. It was a good date, or at least not a bad one. Surprisingly enough. The only good one I had in a while. But . . .'

I looked at her while we waited for the lights to turn green. 'Yes. But?'

She gave me a sideways look. 'I didn't feel a spark. It was more like having dinner with a friend.'

I'd seen the guy look at her. It absolutely was not a friendly dinner for him. But I kept my mouth shut. 'How about we take a cab?' I asked instead. 'You might be willing to walk all the way home, but I'm not.'

The light turned green and we walked across the street. All the while Charlie was smiling at me.

She was about to turn left after we made it to the sidewalk, but I grabbed her hand again and held onto it. She stopped and looked down at our hands, then up at me.

Her lips were slightly open, her cheeks flushed.

'Did you know that holding someone's hand is very intimate?' she commented. 'Our hands are one of the most sensitive parts of our bodies, so it makes sense that it kinda means something emotionally.'

I didn't comment on her little piece of information. 'I want to take you somewhere I think you'll like,' I said instead. Tonight things had changed for me. I was done denying that I wanted this woman in my life. Now all I had to do was show her how good we would be if she gave me another chance at her heart.

Her eyes lit up. 'Oh, food? Please say French fries and brownies.'

I smiled. 'No. Not food.'

19

Charlie

I got out of our rental car and just stood in front of the beautiful stone house like an idiot as William grabbed our small bags from the trunk.

'I can't believe I let you talk me into doing this.'

'We need to work. What does it matter if we do it here or there. I don't know what you're talking about.'

'We're standing in front of your family house in Montauk.'

'Actually *you're* standing in front of my family house in Montauk, I'm getting our bags.'

I looked over my shoulder at William and gave him my slightly hostile look and caught him grinning.

'Stop that. You don't get to smile.' Right that minute Pepperoni stuck his nose out from the window and nudged my arm. 'Hello, big baby, did you finally wake up?' I held his face in my hands and dropped a big kiss on his nose and got a wet one in return. 'You're so handsome after you wake up,' I whispered and smiled when he gave me another kiss on my cheek.

Still smiling widely, I turned to William and found him quietly studying me. 'I can get my own bags.'

'You don't have to do anything when I'm here. I got you. You get Pepp.'

Feeling a little self-conscious, I looked away and opened Pepperoni's door to grab his leash. I got him out and closed the door. When I turned back Pepperoni was sitting right in front of me, almost on my feet, and William was standing right next to me with our bags.

I tried not to act too skittish, but since the night before and his little performance at the restaurant, I was struggling to meet his gaze. Going out on a date with Ralph had been a clear mistake when it was pretty obvious I was starting to feel . . . okay, not starting to, but already feeling attracted to William.

I cleared my throat and kept looking at the house with the red door. 'You're sure they'll be okay with Pepperoni being here? Did you even ask? He seems to be okay with kids, but I'm not sure. Do they know I'm coming too?'

'He is fine. They'll love him. Relax.'

I watched as he put his hand on Pepperoni's head and gave him a scratch that had Pepperoni rolling his head up just so he could look at William with admiration and his tongue hanging out. Hopefully that's not how I looked whenever he touched me.

'Relax, he says,' I muttered under my breath.

Then I felt his hand on the small of my back and my spine straightened. I gave him a sideways look, but I couldn't read his expression. All of a sudden he pulled his hand back, tugged Pepperoni's leash from my hand and started walking towards the house. I just stood there like an idiot, trying to understand what was going on. Why even put your hand on my back if you're gonna pull it away like that? Why put it on my back in the first place? Did he not realize how my heart skipped a beat whenever he casually touched me like it was nothing?

Still walking, he looked over his shoulder. 'Are you coming or are you gonna stand there ?'

Nope. He did not understand what he did to me.

I ignored his amused expression and sighed before following him.

The second we entered the house, the chatter and the kids' screams hit us in all its glory.

Pepperoni froze between me and William for a second, ears pricked. Then he started wagging his tail as two girls came running around the corner. The one who was behind stopped the minute she noticed William and changed course to run towards us.

'Uncle Willie! You came!' she shrieked, throwing herself into William's – *Uncle Willie's* – arms. Pepperoni lost his excitement and remembered that he was actually a little scared of strangers and backed into my legs. I put my hand on his head and gave him some scratches to calm him while I watched everything unfold in front of me.

Uncle Willie caught the little girl, impressively with only a small grunt, mid-air and she wrapped her arms around his neck, closing her eyes and holding on tight. William was hugging her with more care, but it was still tight.

'I missed you. I missed you,' she whispered, her eyes still shut and her face hiding in his neck.

It was a good hug. It was the kind of hug I would've loved to give William too, so I understood her.

'I can see that,' William said, his voice hushed.

I smiled.

The girl opened her green eyes and straightened her head and focused on me.

'Who are you?' she asked, with a small frown lining her forehead.

William turned sideways so he could look at me too.

'Hello,' I said, giving her a small wave. 'I'm your Uncle Willie's work friend.'

She squinted her eyes at me, and I had to hold back my smile. She touched William's cheek and forced his gaze back to her. 'Is she the new Lindsey? We talked, you weren't gonna bring Lindsey. You said no Lindsey.'

William sighed. 'Ivy.'

'Yes?'

'She isn't Lindsey.'

'I can see that. I'm smart.' She put her little hand on William's cheek and my heart melted a little. 'But is she the new Lindsey?'

'Her name is Charlie, Ivy.'

'Hi,' I piped up again, lifting my hand in a wave, and their eyes turned to me. 'I'm Charlie.'

'I like your name, but I don't know if I like you.'

'Ivy, you can't ...' William started, a frown materializing between his brows.

'I can understand that,' I cut in. 'Maybe you can get to know me a little bit while I'm here and then make a decision? That's fair, right?'

She seemed to think about it for a few seconds, then nodded. 'Okay. Fair.'

I smiled at her.

William met my eyes and shook his head.

'Who is that?' she asked, pointing at Pepperoni, who had slowly but surely managed to hide behind me by then.

William gently put her back down. 'That's Pepperoni,' he introduced.

'Can I meet your dog while I'm making a decision about you? I like dogs.'

I tried to hide my smile and nodded. I crouched down and Pepperoni pushed his head under my arm, checking out Ivy and the new surroundings quietly. He wasn't as timid as he had been when I first got him, but new people still made him a little anxious.

'He would love to meet you,' I said to Ivy, right as a gorgeous woman with black hair and eyes identical to William's walked in and stopped next to William.

'Finally, you're here! Why didn't you come last night?' She gave him a big hug and kissed him on his cheek, brushing the lipstick smear with her fingers after. 'Mom's been asking for you.'

'Mom, look, this is Pepperoni,' Ivy piped up as she was reaching to pet him. Pepp gave her hand a quick sniff before lowering his head so Ivy could pet him.

I was caught in that awkward situation of trying to decide whether I should stand up or stay still, but she noticed me in front of her daughter before I could make my move.

'Oh. Hello.'

I rose and looked between William and Ivy's mom. 'Hi. Sorry.'

'Charlie, this is Beth, my sister. And ...'

I offered my hand but the same moment Beth cut William off.

'Charlie?' She gave him a sideways look and then looked back to me. 'You're William's Charlie?'

William's Charlie?

William's Charlie?!

I couldn't help it, a snort escaped my lips. A small one, and hopefully a cute one, but it was a snort nonetheless. 'I wish,' I muttered, then realizing what I'd just uttered out loud, tried to take it back. 'I mean, I'm just Charlie. Not William's or anything. I'm the girl Charlie.' Then I shut up.

Beth beamed.

I offered my hand. 'Hi.'

She ignored it and gave me a quick hug, pretty much like the one she had given her brother. After my tiny word vomit I decided to ignore William's presence completely.

'Nice to meet you, the girl Charlie,' Beth said, still smiling at me. I didn't feel like she was making fun of me, but she was definitely entertained. She was a little shorter than me, and she was gorgeous. Just as gorgeous as Ivy. Just as gorgeous as the brother I was avoiding eye contact with.

I could feel the heat on my cheeks, so I looked straight into Beth's eyes.

'I'm sorry for showing up unannounced. I told William he should ask you first, but ...'

She waved her hand in dismissal. 'Why would he do that? You're always welcome here.'

A giggle caught our attention and we looked down at Ivy and Pepperoni right as he was giving her a kiss on her nose.

'He is friendly,' I said to Beth, just in case she was worried about her daughter.

'Oh, I can see that.' She leaned down and gave Pepperoni a scratch beneath his chin that had him looking up at her with a lolling tongue. A new voice called Ivy's name.

'Come Pepperoni,' Ivy ordered. 'Come play with me.' And then she ran away. Pepperoni looked up at me and rested the side of his head against my leg. Before I could do anything, William was at my side and he was kneeling down to take off Pepperoni's leash.

'William,' I started, hesitating.

'He wants to play too. Stop worrying, he is fine here,' he said simply, but even though he had taken off his leash, Pepperoni was still staring at me while his tail was going a mile a minute.

'Is it okay?' I asked Beth to make sure. 'He is a little big, but he is very gentle.'

Her smile softened. 'Of course.'

I leaned down to give him a kiss on his head. 'Go play, baby.' He was off like a rocket, then we heard Ivy's delightful squeals and a small bark from Pepperoni. Because it very much felt like my baby was making new friends, my heart melted a little.

I straightened and came eye to eye with a grinning Beth. I looked at William and then Beth again, thinking I had missed something.

'What?' I asked, but no answer came.

'Nothing. I'm just glad William brought you. Mom is preparing dinner, come say hi when you're ready,' Beth said over her shoulder and left us alone.

I was about to take a step forward to follow her, but William touched my back and I almost jumped to the ceiling like a scared cat.

'Jesus!' I held my palm against my chest to try and contain

it. When I looked at William he was smiling at me. 'What?' I demanded this time.

As an answer he shook his head at me. 'Are you nervous or something?'

'What makes you say that?'

'You're nervous.'

'Says who?'

Infuriatingly, he just smiled at me. 'Come on. Let's say hello to my mom and the others before she comes to look for us.'

What the heck is going on here?

Before I could utter a single syllable, he had slipped his hand around mine and was pulling a shocked me further into the house. And what concerned me most wasn't the fact that he was holding my hand, but the unsettling fact that it felt so good and natural.

'We're good?' he asked, looking at me over his shoulder.

We're not that good.

I nodded and he nodded back. It was clear he was enjoying this a little too much.

'They're going to love you,' William said, and I looked down to our joined hands then back up again and got caught in his gaze. Got caught in him all over again.

Then before we could make it into the kitchen his mom's voice reached us. 'He brought his Charlie?'

'Charlie, tell us more about yourself,' Evelyn Carter, William's mom said, and I looked up at her. We – all of William's family and a few of their friends – were having dinner and it was the most lively and beautiful thing ever. It was nothing like the dinners at my house. We were maybe around ten, twelve people and everybody was chattering and laughing. Other than William's sister Beth and her family, William's brother and a few of his friends were there too. So far I had met Beth's husband Nico, and his brother Damon and the younger sister Kay who was very much pregnant, and Kay's friend Elijah.

My Pepperoni was lying right underneath my feet below the table. He was completely tuckered out after running around with Ivy and all the love he had gotten from everyone.

I put down my fork and knife and reached for my water glass. Apparently it was tradition to have a big family dinner before someone's birthday in the Carter house because then the birthday girl or boy could focus on what they wanted to do on the big day. But the day before was for family.

'What would you like to know?' I asked Evelyn, genuinely happy to be there. I had smiled and laughed with them the entire day and was probably halfway into falling in love with every single one of them, but I was trying my best to hide it.

Especially from William.

William . . .

He was sitting to my right and in my opinion had somehow been messing with my mind. He had been killing me the entire day. Every time I'd laughed if he was in the room, he'd sent me these long looks I couldn't for the life of me decipher, but which made something flutter in my chest. Whenever I made a face at him, he smiled and looked away from me. And then there was the touching. We were both helping his mom set the table and whenever I handed him a plate, our fingers touched and I swear to God, he lingered. His eyes lingered.

'Tell us about your family. Your mom? Dad? Do you have any other siblings?'

I swallowed and took a sip of water before answering. 'I have a sister, my dad and my grandma. It's just the four of us.'

Some of the others were still chattering among themselves, but most of them had gone quiet and were listening to us.

'Your mom?' she asked simply.

Trying not to feel too awkward, I put both my hands on my lap under the table. 'My parents divorced. She left when I was twelve.'

'You still see her though, right?' Beth asked.

'Beth,' William muttered, and I shook my head, reaching for my glass.

'Oh, I'm sorry, Charlie. I didn't mean to pry.'

'Oh, no, it's okay.' Sometimes it was better to just overshare things instead of making the situation more awkward than it needed to be by dragging it out. 'She moved to a different city, I think it was Oregon, but we heard later that she moved from there too. I have no idea where she is right now. She did call once, it was my birthday, and I think she was a little drunk because she asked me if I'd gotten prettier.' I shrugged. 'We didn't talk much after, I think that was the last time I heard from her.' I lifted my glass from the table and took a long sip of my cold water and then smiled at Evelyn when I caught her gaze on me.

She tilted her head and put her wineglass down. 'Oh, sweetheart.'

I smiled a little more to show that I was actually okay. And I was. My mom . . . she hadn't been in my life for a long time. She didn't affect the life I had now.

I felt the tablecloth move against the skin of my arm and looked to my right to see William's hand secretly inching towards mine. I watched – still almost as surprised to feel his skin on mine as I was the first time he'd done it – as he covered his hand over mine under the table and gave it a gentle squeeze.

You're not alone. I'm here for you.

That's what his touch and that squeeze meant to me. My heart lurched with an extra thud and I could feel a slow heat flood my face. I gave him a sideways glance, but he was talking to one of the guys, one of his sister's friends who was sitting next to him. And somehow just because of that, the gesture meant even more. After giving my hand another squeeze, he pulled it back. I made a fist of my hand and then opened it. He knew what had happened with my mom, I'd shared it with him years back – just as he'd shared how they had lost their father when they were young.

'Charlie, this tastes amazing,' Beth's husband Nico commented and everyone murmured their appreciation, breaking the unexpected tension in the room. I turned to him with a warm smile. He was taking spoonfuls of the Mediterranean potato salad I had made as a contribution to the dinner after much begging to Evelyn. I didn't want to just sit around and do nothing while they were working their asses off in the kitchen.

'I'm glad you like it,' I replied and picked up my fork.

'It is really good, Charlie,' Evelyn added, her eyes warm as she got up from her seat.

I nodded in thanks and took a small bite out of the chicken dish I had on my plate. They were being kind, Evelyn could've been a chef.

'No, seriously,' Kay said. 'I wasn't here when you were making it so I missed out on what spices are in here, but I want the recipe. I love it.'

My heart warmed. 'It's very simple, but of course I'll give you the recipe.'

'You're gonna cook?' William asked, with more than a little suspicion in his tone.

Kay's eyebrows flicked up. 'Ha. Ha. Funny. I cook, thank you very much.'

'Really? When was the last time you did anything in the kitchen?'

'I'm pregnant, you idiot.'

I held back my laughter, but William wasn't that smart.

'What does that have to do with anything?' he asked.

'I get tired a lot.'

'Ah, got you.'

'Shut up, I'm a single mom. I don't have time.'

'You didn't have the baby yet.'

Evelyn caught my gaze and shook her head as if to say *kids, what can you do* and I felt included and smiled back at her.

The conversation picked up around me, and Evelyn and I were talking about life in Montauk until she asked me if I was seeing someone.

'Nope.' I shovelled some more potato salad into my mouth, hoping she'd move on to talk about something else. Beth was sitting right across from me, and Evelyn was next to her.

She moved forward and lowered her voice. 'Can I ask why?' Thankfully, as far as I could tell, no one else was paying attention to what we were talking about.

'Too busy, I guess,' I confided in a lower voice. I was *not* going to tell her I hadn't dated in years. 'And I can't seem to find the good ones.'

She pulled back a little and smiled at me. 'You're beautiful, Charlie. If guys are not getting in line and knocking on your door, they're idiots.' She shook her head and took a sip of her wine.

Kay's friend Elijah was sitting to my left and slightly leaning into me under the disguise of getting the pepper mill, as he muttered, 'She's right.'

I gave him a small smile and glanced back at Evelyn.

'It's a little on me too. I decided not to date for a few years.'

'Oh,' Beth piped up, looking intrigued. 'Is there a story behind it?'

'Other than heartbreak? Not really. My grandma got sick, I had to take care of her. Then I wanted to focus on work. I just didn't want to deal with anyone I think. Not to mention every online date I'd been on just turned into disasters. I just thought it'd happen when it happened.'

'Ah, being single. Sounds like heaven to me,' Beth sighed.

'I heard that,' Nico piped up.

I smiled.

'Good. I wanted you to hear it,' Beth replied.

'You'd miss me if you were single.'

'Hah, you wish. What will you do if I . . .'

'Please don't start flirting at the dinner table,' William cut in. 'Please.' He glanced at a grinning Nico, then at his sister. Nico raised his hands while Beth just shook her head with a small knowing smile on her lips.

I was beaming at everyone around me.

William started scooping up his peas and putting them on my plate while he was talking to Nico. I waited for him to finish, then started gathering my carrot salad and putting it on his. Once I was done and looked up, almost everyone was staring at us.

'I'm sorry, Charlie,' Evelyn said. 'I wouldn't have forced the carrot salad on you if I knew you didn't like it.'

'Oh, no, it's fine. I like it, but William seems to really like carrots from what I've learned at our lunches, so I thought I'd share. Sorry.'

'And she loves peas,' William put in.

I drank some water. I'd forgotten that we weren't alone having lunch near the office. I forgot that this was something natural for us. Usually he gave me his French fries and I gave him whatever he wanted from my plate, but we hadn't done that in front of others, let alone his family.

'How is working with William?' Kay asked, thankfully changing the subject. But I could see her lips twitching.

'He is amazing,' I announced, giving William a sideways glance as he looked at me in surprise. When I turned back to Kay, I noticed Evelyn's smile as her eyes went from me to her son. 'As in, he is a really hard worker and it's been great being on a team with him. Not to mention he is great at what he does. I wish we had more time to work together.' I corrected to make sure they didn't misunderstand me. 'You must be happy now that he is closer to you.'

Evelyn's brows furrowed in confusion as she distractedly passed more of my potato salad to Nico. 'What do you mean, you wish you had more time to work together?'

'Oh, umm . . .' I chanced a quick look at William and he was staring back at me. 'I'm moving to California. New job.'

'Oh,' Evelyn echoed, and I could tell from her expression that she was confused.

'You're working in your dad's company though, right?' Kay questioned.

'Yes. He doesn't know about the new job yet, but he does know that I've wanted to move for a while now.'

'I'm sure he'll be happy for . . .' Evelyn started.

'You talked to Nora?' William cut in.

I turned my shoulders to face him. 'Yes. Yesterday. Before I went out for the dinner we had a quick video call.'

'You didn't tell me.'

Was that accusation or disappointment I was hearing in his voice? 'I . . . I was going to. It was a little hectic yesterday before dinner and . . . well then the dinner and everything else.' I tried to make him a face, but he looked too serious.

He put down his fork and knife, reached for his water glass and took a big swallow. 'It's done then. She wants you. I knew she would, but . . . You're leaving.'

I chuckled nervously. 'She does want me. Thank you for talking to her. Whatever you said worked. If you hadn't offered to help out, I'd still be looking. And I really like Nora, I think it'll be a good fit. I'm excited.'

His eyes wandered down my face and he looked away, forehead creased, his jaw muscles working.

I gave the table a half-hearted smile, confused about William's sudden change of mood.

'We have work to do,' he announced, after clearing his throat, and then pushed his chair slightly back.

'William?' Evelyn asked, and our focus turned to her. 'Surely you mean after dinner?'

He gave her a distracted nod and settled back down. 'Of course.'

Feeling like I'd somehow disappointed him, I shifted in my seat.

While I was confused about William's reaction, Evelyn must've gotten up from her seat, because the next thing I knew she was walking around the table towards me. And much to my surprise, she bent down and wrapped her arm around my neck, giving me a warm hug from behind. I lost my words and felt a slight flush on my cheeks.

'Congratulations, sweetheart. New beginnings are always exciting.'

She pulled back, and I peered up at her with a small smile on my lips.

She grinned down at me and lightly cupped my cheek in a motherly way. 'I was hoping we'd get to see you around more since William mentioned you so much, but I'm sure you'll do great in California. Do you know anyone in the area?'

'Thank you,' I murmured. 'My best friend lives there with her fiancé so I won't be alone,' I explained, but I was mostly stuck at the *William mentioned you so much* bit. I needed to text Valerie asap.

'How come Pepperoni's name is Pepperoni?' Ivy piped up from her seat at the end of the table, next to her dad.

Mentally I shook off the questions swirling in my head and tried to focus on Ivy. 'The first night I adopted him we ordered ourselves pizza to celebrate and I learned that he was a pepperoni stealer. So I thought it fit. I call him Pepp.'

'Pepp,' she repeated, scrunching up her nose as if she were sniffing the air. 'I like Pepp too.'

The handsome boy in question lifted his head up and thumped his tail a few times before putting his head on my shoe and falling back asleep.

'Did you buy me a present, Charlie?' Ivy asked next.

Both Beth and Nico interrupted before I could answer.

'We talked about this, Ivy. Not everyone will get you presents.'

Her red lips turned downward. 'But it's my birthday. When is she gonna buy me a present if not on my birthday?'

'Well,' I started before Beth could say anything else. 'I do have a present for you. It's from Pepp and me.'

Her mood picked up immediately and she was all smiles. 'Can I see it now?'

I sighed. 'Your Uncle Willie told me you were a little sneaky with presents so I left it in the car.'

She sent a powerful William's way, which looked funny more than anything. 'Uncle Willie, I'm not sneaky. I only got a little excited and opened your present early once. If you didn't want me to open it why would you leave it in the kitchen? It wasn't my fault, right, Mom? Tell Charlie it wasn't my fault.'

I peered at William, but he looked preoccupied.

The rest of the dinner was nothing but laughter and smiles, and while half the time I envied what they had since my family dinners were the exact opposite of this, the other half I was really happy William had brought me along with him because it had been a long time since I'd had that much fun. And it only solidified the fact that I wanted and needed a big change in my life so I could feel this kind of happiness every day.

It was around 8.00 p.m. and William was getting a few things ready and wrangling the team around for a video call, where we were going to try our best to make sure they wouldn't realize we were together in his family home since no one else had been invited. I was in the kitchen talking to Kay, Elijah and Evelyn. Beth and her family had already left with a sleepy and excited Ivy, with the promise of showing up early the next day to help with the party preparations.

'Do you want milk in your coffee, Charlie?' Evelyn asked.

'Yes, please. Thank you so much for everything, Evelyn. Dinner was amazing.'

Smiling, she glanced back at me over her shoulder. 'Any time. I'm glad you could come. And tomorrow after the birthday party is over we're going to celebrate your new job.'

'Oh, that's not necessary at all. Tonight was a celebration on its own.'

She walked towards me and handed me my coffee cup. 'Nonsense. We'll just have some drinks around the fire in the back. It'll be cosy. Trust me, you'll need cosy and quiet after the madness that will be tomorrow.'

Feeling a little embarrassed with the attention, and not knowing what to say, I nodded. 'Thank you so much.'

'I'll go and get your room ready.'

I put my mug down. 'Please let me help. I don't want to be more trouble than I already am.'

'It will only take me a few minutes, trust me. Plus William will come looking for you any minute now. I got this.'

Before I could protest some more, she disappeared up the staircase connected to the kitchen.

'Trust me, Mom loves guests,' Kay explained while she was heating herself some milk. 'It's no trouble for her to have you here. The more the merrier.'

'It's true,' Elijah added, coming to stand next to me. 'The Carters love unexpected guests.'

'You would know. You've been an unexpected guest in this house for the last five years.' Opening one of the cupboards, Kay picked a mug and poured her milk into it.

Elijah winked at me. 'And I've been loving every minute of it.'

Watching their easy banter with a smile on my face, I took a sip of my coffee. 'How did you two meet?'

'In college,' they both replied at the same time.

'I was dating his best friend. I kicked that guy to the curb when he cheated on me, but got his best friend out of the deal.'

Kay's phone started ringing and she took it out of her jeans pocket. 'Oh, I'll be right back. I need to take this.'

As soon as she was out of the kitchen Elijah turned to me. 'So, William's Charlie, what do you think about the Carters?'

The curiosity got the better of me. I groaned and leaned towards him a little so no one could hear. 'Why is everyone calling me that? Do you know?'

He mirrored my movement, but because he was almost 6 ft 3 in, he had to tip his chin down to look into my eyes. 'I think if I remember correctly William had called you *My Charlie* on a phone call when he first started working at your dad's company. I don't know the details any more than that, but I know it stuck with them all.'

Surprised, I pulled back a little. 'Oh.'

His right eyebrow shot up. 'Anything going on there?'

'Where?'

'With William.'

I shook my head. 'No. No. It couldn't. I'm going to move. And even if I wasn't, we're colleagues so . . .' I trailed off.

He nodded in understanding. 'Too bad. Carters seem to love you.'

I gave him a distracted smile, but my mind was buzzing.

'I'm a photographer and I have a lot of clients in California. I'd like to give you a call when I'm back over there again.'

Raising my gaze up to him, I tried to focus on what he was saying. 'Ah, yes. Sure.'

'Charlie.'

I spun around to William's flat voice and came face to face with what looked like an annoyed man. The same jaw muscles I had seen jumping at dinner were jumping again, and I felt a flutter in my stomach. I barely held my hand back from touching his face.

I noticed Elijah straightening up and away from me, so gripping my coffee mug tighter I shuffled a step away from him and right into William, who hadn't been there just a second ago. He steadied me with a hand on my back and a sudden shiver worked its way down my spine from our unexpected closeness, my back against his warm and broad chest.

'Sorry to cut into your conversation, but if you're done we have work to do,' William announced, studying me closely right before giving Elijah a quick glance.

'Yes,' I managed to get out. 'Yes, of course. I'll be right there.'

I waited for him to go for a few seconds, but it didn't look like he was about to budge. We stared at each other in a battle of silence.

Trying very hard not to grin, I turned back to Elijah. 'I'll see you tomorrow at the party?'

'Yes. I'd love that,' he replied, giving me a small nod as if to say *we'll pick up where we left off.*

Returning his gesture, I turned around to leave and had to endure the electric feel of William's hand accidentally sliding against the skin between my shirt and my pants. I walked past him – without making a fool of myself – into the living room and towards the office he had shown me ten minutes ago. When I peered back he was still giving the death glare to Elijah.

Something shifted in me and I grinned to myself.

When I made it to the desk and put my coffee mug down, William was right behind me.

'You ready?' he asked, as if everything were normal, and started to take out his laptop from the bag. Mine was already set up.

I gripped the edges of the table and slightly leaned back against it. 'William.'

He ignored me. 'Yes.'

'Can I say something?'

'What?'

I couldn't help it. I grinned and waited until he met my gaze.

When he did, I smiled as widely as I could. He stopped what he was doing and studied me in silence. Then he took two steps towards me until his chest was almost brushing my shoulder.

'What?' he repeated, his voice low and a little rough.

I bit down on my bottom lip and then let it go. 'I'm gonna say something, but you can't be mad.'

His eyes dropped down to my lips, then back up to my eyes.

'Try me,' he said, after letting out a breath.

I dipped my body to the left. Just a little, so my shoulder could touch his chest. His eyes were burning into mine, and I couldn't find it in me to look away. 'I think you're jealous,' I whispered.

He inched just a little bit closer, to the point where I could feel his hot breath against my cheek.

'Jealous?'

'Yes,' I replied simply.

His eyes dropped to my lips yet again. I lost my confidence and straightened from the desk, which put me another inch closer to William. His eyes found mine and he licked his lips. All of a sudden my heart went into a fast and frantic beat and my awareness of his closeness jolted through me.

'You think I don't want guys coming onto you?'

'Elijah wasn't coming onto me,' I whispered.

He took a deep breath and let it out as I watched him in fascination. 'Yeah?' he asked quietly. 'Tell me, Charlie. What do you think he was doing?'

'Being nice and friendly.'

'Yeah?'

I nodded. I was pretty sure he *was* being nice because I hadn't felt anything different from him the whole night.

'I'm not a jealous person. I've never been jealous of anyone before.'

'You could've fooled me.'

'Hmmm,' he grunted, making my lips twitch. 'You're right,' he admitted, much to my shock.

I tilted my head, studying him. 'I'm right?'

'You have honesty on your list, right? I'm following your example. It looks like I'm very jealous when it comes to you, Charlie. I was hoping it would go away, but I don't think it's going anywhere.'

I licked my lips, feeling a little overwhelmed by how close he was standing to me and how deeply he was staring into my eyes as if he were trying to see into my heart. 'William . . .' I started, but wasn't sure exactly what to say.

'Yes, Charlie,' he said, his voice gruff and deep.

My heart thudding in my chest, I watched as he bent down and put his hand right next to mine, almost boxing me against the table. He raised his left hand and let his thumb stroke over my bottom lip. All at once, the world stopped moving and there was nothing – no one but William. I stopped breathing altogether.

He closed the gap between us and my heart slowed down as I felt his nose right between my ear and my neck. He took a deep breath. 'How do you always smell so good?' he whispered into my ear.

My eyes fluttered closed all on their own and instinctively I tilted my head to the side, giving him more access to do what ... I had no idea.

He pulled back a little, but he was still standing too close to me. I managed to open my eyes and stare straight into his. His gaze touched every inch of my skin as we stood there in the quiet of the night.

'Are you going to kiss me?' I breathed out. A little hopeful and maybe a little scared. 'Is it happening?'

His lips twitched, but he was still staring at my lips. 'No.'

'You're going to break my heart,' I said quietly, and his eyes came back to mine.

'You're the last person on earth I would hurt. You deserve the best, and I will ...'

'William? Are you in the kitchen?'

I blinked and William was gone. My body felt oddly cold. Three seconds later, his mom walked into the office.

'Oh, here you are. You haven't started yet. I'm not interrupting, am I?'

William cleared his throat, and still a little shellshocked I looked over my shoulder to see that he was busy setting up his laptop. 'No, mom. But we're about to start.'

I swallowed and turned to face Evelyn. I think I offered her a smile, but I wasn't sure if it actually looked like a grimace.

'Charlie, are you okay?' she asked, her brows knitted.

'Yes. Yes. Great. Thank you.'

'You sure?' Coming towards me, she touched my forehead with the back of her hand. 'You look a little pale.'

'I think it's a little hot in here. Or maybe I'm just tired, that's all.'

She didn't look convinced, but she didn't push it. 'Don't work her too hard, William. It's not a work day, and she is a guest here. She should enjoy her time. Take her to the beach tomorrow to escape the madhouse. Okay?'

William sighed. 'We'll see tomorrow. But now we need to work.'

I watched as he reached for his mom who was much shorter than him and bent down to give her cheek a kiss.

Taking my eyes away from them – away from William – I sat my ass down on the chair and turned on my laptop, trying to focus on work and not on how hard my heart was thumping in my chest. It was going to be a long, long weekend.

20

William

I watched as she walked out of the back door carrying a big bowl of what looked like fruit salad. Beth was standing right next to me, telling me something important I think, but I must've tuned her out completely, because I didn't hear one word after Charlie stepped into the backyard with that big smile on her lips.

She was wearing a dress that I didn't even know how to begin to describe, but it was almost indecent to wear to a kid's birthday party. Or maybe it wasn't indecent at all, but it was just me who thought that. More likely that was the case, because it wasn't like there was much cleavage going on, but I could see the shape of her breasts. There was fabric against her skin, and that alone made it indecent, because I just wanted to see what was underneath all that fabric.

I kept watching with the orange juice in my hand which Beth had pushed at me a moment ago as Charlie looked over her shoulder and said something to Kay, who was following her out. They laughed at the same time, then kids swarmed around them. How they still had energy to even walk after their Bounce House activities I had no idea.

Charlie let out another laugh and it finally reached my ears through all the kids' screams. She sounded happy, and just that sound made it worth bringing her here. I took a step forward, feeling a strong urge to go to her and take her hand, so I could pull her to a quiet corner. To talk to her. To have her look at me and smile that little smile she had just for me. To have her tell me more about her list and what she wanted from life, what she needed. I realized I could listen to her talk to me for hours. And not even for a second did I question that I'd have enough of her, or our random conversations.

Shit.

I was screwed because even in my thoughts I sounded borderline obsessed with her.

But then again, I already knew that. Since last night and with that date that wasn't-couldn't-shouldn't-really-be-a-date she went on, I had come to the conclusion that I wouldn't be an idiot again and wouldn't let her slip away through my fingers. It didn't matter that she had a new job and was officially about to move. We would figure it out.

Just as Charlie turned around and her gaze found mine across all the little kids and the adults standing around, Beth came into my view and ruined it. I squeezed the box of orange juice in my hands. I must've looked ridiculous.

'Yes? You were saying?' I prompted, drinking the rest of the juice and trying to look as if I'd been listening to her all along.

Beth's lips tugged at the corners and she gave me a knowing look.

'You were agreeing with me.'

'About what?' I tried to look over her shoulder, but her damn hair was flying all over the place because of a sudden wind.

'About how beautiful Jenny was.'

I shuffled a step to my right and my brows drew together when I caught Elijah looking down at Charlie and Charlie holding onto his forearm while she pulled at the flowing skirt of her dress.

I was right. Completely indecent.

Then Beth was in my face again. 'When will you go out on the date then?'

'What?' I snapped sharper than I'd intended.

'The date. When will you go?'

I tried to ignore what Charlie was doing or who she was holding onto and tried to focus on my sister. 'What are you talking about? What date?'

Her brows rose as if it were a surprise to her that I hadn't been listening. 'The date you said you'd go on with Jenny.'

I felt a headache coming on. 'When did I agree to go on a date with Jenny? And more importantly, who is Jenny?'

'My friend who lives in New York, remember?'

'No, I don't. And you know I'm not dating.' I pushed my empty orange juice box into her hands. 'You got any more of these?'

'You aren't *dating*?'

It was the sound she made at the last word. That squeaky way she ended the question.

'I'm gonna take Charlie and get back to work. I got a headache just watching your kid bounce around with all the other kids. What do you want from me?'

'You aren't dating?'

'I'm not going out on a date with whoever Jenny is.'

'Because you're dating someone else ... or ...?'

'I'm not dating anyone.'

'Not even Charlie?'

I stopped trying to look over my sister's shoulder to see what Charlie was doing with Elijah, who I had no idea why Kay had invited along. So what if Ivy liked him? She had just turned seven; she was bound to like anyone who brought a good present.

'I need to go back to work,' I muttered, trying to make my way around her. Finally I could see again. And Charlie was now chattering away with my mom *and* Elijah. She just had no idea.

Beth fell into step next to me. 'You're a goner.'

'What the hell does that even mean?'

'Go take Charlie to the beach or something before Elijah rushes in and takes the prize. Bye.'

I lunged for her arm, but she danced away. 'What? What do you mean? Do you know something?' I stopped walking and dodged the crazed children as they ran past me, chasing after some girl Beth had hired who was about to paint their faces. I found my nosey sister walking backwards and giving me a satisfied grin.

'First of all,' I yelled after her as her grin widened, infuriating me further. 'First of all, mind your own business.'

'Second?'

'She is not a horse to be called a prize.' I ignored her laughter and started stalking towards her.

'Third?'

She skipped just out of my reach. 'Elijah isn't taking anything from me.'

Right then I lunged forward and caught Beth's arm as she opened her mouth to scream, most likely. I gave her a good reason and threw her over my shoulder.

Ivy came out of nowhere and ran around us laughing and yelling, 'Do me, do me, Uncle Willie.'

My mouth twitched as Beth got creative with her word choices around her daughter. I didn't hear half of them though, my eyes were just for Charlie as our gazes got caught in each other and she finally ignored Elijah. That was more like it. As soon as I was near their cosy little group, next to the food table, I not-so-gently slid Beth off my shoulder.

'Promise to give you a longer tour than I just did your mom, Ivy, but later okay?' I smoothed down her hair as she stared up at me with her big blue eyes. 'We don't want to make your friends jealous, right?'

I took the last few steps that separated me and Charlie and finally managed to put my hand on the small of her back. Her back arched to some extent, and I couldn't help but slide my hand around her waist and rest my hand on the curve of it. I came eye to eye with Elijah and then watched as his gaze dropped to where my hand was resting.

Good.

'What did I miss?' I asked to no one in particular and felt Charlie shift from foot to foot, which brought her closer to me.

'What's happening with you two?' Mom asked, studying Beth and then me.

'Just ...'

I didn't give her a chance to finish her sentence. 'Nothing. Charlie and I will have to take a break. We have some work we need to finish.'

'Now?' Mom pushed, looking around. 'But I wanted to introduce Charlie to someone.'

Another call from Lindsey came in and I let it go to voicemail, as I always did. My brows furrowed. 'Who?'

'You remember Ally's son ...'

I dropped my arm from Charlie's waist as Beth's barely audible snort reached my ears. 'Are you kidding me?'

Finally Mom focused on me instead of looking for who-ever. 'What?'

'What's wrong with all of you today?'

'I wonder what's wrong with *you*,' Beth commented.

I ignored them all and offered my hand to Charlie. Everyone got quiet. Her gaze dropped down to my open hand, then up to my eyes.

'I'll take you to the beach.'

She didn't think about it. She put her hand in mine and I curled my fingers around hers.

'What time is it?' She checked the watch on her wrist. 'Isn't the video call around four?'

'We have a little more than an hour. Plenty enough.'

Ivy appeared out of nowhere with some whiskers over her upper lip and clasped her mom's hand. 'Mom, can we go to the beach too?'

'Sweetheart,' I cut in before Beth could respond. 'This is just for me and Charlie.'

She tilted her head to the side and her brows snapped together. I'd find it more adorable if she wasn't trying to squeeze herself in with us while I was trying my damned hardest to be alone with Charlie.

'Why? Uncle Willie, everyone can go to the beach. We go to the beach with everyone all the time.'

I held back my groan, instead clenched Charlie's hand a little tighter.

'Yeah. Why, Uncle Willie?' Beth added unnecessarily.

I gave her a long look that she should've recognized, but she didn't back off. I turned my focus back on Ivy.

'You're gonna leave all your friends?'

She shrugged. 'Sunny had to leave to visit her grandma.' She smiled at Charlie and raised her chin up. 'Sunny is my bestest friend.'

I surveyed the remaining kids over my shoulder. Sure enough, more than half of them had suddenly disappeared. I wanted to say no. I really wanted to spend a few quiet moments with Charlie, but it was Ivy's birthday after all and everyone in our little circle was looking at me as if I'd sprouted an extra head, so I had to relent. 'If you really want to then,' I grumbled.

She squealed, damaging all of our eardrums, then ran off to invite a few of her friends with us. Thankfully Beth and Mom followed her to organize everyone.

We might as well have moved the whole damn party with us.

'How about that bike ride? Beach is close enough so you wouldn't be afraid.' Elijah asked, staring at Charlie as if I wasn't standing there next to her *holding* her hand. I struggled for words for a second.

Charlie opened her mouth to answer, but I didn't let her.

'Charlie is not gonna go to the beach on your bike, Elijah.'

'I'm not? I've never been on a bike before.'

I kept my eyes on Elijah, but spoke to Charlie. 'I'll take you out on one. Later.'

'You have a motorcycle?'

'No. I'll find one.'

'Where are you gonna find a motorcycle?'

'From wherever people find motorcycles.'

She gestured at Elijah with her free hand. 'But Elijah already has a bike. We were talking earlier and I promised him I'd try it. We'll meet you at the beach.'

I gave her hand a gentle squeeze. 'I'll find us a motorcycle,' I repeated softly.

'Do you know how to ride one?'

'Where is Pepp?' I shot back instead of giving an answer.

She glanced over her shoulder and a small smile tugged at her lips. 'He's with the kids. He is having the best time of his life. Every few minutes he rushes to my side, says hi, hello, and then rushes back to them. I get teary eyed every single time.'

'Well. If you're so set on getting on his bike, you won't be able to take him with you to see the beach. So it's either the car with me and Pepp, or . . .' I regarded Elijah with barely concealed annoyance, 'or bike ride with Elijah.'

'That was harsh.'

I raised one shoulder and dropped it. 'Your choice.'

'You really know how to ride?'

'Yes, Charlie. I know. I had a motorcycle when I was in college.'

'No, you didn't.'

'I did.'

Her whole face lit up. 'I can actually imagine you on a bike and it's not that bad.'

'Yeah?

She bit on her bottom lip to hold back a smile, then asked quietly, 'Are we bantering, William? Again?'

'I'll leave you two alone,' Elijah spoke up, and I realized I'd already forgotten he was standing right there. It hadn't been the first time I'd done that. It didn't look like it'd be the last either.

Charlie turned to say something to him, and her hand loosened in mine, but I held on.

'Okay kids.' Mom joined us again with a line of actual kids

behind her. 'We're ready. Nico and the others will stay back with some of them, but we can leave.'

'I'm coming too,' Beth piped up.

Everybody headed towards the house. Charlie pulled on my hand to get my attention so I turned to her. She rested her shoulder against mine, leaning in closer.

'Is everything okay?' she asked quietly.

I gave her hand a gentle squeeze, closed my eyes and took a deep breath. 'You're not trying hard enough.' I started following the last kid in the bunch and gently pulled Charlie with me. At least no one had tried to question us on why we were holding hands, because if they did I might have lost it on them.

'Trying hard enough for what?'

'To be alone with me.'

21

Charlie

Don't go to sleep before talking to me

That was the note I'd found in my room in my book *The Girl Who Fell Beneath the Sea* by Axie Oh. I'd left it on my bed that morning when I went upstairs after the video call we had with the CEO of the airline company. I was having the time of my life at Montauk and that was even before you added William and the way he was acting towards me into the equation. With how often he was holding my hand, touching me and putting his hand on the small of my back, I was starting to believe his love language was touch.

As much as I was secretly loving it, it was also wreaking havoc in my soul and in my heart. We were playing a dangerous game.

I still wouldn't have changed the weekend I was having with him and his family for anything.

I'd simply fallen in love with every single one of them.

Leaving Pepp back in my room where he was happily snoring away, I stepped out onto the porch and rested my hands on the railing, peering up at the night sky that was filled with countless stars. Tonight was a big night for me, I could feel it in my bones.

This was the life I wanted to have. This was the life I'd always wanted.

The beach had been amazing. Pepp's first time seeing the ocean. I couldn't remember the last time I had laughed so much. Ivy, Evelyn, Beth and I had all taken turns coaxing him into the lazy waves and he had loved it so much that I'd had to drag him away when it was time to go. And when we got back home it was work time: we'd spent over three hours preparing statements for a new case William had accepted.

Even before I'd found the note in my room, I knew something was bothering William, but before he could say anything after we were done with the conference call, Nora called me. Then Evelyn offered a glass of prosecco.

Then.

Then.

Then.

It never stopped, and I ended up back in my room and saw the note.

'You're a sight for sore eyes,' I heard William say from behind me, and I peered over my shoulder to watch as he stepped out of the house. He was wearing black jeans with a thin light grey sweater and he looked amazing. Cosy.

And unattainable. Not mine.

'Hey stranger.' I smiled at him. Freely. Widely.

His eyes stayed fixed on my smile.

'Stranger?'

'I barely talked to you today outside work stuff.'

'Yeah? Do you want me to tell you how many times I tried to catch you alone today? I haven't succeeded even once.'

My grin got bigger. 'I've had an amazing time.'

'I know.'

'Come look.' I tipped my chin back up to the sky and closed my eyes, taking a deep breath of the sea-salty breeze as it danced through my hair. 'It's beautiful here,' I whispered into the night.

'More than beautiful. Yes.'

'So, did you want to see me to apologize about not finding a bike?'

He sighed. 'That's on Nico. He was supposed to call his friend.'

'Uh-huh. If you say so. I could've gone to the beach with Elijah. Which would've been a very short ride since it's only two streets away.'

He grunted in response. We were both quiet for a moment.

'Honesty?' I probed without looking at him.

'Always.'

I licked my lips, still tasting the prosecco and chocolate. 'You have an amazing voice. Low, husky, strong, deep and a whole bunch of other adjectives. It's a good voice and it was the first thing I noticed about you back then.'

'Thank you, Charlie,' he said softly, causing me to glance at him with one eye open as his voice touched some deep part within me and something melted just a little

He was studying me, so I stared up at the sky again, because that was easier to handle.

'Where is Pepp?' he asked softly.

'Tuckered out, sleeping in the room.'

'Do you have anyone else hiding around?'

That made me look. 'What?'

'I can't seem to catch you alone even for a minute, so I thought I'd check before someone jumps out of nowhere and takes you away from me.'

Takes you away.

Staying quiet, I shook my head.

He raised an eyebrow then inclined his head. 'Good.'

'I really really love your family,' I admitted.

'And they love you.'

Still holding onto the wooden rail, I turned to William. 'You think so?'

A smile tugged at his lips. 'Yeah.'

'You're so lucky. They are amazing.'

'I know.'

'Can I have them?'

'They're yours if you want them.'

They're yours if you want them.

We stayed quiet for a moment and listened to the waves we could hear coming from afar. He was the one who wanted to talk to me, but for some reason I was afraid to ask what was on his mind. And he wasn't saying anything.

'Tell me something happy, William,' I challenged instead.

He didn't even take a moment to think. 'I couldn't even put into words how good it feels to look up from my desk and see you across the room at the office,' he shared, stealing my breath. 'It's my favourite thing at my new job.'

Whoosh – breath gone, just like that.

My heart slowly picked up speed as we studied each other in silence for a while. I waited. I waited because it seemed like I'd always waited for him. When the silence stretched, I couldn't stand it. I turned halfway towards him, resting my hip against the porch rail, my fingers gripping the wood tightly.

I slid him a guarded look. 'I think I'm gonna move sooner than expected. Nora said around a month, so I have to tell my dad, and everyone else, this week.'

'Are you going to meet with Elijah when you're there?'

'What?'

He moved closer, his arm touching mine.

'You heard me.'

I did my best to hold back my grin and gave him the honest answer. 'No. I'm not interested in Elijah. Although I'm pretty sure he was just being friendly anyway.' I paused. 'Do you think we were always meant to say goodbye? That first time we met and now?'

He moved, making my heart skip a beat and my breath rush out. One second he was right next to me, the next he had my back against the wooden rail, his hands gripping the wood right next to where my hands were.

His jaw was tight, eyes burning with intensity. I felt his hands tighten around the wood while his arms flexed with power, shoulders tense and unmoving.

'First of all, he was interested. Trust me, he was. And the fact that you don't see yourself the way I see you ... everybody sees you ... it blows my mind that you're not aware of yourself and the effect you have on people. Also, goodbyes are not what's on my mind right now, Charlie.'

My breath was coming out a little shaky as my chest rose and fell against his body. I closed my eyes and tried to calm down my frantic heartbeat.

'You're standing too close, William,' I whispered, brokenly. Being close to him at all times, or him grasping my hand in his whenever he could, was one thing I could trick myself into believing that he was just a little too friendly, but having him *this* close ... There was no way I could talk myself out of this again.

'What are you gonna do about it?'

I was too scared to open my eyes, but I carefully moved one of my hands, palm open, to rest on his chest. I wasn't thinking of pushing him away, but I needed to centre myself. When he bent down and rested his forehead against mine I was simply gone. I felt my fingers curl, clutching the fabric of his sweater.

'I think it's time. You have to ask me now,' he murmured.

'Ask you what?'

He pulled back. 'Why I didn't come that night. Why I came every night for a week just to see you and sit next to you at that diner, but why I didn't show up *that* last night.'

I took a deep breath and opened my eyes, only to get trapped under his gaze. 'You don't have to explain. It was years ago. It was probably stupid to expect anything would happen.'

'It wasn't stupid. I felt everything you felt too.'

'William, you don't have to say that.'

'I came, Charlie. I was there. I remember you constantly checking your watch. I watched you smile to the waitress and then as soon as she turned her back to you, your face fell. I came for you. To see you. How could I not?'

My mind whirled. Then my heart sank as realization dawned on me. 'You didn't want to walk in.' I let go of the grip I had on his sweater, but there wasn't enough space between us for me to move away.

He took my hand and pressed his lips into my palm right before he placed it back to where it had been, against his heart. It was beating just as heavily as mine. Then with the same hand he reached for my chin and tipped it up so I was open to his gaze.

'No, it's not that I didn't want to,' he said softly. He cupped my cheek and let his thumb caress my skin, sending a shiver down my spine. 'I couldn't. I got a message from my ex right as I got there. She'd been calling before, but I hadn't answered. You were all I could think about. I wanted to spend more time with you, I wanted to know what you looked like when you first woke up in the morning; so I came. I couldn't stay away. But her text . . . I called her back and she told me she was pregnant and she was wrong to say no to my proposal.'

My eyes widened. I knew he had married his ex, but I hadn't known he had asked her to marry him right before we'd met.

'In hindsight,' he continued before I could ask anything, 'I shouldn't have rushed. But I thought if she really was pregnant and I'd gone into that diner, I was gonna have a hard time walking away from this girl. I couldn't put you in the middle of something like that. And you were a stranger. A stranger I desperately wanted to be with, but a stranger nonetheless. And she was . . . I'd asked her to marry me and if she was carrying my child . . .'

He shook his head, dropped his hand away from my face and looked up at the stars for a second.

'I made the wrong choice, Charlie.'

Then his eyes came back to me.

I couldn't make any comments because I'd lost all words.

'Your ex and every other guy you've been with who made you cry? They are idiots. They should've held on to you for all their worth and tried their hardest to make you happy. Just so you'd choose them. You deserve it. Someone who is as real, as beautiful and as honest as you are deserves everything they want to have in life. And I hope like hell you want me now.'

The words hung in the air between us like little ice crystals soothing my tattered heart. I swallowed the heavy lump in my throat and watched William as his eyes moved over my face. My lips parted, and I realized I was clutching his sweater again. I let go of the railing behind me and put my other hand on his chest too. My hands were trembling a little.

'I really wanted you to come that day. I was sure you'd come,' I admitted quietly.

'I know, sweetheart. I could see it. You were wearing the black off-the-shoulder thing you had on that first night we met. I loved how you looked in it. I don't know if you were wearing jeans or something else underneath because you were sitting in our booth and you looked nervous and so beautiful. And I don't know if you'll believe me or not, but it hurt to walk away from you. I went back the following night and a few days following that. I still don't know why. Maybe because I couldn't get you out of my mind, and even then I wasn't sure what was gonna happen with Lindsey because it didn't feel the same anymore. So I came back to the diner, thinking maybe you'd be there. It was a long shot.'

'I didn't go back again . . .' My brows drew together. 'But, wait . . . you remember what I was wearing that night?'

His eyes moved between my eyes and my lips, and I stared transfixed, heart in my throat.

And just then the kitchen light came on, bright and unwelcome. We froze. My grip on his sweater tightened as if I was scared somebody would come out and pry him out of my hands.

William let out a low groan that only I could hear. His hands were still on the railing behind me, but his arms were now tight against my waist and he pushed his body against mine, locking my arms between us. If anyone looked out, they would only see his back. I was resting in a cocoon of William.

'For fuck's sake,' he cursed, his voice low and dark and deep right next to my ear. 'Don't you dare move or make a sound.'

I couldn't help it – I laughed, burying my face against his chest so it wasn't audible.

Whoever was in the kitchen was making an awful lot of noise, opening the cupboards and closing them, but it didn't look like they were about to come our way.

'I swear to you if someone comes out and takes you away, I'm going to lose it.'

He sounded a little desperate and it thrilled me to my bones. And it was a fact that I loved grumpy William. I turned my head just slightly and rested my temple against his hard chest. I could hear his heart beating hard and strong. He took a small step forward and our legs pressed against each other, my chest against his chest.

My whole body against his.

Then I realized it probably wasn't his phone in his pocket.

Seconds passed. I barely held myself back from squirming.

Then the noises stopped, the light went out and it was just the two of us.

'Are they gone?' he asked.

I peered over his shoulder. 'I can't see anyone.'

William waited for another ten seconds, then pushed back just a little.

I drew back from him slightly, but he didn't step back.

I looked up at him.

He looked down and straight into my eyes.

He was just there.

Right there.

Even though there was only a breath separating us, he moved closer until his nose was against the side of my nose.

Out of all the moments, I chose that one to start panicking because I knew . . . I *knew* he was going to kiss me. I could see it in his eyes. I also knew he would ruin me, and I wanted to ruin him for other girls too. I wasn't sure if I remembered enough to be able to do that, but I wanted to leave a mark on him, as insane as that sounded.

'Honesty?' he murmured, and I almost missed it.

I nodded, afraid to move.

'I still have a crush on you, Charlie.' He paused. 'I think more than a crush.'

I raised my eyes to his. 'Honesty?'

He gave me a barely there nod.

'I have a crush on you, too. I think I'll always have a crush on you.' Neither one of us moved as our confessions settled between us.

'Would you like to try me for a kiss?' he asked softly. His words, his voice a caress on my soul.

'William,' I muttered, just as his lips were about to graze mine, and closed my eyes.

'Yes, Charlie?' he whispered, stopping.

'I don't know if I – God, I hate myself for saying this. To you especially. But, it's not like you don't know about it already. To be honest, I don't think I remember how to do this. I don't want to mess it up,' I whispered.

'I don't think that's possible.'

'I watched YouTube videos.' Quickly I covered my hand over my mouth.

He raised a single brow, giving me an incredulous look.

I lowered my hand. 'I didn't say that. Please say you still want to kiss me.'

He laughed quietly and rested his forehead against mine, breaking tension in my heart.

I *was* going to kiss this guy. No matter what happened, no matter how bad I turned out to be, I would steal a kiss from him.

I smiled up at him.

He rested his palm against my cheek, and released a slow breath.

'Yeah,' he muttered, eyes fixed on mine. 'Badly.'

I nodded.

'You're good with that?'

I nodded even more enthusiastically, and he gave me a devastating smile.

Then he was leaning in, closing the little gap we had between us.

My eyes closed on their own. My heart was beating in my throat and the quiet night and world had slowed down to our pace.

His lips pressed against mine.

Once, and shivers covered my body, completely.

Then he pulled back.

I licked my lips, barely breathing, and tasted him when he angled his head and gently nipped my bottom lip. I tipped my head higher, searching for his mouth.

Slowly, he fitted his lip between mine and gave me one little kiss before pulling back.

My breath hitched, ready and eager for more.

'I was very good at this,' I mumbled, swallowing as I waited for another kiss.

'Hmmm,' he hummed.

'I promise, you'd have been impressed.'

'Show me then,' he breathed.

I got another kiss, this time it lasted for three seconds, and I felt his tongue tasting my bottom lip. My grip tightened on his sweater.

Pulling on it.

Pulling on William.

'Breathe, Charlie.'

His voice was nothing but a whisper on my skin. His lips moved over to the corner of my mouth and he pressed a gentle kiss to the spot while his fingers slid into my hair, his palm covering my cheekbone and my ear. My head dropped to the side, giving him full access.

'I've wanted to do this for a long time,' he mentioned, pressing his body flush against mine.

I was quite busy trying to remember how to breathe.

His lips pressed against my jawline. Once. Twice. While his stubble deliciously scratched at my sensitive skin. 'Your smell drives me insane. *You*, sweetheart, drive me insane without even knowing what you're doing.'

Next he kissed right below my ear. 'Charlie . . . Are you real?'

I lost my mind and moaned.

He practically groaned my name again, and his voice was so warm, so sweet, so hard and yet soft. It was anguish I was hearing in his voice, and I loved it. I loved that it was me who made him sound like that. It was my favourite sound in the world. His stubble burned my skin as he shifted back to my lips and his hand tightened in my hair.

He nipped at my lips again, sending a shiver through my spine.

'You're not gonna say anything?'

'Words are lost to me, I think.' I waited to understand what I was feeling. 'I want to make it good for you.'

'You are more than good for me, already. More than I've ever imagined.'

He kissed me softly with his warm and firm lips, and I opened my mouth for him. His tongue broke the seam of my lips and I whimpered – the sound coming from somewhere deep within me. He drew back before I could have enough.

I could hardly think over the beating sound of my heart.

I opened my eyes.

'More?' he asked, and I noticed how dark his eyes had become. How hard he was studying my eyes and then my lips as if he was barely holding himself back.

I nodded, thrilled and vibrating. And just like that he gave me more.

I stopped gripping his sweater with my right hand and slid it behind his neck, trying to make sure he wouldn't leave me, pulling him somehow even closer.

He licked my lips, tilted his head, tongue delving into my mouth, and fireworks exploded behind my eyes.

It started as soft, tentative and careful, but we were both pulling at each other. One of his hands was still in my hair, his grip tight. I pushed up onto my tiptoes just to get closer to him even though it wasn't physically possible anymore. His other hand coasted against my waist and he gripped the back of my shirt, crushing the fabric in his hand.

My head swam, a slow heat moving down from head to toe. We surfaced, two, three times just to draw in some breaths and then immediately went back in. The fourth time we had to stop, I was already feeling lightheaded.

I managed to open my eyes and stared at William's. We were both breathing in short bursts. I watched as something shifted in his gaze. His movements were slow and deliberate when he bent down, eyes still on mine, and picked me up. I let out a shallow gasp and wrapped my arms around his neck. He turned us around, found the little table that was standing between the two chairs and gently put me on it.

I skimmed my teeth over my bottom lip, my stomach fluttering.

Looking at me, William laughed huskily and dropped his forehead on my neck. I revelled in the fact that he was breathing so hard.

'I love kissing,' I whispered, my voice rough and drowsy as I touched my already swollen lips with my fingertips. 'I missed it.'

'I can see that,' he replied, his eyes heated.

I felt his wet and warm lips against my neck as he roughly dragged me forward to the edge of the shaky table by my hips. A little moan escaped from me when he pushed open my legs with his thighs and nestled himself against me.

'Shhh. Quiet. I'm not done.'

I was smiling at him, because I was giddy from our newfound closeness, when he wrapped his long fingers around my neck and tugged me to his mouth.

This kiss.

This specific kiss was to sate hunger, and I went in with all I had.

We kissed as if we had practised for *this* specific kiss in other lifetimes. Everything we lived and went through was so we could have this exact moment in this exact time. And there would never be any other kiss like this. Not with any guy other than the guy in my arms.

I felt the bulge between his legs growing and wrapped my legs around him. He stopped enough so we could breathe, then stroked my cheek with his thumb to hold me still and started kissing me again.

It was a very hard kiss. The kind that got your lips bruised and swollen.

It was more than I could've ever wished for and it was definitely worth all the years I'd waited.

I felt his left hand move under my shirt, and I gasped into his mouth at the contact, shivering as he dragged it up to my rib cage and stopped right below my breast. His hand tightened around me and I arched my back, savouring the way he bowed forward with me so he wouldn't have to stop kissing me. I smiled into our kiss and gripped his hair tighter.

Right when I was about to lose my head even more than I already had, the light overhead suddenly turned on, and I vaguely heard someone open a door from very far away.

I wouldn't say I mewled when William completely withdrew from me, but it was a close call.

'Uncle Willie.'

I was still panting when I looked to the side and saw a sleepy Ivy, holding her arms up so William would lift her up.

Quickly jumping down from the table, I tried to tidy up my hair and clothes which I could only imagine were a real mess.

'I can't find my toy,' she mumbled as she rubbed her eyes.

Beth and Nico had left to spend the night alone and Ivy wanted to stay behind with William.

He picked her up. It did something to my heart that William had to clear his throat a few times before speaking. 'Do you remember where you saw it last?'

'I think in the yard,' she mumbled, resting her head on his shoulder, eyes already shut.

'Okay, let's take a look then.'

'I'm gonna miss you, Uncle Willie. Can I sleep with you?'

William glanced at me over his shoulder so Ivy looked as well.

'Hello, Charlie,' she mumbled.

'Hi Ivy.'

'Did you lose something back here, too?'

'No.' I took a trembling step towards them and forced a smile on my face. It had never been mine in the first place, so I couldn't have lost that something. 'I was just having a . . . conversation with your uncle.'

She nodded sleepily. 'Kay.' Hugging his shoulder, she turned to her uncle. 'If we can't find it, can I sleep with you?'

William's gaze found mine again, and I offered him a small smile. Our night had just ended. I nodded at him and moved to go inside, because without his body heat and closeness I was starting to shiver.

'I'll go inside,' I said to both of them quietly. 'Goodnight.'

I got a *goodnight* from Ivy, but nothing from William, even though his eyes followed my every step. His fingers around my wrist stopped me before I could disappear through the door.

'Tomorrow,' he said.

It was both a promise and warning, but it didn't mean much since I was going to leave New York *and* William in a few weeks. I had to.

Don't ever change your life around for a guy.

I'd made a promise to myself. And I owed it to myself to keep it. So why did my heart hurt then?

22

William

She was avoiding me. I wasn't sure whether I wanted to laugh at her or be annoyed. The car ride back to New York had been a quiet one since it was 5 a.m. when we left Montauk and both pup and woman had fallen asleep on me ten minutes into our ride. Then when we made it to our street it was a rush to get to work in time and get started on the meetings we had lined up with the team. We were three hours into the work day and I hadn't had any alone time with her. At the end of our first meeting, before lunch, other than a fleeting touch here and there when she wasn't expecting it, we had had no contact.

What I really wanted to do was to get her alone so we could talk, but she was proving to be very slippery, as always. I stopped by her office just as Gayle showed up. I nodded in Gayle's general direction but kept my eyes on a flustered Charlie who was standing stock still before me.

'Charlie,' I started. 'Good morning.'

Her gaze moved between me and Gayle, eyes jumping back and forth.

'Good morning?' she answered sceptically.

'Good morning to me too,' Gayle added when there was a silence. 'Not that anyone wondered about me.'

Before I could ask if I could steal her away so we could have a moment to ourselves, Gayle's phone started ringing. She checked the screen and gave us a curious look. 'You two keep being weird, I have to take this one.' She walked a few steps into Charlie's office.

That left just the two of us, with our backs to a crowded office. I glanced around and realized everyone was busy with their day and no one was focusing on us anyway. We were standing right in front of her door and her back was against the wall, so while Gayle was busy with the call, I took a step forward and sneaked my hand around her waist, leaned forward to whisper into her ear. If Gayle turned she would see us, but anyone else in the office would think I was standing a little too close to Charlie and that would be it.

I smiled when I realized she hadn't stiffened. Quite the opposite, she leaned slightly towards me as well, and I enjoyed her breath hitch for a second, as a smile spread across my lips. I stood still for a moment. Taking in her scent, without being too creepy about it. 'Have lunch with me?' I whispered.

'What are you doing?' she shot back quietly, her nose touching my neck when she turned her head. Her chest was rising and falling a little quicker.

I pulled my hand back and took a step away from her.

'Asking you out for lunch,' I said, staring into her eyes and trying to look as innocent as I could. I would've much preferred to taste her lips and her skin once again. And then there was the spot right below her ear towards her neck . . .

She squinted at me as if she was trying to figure out what I was thinking.

'I can't,' she replied after a while. 'I'm going to skip lunch.'

I quirked an eyebrow. She hated missing lunch. 'Why?'

'Uh . . .' She lowered her gaze and glanced down at her phone. 'I have that thing you asked me to write. And something else I need to take care of for my dad.'

'What thing?'

She met my eyes. 'The thing we worked on at the weekend.'

'Ahh . . . that thing.' I leaned down again, but kept both my hands in my pockets. As much as I wanted my hands on her, there was no need to push our luck. 'You wouldn't be avoiding me, would you, Charlie?' I whispered.

She shook her head as I pulled back to look into her eyes. After I took her in, I leaned down again and paused when my lips were right next to her ear. I made sure that our bodies were not touching, but we were still standing a little too close.

'You look beautiful today,' I said simply before leaning back, but I chose to stay closer this time.

'What?' She looked down at herself and her cheeks flushed. 'Thank you, William.'

She was wearing a white pencil skirt with thin black stripes and V-neck thin black sweater. I lowered my voice. 'You look beautiful every day, Charlie. It doesn't matter what you're wearing.'

'That's kinda putting it on a little too thick.'

Noticing who was heading our way, I took another step back from her and waited as her dad came to her rescue.

'Good morning Douglas.'

'William. Laurel Nielson is coming up.'

'What? Why?' Charlie asked, confused.

I checked my watch as Charlie went through her phone to see if she had missed any calls. 'We have a meeting with her at 3.00 p.m. Not now.'

Douglas shook his head. 'You'll have to ask her. I saw her on my way up.' He briefly glanced at Charlie. 'The conversation you wanted to have has to wait for now. I'm leaving the office for a few hours. We'll talk tonight at dinner.'

I watched as Charlie cleared her throat and set her lips in a firm line. 'I'm sorry. I won't make it to the dinner this week.'

'Why?' Douglas sighed. 'Charlie, are you going on another date?

We're busy enough here, maybe you should take a break. You're not having any luck meeting someone decent anyway.'

I watched as her whole body tightened at his words.

'No. Not a date, Dad. Like I said, I won't be there. I'm busy.'

Douglas sighed, rubbing the bridge of his nose. 'Charlie, is this about the babysitting job? I need you in another meeting to get some notes for us. And you'll be working with Kim this week, I don't want you two to . . .'

'If it's okay with you, I need to get to Laurel with Charlie, Douglas. And as we discussed before, she is on my team. She is not going to work with anyone but me. I can't have her distracted with the problems other people should be qualified enough to handle. Try asking Kim for help. She needs the experience more than Charlie does to be honest. She needs to work on her people skills.'

Douglas opened his mouth to respond, but his phone started ringing and the words died in his mouth. 'I need to take this, but we're going to talk about this later.' He kept his gaze on me. 'I'll see you tonight, Charlie. I don't want any arguments.'

I ignored Douglas completely. 'Were you going to tell him about the move?' I asked, quiet enough that Gayle wouldn't hear as she walked towards us. 'Is that what he was talking about?'

She looked over her shoulder to find her friend, but Gayle was still on her phone.

Charlie glanced back at me, and nodded.

'I see. I want to talk to you about that as well. But first let's see why Laurel is early for our meeting.'

'Okay. Gayle?'

Her friend looked up, the phone still clutched against her ear.

'Laurel Nielson is here. Have drinks tonight?' There was a short pause, then she rushed to add, 'Just the two of us?'

She got a nod as a response.

I wanted to cut in and tell her that we needed to talk again, but held my tongue. Obviously she thought she could avoid me not just in the office, but tonight too. Well, she had another think coming. Looked like today I'd keep the promise I'd given her at the restaurant when she was with what's-his-face. Today was the day I would seduce Charlie Davis. It was going to be fun for me because I could clearly see how much she wanted me.

I smiled to myself and followed her out.

In the middle of the impromptu meeting Laurel took a phone call from her agent and I used the small pause in the conversation to put my hand over Charlie's restless pen-clicking hand. It was a habit of hers that had once annoyed me when I was trying to focus on work, and it had become a habit of mine to stop her whenever I was close enough to do so. But as I watched her play with her pen, I realized I'd gotten used to it in time. If she wasn't in a meeting with us, I actually missed the sound. Not as much as I missed having Charlie in the room, but it still made it into the list. It was too quiet without it. The silence too heavy.

Slowly, I covered her hand with mine and the clicking stopped. I kept my focus on our hands, but I could feel her gaze boring into my face, because usually whenever I stopped her by either pulling the pen away or covering her hand, my reactions were always instantaneous, an act without too much thought. This time I didn't move.

Laurel kept talking to her agent.

Suddenly out of nowhere it hit me. I knew I was going to miss Charlie, but it had just hit home just how much. When she left, I was going to notice her absence at every hour, if not minute, and miss her every day because I'd gotten used to having her so close to me. I was going to miss seeing the happy look on her face when I offered her my French fries or when I brought her lunch because she was too busy working for everyone. Even the absence of the damn pen clicking in the meetings was going to be a problem for me. The thought didn't make me happy.

I looked up and into her questioning eyes.

'Okay, I'm sorry about that. Where were we?'

Charlie was the first one to look away and pull out from under my hand. She cleared her throat. 'We need to consider which talk shows you'll appear on for your next press junket for the movie. We'll work with the PR team in the beginning to make the transition smooth for you. We don't want to have . . .'

In that moment I did something I'd never done in my career and stopped listening, stopped focusing on work. I pushed my hand under the table and put it on Charlie's thigh over her skirt. I watched as she stumbled over her words and looked down to the papers in front of her to realign her thoughts. I did nothing but watch her because I couldn't take my eyes away. I hadn't been able to take my eyes away from her for a good long while now.

And after kissing her this weekend . . .

I never wanted to stop.

As I watched her share our plans – plans that we had both worked on – I remembered something from her list that she had shared.

Find someone who is afraid of losing you.

Well, it looked like I was afraid. She had achieved that one too.

I gave her thigh an involuntary squeeze where her skirt had ridden up, as if I could keep her anchored here by my side, and noticed Charlie slowly putting her hand over mine. I waited to see if she was going to move it, but she didn't. I turned my palm upwards and laced our fingers together.

Slowly I started tuning into what they were talking about and looked up when Gayle entered the room.

'I'm sorry for interrupting, but I have some news I need to share if you could spare me a minute.'

A few seconds had passed by the time I realized she was actually addressing me. So much for seducing Charlie Davis. She was successfully seducing *me* without even lifting a finger or realizing what she was doing. When I thought about it . . . she had been seducing me from day one.

I cleared my throat and looked at Charlie. 'You have things in hand. I'll be back in a minute.'

All professional and lovely and beautiful, she nodded to me with a warm smile and turned her focus back on Laurel, whereas I was still sitting and staring at her like a lovesick boy.

'William?' Gayle tried again.

I quickly stood up and followed Gayle out.

It was an hour later when I found Charlie in the crowded kitchen. She was standing at the edge of a group, listening to someone giving their account of what sounded like an important meeting, while sipping on water. She always stood on the edge of life for one reason or another when she deserved to be at the very centre of it.

I stopped right behind her and spoke into her ear. 'Why am I missing you so much today?'

She stiffened for a moment, but then her body relaxed just as quickly.

'Maybe a flower pot or something fell on your head?' she whispered back over her shoulder with an amused tone.

I smiled, but she couldn't see. 'You want cheese, right? Here you go. Maybe you kissed the hell out of me and I don't know my up from my down anymore.'

As cheesy as it sounded, it was also very true.

There was a pause and then suddenly she burst into laughter, causing everyone to turn around and stare at us. I gave them all a small head nod, with my most stern look, reached in front of Charlie and grabbed a water bottle and fled the scene while Charlie was apologizing about a text message she had gotten.

The entire day became a cat-and-mouse chase across the office and I was enjoying the hell out of it. She had stopped avoiding me, but we were so busy that we couldn't stand still next to each other. I staked out her office for a good portion of the day and as soon as she left her room, I sneaked in and left a note. Managed to get in four notes in total.

They read:

I need to kiss you again.

I can't stop thinking about you.

What did you do to me? I can't keep my eyes off of you, I can barely work.

Happy looks so beautiful on you.

And she was happy, I could tell. She was looking for me with her eyes just as much as I was looking for her. And at the end of the day I don't know which one of us was more charged and on edge. When I realized she wasn't joking about skipping lunch, I went out and bought her French fries and left them in her room with no note.

'You're my inevitable, Charlie. I'm just as into you as you're into these French fries.'

When we had another conference call with the CEO of the airline company as a team, I waited until she entered the room and held her chair, then quickly sat right next to her. Before the call ended, when I got up to get myself coffee, I brought her a fresh one as well under the scrutinizing gaze of Rick and Stan. I ignored them all. When the meeting ended and each one of us exited the small meeting room, I held the door open for everyone, and when Charlie was the last one to leave, I made sure to place my hand on the small of her back to guide her out. It lasted only for two or three seconds and by the time she looked at me with a blush spreading across her cheeks, I was nodding at her and leaving also.

The whole day passed with more fleeting touches. And there was a whisper here and a whisper there without being too obvious about it.

She was sitting in front of her laptop in the shared working space and Trisha had just got up and left when I stopped by her side. Crouching down, I looked at the screen right over her shoulder. Her fingers stopped moving on the keyboard and she held her breath.

'What are you doing?' I asked quietly.

'Finishing up the last press release for Michael Ashton. Would you like to read it?' Her voice was just as quiet and soft.

'I need to,' I responded. 'But maybe not today. It seems I'm not able to focus on anything.'

Someone walked past from the other side of the desk and both Charlie and I stared at him; the guy didn't even glance our way.

She turned her head just slightly and met my eyes. 'Thank you for my lunch,' she whispered, and I had to physically hold myself back from cupping her face and giving her a soft kiss that matched her tone.

'This is killing me,' I said as a response.

Her brows furrowed.

'Not being able to touch you. Not being able to kiss you in front of everyone.'

Her eyes, her lips, everything about her softened and for a second there I thought I saw regret flash across her features, but as quick as it came it disappeared.

'You've done nothing *but* touch me today, William.'

I looked straight into her eyes. 'I touched you eleven times, Charlie. Not nearly enough. We're gonna have to talk eventually.'

'I know, but I'm a little afraid, if you couldn't tell.'

'I never saw you as someone who ran away from things.'

'I'm not running away.'

'Then what are you doing?'

She faced her laptop screen again. 'I don't know.'

All I wanted to do was reach out and gently bring her eyes back to me, but I couldn't push my luck, our luck, that much. The last thing I wanted before I could talk to Charlie and figure out our situation was to deal with Douglas or even her sister, who thankfully hadn't been in the office during the day. 'You won't until we talk about it.'

She started typing on her laptop again, which was my cue to leave.

I stood up, but then leaned down again because I had to. 'I won't hurt you, Charlie.'

She turned halfway to me, her shoulder resting against my chest. 'I know that.' She forced a smile on her lips, and it looked all wrong.

'We are a losing game, William. We both know it. That's all, but I don't know how to stop wanting you either.'

I frowned. What the hell was that supposed to mean?

'William, sorry to interrupt.' I looked up and saw Douglas's secretary waiting for me. 'Douglas is waiting for your meeting.'

I sighed and straightened up as Charlie faced forward again and began typing as if nothing was wrong.

Wilma gave me her usual smile and turned around and left. Before I could ask Charlie what she meant, Trisha came back and took her seat.

'Hey William. Is the press release done, Charlie?'

'Yes. Let me go over this last part again, then I'll send it to you to double check.'

I left them to their work and headed towards Douglas's office. The meeting took us an hour. When I first went into his room, I tried to catch Charlie's gaze a few times, but she didn't glance my way. Once I managed to focus it was almost the end of the meeting.

When I left his room Charlie was gone, but when I went into my office I found a piece of chocolate cake, my favourite, waiting for me on my desk with my very own note from her.

I don't know how you make me the happiest person, but you do. Thank you.

23

Charlie

I unlocked my door and entered my apartment, locking it immediately before resting my back against it. Trying to stay away from William, at least at the office, had become necessary to protect my sanity the entire day, and I had failed to do so multiple times. As many victories as he had won today, I had won the battle by managing to give him the slip. I wasn't sure what was happening between us, and I wasn't looking forward to the torture that I'd be going through if my heart didn't get what it wanted. It didn't matter that I was kind of hurting my heart anyway.

The torture aside, running away from William took some finesse, but I had managed it. My lips started to stretch in a big smile, I was proud of the hard-won battle. I heard Pepp jump down from my bed, where he loved to rest while he was waiting for me, with a happy yip followed by even happier tip-taps. I leaned down and gave him kisses whenever I could get them in and got hit in the face with his tail as he generally went crazy around me.

'Hi. Hey, handsome boy. Did you miss me?' I laughed. 'I missed you. I missed you like crazy. Yes. Did you have a good day? I had the best one.'

After our enthusiastic hello, he left me to go and drink some water while I took off my jacket and let out a long breath. My cheeks were all flushed from the cold, but whenever I thought about William and our kiss *and* his hand on my thigh, my whole body started burning anyway.

'What should we eat?' I asked the good boy, trying to keep my smile to a minimum as I took off my clothes and changed into my comfy oversized tee-shirt.

I grabbed my phone and sent Valerie a quick text. She'd been texting me non-stop the entire day, but I was enjoying making her squirm.

> **Charlie:** I no longer need to say that I need to be kissed.
> I've been kissed to my very limit.

I opened the cupboard and both Pepp and I stared at our options. 'We could make hummus. Or maybe the chicken in the fridge. Or tacos. Or . . .'

> **Valerie:** It happened on the weekend, didn't it? How could you not tell me? I've been dying here. You're evil!

Before I could respond I got another text from her.

> **Valerie:** And you don't even text me this morning with this news? Right as you wake up? Or was William with you? That's the only reason I'll forgive you.

> **Charlie:** Busy day at work. Sorry, no William.

> **Valerie:** You're the worst friend I've ever had. I'm waiting in line at this restaurant they've dragged me to. I'll call you tonight! Do not even dare to sleep before talking to me.

Charlie: I'll do my best.

Valerie: Just try me, Charlie. Just try me.

I was still smiling and had started taking out random ingredients I had no idea what to do with when the doorbell rang and Pepp let out a soft woof as if to let me know there was someone at the door. Cautiously, I put the cucumber I was holding on the counter and moved towards the door, but by the way my heart had started to beat in my throat, I had a good idea of who was on the other side of it.

I put a finger over my lips and shushed Pepp, waiting. I made sure to stay a little away from the door so whoever was on the other side couldn't hear me there.

Then there was a quiet knock.

Pepp let out another bark and kept looking at me and the door, his tail wagging happily.

'Come here,' I whispered, but he was already busy sniffing at the door and pawing it.

I winced and tiptoed closer. I stopped when I was inches away, feeling my heart in my throat already. I crouched down next to Pepp, trying to hold onto his wiggly body, but I underestimated his strength and with his excitement to see me on his eye level, he pushed me onto my ass.

'Ouch,' I exclaimed, forgetting I was trying to be quiet.

I froze.

Pepp licked my face.

'I know you're in there, Charlie.'

Yep. It was William on the other side of the door. I had spidey senses.

I stood up and tried to think of what I should do. If I opened that door, I didn't trust myself. Or him, for that matter. And if I didn't open it . . . I knew I'd regret it for a long time.

'Hello, William.'

I moved closer until I was touching the surface with my palm. Pepperoni looked at me for a beat, then moved back to his water bowl, leaving me alone with William. It didn't change anything that there was an actual door between us. My heart still sped up and ran with the fact that we were close to each other.

'Charlie,' William sighed, the sound muted through the wood.

His voice felt like warm liquid on my skin, causing me to close my eyes and rest my temple against the smooth surface. What was the worst thing that could happen?

'What are you doing here?' I asked, just as low as he had.

'We need to talk.'

I moved my head so my forehead was against the door and splayed my fingers as if I could push through and touch William. Talking inside my apartment would not be the best idea. There was no one to make sure we behaved. And if I had to be honest, behaving when it came to William was the very last thing I wanted to do. I glanced at Pepp and he was sprawled out in our tiny kitchen area, having already forgotten that someone was outside. So no saviour there.

'About?' I asked, trying to sound matter-of-fact.

There was a pause on the other side.

'You want to do this through a door?'

'What do you mean?' I asked, playing the innocent.

I heard a chuckle.

'Did you think I wouldn't come after you left me such a note?'

'I was just being honest.'

'Open the door, Charlie.'

'Why? What are you going to do?'

'What do you want me to do?'

'I don't want you to do anything.'

'Are you sure?'

'Very sure.'

'Then it should be okay to open the door.'

'I'm kind of not decent.'

'Open anyway.'

'No kissing, William. I mean it.'

I heard a chuckle coming from the other side.

'Why no kissing?'

I could tell he was very amused just by the sound of his voice.

'You know why.'

'Enlighten me again.'

'With my kiss?'

This time when he laughed it was louder.

'Just open the door, please. We'll see how it goes with the kiss and you enlightening me. Just . . . open the door first, please.'

With one hand on the lock, I sighed. 'William, I don't know if I can. You're going to hurt me.'

'Impossible.' There was a pause. 'I'll hurt myself before even imagining hurting you, you should already know that. I have things to say to you. *We* have things to say to each other. You know we do. We can't run anymore.'

We did have things to say to each other. I couldn't avoid him wherever I went. Not to mention if today was anything to go by, he had no plans to make this easy on me.

I opened my mouth to speak but he got there before me.

'Tell me you didn't know this was exactly where we'd end up after that first day at the office.'

Opening my eyes with a frown, I unlocked the door and slowly opened it, peeking through the little space I'd allowed myself first.

'What gibberish are you talking? Of course I didn't know we'd end up here.'

He was standing there, with his hands in his pant pockets, still wearing the same suit he wore that day, but he looked messier. A little undone and roughed up at the edges as if he was nervous. As if *I* made him nervous.

True or not, the idea thrilled me.

I met his eyes and he let out a long breath and smiled as if seeing me – well, a small part of me – had made his day *and* night all the better. As if he hadn't just spent the entire day working beside me.

'Hello, Charlie,' he murmured, his shoulders relaxing.

'Hello,' I returned. 'How can I help you?'

His lips stretched into a smile and he never moved his eyes from mine, forcing me to keep the eye contact.

'You can help me by inviting me inside.'

I thought about it, but there wasn't much to think about. He was at my door, and my heart was beating in my throat.

Before I could say something witty, Pepp took it out of my hands by nosing the door open wider and getting all excited around the newcomer.

I had to pull back so both of them could come inside unless I was willing to leave my dog out, and I wasn't willing to leave either one of them out now that he was here. William kneeled down so Pepp could be at eye level and show his excitement at seeing a friend more enthusiastically. He barked twice.

'Hello to you too, Pepperoni,' he replied, giving him a full rub-down.

I hung onto the door and waited for them while I considered what he thought we needed to talk about. We had kissed. It had been a spectacular kiss, but I think I was afraid to believe it could go any further than that. Not because I didn't want him, but because I was scared to have the talk he wanted to have. But did it make my heart ache? The fact that I had to move and the one that got away could finally be mine after all these years, yet I couldn't just let go and fall? Did I have to make a decision? I knew I did, but my heart . . . I wasn't sure how to handle anything.

Eyes heavy on me, William straightened. Pepp made circles around him and started chattering away with soft growls and soft barks as he literally led him into our home.

'You don't say,' William responded to the growls, eyes on me the entire time as he walked inside. 'I was thinking the same thing.'

Pepp ran ahead and grabbed his favourite rope toy and was already playing with it. Probably hoping the guy who was standing right next to me would come and play too.

William pushed the door closed for me. I turned around and pulled at the hem of my tee-shirt as I walked the few steps to the kitchen.

'Can I get you anything?' From my peripheral vision I saw him pet Pepp's head when he offered him his toy and then come straight towards me. 'Water?' I reached for a glass and decided to get myself some. 'Or I have soda? I was about to start cooking so I don't have too much time to talk, so whatever it wa—'

I stopped moving towards the fridge to get the water when I felt his body heat right behind me and my elbow bumped his hard stomach.

He grunted, and mortified I'd hurt him, I turned around, only to be imprisoned against his hard body and the counter behind my back. How did I keep finding myself in this position with this guy? I tried to let out a calming breath and stand taller. I looked straight into William's eyes because I couldn't not do it.

'Pepp? You want some water?' I asked, eyes still on him, and my beloved dog, the little traitor, was too busy snacking on his favourite toy to notice my predicament.

William just waited.

And waited.

'So, no water for you either, I take it?'

He tilted his head, his lips so inviting as he gave me a small smile. Then he took another step into me and I had to grab the edge of the counter so I wouldn't touch any part of his body. Which was pointless, since he was close enough that our chests were already touching and I was dying for him to kiss me, touch me.

'No water for me either,' he repeated.

'Hot Cheetos, maybe?'

'That was random. But, no, I don't think so.'

'I love Hot Cheetos.'

'I'll bring some over.'

He moved for me, so I moved my upper body slightly back, my heart doing happy cartwheels in my chest against my brain and logic. Logic saying that having William in my apartment and this close was bad bad bad. But my heart . . . my heart was a hopeless romantic.

'Okay.'

'So I was a one-night stand for you?' he asked, shocking me out of my stupor of having him so close.

'What?'

'I must be if I have the no kissing rule enforced on me.'

'I think you have to have sex to be a one-night stand.'

'Hmmm. You think so?'

I nodded, my gaze jumping between his lips and his playful eyes.

He closed his eyes and rested his forehead against mine, humming as he stood just like that. 'I've wanted to be exactly right here ever since last night.'

My traitorous body relaxed at his words, my eyes falling closed, but my fingers gripped the edge of the counter tighter. I felt him nuzzle his nose against mine and although I felt like my heart was about to burst with something building in my chest, I found myself tipping my head just slightly up, responding to him.

Then his lips were *right* against mine. Almost touching as he breathed me in, making me feel dizzy and breathless and all out of words. I don't know what exactly got into me, but suddenly I swayed a little.

I felt his hand pull on my grip on the counter, then his fingers slipping through mine as he held on to me.

Truth be told, I was afraid to open my eyes, so I didn't.

'I've been wanting to do this again all day, too,' he admitted, his voice soft against my skin.

'It feels like I've wanted you since forever.'

I reached up and pushed my hand along his chest while our foreheads were still resting against each other and curved my fingers around his shoulder, holding on for dear life.

He gave my fingers a soft squeeze.

'Can you open your eyes for me, Charlie?'

'I'm not sure. Do I have to?'

He chuckled and the sound travelled over every inch of my skin.

My eyes were still closed, but I sensed his hand push back my hair, his fingers moving against my neck, leaving goosebumps in its trail. 'I need you to be honest with me right now. Why don't you want me to kiss you?'

'Because it can't be good for us.'

'Says who?'

I didn't have a good answer. I opened one eye. *Our situation* didn't seem like it was doing the trick anymore when I was almost done caring about the fact that I was going to move in a few weeks. My heart was gutted.

He nodded at my silence as if it was the right answer.

'Okay, this is what we're going to do. We're going to tell each other things we couldn't before now. Things we wanted to but couldn't, okay? Everything you have locked up here ...' he placed his palm over my heart '... we're going to share it with each other, because that's what we're good at. We're good at telling each other everything. And that's exactly what I want from you. Everything. That's it. We're not going to think about the why or the how. Not in this moment.'

My heart rate picked up.

Everything sounded like a lot.

'But first, do you want me to kiss you again? Because, Charlie ...' he sighed and his gaze dropped to my slightly parted lips. 'I really need to kiss you.'

I nodded and unconsciously licked my lips. That little movement seemed to be the only thing I was capable of at that moment in time.

'I need the words, Charlie.'

'I do,' I breathed out.

Then, he finally *finally* gave me a kiss and my heart sighed in happiness. His teeth gently bit on my lower lip, causing a shallow gasp to slip from me, and then his tongue was there and he was softly kissing me.

This was our second kiss, and it was somehow even better than the first one. And the first one was already insane. But maybe because we were in New York, and in my apartment, it somehow felt more real. Back at his mother's place, as mind-blowing as the kiss had been, it had felt like a one-time deal.

This one felt . . . more.

I groaned, pushing my body against his as he curled his arm behind my back and squeezed my fingers while pulling me towards him with our joined hands.

What started as a small kiss suddenly turned hotter as he coaxed me deeper into it. And then his free hand made its way up to my throat as he gently tilted my head back so he could give me more. And I pretty much lost it, because his hand on my face, on my throat, on my skin . . . It was the sexiest thing in the world. He was absolutely without a doubt my best kiss. I remember groaning and then all of a sudden he pulled back and my eyes snapped open in disappointment. Both of us breathless, we just stared at each other and the fog he seemed to create in me dissipated and I watched his eyes burn for me. I found myself leaning forward, and he didn't make me ask for it twice. He came back to me, his fingers pushing, delving deep into my hair as he cupped the back of my head.

'You're dangerous for my sanity,' he whispered against my burning lips as we both tried to catch our breath. I felt his lips stretch against mine and I knew he was smiling. 'I don't think I'm ever gonna get used to the taste of you.'

Something pushed at my leg and we both looked down to see

Pepp nudging his way right between William and me and just standing there, one of his paws on William's foot as he gave me puppy-dog eyes – something he had mastered on day one.

'Hey you,' I said quietly. 'I know it's dinner time. It'll be ready in a few, promise.'

'I don't think he is after food. He is jealous, I believe,' William muttered, his voice thick. I blinked back up at him, still feeling a little disoriented. 'Can't blame him. How could he not want you just for himself?'

'It's food. Trust me. We love food in this apartment.'

William's lips curled up and my eyes locked on to them.

'I know you do,' he answered softly, his hand coming up to caress my cheek, 'I wanted to pick something up for you, but I needed to be here more. I couldn't wait in a line. I'm sorry.'

My blood boiling in my skin from the look he was giving me, I found myself leaning towards him again as he mirrored my move and I skimmed his bottom lip with my teeth.

'As much as I want to make up for all the years I've missed doing this, we need to talk,' he mumbled, his eyes betraying his words as he aimed them to my mouth again.

Then there was a soft growl.

Shocked, I looked down at Pepp to see he was wagging his tail, eyes on me. I watched as he turned his body, successfully pushing William away a step. His hand dropped from my face and I turned my focus back on William.

'He *is* jealous!' I exclaimed with a big smile.

William returned my smile and took another step back. 'He loves you. Of course he is jealous.'

Our gazes stayed locked and something big bloomed in my chest. I kneeled down to give Pepp a hug and many kisses on his face. 'I love you too,' I whispered. 'Wanna have dinner?' His tail picked up speed, and I straightened up so I could feed him and give myself some time to come down to earth.

I picked up Pepp's food bowl and busied myself, feeling William's gaze on me the entire time.

'Can I get you anything?' I asked, looking at him over my shoulder, but not really looking at him.

'Just you.'

I started laughing. 'Stop, please. You're killing me here.'

'I'm just being honest.'

'Okay. Have it your way.'

I finished filling Pepp's food and water bowl and turned around to face William, who was standing with his back against the door, arms crossed against his chest.

I gestured towards the couch. 'Would you like to have a seat?' Compared to his, my apartment was probably half the size, but I liked my place. It was cosy and inviting.

Instead of taking a seat, he came to me. He didn't crowd me, but he was standing closer than he had been a second ago.

'I don't think that's going to work for me anymore.'

'What won't work for you anymore?'

'Space. Between us. Here is the thing, Charlie. I'm crazy for you. It's been like that for a while. And I remember what you told me at that bar we went to with everyone else, my first week here. You said, *I want a man who knows what he wants and isn't scared to ask for it or work towards getting it.* I know exactly what I want right now. And I'm not scared to ask for it.'

My pulse sped up, and I worried my lips between my teeth, trying to *think.* I had a wild guess about what he wanted and I wasn't sure what that meant for our future.

'William,' I started and shook my head, heading towards the couch to take the seat he had refused to take. 'I can't do that. I can't . . . I wouldn't be able to . . .'

Before I could finish my sentence he was kneeling in front me.

'Tell me what you think I want from you? If I had to guess from the look on your face . . . sex?'

I hesitated.

'Remember, we're going to follow your list and we're going to be honest with each other. We're not gonna lose another shot at this, Charlie. Anything you want to or have to say to me, I want it to be true. Don't think. Just tell me whatever you're feeling.'

I was still stuck on the fact that he was on his knees in front of me, but I tried to be as honest as I could. 'I'm leaving in less than a month, William. The only thing you could want from me is probably sex. Until I leave. To get it out of our systems. I can't do that with you. You're more . . . you mean more to me.'

'That's the only thing you can think of?'

I nodded. There was no other way for us.

'Okay. Point to you. Since we're being honest, you're right, I do want to have sex with you. Badly. I can't stop thinking about the look you'll have on your face when I push myself inside you for the first time. I want to know what your eyes will tell me when I'm moving inside you.' He moved forward and I held my breath. 'I'm dying to know what you like, how you like it. Fast? Slow? Deep? Will you let me take my time with you or will you beg me to go faster. I want to learn and memorize every inch of your skin. I want to know your favourite position. And I want to learn the noises you make and what each and every one of them means so I can take care of you.'

I swallowed. Hard. But didn't move a muscle.

'Are you loud? Quiet? Would you want me every day or less? As it is with everything when it comes to you, I want to learn everything about you, Charlie.'

Whoosh . . .

There went the air in my lungs.

He stared at me, and I stared back.

'You don't have anything to say?'

I shook my head, my cheeks heating up. Not from embarrassment, but need.

His lips twitched and he reached forward to tuck a piece of my hair behind my ear. Just that small action and the familiarity of it caused all kinds of emotions to stab at my chest. I wanted this guy that was kneeling in front of me more than I'd wanted any single person before. In my bed *and* in my life.

I heard Pepp finish his dinner and start drinking his water. Soon enough he'd be back.

I cleared my throat as William's hand dropped from my face.

'I . . .' I started, but he shook his head.

'I'm not done, Charlie. So yes, I do want you in my bed, on top of me, under me and next to me. In any way I can get you I want you. But that's not all I want.'

I watched as he put both his hands on my thighs and gently parted them so he could get closer to me. Coincidentally, I was seconds away from hyperventilating. I didn't think I could have him in my bed and then act like we were just friends at the office. I didn't even handle just kissing him well, since I spent the entire day trying to avoid being alone with him worrying I'd give in and kiss him in front of everyone. If we were to have sex, it'd be even worse. Not to mention I'd have a hard time not thinking about our expiration date.

'Then what do you want from me?' I asked, my voice low and surprisingly a little shaky. 'In the spirit of being honest, I feel like I'm on the edge of a cliff right now.'

He squeezed my thighs with his hands.

'You,' he said quietly and simply.

My brows furrowed, not catching on what he meant. Yet the fact that he was saying that word still lit a fire inside me.

'What do you mean?'

'Everything about you makes my heart happy, Charlie. After my marriage, I didn't trust women. But you? You're different. You've always been different. I trust you. I didn't want to date. I wasn't interested whatsoever. Just wasn't the time. But you? I'm interested in you. A lot. I want to be what you need. I *know* I can be what you need.'

My heart thudded in my chest.

'Your eyes and your smile? I can talk about those two forever. The way your eyes look at me when you think I don't know you're doing it . . . there is always a shy smile accompanying it – as if you can't help yourself. And that secret little smile you have when you're trying to hold yourself back from smiling full-on? You lick your lips and bite on your lower lip, but I can still see how much trouble you're having holding it in and all I want to do when I see it is just laugh with you. But the way I can see how sad you are when I look into your eyes, even when you're trying to give smiles to everyone around you? That one hurts me and it makes me want to hurt whoever made a chip in your heart. And then your eyes give me more and they start to shine when I look into them and silently try to tell you I know how sad you are right now and I'm here for you, I will always be here for you. Then I watch your beautiful, beautiful eyes as they fill to the brim and you blink back your tears and avoid my gaze. Because you know . . . you know I know you. You know in your heart we've been waiting to find each other again and you can't hide yourself from me. So Charlie, I want you. In every aspect of my life.'

Just like he said, my eyes filled with unexpected tears and I blinked them away. Missing just one tear as it found its way down my cheek. He wiped it off before I could.

'I don't want you to cry. I never want to see you cry again.'

'William, I . . .'

The doorbell rang, and I jumped in my seat as Pepp started barking at the door.

William got up, way slower than I did, and offered me his hand, pulling me up from my seat. I needed the support because I was too shocked to be able to move on my own, but I somehow made it to the door and opened it, with Pepperoni gazing behind my legs.

It was Antonio, Josh and Daisy, so Pepperoni stopped hiding and joined his friend for an enthusiastic hello.

'Uh, hi guys,' I mumbled and with a small jolt realized William was now standing right behind me, his chest on my back. After everything he had just said, the closeness of him had gained new meaning, and I realised I wasn't wearing all that much.

'Hello,' Antonio said, eyes going from William to me. 'We ... wanted to ask if you and Pepp wanted to join us for a walk with Daisy since the weather is getting softer, but you have company, so ...'

My brain was still a little fuzzy so I couldn't find my words. 'Ummm ...'

'You must be Antonio and Josh,' William said, extending his hand.

'Ah, sorry guys. I'm a little distracted tonight. This is William. He is my ... colleague from work.'

They shook hands.

'And her friend, too, I would hope,' he added, giving me an inquisitive look.

'Yes, friend, too,' I repeated.

'If you two are busy ... with work or something else, we can happily take Pepp with us,' Antonio put in, his eyes going back and forth between William and me.

'I'm not sure ...'

'We'd really appreciate it. I wanted to have a talk with Charlie,' William said over me.

I started shaking my head, not because I didn't want to or was afraid to be alone with him, but because I liked the idea of having Pepp around as a buffer if needed.

'You really don't need to,' I stated. 'You know he isn't the best on a leash yet, I don't want him to tire you guys out. He's gaining weight by the day it seems and you already have Daisy and ... I was gonna take him out myself later,' I ended my ramble lamely.

Both Josh and Antonio smiled. 'Sweetheart,' Josh started, clearly amused, 'it's safe to say both Josh and I are bigger than you. We can handle a pup if you can.'

I flushed a little. For crying out loud, of course they could. And it wasn't the first time he had gone out for a walk with them. Heck, I left him with them while I was at work so many times.

'Come on,' Josh prompted. 'Get his leash. We'll take care of your baby.'

'I— okay. Uh . . .' I looked around, avoiding William's gaze, and left them to go and get Pepp's leash. The good boy followed me and patiently waited as I put it on him. 'I love you,' I murmured. 'Be a good boy, okay?' I gave him a kiss and then another one and we walked back to the door where William and the boys were chatting.

'He's ready,' I announced and William's eyes came to me.

My stomach flipped, so I looked away and handed Antonio the leash. Pepp took a step towards him, but then turned and glanced at me to see if I was following him. I gave him another quick kiss as Josh laughed at me. 'Bye, baby. Be good.'

'We'll take care of your boy, don't worry, sweetheart,' Josh said, before another round of goodbyes between everybody, and then I closed the door and that was it.

We were alone.

My mind racing, I stood facing the door, my hand still on the handle.

'You're not gonna look at me?' William asked, his voice low.

I took a deep breath and turned to face him and tried to steady my heart because it didn't look like he was done with it yet.

We locked eyes and William closed the distance between us. I linked my fingers behind me so I wouldn't be tempted to touch him. Not yet. Not until I understood exactly what he was asking of me.

'Honesty?' he asked quietly.

'You like me?' I shot back. 'A lot?' More than a question, it was a statement, but I was trying to make sure.

He smiled with his eyes. 'I have the biggest crush on you, Charlie. I like every single little thing about you, yes.'

'Why?'

'Remember how I told you your ex and every other guy is an idiot. I'm not an idiot, Charlie. I want you, you must know this. I hope I'm someone you want to have in your life too.'

I swallowed the heavy lump in my throat. I was rooted to my spot.

'You are,' I whispered.

He took one more step and put his hand on my waist, pulling me just a little more firmly against his body, and rested his forehead against mine. My eyes shuttered closed and I let out a big breath.

'Tell me more,' he whispered back, his hand cupping my face, his thumb touching my bottom lip. 'I told you everything I was holding in. Tell me more.'

Feeling a little dizzy with all the emotions and possibilities rushing through me, I tilted my head and let everything I was holding inside when it came to William loose. 'I always wondered how it would be to be loved by you. Even back then and now. How I would feel. What it would do to me. Would I be ruined for any other men? Would I always keep it with me? Would you be ruined for every other person that would come after me? I have the biggest crush on you too. Always did.'

'Charlie.'

My name was a sigh coming out of his mouth and it warmed something inside me, made me relax into his touch.

He reached around and took one of my hands into his, linking our fingers. I realized how much he loved doing that, after the first time he'd done it at his place.

'Do you remember telling me how lonely you felt? And that you wanted to belong to someone or someplace? And that you wanted someone to belong to you?'

A little shocked that he'd remember any part of my ramblings, I nodded so he could keep going.

'That's my offer. If you'll have me. I still don't understand how someone like you can even begin to feel lonely, but I'm going to take advantage of the situation and not look a gift horse in the mouth. Their stupidity and loss. You're my biggest wish to date, Charlie Davis.'

'William,' I started, trying to think, but failing miserably. 'I'm moving. Yet I want you so much too. I don't know ... I still want to ... and you know I promised myself and I have to do ...'

'I know ... I know. We'll figure out a way. I just want a chance. I can't miss my shot with you again. I just know it'll be one of the biggest mistakes of my life if I do that. Again. So we'll figure out a way.'

My mind worked a mile a minute.

'Long-distance?' Even I could hear the unenthusiastic tone in my voice. 'I can do that, but can you?'

'You like honesty and certainty. Here is what I can offer. We have a little less than a month before you go. We're going to make the best of every second. And when our time is up and it's time for you to leave, we'll try long-distance for a little. If you love your new job and want to stay in California, then we'll figure out another way. My contract ... I can't leave your dad's firm for the next few months, but after that, if you still want me, you'll have me wherever you want. If this thing we have between us stays exactly like this without showing any signs of disappearing, then I'll move.' He nuzzled my nose. 'I'll come to you.'

Now I was seriously getting lightheaded and I leaned more firmly against the door. Sitting would've been the better option, but I didn't think I could make it to my couch without ending up on the floor on my way over there ... I didn't think it would look cool on my part.

Craig, my ex, who had been with me for almost a year prior to leaving for London, had never uttered anything like that to me. I was going to go to him. I was going to change my life for him or to be with him. It was never him doing anything for me. And then he had ended the relationship because he had met someone new.

'But you just moved from California. You said you didn't like it. What changed?' I shook my head, trying to clear the fog. As much as I loved everything coming out of his mouth, I couldn't disregard his earlier thoughts. 'You said you missed being near family. You wanted . . . I don't want you to resent me down the road . . .'

'You, Charlie. I want you. And if this thing between us can go somewhere, I can't have you that far away from me. I'm already jealous over you. For the first time in my life I'm jealous about someone. Blind dates? No. Even if it's just for practice or whatever reason, I can't take it. If you're smiling and laughing with somebody at the office, it drives me insane. I want to come and just stand near you, be a part of your conversation, so they know that I'm in your life. That I matter to you more than they do. I want to be your number one.'

He stopped speaking and I met his eyes. He hadn't asked a question, but I could see he needed an answer.

'You are.' I put my hand on his chest, slightly clutching the fabric of his shirt in my hand. 'You matter to me. I don't see anybody but you. You must know this already'

'And they can't have you. You said you loved clichés. You must love that you're making me jealous.'

I smiled at that. 'I think I do love hearing it.' I paused. 'Yeah, I love the idea of you being jealous. I didn't know. I wouldn't have guessed. I thought you were acting and pretending with Elijah just to make me smile. I thought you were playing.'

'You make me go crazy at the office. Trust me. I'm not used to being jealous, I don't particularly like it, but I'm crazy about you. I barely hold it together when you get close to another guy that is flirting with you.'

'They're not flirting with me.'

'Yes. You keep thinking like that, please.'

For a few long moments we just stared at each other.

'Every single day I'm astonished that you don't see the effect you have on people. Men especially. You're like a magnet.'

I felt he was exaggerating a little bit, but didn't make a comment. I worried my bottom lip between my teeth and his attention snapped to that. My back still to the door, I got on my tiptoes and pressed my lips to his and in a second he pushed his body harder against mine, groaning as he forced my mouth to open and gave me a hard kiss that took my breath away and made me go weak at the knees.

'Yes?' he asked, out of breath when he let me go for a breath of air. 'You're in? You're okay with this? Us, trying? Long-distance and everything.'

Smiling from ear to ear, I nodded. 'I never thought I'd get excited about the idea of having another long-distance relationship, but I think this is one of the promises I don't mind breaking because I'll get to have you.'

He moved his hand to my hips and kind of forced me to jump so he could have me plastered against the door. I wrapped my legs around his waist, my arms around his neck. I was still laughing and feeling a little tipsy on all the excitement and happiness in my heart and lighter than I'd felt in a very long time.

'I'm a little heavy,' I breathed, having a hard time breaking our eye contact.

'You're perfect.'

'You know hearing that will start to go to my head, right?'

'If you knew the things I wanted to do to you, I don't think you'd say that.'

I tightened my legs around his body, feeling him harden against me.

'I don't think I gave you a tour. Did you want to see my bedroom?'

He burst out laughing, and I smiled into his eyes. Not being able to stop, I gently ran my fingers through his hair.

'I've always wanted to do that.'

'I can't stay away from you, Charlie.'

I tilted my head and smiled down at him. 'I don't think I'd want that. So what now?'

'Now comes the best part.'

'Sex?'

Smiling, he pressed a kiss on my neck and gently dropped me back down on my feet.

'Now, I take you out to dinner.'

A small thrill went down my spine. 'Like a dinner date? Our first date? Not even a fake date, a real real date.'

'First official, as real as it gets, date, yes. If you're going out with a guy, that guy is me.'

Feeling giddy, I bit down on my bottom lip and didn't even try to hide my big smile.

24

William

It was the sweet and happy smile on her face that did me in. I waited for her as she texted her neighbours to see if they could watch over Pepperoni until we returned. They texted her back to say they wouldn't mind keeping him overnight if she wanted to stay out late and I watched as she blushed – then I waited some more as she disappeared into her room to change. But then she was standing right in front of me in a polkadot dress under her coat and a beanie, and all I could think about was taking everything off her and staying inside. But she was almost all mine, and soon we'd have all the time in the world for me to do anything and everything I'd always wanted to do to her.

'What are you thinking?' she asked, her eyes twinkling.

'No more blind dates anymore. No more looking or trying or anything.'

She raised her brows and waited for me to go on.

'I'm going to kiss you every day, so you never forget how it feels.'

'Every day, huh? That's a pretty big promise.'

I reached out to her because now I could. Now I didn't have to stop myself when my instinct was to touch and feel. Something inside me settled. This was what I wanted with her. Always close to me. She came towards me without a second of hesitation.

I pushed my fingers into her hair and tilted her head with my thumb against her jawline.

I stopped when my lips were against hers. Hers parted.

'I will gladly kiss you every day; that's not something you ever have to worry about again.'

She started laughing, and that's when I kissed her – pushing my tongue into her mouth and revelling in her gasp and then soft moan.

When we stopped, we were both out of breath, and our bodies were flush against each other.

'If we don't leave now, this is gonna be a problem,' I whispered.

'I don't see the problem,' she whispered back, softly. 'And what if I started to enjoy going out on blind dates?'

I sighed. 'I'll take you out and we'll pretend we just met.' I turned her and headed towards the door. 'Knowing you, you'll probably like that more than the real thing.'

'Oh, do I get to be whoever I want to be?' She asked over her shoulder, her eyes sparkling with mischief.

'We'll see. I want to take you out now. Can I do that?'

She smiled her gorgeous smile. 'I'd like that.'

I grabbed her hand and stepped out. 'I've got a surprise for you.'

Rushing her out the door wasn't one of my greatest ideas, but it was necessary if I didn't want to lose the battle against myself. The weather was starting to turn properly into spring and it wasn't as cold as it had been just days ago, so it was the perfect timing for the motorcycle ride I'd promised her.

'You're lying,' she exclaimed as I stood in front of the motorcycle and she did a slow walk around it. 'This isn't yours.'

'Why would I lie?'

'You bought it for me?'

'No,' I repeated, 'I didn't buy it for you. I rented it.'

'It's the same thing.'

'No, I've rented it for twenty-four hours. There is a huge distinction.'

'It's the same thing,' she repeated, eyes still on the bike. 'You like me so much that you bought a motorcycle. So you have a licence to use it. I'm actually going to drive a motorcycle.'

I laughed quietly, shaking my head. 'No, you're not gonna be driving anything. I'm the one who has a licence so I'll be doing the driving.'

She waved her hand my way. 'We'll see.'

'No. We won't see, I need you to stay in one piece. Do you want to go to dinner or do we have to stand around and just stare at it for another ten minutes?'

Finally she looked up at me with a huge smile. 'We can go. Definitely. Dibs on the black helmet.'

'I'm not wearing the pink one, Charlie.' I moved forward to get the black one from her hands.

'Then let me drive. I'm not saying I want to drive in traffic, I don't want to die just yet. But down the street? I can totally do that. Please?'

'I don't think so. I'm starving, let's go.'

'Do you get grumpy when you don't eat?'

'I never get grumpy.'

'Okay, whatever you say. So . . . it's a no on the driving? Still?'

I shook my head and got on the motorcycle before she could jump on and try something. I patted the seat behind me. 'Come on. I made reservations.'

Smiling, she took a step towards me and all I wanted was to wrap my arms around her waist and pull her in.

'Just one more thing,' she whispered, her body now brushing against my thigh. 'Are you telling me you really rented a bike for me because I told some guy I've always wanted to go on one?'

I decided to let go of the hold I had on my instincts and wrapped my arm around her waist and pulled her in until I was very close to her face. I had to close my eyes to stop myself from going for her lips.

'All I want to do when you look at me with those eyes is kiss your beautiful lips, Charlie.' I took a deep breath and opened my eyes to stare into hers. 'Yes, I got it for you. But this isn't anything big. You shouldn't be impressed. You deserve so much more. But I do want you to know that I listen to you, and I hear everything you tell me. I told you I'd get you on a bike. Get used to having someone in your life who keeps his promises.'

She nodded, her eyes half-closed already.

'If I kiss you, we might still end up going back inside, so let me take you out to dinner, okay?'

I got another nod. Then she got up on the seat behind me, put on her helmet and wrapped her arms around my waist.

I sat up straighter and my dick hardened in my pants. It was going to be a long, long dinner.

Three hours later we were back on our street. Charlie got off the bike and I followed her.

'That was the best thing!' she announced, louder than her usual volume. I took off my own helmet and then helped her take off hers. Her cheeks were flushed, her hair mussed in the best possible way, reminding me of all the things I wanted to do with her that would give her that kind of hair, but even better. And she had such a big smile on her face that it was hard not to smile back at her.

'I'm glad you enjoyed it, Charlie.'

'I loved it. Should we go again?'

'I think driving for the last hour was enough for your first time.'

She bit down on her lower lip and touched the handles on the motorcycle, then she was right in front of me and her palms were on my chest. She leaned up to place a kiss on my cheek and rested her face against mine. 'Thank you for letting me drive in the parking lot, William.'

I put my hand on the small of her back. 'You're welcome, Charlie,' I whispered softly. I felt her shiver in my arms and my body responded accordingly.

She leaned slightly back, but didn't pull her hands off me.

I grasped the back of her coat to keep her near, because I wasn't ready to let her go yet.

'And thank you for taking me to a diner. I can imagine some people wouldn't find that romantic, but considering we met at a similar place, it was perfect.'

'I thought you'd like that.'

'And the fact that you remember what I ordered that first night we met . . . mindblowing.'

I smiled.

'What do we do now?' she asked softly.

I kept my eyes on hers. 'Whatever you want to do.'

'Are you sleepy? It's getting a little late.'

I shook my head.

'And we can't go for another bike ride?'

I shook my head again, but this time with a smile on my face.

She sighed. 'It was worth a try.'

I laughed, somehow managing to pull her even closer, and went for her lips. She melted in my arms and opened her mouth so I could seek out her tongue. She let out a soft moan that sent fire rushing through my blood and I pulled back to get some fresh air to clear my head.

'I love kissing,' she muttered, her eyes half-closed, and touched her lips with her fingers. 'But I think my lips are swollen.'

'I love kissing *you*.' My admission caused her eyes to open fully and her gaze softened. 'And you wear it so beautifully. We're making up for lost time, remember? Be prepared to have swollen lips every day from now on. Seeing you like this makes me want to kiss you even more.'

A group of five people walked past us on the sidewalk and we stood in each other's arms until we couldn't hear them any longer.

'How do you make me smile so easily?'

'Because I know you.'

'Would you like to come upstairs for a cup of coffee?' Charlie asked. 'I know it's a little late for coffee, but I . . . kind of don't want the night to end just now. Is that weird?'

I took in every little detail of her features. From her beautifully pink lips to the small dot of a beauty mark below her right eye. 'You know it's not weird, Charlie. I never want to leave your side as it is, but tonight it's worse. It was really hard seeing you at the office yet not realizing what was missing between the two of us was this. Being able to touch you. Hold you . . .'

She bit on her lip. 'We're really doing this, huh? My heart is racing.'

'If by *this* you mean a relationship, then yes, we are definitely doing this. And you have no idea how much I love the fact that you're so open and honest. I might be a little obsessed with you, just so you know.'

'You don't have to say that.'

She gave me a small smile and took a step back. I reached for her hand as we walked up the steps to her apartment.

'It's weird without Pepp welcoming me home.'

She let me walk in and then closed the door.

'Do you want me to go get him from your neighbours?'

'It's past midnight. Antonio wakes up too early I'm sure they're already in bed. I'll go get him before work. It's okay.'

She locked the door behind us and slowly turned to face me. I could see the nerves playing on her face just as easily as I could see whatever she was feeling right in her eyes on any given day. She was like an open book for me to read.

'So,' I started gently. 'Do I get to see your famous list?'

'You want to see it?'

'If I'm allowed.'

She gave me a small smile. 'Of course.'

Pushing away from the door, she went into her room and came back with a single page in her hands.

She put it on the kitchen counter behind me and waited just next to me with her hands clasped behind her back, as if she was barely holding herself from snatching it away again.

I raised my eyebrow. 'Why are you nervous? You already told me about most of them.'

Keeping quiet, she shrugged. 'I'll make us coffee.'

Instead of going for the list, I turned around and reached for her hand, pulling her to my front, fitting her against me. I wrapped my arms around her waist and rested my chin on her shoulder. Her body relaxed and I closed my eyes, savouring the feel of her.

She drowned my mind. Whenever I was near her, she made me feel out of my depth.

'I love this,' I muttered.

'What?' she asked quietly as she tilted her head to rest against mine.

'This. Having you this close. Being able to touch you like this, finally. We waited years to have this. I'm a lucky bastard to have this second chance with you.'

'Sounds like our own second chance romance. Are you giving me this cheese because you know it's working on me?'

I laughed.

She moved in my arms and faced me, so I used the opportunity to pull her closer. My arms still safely around her, I leaned down and rested my temple against hers.

'I might be a little scared,' she whispered into our quiet.

I pulled back so I could see her eyes. 'Scared? Of what?'

'You. This. Of what's happening. I've had a crush on you before and it didn't turn out so well. And all of this, you, feels like a dream. I don't want to wake up from it'

'I want you, Charlie. I'm ready to do whatever it takes. I can wait if that's what you want. Anything you want from me, it's yours.' I lifted her chin with my finger to catch her gaze. 'But if it's up to me, I don't want to wait. I'd struggle to try and stay away from you.'

She exhaled and I watched her eyes flutter to a close.

'You really came back for me? Back then, at the diner?'

Her voice was barely audible: it was just the two of us, in our little bubble in her kitchen.

Her list forgotten.

The world forgotten.

'Yes. A few times. I knew I wouldn't find you, but I wanted to make su—'

Before the last word was even out of my mouth she lifted her chin up and kissed me. And this time it was me who groaned. Bending a little, I caught her right beneath her butt and smiled into our kiss when she wrapped her arms around my neck and did a little jump into my arms.

After pushing her back against the fridge and kissing the hell out of her lips until I just couldn't wait any longer, I managed to drag myself away to get some clarity back to think for a second, so our first time wouldn't be against the fridge. Not that it wouldn't be amazing. Hell, maybe it was a good idea.

'Where do you want me?' I asked into her neck, my voice hoarse and breathless.

'You don't want coffee?'

'I want you. Where do *you* want me?'

'In my bed.'

She didn't hesitate in her answer and it made me smile. In the blink of an eye we were in her bedroom. I didn't even take a second to look around because I had something more interesting to look at in my arms. I gently lowered her to her feet, her body sliding against mine in a maddening way that left nothing to the imagination about how ready I was for her. The moment her feet hit the ground she pulled my head down for a kiss.

I smiled. My heart was racing. I couldn't remember the last time my heart had raced because I was about to have sex with someone. Yet there we were.

I was finally going to touch this woman in all the ways I'd wanted to touch her in the last few weeks, and I couldn't wait a second longer. Reaching down, I started to pull up her dress and stopped kissing her to take it off. She reached for me again, but I took a step back to take it all in.

She was wearing a pale lilac matching set of underwear and she was so fucking beautiful that I didn't know what to do with her, other than just stare like an idiot. She was absolutely made for me.

I watched as she started blushing. Just a pretty pink at the top of her cheeks. And I smiled because she had no idea what she did to me.

'I'm speechless,' I muttered, just to repeat myself, my eyes roaming every inch of her skin.

She swallowed. 'I'm a little shy . . .'

'No. Don't you even dare finish that sentence, Charlie. You're absolutely stunning and I don't even know where to start with you.'

I moved and reached for her hips, my fingers grazing her warm skin and squeezing the flesh because I couldn't help myself. Slowly, I pushed my hands beneath her underwear and pulled her flush to my body so she could feel me. A small gasp left her pretty mouth when I squeezed her butt harder and slightly pulled her body up so she could slide against my cock. I was probably going to leave a mark on her skin, but I could barely think straight with her in my arms.

I realized all too suddenly that I couldn't feel her skin against mine, and I hated it.

Thankfully she was thinking along the same lines, because she started clumsily unbuttoning my shirt, her hands slightly shaking. Letting her go, I unbuttoned the rest and took it off.

She watched my every movement, and I watched her the entire time.

I reached for my belt, slowly unbuckling it as she bit her lip, her chest falling and rising rapidly.

Then instead of taking off my pants, I grabbed her arm and pulled her in for a long kiss, because I couldn't stay away. I was overwhelmed just by having her eyes on me.

I greedily swallowed her moan and as she was lost in the kiss, lifted her up and wrapped her legs around my waist. When I felt her wetness through her underwear against my stomach, I almost lost it.

Half-drunk on her, I put my knees on the bed and slowly laid her against the pillows, keeping my body between her legs. I was about to straighten, but all breathless, she pulled me back down to her.

I rested my forehead against hers and tried to steady myself.

'You want to stop?' I asked. It would kill me, but if she didn't feel ready this would be as far as we went until she wanted more.

Her eyebrows drew together and she put her palm on my cheek. 'No,' she whispered, her voice deliciously hoarse. 'It's . . . you know it's been a while . . . a long while, and . . .'

'And . . . ?' I prompted as my hand started caressing the dent of her waist. I didn't even have to look, I was clearly mesmerized by her. My fingers grazed the side of her bra and then my palm made its way back down to her hips. Her body shivered underneath me.

'And I'm not sure what to do right now. I . . . Honesty?'

Gently I squeezed her waist. 'Always.'

'I'm probably gonna suck right now, considering it's been years, and I don't want to. I want you to be very impressed by my skills in bed. So impressed that you will never want to sleep with anyone else because I'll be the best one you've ever had. Or even if you do, you'll always think of how good I was.'

Somewhere in the middle of her confession she had closed her eyes and when she opened them I was smiling down at her.

'Don't make fun of me.'

I shook my head, my lips stretching even more. 'You know I'd never do that. You trust me, Charlie?'

She nodded.

Deciding we had done enough talking, I straightened, and still on my knees between her legs, I gripped the sides of her pretty underwear and slowly slid them off her legs and threw them over my shoulder.

I was too far gone to think of turning on the lights when we first came in, but the soft light streaming in through the living room was enough for me to see her.

Heat like I've never known before spread through my veins, and I could barely stop myself from taking my cock out and slamming into her until I could feel her pussy spasm around me. I lost the smile on my face.

Lifting her foot, I kissed the inside of her ankle and trailed my lips up on her leg, sliding my hand up until I positioned her leg over my shoulder. I would've loved to see the look on her face, but I made do with her deep intake of breath.

Her body was still tense, so I needed to loosen her up and calm her down before I could even think of going deep inside her.

I settled myself between her legs and smoothed my hand over her pussy. She was dripping wet already. Not having the strength to wait a second longer, I wrapped my arms under her hips, parted her pussy lips and started eating her out.

She moaned my name and I lost my head as I kept licking her pussy, swirling my tongue around it and gently sucking. She tasted fucking amazing and my cock swelled painfully in my pants. Another small groan left her lips, and I felt her fingers in my hair, holding on. I flattened my tongue and pushed against her clit and she gasped. I unwrapped one of my arms around her hip and slowly pushed two fingers in. When I felt how tight she was, I let out a groan and pushed my fingers as deep as they could go and then curled them to hit her spot.

'Will,' she gasped my name out. 'Please don't stop.'

I could tell from how she was tightening around my fingers that she was close to coming. And there was a roaring sound in my ears, because if she was so tight around my fingers how was she going to feel about having my thick cock in her pussy? I moved my fingers a little faster and sucked her clit into my mouth a little harder, trying to push her over the edge.

I dared to look up at her and saw that she had one arm over her eyes and her body was arched, her breathing excited and uneven. Her fingers tightened around my hair, pulling, but I couldn't care less about the pain. Nobody could take me away from her in that moment.

'William,' she whispered this time, and I knew she was seconds away from coming all around my fingers and all I could think about was making her come around my cock. All night long.

I doubled my efforts, pushed in faster with my fingers and sucked her clit into my mouth. She groaned my name again and tried to close her legs around my head, but I used my hands to push her thighs open and kept going as she started coming all over my face, her thighs shaking – hell, her whole body shaking.

I gently pulled my fingers out of her and licked her pussy for the last time.

My whole body felt on edge, my skin burning. I crawled up her body, dropping kisses on my way to her lips. First her stomach, then the tops of her heavy breasts, her throat, and then finally I was at her lips and gave her a searing kiss as I ground my erection trapped in my pants against her pussy. Dying to get in there.

She groaned into my mouth as I grabbed her jaw and kissed her, playing with her tongue. I'd decided it was a sound I'd happily listen to for the rest of my life. I felt like a teenager because I knew my pants were wet from all the pre-cum, and I didn't even give a shit. I slowed down the kiss when she calmed down a little more from her orgasm and she wasn't shaking anymore. I ground my cock against her again and her breath hitched.

'How did that feel?' I asked quietly against her ear. I couldn't help but smile when her fingers tightened around my hair again. 'Good?'

She gave me a small nod.

I pulled back and met her eyes.

'Let me hear you.'

She slid her hand to my cheek and stared straight into my eyes. 'I loved it.'

I didn't let her breathe and kissed her again, our tongues tangling together.

Realizing I might just come by kissing her and feeling her body underneath me, I slowed the kiss down and slid my lips to her neck, gently biting and licking her skin while I gripped her chin with my thumb and forefinger so I could tilt her head the way I wanted. She was still frantically trying to slow down her breathing. While we were kissing she had moved one of her hands to the back of my head, running her fingers through my hair.

'Do you have any idea how long I've wanted to do this?' she breathed out.

'Do what?' I asked, gently biting her lip and pulling down the tops of her bra cups as I made my way to her nipples. I swirled my tongue around one pink and hard nipple, sucking once, twice. When she didn't answer me, I bit down on her skin, causing her to gasp. 'Do what?' I repeated.

'Have my fingers in your hair,' she rushed out, arching under me.

'Yeah?'

I pulled down the other bra cup and went for her nipple while I palmed her left breast, pulling on the taut bud, gently.

'Tell me you have condoms. Please.'

Her face lit up. 'I do. For emergencies.'

'You have emergencies a lot?'

'Haven't had any in years. But you never know. Hope is a powerful thing.'

I started laughing and she gave me a small, shy smile.

'You're beautiful,' I said softly and brushed away her hair. 'Now, can you tell me where your condoms are before I die?'

She pointed to her bedside table. I leaned forward and opened the drawer, finding a few condoms at the very back of it.

I ripped a wrapper open with my teeth, and put the condom on her stomach as I slowly got off her. Leaving another kiss on her hip and then her thigh before I straightened, keeping my gaze on hers the entire time. She got on her elbows to watch and I unbuttoned my pants and . . .

The doorbell rang.

I stopped. 'Are you fucking kidding me?'

Charlie's eyes widened and we both froze for a second.

'No. Absolutely no,' I forced out, and leaning down, saved her boobs from their unnecessary confinement.

She slapped my hand away to fix it. 'But . . .'

'No, Charlie. Not happening.'

There was another knock and Charlie rushed to fix her bra, hiding her breasts from me, then attempted to get up. I was on her in a second, covering her with my body.

'I refuse to entertain the idea of someone interrupting this,' I announced in a whisper, just in case someone could hear us. Which was unlikely, but it always paid to be safe. 'Forget about it, no force on earth will take you from my arms.'

'What if it's Pepp?'

'They would've called you.'

'You don't know that.'

'Would they have called you to see if you were up first?'

'Yes,' she admitted grudgingly. 'But that doesn't mean it can't be them.'

'If they call, I'll let you up. If your phone doesn't ring in the next ten seconds, we're going to let whoever is on the other side of the door go.'

'You aren't curious about who is out there? I kinda want to know.'

I held her head in my hands and stared into her eyes. 'I'll make you forget about being curious, don't worry.'

She smiled at me playfully. 'You think you got that in you?'

I quirked an eyebrow at her. 'Are you challenging me?'

'Oh no. I'm just saying. It's been years, as you know, and I might have built things up in my mind. It's probably going to be hard to impress me.'

'I know you. I know what you want. Don't worry.'

'If you say so.'

'Do you want me to tell you what you want then?'

'Yes. Please enlighten and impress me.'

'My pleasure.'

Whoever was or had been on the other side of the door disappeared from our minds and it was just the two of us again. Still holding the back of her head in my palms, I pressed my lips to her forehead, then lifted up from her body.

It took me only a few seconds to get the boxer briefs off and the condom on before she could utter a word. Then I took my now favourite spot in the world and gave her a long and satisfying kiss while I gently pushed her thighs open to give myself more room.

'I'm feeling both enlightened and very impressed, I should say.'

I chuckled. 'Glad to hear that, but that's not how I was thinking of impressing you. Or not just that, at least.'

Her smile grew and she moved her hands on my shoulders as I settled more firmly over her. My elbows were resting on the bed, right next to her shoulders, as I sank my fingers into her hair.

'Now,' I started as our eyes met, 'where were we?'

She smiled at me and some forgotten emotion stabbed at my chest, my mind racing.

'You were going to tell me what I wanted.'

'You want to hear?'

Her chest falling and rising, she bit the edge of her lip and nodded.

Keeping my left hand exactly where it was, I moved my right hand down her body, squeezing her hip on the way to her thigh. Then I was gently, very gently caressing her pussy again. My touch a whisper against her wet and quivering skin.

I leaned down until my lips were right next to her ear. 'I've wanted you like this for a long time now. Under me. Needy. Hungry. Ready for me.'

She tilted her head to the side as she closed her eyes.

Looking down between our bodies, I grabbed the base of my cock and moved it up and down against her wetness.

Charlie let out a small groan, her hand grasping my arm.

'Tell me,' she whispered.

'You want to be fucked, don't you? Hard and fast?'

I slowly thrust forward, entering her, and watched as her brows drew together with every inch she took of me.

She gasped when I pulled out and this time thrust just a little deeper.

I kissed her lips to swallow the sound, but I could barely hold it together myself.

'You want it as deep as you can take. You want to feel full. You want to be breathless. You want to be touched and loved.'

I pulled back my hips again, and this time thrust all my length inside her. Squeezing her thigh, I held her in place. Utterly and completely open for me.

'You want someone to take over and take care of you. And most importantly, you want someone who knows how to take care of you.'

When I knew she had finally adjusted to my size, I started moving, my voice thick and breathless as I tried to keep it together. 'You want someone who knows what they're doing with your body.'

As my pace quickened with her breathing, and I was drowning in the little noises she was making, the words just tumbled out of my mouth. 'You want *me*, Charlie. You want me to push deep . . .' My body echoed my words and half-growling, half out of my mind, I pushed deep, watching her face as her mouth dropped open, her glazed-over eyes looking into mine as her back arched underneath me. 'And you want me to keep talking to you, don't you?' I dipped my head down until my lips were grazing her ear lobe. 'You want me to tell you all the many ways I want to fuck you, and all the ways I imagined I'd take you once you were under me or over me.'

'Will,' she moaned and lifted her hips, moving them in time with me. She tilted her head back, opening her throat for me as her moans got louder the harder and deeper I pushed into her.

'You want to know how I'm going to pull you to the edge of the bed and go as deep as I can and make you scream. You want to know every little thing I'm going to do to you.' I stopped talking because just by looking at her face and feeling her burning skin against mine, I was about to do something I hadn't done in a very long while and lose it. I squeezed my eyes shut and let out my own groan as her pussy tightened around me. 'How am I doing so far?'

By the time I got it together and pulled back to meet her gaze, her pussy was already fluttering around me.

'Can I have an answer?' I asked and stopped moving inside her. It was killing me to stay still, but I didn't want her to come just yet. Letting her thigh go, I put both my hands on either side of her head.

Her eyes were half-open, her cheeks already flushed when she focused on me. 'I want all of that. I want everything you want to do to me.'

'Yeah? You want to see what you do to me?'

She nodded, and I felt her whole body shiver underneath me when I pressed a kiss on her throat and then on her right breast, and pulled out of her warmth.

I stood on my knees, still very much between her legs and looked down at my swollen cock and then at Charlie, who was staring back at me with barely concealed hunger. Grabbing my cock from the base, I softly moaned. 'Do you see my throbbing cock? All covered in your juices?' I swiped my thumb around the thick head and then, being as rough as I could, rubbed it from base to tip. 'I wanna give it all to you, Charlie. And I wanna see how it looks in your mouth.'

She got on her elbows and tried to get up, but I grabbed her ankles and kept her in place.

Swallowing thickly, I shook my head in regret. 'Not tonight, I don't think. Not this round, at least.'

'Why not?' she asked, her eyebrows drawing together as I slowly got off the bed.

'I'm afraid I won't be able to hold it any more than a minute if I feel your beautiful lips wrapped around me.'

Reaching for her ankles, I turned her and pulled her all the way to the edge of the bed. She squeaked, but didn't utter another word when I guided my cock right back into her pussy.

'I want to feel you on my cock,' I murmured and just thrusted in.

She was still on her elbows, watching the show, but dropped back when she was full of me and the moan she let out . . .

Jesus fuck.

She was making me last so fucking long.

I pushed my hands under her ass and pulled her even closer so I could go in deeper.

'Will,' she moaned, hard and long.

'Yeah sweetheart?' I managed to grunt out, but I was in a losing battle.

'Shit,' she groaned. 'You're gonna make me come.'

'Hold it off for a little longer,' I forced out through gritted teeth as I pressed the backs of her thighs against my body and slightly changed my angle.

She groaned loudly, her hand going for her clit. I hugged her tightly and stopped her before she could touch herself.

'Please,' she begged, but all I did was interlock our fingers and hold them straight in the air.

'Not yet. Just a little more. You're doing amazing. Just give me a few more minutes. You're going to love it, I promise.'

'Will,' she groaned, her back arching, her beautiful boobs in the air just waiting for me to lick and bite.

Still holding onto her hand, I let her thighs go and went harder and deeper in her. She just dropped her legs, doing her best not to come all over my cock.

'You want to come on my cock?' I asked, my voice barely recognizable to my own ears. All she did was moan, too far gone in the moment.

My body burning and my cock about to explode, I went for her other hand, locking our fingers together as I pulled her up until our bodies were flush and my cock was slamming into her.

'I'm so wet,' she whispered, eyes far too gone.

'Soaked,' I whispered back.

'You feel so good,' she mumbled.

'Deep enough for you?'

'Yoooo. I'm gonna come, Will. You're gonna make me come.'

Gritting my teeth, I kept up my rhythm, working her hard and watching her every reaction to every thrust. 'You're taking me so fucking well.'

She started whimpering, her moans echoing inside the walls of her bedroom, and I knew she wasn't going to be able to hold it any longer. I dropped one of her hands and pressed my palm against her lower belly.

'Will,' she groaned as her eyes popped open, her breathing all over the place. The added pressure catapulting her orgasm.

I don't think my dick had gotten that hard before Charlie, but I let it go and pounded into her with all my strength as I felt her legs start to shake.

'Yes, Charlie. You can come all over my cock now.'

Her pussy started tightening around my girth painfully, and I had to push just a little harder into her with every thrust.

'Oh god.'

'You can take it, come on Charlie. Give me what I want.'

Every muscle in her body seized and her pussy slowly started contracting all over me. She whispered my name, once, then gasped loudly. Then it was nothing but moans and groans in my ears and I realized a little too late that I wasn't gonna be able to hold it either. Not when she was squeezing me like that and nothing had ever felt that good. I dropped her hand as she gripped the bed sheets and pushed her hips downwards, letting me reach so fucking deep while her body tried to push me out at the same time.

My jaw clenched and I hissed out a breath as I felt it start to take over me. I grabbed her hips and fucked her as hard as I could, as her orgasm kept going when I picked up the pace.

'Oh, Charlie, your pussy . . .' It took me only a few seconds to start to come, and when it started I felt all the air rush out of my lungs as I went lightheaded.

I planted myself deep inside her pussy and my body dropped right on top of her. Just so I wouldn't crush her, I put my hands on the bed and buried my head in her throat.

I noticed how much her body was shaking underneath me and how fast she was still breathing, but I was too lost in my own orgasm to help her calm down. Every time she pulsed around me, my dick jumped inside her.

When we both finally started to settle, I licked her throat and gave her a gentle bite. Not enough to leave a mark, but just hard enough.

I moved my hips forward, just to feel her pussy grip me again.

Moving one hand, I grasped her head and moved my forehead against hers. 'I don't remember the last time I came that hard,' I whispered, out of breath. I pulled back to stare into her soft and very satisfied gaze. 'Am I crushing you?'

She moved her head from side to side.

I raised an eyebrow. 'Was that worth the wait?'

She nodded.

I smiled. 'Not talking to me, huh?'

Her hands framed my head and she pulled me down for a kiss. It was the laziest and sexiest kiss as our tongues gently tangled around each other.

When we stopped, she whispered against my lips, 'You fucked the words out of me. I'm not feeling my legs. When can we do it again?'

I chuckled and breathed in her sexy scent, very, very slowly pulling out of her.

'Does that mean I get to spend the night with you wrapped in my arms?'

Her eyes softened even more. 'I'd like that. Very much.'

I pressed my palm against her cheek and started another slow kiss. This one just for my own sake. I didn't think I'd let her get any sleep if I stayed over, but the other option, which was me leaving Charlie in bed all alone and crossing the street to get in a cold bed, was not even an option anymore.

'Then I'll stay,' I whispered, and straightened up.

I gave her another look, taking in every inch of her body, especially where I could see the imprints of my hands on her soft and pink skin, and headed towards the small bathroom connected to her bedroom to get rid of the condom. I was back in a minute before she could even get to her feet to help clean her.

'Thank you,' she whispered, and I kissed her.

'You're welcome.'

In a few seconds we were both in bed and under the covers, and my naked body was wrapped around her. I sighed and tried to get closer even though we were touching from head to toe. Her head was lying on my arm and I had my arm thrown over her stomach. She gripped my forearm with her hand, keeping me close.

It was silent for at least a minute, if not more, our heartbeats and breathing the only sound in the room.

'Maybe I could be your only one,' she whispered, quietly.

'Maybe you could stay,' I murmured back against her ear.

'Maybe we could . . .'

I didn't let her finish the sentence, this wasn't the time to have this talk. So I gripped her chin and turned her towards me so I could kiss her lips to quieten her. She lifted her chin up and let me have more of her. When we were both out of breath and I could still taste her lips against mine, I stopped.

'Are you happy?' I asked into the quiet.

She looked at me over her shoulder. 'Very happy. You?'

'I couldn't be happier.'

She smiled and rested her head on my arm again. I moved until my lips were against her ear.

'How do you feel about sleep?'

'Overrated.'

I chuckled. 'I was thinking the same thing, but I'll let you rest a little. It's been a while for you, and I don't want to hurt you.'

'Do you th— never mind.'

'Hey,' I whispered, pushing up and meeting her eyes. 'We're not going to hold back from each other. You tell me everything. I don't want that to change now.'

She took a few seconds to keep going. 'That was a little intense. Do you think it felt that way because I haven't had sex in a while?'

'What do you think?'

'I think it might be you.'

I moved back, turned her a little so she was lying on her back and lightly put my palm on the side of her throat, holding her for my gaze as my thumb moved over her red and sensitive lips.

'It's not me, Charlie. It's us. If you don't want to say it, I can say it for both of us. That was the best sex of my life.' I leaned a little down so my lips were just against hers. 'You didn't see the condom, but I don't think I ever came that hard and that long.'

She bit on the edge of her lip, her eyes jumping to mine. A slow smile stretching across her lips. 'Honesty?'

'Always,' I murmured. Already feeling my cock come alive, just with the way she was looking at me.

'I'd never come without playing with my clit before. This was the first time. I didn't know I could.'

I pulled back and gave her a long look as she studied my features.

My hand moved down till my palm was cupping her breast, lightly moulding and playing with the nipple.

'Yeah?'

She dipped her chin as answer.

My heartbeat started to quicken as I felt my cock harden. I let my hand roam down her body, memorizing every inch and learning every curve. Then I reached her pussy and gently, very gently started touching her clit with the tips of my fingers.

I had to smile when she slightly opened her thighs to the side to give me more space to play with her.

'I called you Will a few times, I think,' she whispered gently.

'I know.'

'Sorry.'

'Don't be.'

'But you said you don't like anyone calling you anything other than William.'

I pressed on her clit, just slightly. 'You get to call me anything you want. And I like Will coming from your mouth.'

'Can I call you Willie, too?' A mischievous grin tugged at her lips, her eyes sparkling and transfixed. I just stared. For a long moment I didn't know what to say or what to do. I wasn't in trouble anymore when it came to Charlie. Whatever I was was irrecoverable. And I had no problem with that fact.

I shook my head with a small smile teasing my lips. 'Maybe not that one.'

The corner of her mouth lifted.

'Can you take me again?' I asked softly, gently pushing the tip of my finger in her warmth.

Her lips parted, her body slightly arching off the bed and she quietly moaned, just the sound and the feel of her body against me making me dizzy.

'I can,' she whispered meeting my gaze.

'You want me then?'

'Always.'

'That's good.'

Leaning down, I pulled my finger out and spread the wetness on her skin.

'I'll be very gentle this time.'

And I was. Very gentle. I lost count of how many times I coaxed her orgasm out of her and our bodies burned through the entire night.

25

Charlie

Ever since the second I'd woken up with William next to me, I had this ridiculous smile on my face, and I didn't think anything could wipe it off. It was permanent. Or at least, it felt permanent to my heart and my face.

I walked into my office, my phone pinging with a new message from Valerie. Her tenth message of the day after the only one I had sent her. After her third message, all I'd gotten from her had been my name. Around seven texts with just my name with one or several exclamation points. Every time I saw them made me smile. But every time I saw William walk across the office or pass by me, my heart did a somersault in my chest, my breaths coming in faster. I had to bite down my lip to keep myself from smiling like a lunatic if we made eye contact when I was trying to talk to someone about work.

Valerie: You're the worst friend in the world for not responding to any of my messages. You better call me during your lunch break because I'm getting no work done, so I need the details to actually focus on what I'm doing instead of checking my phone every five minutes.

Valerie: I mean it, Charlie. Call me.

I was still smiling and pulling Val's number up so I could give her a call when someone behind me cleared their throat.

'Anything you want to share with the class?' Gayle asked, as I looked over my shoulder and noticed she and Rick were just standing at the doorway.

'Like what?' I asked, trying to sound normal and heading for my desk as they walked in.

'Why the good mood?' Rick added.

'I'm usually in a good mood. What are you two talking about?'

They both stared at me expectantly as I took a seat and gave them an innocent look. Gayle pinched her brows together, squinting at me.

My eyes landed on my book that was on its regular spot, and I spied a tiny piece of paper sticking out of the pages. My heart rate picked up. William's notes had become some of the best parts of my day. My hand reached for the book – *The Girl Who Fell Beneath the Sea* – but instead of pulling the paper and reading the note, I focused on my friends.

They were still staring.

'You're freaking me out.'

'And you're making us very curious.'

'I have no idea what you're talking about.'

Rick kept standing in the middle of my room with his arms crossed against his chest as Gayle put her palms on my desk and leaned forward, I assumed to intimidate me. It took a lot not to lean back.

'Hmmm,' she muttered. 'I see.'

I tilted my head and waited. She said nothing more.

'What does she see?' Stan whispered.

'Beats me,' I said, moving my gaze from Gayle to Rick.

'Is there a reason you two are here, or did you just . . . ?' I trailed off, waiting for an answer.

'Maybe you should leave, Rick,' Gayle offered, which came out more like an order.

'I'm not leaving. Interrogate her in front of me. I want to hear too.'

I shook my head. My phone started ringing, and I picked it up and rose from my seat. 'Okay. As fun as it was to talk to you two, I was waiting for this call, so if you both could leave that'd be great actually.'

'Who is calling? Someone we know?' I watched Gayle ask as she looked out of my office, her eyes searching for someone.

I grabbed her arm and then pushed Rick with the back of my hand and marched them right out of my office. 'It's actually from the airline. You know, the call we've all been waiting for today? Ring any bells?'

'Fine. Take the call. Then you'll talk to us.'

'Bye guys.'

I closed my door in their faces and they lingered until I rushed back to my desk and answered the phone.

'Hello, Mr Dunne. Did you come to a decision?'

After everything we'd released to the media, and after Mr Dunne himself had gone online with a major news outlet and talked about the situation, we had still recommended that it would be better to sever ties with their racist pilot as soon as possible. Especially after everything Gayle had found out about him just by deep-diving into his social media. It was shocking that this was the first time they were having a problem with him.

As Mr Dunne kept talking, I couldn't help it, I reached for my note.

Stop looking at me over your shoulder. I can't handle it. You're making me crazy.

I grinned. Completely forgetting that I should be focusing on my call, I still lifted my head and searched for him in the office. I found him in front of his office door, talking to Trisha. As if he could feel my eyes on him, he turned his head and our eyes met. His lips still moved, but I had all his attention. After a few seconds, I looked away first, but he had seen my smile.

'Okay. Mr Dunne. I'll get the team together and we'll jump on a video call to discuss our next step and how to handle the situation carefully. Will you be available in an hour?'

Just a few minutes later, after I had ended my call with Mr Dunne, I practically ran out of my office so Rick and Gayle couldn't corner me again. I tried to look for William to fill him in on the call with Mr Dunne, but he wasn't in his office.

I headed for the kitchen to get myself some coffee. My very first one of the day at 11 a.m. I grabbed a pod from where I had my favourites stashed in the back of the cupboard and Kimberly chose that very minute to walk in and startle me enough that the pad of my finger caught on something against the cupboard as I pulled it back.

'Hello, hello.'

'Dammit,' I muttered, holding onto my finger. There was no blood, but the skin was scratched and it burned like hell.

'Why so jumpy?' Kimberly asked, getting herself a water bottle from the fridge. 'How is your little office romance going?'

'There is no office romance,' I muttered, not even meeting her gaze. I tried to ignore the pain and focused on working the coffee machine.

'Heads up. I think Dad wants to have a meeting with us.'

'Okay.' I hit the button and finally the sound of the machine drowned out Kimberly's voice.

Stopping next to me, Kimberly laughed. 'You can be so dramatic sometimes.'

'Thank you,' I said. 'I try. Have a good day.'

Shaking her head, she finally left me alone. I sighed, letting out a long breath and closed my eyes for a moment as my coffee cup filled and the smell flooded my senses. I have no idea when it had exactly happened, but now whenever Kimberly talked to me, or, hell, even looked in my direction, my shoulders tensed up. One of the good things about working with William, other than looking at his face, had been that I didn't need to deal with Kimberly as much, if at all.

I forced my shoulders to drop and tried to relax. Soon enough I wouldn't have to worry about tiptoeing around anyone.

I glanced down at my hand, frowning at the angry red line and squeezed my finger, hoping to quiet the thrum of pain.

'There you are,' said a soft and familiar voice and then I felt his warm body against my back.

My heart galloped, not heeding any of my warnings to play it cool whenever he was close. Every inch of my body warming with his words, not just with his body pressed against mine. I couldn't help but smile.

Before I could utter anything, he hummed right next to my ear and reached for a coffee pod from the cupboard right above me. And then his other hand grabbed my hip, pulling me back so I could feel him. His fingers tightened, burning my body from top to toe. I could still remember his skin sliding against mine, his breath warming my sensitive flesh as he whispered all the things he still wanted to do to me the night before.

I swallowed hard. My throat bobbing. It was hard not to moan.

After getting what he wanted from the cupboard, he pressed his fingers a little harder and forced my body to turn in his arms so I was facing him.

He looked down at me with hunger in his eyes. I don't think my expression was any different. It really didn't matter that I'd been smiling from ear to ear ever since I woke up in my bed with him right next to me. Or that we had woken up countless times and kept going on and off the entire night, I still wanted him.

My eyes slid to the now-closed kitchen door.

'William, someone . . .' I started, but he didn't let me get any-where with that.

'Just a minute,' he muttered, as he tilted my face back to him with his knuckles against my chin.

'Hi,' I mumbled stupidly.

'Did you get my note?' he asked, his eyes smiling at me.

I nodded, too lost in his gaze to try and find the right words to speak right away. 'You're looking at me too much. Everyone will know what's going on.' As his eyes moved over my face, I frowned up at him.

'I'm looking at you too much? Whenever I see you, you're always looking at me.'

'That's because you're looking at me.'

'No. Whenever I see you, *you're* the one who is already looking!'

His lips stretched into a familiar smile, and my frown smoothed out. He was bantering with me because he knew I loved bantering. He knew it was one of my favourite things. I barely managed to hold back my laughter, feeling happiness bubble up inside of me.

'I can't take my eyes off of you,' he admitted, his voice rough and deep.

'You already said that,' I reminded him. I couldn't remember when exactly, but he had told me that before. It still had the same effect, though; it sent a tingle down the length of my spine. 'And I can't stop thinking about you. About us.'

Fingers flexing and moving towards my waist, he dropped his head so he could speak into my ear, as if he was trying to make sure only I could hear what he was about to say even though we were utterly alone.

'Every time I catch you looking for me over your shoulder, I keep imagining you in bed as I'm taking you from behind.'

His words caught up to my brain and I felt the world tilt.

He was killing me.

His stubbled jaw scraped over my skin and my eyes fluttered close, my body trembling before I could stop it.

'You have nothing to say?'

'Nope. Can't think.'

'You can't think?'

'Nope.'

'Do you think I can take you from behind tonight? Hold onto your waist while I pull you back onto my cock and you . . .'

I forced myself to open my eyes to see why he had stopped and saw that he was looking down between us. My chest was rising and falling, but that's not where his focus was. I realized I was still holding my finger in a firm grip.

'What's wrong?' he asked, his voice deeper than it was just a moment ago.

'Nothing. I just scraped my finger when Kimberly surprised me.'

'Did you cut it?' His warm, long fingers untangled my grip on my finger and gingerly took it into his so he could inspect it. He brushed the edge of the scrape, sending a shiver throughout my body. I winced. As I watched, he lifted it and put the inside of my finger between his lips, ever so gently sucking on my ghost of a cut.

With every pull of his mouth my body came alive. Every atom of my being pulsed with want and need for this man in front of me who was trying to take care of a cut that wasn't even a cut. A man who had gotten on his knees just the night before to hear me say yes to him.

He hummed, softly, and I just stood there frozen on the spot.

'What are you doing to me?' I whispered, my voice coming out as nothing but a rasp.

'Hmmm.'

He stopped sucking on my finger, took his lips away from my skin, and met my gaze. I moved slightly forward. The fact that we were at the office entirely forgotten.

He smiled. Unfazed at my state. Letting me go, he handed me my coffee cup and then started to make his own.

'Please be more careful with yourself,' he muttered.

I opened my mouth to speak, but someone – no, three new people walked in, but their focus wasn't on us. They were discussing something I couldn't understand. One of them said hello to William. I stood straighter, visibly collected myself, and turned to William. He had his back to the newcomers, but his eyes were quietly watching me with a small satisfied smile tugging at his soft lips.

Two could play at that game. I took a sip of my coffee, which was lukewarm at best. After making sure no one was really looking at us, I leaned towards William, just a little, nothing that would draw too much attention, and whispered, 'Would you like to know one other thing I had on my mind, but didn't put it on my list?'

I waited as he gave me a nod.

'I want to be with someone who has that I-can't-wait-to-be-alone-with-you look on their face. You have that face, right this minute. So, thank you, William. Oh,' I leaned even closer and murmured, 'I didn't answer before, but yes, please take me from behind like that tonight. I love your cock, especially when it's inside me.' I pulled back as waves of heat came off of him. His jaw was clenched, eyes telling me a million things without any words.

By the time I gave him my smile and left the kitchen, he wasn't grinning anymore, but his eyes . . . his eyes had been too open to hide the effect my words had had on him. And I had watched his fingers twitch as if he was barely holding himself back from touching me.

An hour later, I was back in my office after running around trying to get things ready for our video call and doing my best to avoid Dad at the same time. My gaze fell on my book and of course, there was another piece of paper sticking out of it. My pulse quickened, my heart just purely happy.

I looked around and, making sure nobody was watching, I pulled at the note, devouring the words at once.

You'll be the death of me.

I bit down on my lower lip and rushed out of the room, heading straight towards the small meeting room, knowing he was already in there.

When I opened the door and walked in, only Stan and Trisha were present.

Hiding my surprise, I gave them a nod and took a seat. He was right behind me; the door opened and William walked in with Rick and Gayle. I turned on my laptop and tried to focus on work and not on William so as not to draw the attention of my friends. It was easier said than done.

I listened to his voice, trying my best to look busy, busy, busy. He took the seat to my left, the head seat.

I was opening the file we'd need, but suddenly my chair was moving. I squeaked, a barely audible sound escaping my lips. My gaze jumped to William, and I realized *he* was the one pulling my chair to his side. The heat rushing to my cheeks started on my neck and I could do nothing about it. Well, there you go, I thought. Now Gayle and Rick know, because a quick glance at the room showed me that Stan and Trisha were deep in their conversation, arguing about a point they needed to make to Mr Dunne, but Gayle and Rick had seen the quick pull of my chair. Rick's eyes were slightly bulged, but Gayle ... Gayle was smiling her Cheshire cat smile while trying her best to look away. And William was either oblivious to their stares or he didn't care who saw.

I winced. There was nowhere to hide from them after this. Not that I was sure I actually wanted to hide anything.

I moved my surprised and slightly astonished gaze to William, but he looked absolutely serious as he gestured to my laptop with his chin.

'Please, show me the statement you prepared.'

I made sure not to look at him the entire meeting, but he made it almost impossible for me with every touch of his knee against my thigh. He was one of the most hardworking guys I'd ever met in my life and knowing that he was struggling to stay away from me or to hold himself back from me caused my heart to give a little extra kick.

In the middle of the meeting, right after I'd made my speech to

Mr Dunne about considering changing some of their policies on people they hire and the trainings they should go through and the positive reaction it would get from the public following the firing of their pilot, Stan and Rick took over the conversation from me. It was right then that William put his hand on my thigh – just as he had done in his mom's house and only a few days ago at another meeting. But then there hadn't been so many people around us.

And now, after having had his skin against mine the night before, the burn I felt from his hand was not comparable to anything I'd ever experienced. I was seconds away from combusting. His hand slowly moved higher, pulling my knee-length pencil skirt, which had a slit in the middle, with it. I cleared my throat and focused on the laptop in front of me. He stopped midway and I dared a glance at him. The tension in the room was palpable. I didn't understand how nobody could feel what was happening, how nobody could hear my thunderous heartbeats.

Our composure didn't falter because he was the perfect picture of a team leader who was following every word of the meeting, whereas I couldn't even count to ten if someone had asked it of me, or even tell them my name.

Charlie, who?

I was thankful that his hand had stopped. I wasn't sure how I'd react if it had kept moving another few inches, because I was bound to embarrass us both if a moan or groan escaped from my lips. My gaze dropped to my lap and I saw his open palm, the back of his hand still burning a permanent spot on my leg. I bit my lower lip, trying to catch up on who was saying what, as there was a roar in my ears. Both my hands were poised on my laptop, but I moved one down and fitted my palm against his waiting hand. Agonizingly slowly, he laced his fingers through mine. My breath caught in my throat when he gave my hand a squeeze and didn't let go. We sat like that for the next ten minutes with his hand holding mine, my emotions running wild in my chest.

And it felt so right.

So beautiful.

Just as the meeting was coming to an end, he leaned towards me, our shoulders brushing. 'Have lunch with me?' he asked softly.

I smiled, and replied just as softly. 'I have to get on a call with Nora. I can't.'

The meeting wrapped up and before we could say another word to each other Gayle scooped him away to discuss another account, and Rick pulled me away to prepare for another meeting. I dared to look over my shoulder and watched his eyes burn as they followed me all the way. I turned around so I wouldn't walk into a wall and realized I was already missing his touch. And how was I supposed to survive in California, so far away from him, when I'd just got him to myself?

Even though I'd skipped lunch myself I went out and got him something, leaving it in his office with a note.

How can I be missing you like crazy when I'm looking at you from across the room? You'll make me go insane.

'How could you not tell me?' Gayle pressed for the hundredth time ever since I admitted to her that, yes, William and I were actually, maybe, quite possibly now dating.

'I just told you half an hour ago.' I exited the bathroom after washing my hands.

'You only told me because I pushed.'

I headed straight towards my office. Not only had I not had time to go out for lunch after my call with Nora, I hadn't even had extra time to sit down. 'Let's not fool each other, you already knew.'

'Of course I knew. I won a bet, thanks to you two.'

That stopped me in my tracks.

'Excuse me? Did you say you bet on us?'

She snorted and kept walking. 'Do I look like an amateur? Of course I did. Easy money.'

I rushed to catch up with her. 'With whom?'

'Rick, of course. He was sure you wouldn't dare.'

I scoffed, irritated. 'Dare? Why wouldn't I dare?'

She shrugged and went straight into my office as I trailed behind her.

'After the first week, I knew you wouldn't stay away from each other for too long. Either he was tracking every move you made, or you were sending him longing looks whenever you thought he wasn't looking.'

Appalled, I froze before I could sit in my chair.

'I was not.'

Gayle just stared at me, and I shook my head.

'I wasn't. Trust me. Sure, I like looking at him. He looks good. But I wasn't sending longing looks his way.'

She huffed and took her phone out of her back pocket. 'Could've fooled me. I'm heading upstairs if you need anything from me?'

'Nope. Not at the moment.'

'Anyway, I'll be out of the office, running after a few other things. Make sure you miss me.' Gayle studied me with an arch to her eyebrow. 'Anything else?'

I smiled. Grinned even. Feeling the happiness slowly rise from somewhere deep in my chest again. Was this going to be constant whenever I talked about William? 'He was tracking my every move?'

Gayle grinned back at me, her eyes lighting up. 'He stood no chance. Trust me. Whenever we were in his office talking about something, if you happened to walk by, his eyes followed all the way to wherever you were heading. Then if he saw you talking to someone, he'd ask me who the guy was and what he did. And if I told him you weren't interested in them he'd frown at me and change the subject, as if I'd said the most ridiculous thing in the world. Then the meetings ... let's not even talk about how he was hypnotized when you spoke.'

With every word out of her mouth, my lips stretched wider.

'He likes me.'

Gayle let out a laugh. 'I'd say so. God save me from new love-birds. At least I get to reap the benefits.' She rested her elbows on my desk, trying to look as innocent as Gayle could manage to look. 'So ... you kissed someone after years and years and years. How do you feel?'

'Incredible,' I whispered, leaning towards her. 'I ...'

There was a soft knock on my open door.

'Am I interrupting something?' William asked softly, eyes on me.

I stood up and Gayle straightened.

'Not at all,' she replied before I could get out a word and passed him on her way out. 'Talk to you soon, Charlie.'

William walked towards me. 'I bought you lunch.'

'Oh, but I didn't order lunch.' I watched as he opened the paper bag and took out a cold sandwich – one of my absolute favourites for lunch – and a small box of still hot French fries.

'I know.'

'Parmesan truffle fries?' I asked, my hands going for the food immediately.

'Your favourite,' he murmured, his voice a caress. 'How was your call with Nora? Everything good?'

'Yes, it was good. We're both excited to work together.' I refused to think how I would leave him behind. 'Did you eat your lunch?'

He nodded.

My eyes moved to him, I couldn't help it.

He took another step towards me, closing the distance between us just a little more. It was intoxicating, the way he was taking me in.

'Too close, William,' I muttered. 'I can't think when you're too close.'

'So, it's not just me,' he said quietly. 'That's good. Will you have dinner at my place tonight? I'll cook for us. With Pepp, of course. Or I can take you out again.' He skimmed the back of my hand with his knuckles and pulled back far too soon.

We were the worst at trying to keep things under wraps at the office until we figured out what we wanted to do with each other.

'Your place would be good,' I rasped out. I could have him all to myself.

'Sorry to interrupt you guys, but Douglas wants to see us three. I'll come and get you in five. I have to deal with something else first.' Gayle said from my door, then quickly disappeared down the hall.

'A meeting?' I asked into the quiet.

'Not a scheduled one. Eat your lunch, then we'll go. He can wait.'

I grinned. 'I really like it when you're bossy. It makes me a little tingly.'

'Yeah?' His eyes burned into mine with a world full of promises. 'What else do you like?'

I lowered my voice, my body facing his as if he were a magnet to my heart. I clenched my hands so I wouldn't plaster myself to him. 'I like it when you bring me lunch when I'm too busy to take a break. I like that you think of me even when I forget to think of myself.'

His jaw clenched. 'Give me one more.'

I swallowed, hands itching to touch and feel. I could give more than one.

I was thinking maybe I was losing my mind. I wasn't quite sure if what I was feeling was because this was us, that it was just something special with him and me, or if it was because I hadn't been with anyone for so long.

'This isn't exactly something I like about you, but it also is.'

'Keep going.'

'You remember how this morning, after you went upstairs and got Pepp for me from Josh? We did something right before you left and then when we were outside walking him: I love resting my body against yours and putting my chin on your chest and looking up when I'm talking to you. And you look down at me too, and push my hair back.' I closed my eyes for a quick moment, savouring the phantom sensation of his fingers in my hair.

When I opened my eyes he had moved a step closer; his jaw muscle ticking, his chest falling and rising with his heavy breathing.

'I guess I like being that close to you and touching you. I also love that you look at me like that. As if you're happy just looking at me.'

He took another step forward, his arm brushing mine.

'I am happy just looking at you, sweetheart. That is more than enough to be happy.'

I cleared my throat when I heard someone passing my door while they almost shouted into their phone. William took a step back; the heavy tension broken.

I cleared my throat. 'I'll eat the rest when I come back actually. We have thirty minutes till our next call with Mr Dunne.' I popped one last fry into my mouth and then quickly another, because I was very hungry. 'Any idea what my dad wants?' Giving my French fries one last longing look, I put everything back in the paper bag.

His eyes bore into mine, his expression a new one that I couldn't name.

'No idea. Can you give me a piece of paper, please.'

Confused at his hard tone, I nodded and handed him one. He reached for a pen himself, bent down to write something on the paper and then as his back brushed my front, he got my book, pushed the paper in and straightened again. I hadn't seen what he had written at all.

'Ready to leave?' he asked.

'What was that?'

'Something for you to read after.'

We were already heading out of my office when we saw Gayle coming towards us.

'You know what this is about?' I asked as we fell in step with her.

'New account, I think.' She leaned forward a little and threw a glance at William, who was to my left and looking at his phone with a frown etched into his eyebrows. 'Someone he knows I believe.'

We stopped in front of my dad's office and Gayle started chatting to Wilma.

William was still staring at his phone, but his frown had gotten deeper. 'Everything okay?' I whispered. 'Bad news?'

He looked up at me and was almost surprised to find me next to him. Shaking his head slightly, he turned off his phone and put it back into his pocket. 'No. It's fine.'

I wanted to ask what was wrong and smooth out the frown on his face with my fingers, but this wasn't the place or the best time to pull him aside for a quick chat.

'Let's head in,' Gayle murmured, following Wilma into my dad's office so I had to move, leaving a distracted William to follow behind us.

Just as we filed into his office, all three of us choosing to stand up, my dad ended his phone call.

'Did you let Kimberly know?' he asked Wilma. She murmured her yes and left the room after leaving some documents in front of him.

My dad got up, rounded his desk and leaned against it as Kimberly and Dean walked in.

'Good, everyone is here. William, one of the companies you worked with a few years ago called today after your firm in California told them you were here. Ephesus Airlines. Apparently, someone is blackmailing them, accusing them of using old plane parts for their new fleet. They want to work with you again.'

'When were they contacted?' William asked next to me while I was still trying to understand what Kimberly was doing in here if they had called for William.

'This morning. A few hours ago.'

'I'll call them right away. Charlie.'

He took a step forward, but my dad lifted his hand, stopping him. 'You and your team', he gestured towards Gayle and me, 'are already working with another airline company at the moment. I don't want you to lose focus on that. Kimberly was interested in this one, so I thought you could fill her in about the company and she'll take over from there.'

26

Charlie

William frowned, confusion emanating from his features. And a little anger too, if I wasn't mistaken. 'Excuse me? Doesn't Kimberly focus on risk management consulting, rather than this?'

'Yes, but you're already taking care of three different situations. I'm not sure if you can take this on as well.'

I didn't even utter a single word because now I could actually feel William's anger coming in crashing waves.

'I'm sorry, did we have any complaints that I'm not aware of?' My dad frowned.

I didn't even glance Kimberly's way, but she and Dean weren't making a sound.

Gayle bumped her shoulder to mine as both our gazes jumped from Dad to William. It was like watching an uncomfortable tennis match.

'Of course not. But I don't want you to be stretched thin.'

'Let me worry about what my team and I can do.'

'Ouch,' whispered Gayle next to me, and I bit my lip to hold back my smile.

'That is not your decision to make,' my dad returned.

'Oh? Is it not? I thought we had an understanding when I accepted your offer. I get to choose the companies I want to work with.'

'And you have. But I don't want you to take on more than you or your team can handle.'

'I want to work with them,' William repeated in a tone that allowed no discussion.

I almost, *almost* felt bad for my dad, but I knew he wouldn't be easily persuaded.

'I'd like to help, William,' Kimberly jumped into the conversation from her side of the room.

William's voice was steel when he responded. 'This isn't about help. Did they not get in touch asking to work with me, Douglas?' He briefly glanced in Kimberly's direction. 'I'm sorry to say this, but you don't have the experience to handle their situation. If Douglas was coming to me and saying I want Charlie to handle this, I'd trust her with anything. Not you. No offence, but I don't know you. I don't know your work.'

I had the sudden urge to grab his face and pull him down for a long kiss.

Kimberly's back went straight, her eyes narrowing.

My dad spoke before her.

'This is not for Charlie. She doesn't have her own team. She isn't there yet.'

'Okay, you can fool yourselves into thinking that. This way I get to have her in my team. It's my win.'

My dad paused. 'Okay. Okay. Then it's up to the airline to decide. I want you and Kimberly to talk to them together. We'll let them know of both sides' plans to fix their problems, and we'll go from there.'

William shook his head. 'This wasn't our deal, Douglas.'

Dad rubbed the bridge of his nose. His telltale sign of stress.

'Let's do this my way.' He looked up and met my gaze. 'Charlie, you can leave. I didn't need you here.'

I was holding onto my elbow with my hand, and I dropped it, glancing at Gayle briefly. 'I was . . .'

'I thought . . .' Gayle started, but neither one of us got to finish.

William stiffened at my side. 'I seem to be very confused today, Douglas. I thought Charlie was on my team. I thought we went over this multiple times, actually. I'm getting tired of having the same conversation, to be honest.'

That was news to me. The tension in the room multiplied.

Dad straightened up and got back into his seat.

'Charlie, Dean, leave. I'm sure you have other problems that need your attention. I need to call the airline back, and having Gayle, Kimberly and William in the room is sufficient. They'll fill you in if need be.'

I moved to leave, but William's hand on my arm halted me, then he moved his hand away.

'We're both going to leave. I'll let Kimberly know when I'll be available to make the call. As you mentioned a few moments ago, my team and I are busy.'

You could've dropped a pin, and it would've echoed in the heavy silence. He didn't let my dad get in another word as he gestured for me to move. I swallowed, trying my best not to show my discomfort and surprise at the turn of events. If William hadn't interrupted, I wouldn't have minded leaving them to handle the phone call. I did have other things I could be working on, so I wouldn't have cared. But anybody could see how William's shoulders had tensed up, his jaw set. I moved as quickly as possible, with him following at my back.

I chose not to meet anyone's eyes, and Kimberly moved out of our way. Before I could, William reached for the door and held it open for me. As soon as we were out, I opened my mouth but closed it pretty quickly after seeing his furious expression.

He walked next to me all the way to my little office.

'Hey,' I said softly when we stopped just outside. 'You okay?'

His gaze softened as he looked down at me, but I could tell it took some effort. He pushed his hands into his pant pockets as if he needed some kind of barrier between us.

'I didn't like the way he was talking to you.'

My heart melted a little. I gave him a small smile and crossed my arms against my chest so I wouldn't be tempted to hug him. 'I'll get some work done. You go do what you need to do. Text me if you need me; I'll be here. I need to make a few calls.'

He studied me for more than a few seconds, then, giving me a nod, he turned and headed towards his office.

I pushed my door open and took a seat behind my desk. My phone pinged with a new message.

William. I need you.

I looked up and found him looking at me from his office door.

Quickly, I texted back.

Charlie: I'm right here.

William: Good.

I watched as he turned around and headed towards where Stan and Trisha were working. So he really was going to make my dad wait.

Letting out a long and heavy breath, I turned on my laptop and picked up my phone right as I received a new text.

William: Check your book.

Then I remembered he had left me a note. I reached for it and found it in a heartbeat.

Meet me at the stairway in 1 hour. 19th floor.

*

An hour later, I was waiting exactly where William had asked me to. It'd already been a few minutes since I'd showed up, but he still hadn't come. It helped that I knew nobody would be coming out of the door behind me, since the office space on the 19th floor was empty at the moment.

I paced on the small landing, then stopped as I heard a door open. The buzz of the office reached my ears for a second or two, then it was all quiet again. A few moments later, I heard footsteps. My heartbeat picked up at the sight of him. He came straight towards me, which did nothing to help my nerves. But the way his eyes tracked my every move, jumping from my eyes to my lips . . . and that hungry look . . .

I was done for, and I didn't even mind.

He pressed my back against the wall, covering the back of my head with his hand, and rested his forehead against mine. Something settled in my stomach; I loved doing this. Slowly, he took another step and fitted his body against mine. His eyes closed, and he released a long breath.

'Your dad is . . . something else.'

'Is there something I can do?'

'Just keep doing whatever you're doing right now.'

I couldn't not take in his features, and as I watched him let out another breath, all the signs of stress melted off his face and he gave me a soft smile.

'You're staring,' he murmured, his other hand reaching for my waist and gently squeezing, as if that would make me stop.

'Was I not supposed to?' I raised my hands and placed one on his neck and the other atop his heart.

The smile tugged at the corners of his lips again. 'I can do this all day.'

'You okay?' I couldn't help but ask into our quiet little bubble.

'I am now.'

His eyes opened and he took me in. He sighed as his hand came up and cupped my cheek with his palm.

'I like this,' he admitted. 'I like this a lot, Charlie.'

'Secretly meeting in stairways?'

'That, yes, and having you in my arms like this.'

This time it was my turn to let my eyes fall closed and tilt my head.

'Your turn to tell me something you like about me.'

He hummed right next to my ear, and a shiver worked its way down my body. I clutched at his shirt and slid my hand up to his neck to gently massage the tense muscles.

'I love the feel of your hands on me in the dark hours of the night,' he whispered, and my body swayed just a little. 'I might love it even more than having my hands on you. And that should tell you something, because I can't keep my hands off you.'

'Will,' I whispered, my body burning as bright as the stars in the night sky.

He leaned even closer, pulled his hand away from my head, and placed his palm against the wall, securely trapping me in. His lips brushed the shell of my ear, his stubbled cheek against mine, and he sneaked his hand to the small of my back, pulling me closer. Just like that, I could feel him hardening against me.

'That's another thing I like. That you call me Will whenever you're half-lost in me. Coming from these lips ...' I felt the pads of his fingers move over my bottom lip, 'you have no idea what it does to me.'

'I think you like me very much.'

'I think you're right.'

'Are you going to kiss me?' I whispered, forgetting the rest of the world around us.

Even though I still hadn't opened my eyes, I could feel his smile.

'You want me to kiss you?'

I nodded, and his thumb made another pass against my lower lip. I held my breath, feeling a little lightheaded with anticipation.

He moved his lips from my ears, pressing a soft kiss on my cheek. I moved my head a little, and he pressed another on the corner of my mouth. Then his lips were almost brushing mine when he whispered, 'You like how I kiss you?'

My pulse fluttered. 'I love it. Perfect.'

He moved me in his arms gently as if we were dancing, and I found myself with my back against his chest, his arms under mine and around my waist. I took a sharp breath. Then he settled his chin on my shoulder and gave me a soft squeeze around my waist.

'Honesty?' he whispered, and I nodded as a sweet and slow heat flooded my chest.

'I've never known anyone like you, Charlie. I don't think I ever will.' He paused, and I reminded myself that I needed to breathe again.

In and out, Charlie.

In and out.

I swallowed, trying to ignore all the emotions swirling in my heart.

A few moments passed in silence as I tried to savour the feel of him against me and the warmth in his voice.

'Too much honesty?' he asked, pressing another soft kiss against my neck. As if it were second nature, as if I were made to be in his arms and it was the most natural thing in the world, I tilted my head to the side and closed my eyes, holding onto his hands around me to anchor myself to the moment. My lips stretched into the biggest and happiest smile. Because it felt like this was it. This was all I'd ever wanted.

He was what I'd been hoping for myself.

Someone who could see me.

I turned in his arms and rested my cheek against his heart.

'Not too much,' I whispered. 'I wish we were at home.'

His arms tightened around me; no words could've been better.

'When did you say Nora wanted you there?'

'April 25th.'

He sighed. 'Okay. Okay. Three weeks. We have a long time still. And maybe if everything is calm enough, I can come with you for a day or two. If you'll have me, of course.'

'I'd always want to have you.'

And a long time? It didn't feel like it. But I didn't want to say anything; I didn't want to think about my departure and how it would affect us. The unknown was my worst enemy.

But then I realized he was holding on just as tight as I was. On another floor, a door opened, bringing the buzz of office noises. We heard footsteps and froze just as we were, but neither William nor I let go. Then the quick footsteps slowly faded away. Only to be replaced by his phone's ringtone.

'You're not getting that?'

He tilted my head back with a finger and studied my face as an answer. 'You're quiet.'

I shook my head. 'Long day, nothing else.'

He cupped my face. 'I wanted a stolen moment with you. I need every moment that I can get with you. That's why I asked you to come.' A smile played on his lips. 'And now that you got me here, what do you want to do with me?'

I smiled a brilliant smile as he had intended. '*You* invited *me* here, not the other way around.'

His eyebrows lifted as his phone stopped ringing. 'Does that mean I get to do whatever I want to you?' He lowered his head until his lips were against mine, and then he whispered, 'I think you're the one for me, Charlie.'

His lips pressed against mine, his tongue pushing inside, and then I couldn't think of anything but the kiss.

I barely noticed his hand moving from my waist, its path leaving goosebumps under my clothes, as he wrapped his palm around my neck, his thumb against my jawline.

I moaned, and he forced my head back, deepening the kiss, making me forget about anything and everything around us. All of a sudden, I felt the wall against my back, not even realizing he had made me move.

I was completely out of breath when he stopped kissing me, and his lips reverently moved against my skin, heading lower and lower. A small moan escaped my mouth when he kissed my collarbone and I arched my back, pushing off the wall. I felt his fingers play with the small button of my shirt. I pulled at his hair and got back to his mouth, sinking my teeth into his lower lip. Something snapped for both of us and suddenly we were both pulling at each other.

He wrapped his arms around my waist, drawing me near, and I lifted my leg as much as my skirt let me so I could get closer to him. One of his hands pushed my skirt higher to make it easier for me.

His heavy breaths mingled with my own. 'You have no idea what these skirts do to me.' His words rattled my bones.

Our kiss turned reckless and wild in a short few seconds as he angled my head, his tongue slipping deeper into my mouth.

I was breathless, my mind all scrambled. I drew my fingers from his hair and sneaked my hand between our bodies and pulled down his zipper, because I needed him in me like I needed my next breath.

And that was the exact moment another door opened.

He paused, lifting his head to rest against my forehead. Both of us were out of breath, and we waited for footsteps, but they never came. My heart was out of control.

He took a step away from me, and I felt his loss so acutely.

I was still trying to catch my breath as he fixed himself up, avoiding my gaze. 'Sorry, I lost my head a little there.'

He was welcome to do so anytime.

I watched as William sighed and buttoned up my shirt. His phone started ringing again, but he didn't even look at who was calling. I vaguely realized that I'd forgotten my phone back in my office, but I couldn't summon up the worry when William was so close.

I blinked up at him when I felt his lips against my forehead as he held me to himself with his fingers in my hair.

'You take away the stress. I feel better with you,' he whispered, his beautiful eyes meeting mine. 'Hell, I feel better just looking at you.' He held my head in between his palms and returned my slightly bewildered gaze. 'Your lips ... I have to tell you, Charlie. I might be a little obsessed with your lips and now that they're all swollen and red ...' He shook his head and I wanted him to finish his sentence because I wanted to know what he'd do ...

But his phone went off again.

'You need to get that, I think,' I whispered. 'It could be important.'

'Tell me something you like about me,' he returned instead.

I didn't even have to think. 'That's easy. I love that you found me again. And I love that you're not afraid to admit that. And I love that your love language is touch.'

He smiled, his eyes still heated. 'I have no idea what that is, but I'm gonna take your word for it.' He took a step away from me. 'You head up first. I need a second or two. I'll follow you.' He glanced down towards his pants, my eyes following the path, and then I smiled the biggest smile when I saw the outline of his dilemma.

'Don't be so proud of yourself.'

My smile turned into laughter. 'I didn't even say anything.'

Sighing, he physically turned me around and gave me a push towards the stairs. 'We're probably late to a meeting. Go.'

'What are you going to do?' I tilted my head towards a specific part of his body that was not going away.

'I'll stop thinking about you for starters; that should help.'

When I entered the office again, I was still smiling.

'You're in a particularly good mood,' Gayle commented, suddenly falling in step next to me.

'Where did you come from?' I asked, startled.

'Upstairs.' She pointed towards the ceiling with a finger. 'And you?'

'Just a quick meeting. On the phone.'

'Oh, and which phone did you use for this meeting?'

I stopped at the doorway of my office, trying to avoid her knowing gaze. 'What do you mean?'

'Nothing in particular. Just that I called you twice and you didn't answer, so I checked your room and saw your phone on your desk. I'm assuming you were in a meeting with someone else's phone? Maybe someone who is quite tall and struggles to take his eyes off you? Maybe you were in a meeting with that person? And what could be wrong with your lips, I wonder?'

I touched my tender lips with my fingers, frowning. 'What's wrong with my lips?'

'Not much. Just that a certain someone kissed you senseless.'

I got into my room and closed the door on her grinning face.

27

William

I emerged out of the stairway a few minutes after Charlie, ignoring another message and then another call while I was trying to calm down. On my way to my office, my eyes found Charlie in her office, already busy on her laptop.

'William?' Rick called out, heading towards me, and I had to look away.

'Yes?'

'We're going to watch the game tonight; you coming?'

I didn't even know which game they were talking about. 'Maybe next time. I need to go over a few things.'

'Gayle told me about the new airline company. Do you need me to prepare anything before the meeting?'

It took me a few seconds to focus and think about what needed to be done before our call. Not only by my team but also by Kimberly and whomever she chose to bring to the meeting.

My phone went off again, distracting my thoughts. Rick looked at me expectantly.

'Talk to Gayle, and you two do some research and see if they've faced any accusations like this before. Don't share anything at the meeting; we won't be alone. I need to take this call.'

He nodded and left.

I got into my room, closed the door, and let out a long sigh.

My phone wasn't ringing anymore. That was a good sign. But my mind was still full of Charlie. I avoided looking in her direction because once I started, I knew I wasn't going to be able to forget how she looked last night under me. Her eyes half-closed, her moans and cries echoing in my ears. I could still taste her. And the way she was looking at me just ten minutes ago, I could still feel her trembling in my arms, completely unaware of what she was doing to me.

I thought of how I didn't want to get involved with anyone for at least another year. Not only because I didn't have time for a relationship but also because I just wasn't interested. After the last few years with Lindsey, I needed a break.

And then I'd found Charlie again. How life threw our words back into our faces.

Rubbing the bridge of my nose, I took out my phone and stared at the screen – knowing at least one of the names I'd find there. We had finally sold our house just a few weeks ago. We had nothing more to say to each other, yet she had been calling constantly.

I ignored the calls that weren't emergencies and clicked on Lindsey's name.

Lindsey: I'm in New York. I want to talk to you. Please.

We had worked past our normal hours, having dinner in the office. Each team member tried to prepare an action plan for the Ephesus Airlines problem and some leftover things we needed to get done for our remaining accounts. As soon as we got out of the office, we headed home, Charlie's hand always in mine.

We grabbed Pepp from her neighbours' and took him out for a short walk, and then stumbled into my apartment. Because Charlie was barely standing on her own two feet, I told her to lie down on the couch and relax; all she gave me was a tired nod. Pepp took it upon himself to smell the house from top to bottom, even though this wasn't the first time he'd been here. He went to Charlie's side every now and then, gave her a nose bump, and continued on his quest.

After I had prepared a quick snack for Charlie, I took the plate to her side with Pepp trailing me.

When I saw she had already dozed off with a hand under her head, I took the blanket at the end of the couch and gently arranged it over her legs.

'Oh, I'm sorry,' she mumbled, eyes opening slowly as she straightened. 'I didn't mean to fall asleep.'

'It's okay; you've been on your feet all day.'

'So have you. I'm not even that sleepy,' she said, while yawning behind her hand.

I sat next to her, our arms touching, then reached for the plate as Pepp sat right in front of us, expecting his share. He was still eyeing me like he had done that first time I'd met him. But his gaze softened when Charlie reached out and brushed her knuckles against his cheek. He jumped up on the couch and made himself comfortable next to Charlie's other side.

'Is it okay if he is up here?'

'Of course it is.' I held the plate in my hand.

'Oh, what is this?'

'I know you like to have something sweet before you sleep. I promised to cook for you tonight, but we didn't know we'd be working late. And I don't have too much on hand, but I have your favourite.'

'It's okay, we'll do it another night. What is this?'

'Apple sauce. So apple sauce on toast it is.'

She gave me a long look, her eyes sparkling under the low light in the room.

'You bought apple sauce for me? When?'

'I heard you tell my mom it was your favourite thing when you were a kid, and your mom made it from scratch. I know you don't like to talk about your mom, but it sounded like a good memory.'

'So you got me apple sauce.'

'I bought myself apple sauce. You happen to be here.'

A beautiful smile broke out on her face, and she cradled my head in her small hands. 'You bought it for me to have when I came over?'

'Something like that,' I mumbled, feeling as if I was getting lost in her gaze.

She leaned closer and pressed a quick kiss to my lips, pulling away with a grin before I could deepen it.

Then she stole the plate from my hands and picked up one of the slices, biting into it with the most erotic look on her face. I couldn't do anything but watch. She swallowed her bite and turned her eyes to me, offering the next one to me.

I neither loved nor hated apple sauce, but I took what she offered as I stared into her gaze and chewed as she studied me.

Licking her lips, she reached forward, put the plate back on the coffee table and focused on me.

I remembered a question she had asked me just yesterday.

'What do you want from me?' I repeated her words softly.

'You,' she replied just as softly, eyes stuck on my lips.

I gave her what she was asking for and went for her lips. Her soft, bare, and beautiful lips.

28

Charlie

I had spent the night at William's place. I'd only slept with him a total of two times, and when I mean slept, I mean actual sleeping was taking place: eyes closed, bodies wrapped up in each other, and all smiles galore on my part. I had kissed him maybe a little over twenty times in total, counting the kisses at his mom's place. And had sex with him six times in the last two days. Yes, I had absolutely counted.

After all of that, I didn't want to sleep without him again. When I had whispered that to him in the early morning hours, William had just smiled at me, brushed my messy hair away from my eyes, and gently kissed me with a smile on his lips, right after whispering, 'That's not happening anytime soon. Trust me.' A few moments later, we were making number six a reality.

Just a little after he had left for the office, I took Pepp out for his short morning walk, then crossed the street to my own apartment, running into Antonio as he was leaving for work.

'Look who is doing the walk of shame this morning.'

I grinned, not in the least bit ashamed. 'That's me.' Mostly because it was a very short walk across, and I didn't mind Antonio seeing me at all. He got down on his haunches to give Pepp some scratches while his eyes were on me.

'So he is in? It's official?'

The grin just widened on its own. 'He's in.'

'He looks good on you, beautiful.'

I could feel my cheeks heat up a little. 'Thank you, Antonio.'

'We're having a little party between close friends tonight. Celebrating Josh finishing his first draft. If you don't end up working late, bring your guy and drop by.'

I hadn't been around other people with William yet, when we didn't have to hide that we were together. 'I'll ask him. Thank you so much.'

Antonio straightened and Pepp leaned against my leg, his tail thumping the door.

'If you need us to walk Pepp, let Josh know. I think he was planning to take Daisy to the dog park today. She'd love this gentleman's company.'

I petted Pepp's head and shook my head. 'You guys are doing too much already by walking him in the evenings when I'm late.'

'It's not work at all, we love having him around. And have you forgotten all the times you've looked after Daisy when we're away?' His phone started ringing and he distractedly checked the caller. 'Okay, Charlie. I need to take this.'

'Of course.'

He rushed down the stairs, looking over his shoulder. 'Bring William by, we'd love to get to know him better. See you tonight.'

'Have a good day at work!' I shouted as he raised his hand and waved at me while heading down the street.

It took me almost an hour to get to the office after feeding Pepp and getting ready so I was worried I'd be late, but I made it in around 8.45 a.m. so it was still kind of quiet. And most importantly, my dad hadn't showed up. My phone pinged with new messages.

William: When are you getting in?

William: Next time remind me to either wait for you so we can come in together, or just be aware that I'm planning on taking you with me.

Charlie: Why? What's wrong?

William: I keep looking towards your office every minute to see if you're in yet, and it's making it hard to focus on work. That's what's wrong.

William: Are you close?

William: I'm shocked to say that I've missed you in the two hours we've been apart. And I'm slightly appalled that I'm admitting it in a text message.

Laughter startled out of me. Feeling a flutter in my chest, I dropped my bag and everything else in my office and tried not to look as if I was rushing across to his room where I was expecting to find him.

To my surprise, instead of finding William, I found Kimberly, just standing in front of the windows.

She looked over her shoulder when I opened the door hesitantly and walked towards me.

'Good morning, Charlie. I was waiting for William.' She glanced at the phone in her hand. 'The meeting is gonna start soon. I heard that he wanted to see me to fill me in on something about the Ephesus case, but he isn't around and I need to leave.'

By the time I could take a few steps further into the room, she had reached my side. I looked over William's desk. All his stuff was still there.

'He hasn't been here?' I asked with a frown, confused to the point that I forgot I wasn't exactly friendly with Kimberly at the moment.

She gave me a long look, head to toe. I stood straighter, ready for her nonsense. 'He has,' she replied at last. 'I mean, he was here ten minutes ago when he called me in, that's why I came.'

'What was he gonna fill you . . .'

'Meeting will start soon, Charlie. I have work to do.'

Just like that she walked past me, leaving me to close my eyes and count to ten. I released a long breath and turned around to leave, only to come face to face with Gayle as she pushed open the door.

'What were you doing with Kimberly in here?'

'Beats me,' I said with a sigh, shrugging. 'She was already in here when I . . .'

She raised her hand between us. 'Doesn't matter. Where is your phone?'

'In my room. What's going on?'

With two coffee cups clutched in his hands, William appeared next to Gayle. The small crease on his forehead which almost always appeared when he was thinking or distracted smoothed out the second he saw me standing at his doorway.

'Charlie,' he murmured, completely ignoring Gayle's presence.

I smiled and his eyes dipped to my lips for the briefest second until Gayle reached out to grab one of his coffee cups. William turned to her, his brows knitting together as he held on to his mug.

'Not for you, Gayle,' he grumbled. 'Go get your own.'

He moved towards me, standing by my side, and offered one of the two black mugs to me.

I smiled up at him. 'Oh, thank you. Is this your first one?' It must be if he was this grumpy.

Keeping his gaze on me, he nodded and took a sip. 'What are we all doing here in my office? Specifically you, Gayle.'

He broke our eye contact and my heart returned to its normal state.

Gayle rolled her eyes, shaking her head. 'Charlie, you're gonna get a call from our dating app,' she paused, 'in ten. Find Rick, he was the one who helped me with the research so you'll need him.

And you . . .' She turned her gaze to William, who was now standing arm in arm with me. I tried to hold back my smile, but Gayle was all too aware of our closeness. 'You need to be in Douglas's office in fifteen. They moved up the meeting. Did you even leave any coffee in the pot for the rest of us?'

Before William could answer, she was gone. I didn't think he was interested in answering her anyway. He closed the door and faced me with his back to the rest of the office. Only a few steps separated us as he took another sip, eyes intently watching my every move.

I took my time, glanced down at my coffee, noticing that he had already added milk to it. I could guess that a packet of brown sugar had also been added. I blew on it a little and then tasted it. Yup. He made it just as I liked. But then again was it even a surprise?

'I'm struggling not to touch you right now.' His voice was the kind of low and gruff that made me feel pure happiness. 'Or kiss you. Or hug you. Or fuck you. Or hold your hand. Struggling in general, I should say.' He drank from his mug again.

I raised my gaze to his and realized that he was taking me in from head to toe. His eyes lingering on my skirt, or if I'd guessed right, on how it hugged my hips and waist.

'You look beautiful, Charlie,' he added once he was done. 'But then again, when do you not.'

I took in his dark grey suit that fitted him perfectly.

'The same goes for you,' I countered.

He cocked an eyebrow. 'I'm beautiful?'

My lips stretched into a smile. 'Beautiful and sexy and very irresistible.' I bit down on my lower lip. 'And your voice . . .' I closed my eyes for a minute and released a long breath as I took an involuntary step towards him, 'your voice when we're in bed . . . it's deep and when you're talking close to me . . . it's very good.'

I opened my eyes to see his were burning, his pupils dilated. He had moved a step closer to me, his free hand clenching and unclenching constantly.

'So you like when I talk to you,' he muttered.

'We could say that.'

He nodded, his eyes intent. 'I understand.'

I bet he did. I blew out a breath and tried to ignore my body's reaction to him by changing the subject and downing half my coffee. 'So you were shocked that you missed me, huh?'

He tilted his head, studying me quietly. 'Honesty?'

'Yes, please.'

'I'm more than struggling right now. If this wasn't your dad's place I wouldn't give a shit about anybody's opinion and you'd be in my arms in a heartbeat.' He paused and cleared his throat, visibly swallowing. 'But yeah, you could say I missed you,' he answered softly. 'Only because I thought I'd have better control of myself. You didn't miss me then?'

The urge to kiss him grew stronger. There was a knock on the door. I peered around William's body, only to see an exasperated Gayle staring at us through the glass door, pointing at her watch before she walked away.

'Looks like I'm wanted.' We kept studying each other, my body almost swaying towards him. I felt a ghost of a physical pain with the tension in the room and the fact that we were holding back from each other. 'Do you know what's happening with the dating app?' I asked, trying my best to ignore how he was looking at me. 'I thought we were done for the week with them.'

William took a step away from the door, letting me pass. My shoulder brushed against him, causing goosebumps to erupt on my skin. He pushed one of his hands into his pant pocket, the other still holding onto his mug. There was something so sexy about him in a suit with his hand in his pocket. And the grumpiness that came with the lack of coffee just added to it. I almost wanted to jump on him and wrap my legs around him and never come up for air.

With my hand on the doorknob, I waited for his answer.

'They want to pick your brains about a move they want to make, I believe. They wanted to talk to you specifically so I don't have all the details yet.'

'Oh. That's . . . nice.'

'I hope it is. I had to listen to that Darren guy from their team ramble on about you for five minutes.' He had been talking with his back to me, but now he glanced at me. 'Do you even know how hard it is to hold back from kissing you right now?'

My body jolted at his words, a second wave of heat spreading. 'Are you jealous, William Carter?'

His gaze turned intense. 'You never called me by my full name before.'

'Should I not?' I opened the door. From the gleam in his eyes I could tell he liked it.

He put the coffee mug on his desk and stalked towards me. My grip on the door tightened as I heard Rick calling my name from somewhere behind me. William drew closer until he was almost a breath away – as close as he could get to me at the office.

'You should do it more often,' he muttered, gripping the door right next to where my hand was. 'You're avoiding my question.'

I let go of my hold on the door when our fingers brushed, taking a step back. 'I guess I missed you too,' I replied lightly, before we quietly lost our minds.

One of his eyebrows shot up. 'You guess . . . ?'

I gave him a happy smile. He took another step forward. I backed up again. 'You're good to go for the meeting, right? Anything you need from me?'

'Yeah. You.'

Both Rick and Gayle showed up at the same time at the tail end of his words. Gayle dragged William into his office, and Rick guided me towards mine.

When I looked over my shoulder, William's gaze was still on me.

*

I had my phone call with Darren which didn't last long. Then I went into one of the smaller meeting rooms with the rest of our team, waiting for William to come for the last half an hour.

When he did show up and we saw his face, we all tensed up. I'd never seen him really angry so I couldn't compare, but anybody could tell he was fuming. The way his jaw was ticking, his lips pressed into a tight line, not to mention the hard look in his eyes. He didn't glance at any of us as he walked in. With his hands in his pockets, he moved to the windows and gazed out at the New York skyline. We all gave each other a questioning look, but none of us knew what was going on.

Stan, Trisha and I were sitting at the table. I twisted to look back. Rick was standing next to the coffee bar, having topped up his mug just a minute before William had walked in, so he was the closest to him. His gaze darted to me first, but then he turned back to William.

'What's going on?' he asked.

William took a few seconds to face us, his jaw muscles still working.

'We didn't get Ephesus.'

'They picked Kimberly?' I asked, my voice laced with surprise. I had no idea what my sister had prepared to showcase, but we had worked very hard to come up with the absolute perfect plan. There was no way Kimberly would've been able to do that. Not with her experience compared to William's.

His angry eyes landed on me. 'Yes, they chose Kimberly.'

'What was her plan?' Stan asked, just as surprised as the rest of us.

William smirked but it held no amusement. 'Her plan? Well her plan was our plan. That would be the short answer.'

'What do you mean?' Trisha questioned.

William released a long breath. 'She chose to go first, presented what she prepared and it was the exact one we had worked on.'

'How could that happen?'

He faced me. 'Maybe you could tell me that, Charlie.'

There were crickets in the room. An awful feeling filled my chest. 'What?'

'I asked Wilma and she saw you and Kimberly talking in my office.'

'And?' I continued.

'And?' he repeated, his brows shooting up.

'She was in there waiting for you when I came in to . . .' Before I gave away too much, I stopped myself, my brows knitting together in genuine confusion at his tone. I sat up straighter, leaning forward on the desk, meeting his gaze head-on. 'She was already in there William, waiting for you. What does that have to do with anything?'

I forgot that there was anyone but us in the room

He lifted an eyebrow. 'What does that have to *do* with anything?'

My mouth tightened. 'Yes,' I said curtly.

'Did you think that she could be in there looking at our plan? Maybe?'

My brows drew together. 'She was nowhere near your desk.'

William scoffed and turned around, stalking back to his corner in front of the windows. He was rubbing the bridge of his nose.

I stood up, turning towards him, my frown deeper. 'Why would she risk going in there to look at your plan? She wouldn't dare to do something like that.'

He spun around. 'Are you telling me you're protecting her?'

'No!' I rushed out.

'Okay guys,' Rick started, coming to stand between us even though we were nowhere near each other. 'You both need to take a break here. You're raising your voices and people are taking notice.'

I ignored Rick, but stayed in place. 'I'm telling you, she wasn't near your desk. And hell, even if she did look at your plan, are you saying the blame is on me? That I let her look at it or something? Don't you know the relationship I have with her?'

William shook his head, looking away.

'Tell us what happened,' I forced out through gritted teeth. 'Is it a similar plan or the *same* one? Did you present ours?'

'How do you think it'd look if I repeated her exact same plan? I told them Kimberly's was the better option and she should take it on.'

'You did what?'

His expression turned thunderous. 'What did you expect me to do? Look like a fool by repeating her words — words that I wrote down? They already thought I was unprepared. I worked with this company before. This will affect how I look in the industry. This is my job. This is something I'm very good at and it's something I take very seriously. I was distracted with you and this happened.'

That shut me up. I distracted him? And did he think I didn't take my job seriously?

I backed up and sat down. Stung beyond words.

Nobody spoke for at least twenty seconds.

Trisha's phone started ringing. 'I need to take this,' she muttered and quietly left the room, leaving me with William, Stan and Rick.

Stan was the last person I expected to take my side, but he did. 'Okay, so she was in your office and maybe glanced at the papers, did whatever. She sees Charlie coming and she walks away. What did she say to you, Charlie?'

I looked up when there was silence. He was waiting for me to respond. 'She said she was waiting for William so she could ask him something about the meeting. She left before I could say anything, then Gayle walked in and William came right after that.'

'You should've told me,' William mumbled.

My heartbeat accelerated, my face heating. 'I would've never thought she would do something like that. I'm sorry. I ... I wasn't thinking.' I frowned down to the desk. 'I guess I was distracted as well.'

William shook his head. He took his phone out and glanced at the screen briefly, then lightly threw it on the desk.

'What happens now?' Rick asked the obvious.

'Nothing. I apologized and told them they were in good hands. If Kimberly can manage to put everything she stole into action, they should be good.'

'You're not going to say anything to her?'

'Do we have proof that she looked at our work?'

'No,' Rick mumbled, whispering some colourful curses.

I stood up as Gayle and Trisha walked in.

'I'm going to talk to her,' I muttered, half to myself.

'You're not gonna do anything,' William objected, his voice rising again.

'I don't think that's the best idea,' Rick put in at the same time.

'What's going on?' Gayle piped up before I could answer them.

I walked stiffly around the desk and stood next to the open door, ignoring Trisha's and Gayle's inquisitive looks.

'We're not doing anything about it then? That's it?' I avoided William's gaze – if he was even looking at me, that is.

'That's it,' William retorted harshly and my eyes found his.

I completely ignored his scowl and nodded. 'Then I have other work to do.' Turning around, I walked straight out of the meeting room without a glance back, leaving them all in there.

I wasn't the same person I was months ago. I'd promised myself that I would be my own number one, and I was going to follow my own advice. I wasn't going to let *anyone* – *anyone at all* – talk down to me.

After stewing on it for a while, I decided I was still going to have a conversation with Kimberly. I wanted to hear it from her. All I had to do was wait for William to leave for lunch.

After dealing with a phone call from a very excited Laurel Nielson, I walked into my quiet office and closed the door. I rubbed my temples, trying to rid myself of my overwhelming headache. On my desk – not in the pages between my book, but on top of it – I found a note. I glanced down at it, but didn't feel the compelling urge to pick it up, like I usually did.

We'll talk.

I didn't look up, and I certainly didn't try to look for him. I didn't want to talk to him at the office. After the work day was done, maybe. Big maybe. But now, here? No.

My phone started ringing and, hoping it wasn't Laurel again, I glanced at the screen with a grimace. Nora's name flashed on the screen, I didn't feel like I could hold a conversation so I let it go to voicemail.

'Charlie?'

I looked up to see Gayle at my doorway.

'Can I borrow you about the dating app account? I need you to confirm something.'

'Of course,' I muttered, walking towards her.

'Are you good?' she asked, her eyes trying to meet mine.

'I am. Just a headache. Don't worry.'

'You talked to Kimberly?'

At least my friend knew me enough to guess that I would talk to Kimberly. 'Not yet.'

She acknowledged that with a small nod. 'I'm working out here today, just to keep an eye on things.'

I followed her to the open work space and sat next to her. We hadn't even settled down when we heard William's voice. Both our gazes snapped up in the direction of his office, which was almost right next to us. I had purposely avoided him and his room for the last few hours, but now I was too curious to look away.

A woman stood before him in front of his office door. And William looked surprised and uncomfortable. At least from what I could tell.

'Do you know who that is?' Gayle prompted.

'I can't see her face.'

We both watched as William recovered and guided the woman into his office. His eyes darting around only for a second. They never landed on me. When he moved away from her, I realized the woman was pregnant. Her clothes almost hid her belly, but from the side you could tell she was expecting.

A sense of dread filled me as I struggled to take my eyes away from them. The woman was holding her stomach protectively, and talking. William didn't move and I couldn't see his face or his expression.

'Charlie?' Gayle spoke, but I couldn't look away from the scene in front of me because I had a sinking feeling in the pit of my stomach: the woman was his ex. I hadn't seen her in person before, but she looked like the woman in the photo William had shown me.

I suddenly had a heart-clenching moment when William put a hand on her back, guided her out and walked out of his office, pulling the door closed behind him.

As they walked past us, I wanted to clear my throat or do *something* to get his attention, but he didn't notice me, and I couldn't find the voice to make a peep.

'Charlie, are you sure you're good?'

I swallowed the heavy lump in my throat while looking down at the papers strewn in front of me. I was trying my best to remember what Gayle needed me for instead of thinking who William had walked out with.

'What am I looking at here? What did you need me for?'

'We don't have to do this now. This hasn't been the best day for anyone and . . .'

'Gayle, show me what you need from me.'

My phone vibrated on the desk.

Nora calling.

I ignored it and tried to concentrate on Gayle's voice.

'Charlie.'

I looked up and met the gaze of my dad, who was standing right next to me, his expression telling me I was not going to enjoy hearing what he was about say.

29

William

I still had a headache and the painkiller was taking its time to work. Tired, I looked up from all the documents I'd been looking at for the last half-hour and my head jerked back slightly when I saw Lindsey striding towards my office, eyes on me. My jaw clenching, I slowly got up and opened the door. She waited for me to be the first one to speak, her expression calm.

She'd done that a lot in our marriage. She'd always waited for me to speak my mind and shared hers accordingly, if she shared it at all. Some days she would refuse to respond. I'd tell her everything that was bothering me about our relationship and ask for her help to try and change the course our marriage was taking. If she didn't like what I was talking about, or if she didn't like where the conversation was going, she'd just get up in the middle of my speech and walk away – leaving me sitting on our couch alone. And sometimes she would shake her head and apologize, *not now, William. I can't do this right now.*

Charlie crossed my mind and I couldn't help but compare them. Charlie, who was big on honesty and letting me know everything that was on her mind – good or bad. And Lindsey, who wanted to be left alone to the point where we were just roommates who spoke a few words to each other in passing. At the end, I didn't even think we liked each other, let alone cared for each other.

And whereas you could read Charlie's heart just by looking into her face and eyes, with Lindsey you never knew what she was thinking.

I tried to hide my surprise at seeing her in front of me and *pregnant* as best as I could, but I wasn't sure if I succeeded or not. For a split second I thought about how that made me feel – her being pregnant – but nothing came to me. Not anger, not frustration, not disappointment and definitely not sadness.

She studied me in silence. If I had to guess, she was waiting for me to react to this new development I had no clue about.

'What are you doing here?'

'You didn't return my text messages. Or phone calls for that matter. I told you I was in New York.'

My eyebrows rose. 'Something wrong with the house? Escrow didn't go through?'

She shook her head. 'No, everything is fine with the house.'

'Then I don't know what we'd need to talk about. I'm in contact with the real estate agent.'

She shifted on her feet, sighed and glanced inside my office.

'Any way you can invite me inside instead of having a conversation in front of everybody?'

My gaze went to Charlie's office by instinct, but she wasn't in there. She had barely spent any time in her office today – making it hard for me to put right what had gone wrong earlier.

I sighed and stood to the side so Lindsey could walk in. She wrapped her arm around her stomach in a protective gesture and stopped near my desk. I'd invite her to sit, but I didn't want to encourage her to spend more time here.

'How can I help you?' I asked, standing a little away from her.

'There are things I wanted to talk to you about. About the divorce and everything else that happened. You weren't accepting my phone calls so I thought it'd be better if we did this face to face.'

'You should've taken it as a sign that I didn't have anything I wanted to discuss with you.'

She huffed a little with annoyance and took a deep breath. 'I'm pregnant, William.'

My gaze fell to her stomach. 'I can see that.'

'That's all you have to say?'

'What else would you like to hear? You don't think I would fall for *I'm pregnant with your baby*, right?'

'That was harsh, William. Even for you.' She paused, taking in my distant stance and expressionless face. 'This isn't you. Holding things in. You always say whatever is on your mind.'

'I just told you what was on my mind.'

My office phone started ringing.

I let out a breath and rubbed my temples. No painkiller would come to my aid today, and I needed air. And to get Lindsey to leave.

'It's lunch hour. If this is gonna take you long, I don't want to do this at my workplace. We'll sit somewhere so you can say what you came all the way here to share.'

Her mouth was set in a straight line when she nodded. I guided her outside my office and walked right next to her towards the elevators.

Charlie still hadn't return to her office. I felt a tinge of regret for our argument this morning, but confused and overwhelmed by Lindsey appearing at my office unannounced, I kept my eyes to the ground to avoid any unnecessary interaction with anyone and tried to focus on the situation.

The elevator doors opened and Lindsey stepped in, waiting for me.

I left.

30

Charlie

An hour and a half had passed since William had walked out with his ex-wife and still they hadn't returned. I wasn't obsessing. I had by chance checked the time once or twice and simply noticed it. Not because of curiosity whatsoever. What did I even have to be worried about? Not much.

Considering I was still pissed at him, he could do whatever he wanted.

I turned around when I heard Kimberly's office door opening and she stepped in with a curious look on her face.

She paused in the doorway. 'What are you doing in here?' Sighing, she shook her head, heading to her desk. 'I'm very busy, Charlie. Whatever it is can wait.'

I took a few steps towards her. 'Not this.'

She took a seat, but I stayed where I was.

'I guess you decided you're talking to me again?' She raised an eyebrow, putting her knuckles under her chin.

'I wouldn't say so. I just wanted to ask something.'

'Well, go ahead since you're already here. How can I help you?'

'What is your problem?' I took another step forward. 'No, seriously, I'm genuinely curious. What is it?'

She rolled her eyes. 'Charlie, stop being so dramatic.'

'I'm not being dramatic. I want to hear what your problem is with me. I'm pretty sure you're not stupid enough to think that I would flirt with your husband, nor are you that jealous. Why? I think I'm at least entitled to an answer.'

'You want to do this right now? Here at the office?'

'It's just as good as any place.'

She leaned back in her seat. 'You did flirt with him. You two were always laughing in a corner. Or he'd be in the kitchen with you for the monthly dinners.'

'And that is my fault, how? Did I call him to my side to keep me company? Did I ever in my life do anything similar to what you accused me of?'

'That means nothing. I know you two get along.'

'Yes,' I hissed out. 'Yes, we do, because we're family. He is your husband, for fuck's sake! How could you even think that I'd do anything like that? Do you not even know your sister?'

She let out a long breath. 'Why are we discussing it again? Especially now?'

'Because you never let me talk about this. You accused me in front of everyone at the office and then just acted as if nothing was wrong with your husband. You never let me get a word in.'

'Again, why are we discussing this now? I said what I believed was happening and what bothered me. There is nothing else to say.'

'So your husband is just fine even though you think he flirted with me, but your sister is not?'

She rubbed the bridge of her nose as if I was inconveniencing her, and then checked the time on her phone. 'I don't want to talk about this again. I have a meeting in fifteen, if that's all . . .'

'No, that's not all. Did you think it would be okay if you just sneaked into William's office and stole his plan to present it as yours? Are you that insane? Or is this just who you are and I've just never seen it?'

'I'd be very careful with what you're accusing me of.'

I put my hands on the chair in front of her desk and tilted my head. 'Oh? And that should do what? Scare me, I guess?'

Rising from her chair, she met my gaze head-on.

Before she could get a word in, I spoke up.

'I'm done with you, Kimberly. I'm just done. I don't care if we talk or don't.' I lifted a shoulder and dropped it. 'I genuinely don't care.' I'd felt this way for a while and saying it out loud made me stand straighter and somehow feel lighter. 'I'm done trying to look okay in front of Dad and Grandma. I'm done avoiding you or tip-toeing around you. More importantly, I'm done letting you treat me like shit for something I didn't even do. But stealing plans my team worked on? That's low even for you.'

'Do whatever you want, Charlie. That's what I'm doing. I told you I didn't want to talk about this with you again. I know what I saw and how you were with him, I'm not going to apologize for wondering what you were thinking while you were getting close to my husband.'

'Honestly, I don't give a single fuck about you or your husband. Not anymore, not after today. But stealing. That part I'm very interested in.'

'Why would I need to steal anything? I'm very successful at my job.'

My eyes grew big. 'I'm wondering the same thing. Why do you think? And please, you're nowhere near as good as William and we both know it. Even Dad knows it.'

'Get out of my office.'

'You were alone in his office when I walked in.'

'And? That means I stole your plan?'

'Show me what you presented then. I know how you work. You write everything down a million times. Show me this imaginary thing you worked on.'

Her phone started ringing, but neither of us paid it any attention – we were too busy staring each other down.

'You're pushing it, Charlie. Leave my office.'

'If you don't have anything to worry about, show me your files. William won't ask you, but I want to see.' She was quiet. 'Come on, you should love the opportunity to make me look bad. Hell, I'll even apologize to you if you have this extensive plan you prepared that is somehow the exact same as ours.'

'I'm not showing you anything.' Her chest rose and fell in anger and she was gripping the edge of her desk.

'I thought so.'

'What's going on here?'

We both turned our heads to see my dad standing at the door with a crease between his brows.

'I can hear your voices from my office. What the hell is going on?'

'Nothing Dad, don't worry. Charlie was leaving.' Kimberly met my gaze. 'We're done here.'

I smiled at her sweetly. 'I don't think we are.' I slid my dad a quick look. 'I want to see the project she prepared for Ephesus Airlines. You think she is so great, so I want to learn from my sister.'

'Why? Did William ask to see it?'

I gritted my teeth. 'No. *I'm* curious.'

'About?'

I fisted my hands at my sides. Why would he never take my side about anything? 'About the work she did that was supposedly better than my team's.'

He released a long-suffering sigh. 'Charlie, stop acting like a kid. Please, go back to your work.' Just like that he left.

When I looked at Kimberly she had a small smile playing on her lips.

Realizing talking to her was pointless, I followed my dad. I caught up to him in front of Wilma's desk.

'She presented the exact same plan as ours. There is no way it was a coincidence, Dad. I found her in William's office this morning, she must have looked at our work.'

He looked around us, and I noticed people were listening to us intently. I didn't care. I saw Gayle and Rick heading my way in my peripheral vision, but I kept talking.

'I want to see her project. We know how she jots down on every inch of a paper. I want her to show her hard work. I want to make sure that she didn't steal from us. If she has nothing to worry about, this should be easy for her.'

'You're being a bit too much, Charlie, don't you think? Why would she need to steal from your team? She wanted this account, and the airline company chose her. Even William recognized it was a good plan in the meeting.'

I took a step forward. 'Oh, yes. Let's talk about William. Do you really think Kimberly would come up with a better action plan than him?' I raised and dropped my hands. 'He has experience with this company. The company originally wanted to work with him. And if that's the case, she should show what she worked on. Hell, I want to learn from her infinite wisdom.'

His gaze hardened as he faced me. 'She doesn't have to show you anything. What's gotten into you? You weren't even in the meeting, so what would you know? Does William know you're accusing your sister?'

I ignored the William part. He had nothing to do with this. 'He told us it was the exact same plan. He doesn't have to know everything I'm doing, so to answer your question – no he doesn't know. We already know she took it, but it doesn't look like you care about that part. Which I guess shouldn't surprise me.'

The entire office was silent other than a random phone ringing in the background. In a second that was silenced as well.

'Excuse me?' His eyes flashed, brows furrowing. 'You're testing me, Charlie. Kimberly told me she saw you with William outside of work. Just because I'm not mentioning it, don't think I'm clueless.' His eyes moved on me in distaste. 'Is that why you've been dressing like this? Do you think it looks good on you? You look like some-body stuffed you in that skirt.'

My body heated, from head to toe. His words broke my heart – and the fact that he was just fine saying them in front of an audience caused me to see red instead of feeling ashamed. As much as I loved him, I didn't give a shit what he thought about my clothes now.

However, I still felt like an active volcano about to go off at any second. 'Of course, she told you,' I forced out, ignoring the last bit of his words.

'Yeah, so go cool off before I say something that'll hurt. We'll talk about this when you get home. I'll drop by.'

I snorted, hot flames coming off of the top of my head. My mind felt numb. Even my fingers were tingling with rage. I watched as his jaw started ticking when I didn't move.

'When did you ever hold back? Why do so now?' I asked softly, not expecting an answer.

'Get out, Charlie. You're done for the day. And I'm taking you off William's team.' He turned back to a slack-faced Wilma, dismissing me.

'Charlie,' Gayle whispered behind me, putting her hand on my back. 'Maybe you . . .'

My dad was already back to business as if I'd been a speck of inconvenience in his day. 'Wilma, let me know when . . .'

'I quit,' I announced into the silence and, clearly annoyed, he slowly looked at me over his shoulder.

'Charlie . . .'

I raised my chin, standing straighter. 'I took a job in California. I leave at the end of the month.'

Now he faced me fully once again, his brows knitting. 'What job? What are you talking about?'

'I quit, it's that simple. I love you because you're my dad, but I don't like how you've been treating me or other people. I love that you took care of us after Mom left. But I can't work with you. I can't stay around this family and be the punching bag anymore. You have no idea how wrong you are with some things. Hell, you don't even know your own daughter. You just think your way is right and nobody else's opinion matters. You never listen to me. You never take me seriously enough. And I'm done. I can't do it anymore. I *won't* do it anymore.'

He opened his mouth to speak, but then stopped. His tongue pushed against his cheek, his expression hardening. 'I won't help you.'

'Please don't. I didn't ask for your help. I was going to give you my two weeks' notice soon, but I think you'd rather have me out of here now, and to be honest nothing would make me more happy. I'll pack my stuff.' I turned around to leave and Gayle quickly stood to the side, her eyes wide in shock. Considering not much could shock Gayle, I thought I'd done rather well, even though I wished the entire thing hadn't happened in front of everyone at the office.

I paused and glanced over my shoulder. 'Oh, I'll leave the apartment first thing tomorrow morning and stay with a friend till I leave.'

'Who's gonna take you with that dog of yours?'

I raised a brow. 'Don't worry, I have friends. I won't knock on your door. And I'll leave my laptop and office phone on the desk just now.'

Without waiting for another word, I walked away.

I met Kimberly's eyes as she watched me from the entrance of her office. I couldn't tell what she was thinking, but I realized that I genuinely didn't care anymore.

I walked past her and away from them.

It felt as if I was walking on air.

I was walking out with a small cardboard box in my arms when Gayle and Rick came running after me.

'I didn't know you were trying to find another job,' Rick started. 'And in California of all places.'

I gave him a quick glance. 'Sorry for not sharing before, I thought maybe it would fall through or something. That's a lie.' I shifted on my feet and focused on Gayle. 'I was a little scared to tell. Obviously this wasn't how I wanted you guys to hear it.'

'When did you find it?' Gayle asked, and I couldn't tell if she was angry at me or not.

'A week or two ago.'

She sighed, and I felt bad all over again for not finding the courage to tell her the second Nora had said they wanted me there. We made it to the curb where I'd wait for my Uber. I turned to them. 'I'm sorry. A lot of things were happening and I just kept pushing it back. I also didn't imagine I would quit today and look where we are.'

Gayle looked away. 'It's fine. I knew you wanted to leave, that's not the surprise. It just caught me off guard.' She met my gaze and gave me a small smile. 'I'm happy for you. I'll miss working with you, sure, but I know this is better. And I'll visit you plenty of times, it's not like you can get rid of me that easily.'

I turned to Rick, feeling my eyes start to water, just a tiny little bit. 'You'll come too? With Linda and everyone?'

'We will.'

'Hold this.' I pushed the fairly light cardboard box into Rick's arms before he could protest and hugged Gayle and she hugged me back.

'I know I'm still here, it's not like I'm leaving tomorrow, but thank you for being one of my best friends,' I whispered, feeling choked up. 'For everything.'

'Oh shut up. I'll pick you up tomorrow morning and you'll stay at our place till you're leaving.' She pulled back. 'That is, of course, if you were serious up there when you said you'll leave the apartment too.'

I grabbed my box from Rick and gave him a tight half-hug – as tight as I could hug him with one arm.

'No, I'll find some other place to say.'

'Excuse me?'

'I don't want to bother Kevin, I know he likes his alone time with you.'

'You're welcome to stay with us, Charlie,' Rick added before Gayle could snap at me again. 'If you don't mind the kids, that is.'

I smiled at him. 'You have a new baby on the way. And a whole schedule with the kids. I'm not gonna add myself to the mix for you to worry about.'

My phone pinged with a message. I reached into my box and checked the screen, looking around the street after seeing it was from my Uber. For half a second there I'd hoped it was William and that hurt.

'Okay, that's for me.'

Rick looked between me and Gayle and sighed. 'I'll head upstairs, Charlie. I'll give you a call tomorrow just in case you change your mind, yeah?' He leaned down and gave my cheek a kiss.

I smiled. 'Sure. Talk to you soon.'

When he left it was just the two of us.

'You're staying with me until you leave.'

'I . . .'

'I get it, you probably want to stay with William, but I get to have you for at least a few days.'

William . . .

Sure I'd love to stay with him, but he was renting his place from my dad, and I didn't want to get out of one of his houses only to move into the next. Plus, would William even want me to stay with him? I knew he would . . . but maybe he was still mad after this morning.

'I have no idea if he'd be interested in that. And I have Pepp, too. Would Kevin even be okay with that? He isn't exactly a small puppy any more.'

'That's because he isn't a puppy. He is a horse baby.' She lifted her shoulder and then dropped it. 'Kevin loves you, he'll be just fine with Pepp because of that.'

The protest was at the tip of my tongue, but she stopped me by seizing my arms, forcefully turning me around and pushing me towards my waiting Uber. 'Stop worrying. We're actually doing better, slightly, but still better. And not only that, it'll be good to have you around. You know he likes you, so again, stop worrying. You'll stay at my place. You owe me at least that much now that you're gonna be full-time with Valerie.'

'Is that jealousy I'm hearing, Gayle? Colour me surprised.'

'I'll colour you red tomorrow. Come on.' She opened the door on the waiting black Prius and I sat on my ass. 'Go pack up, I'll come by after I get out of here and help out.'

I put the box next to me as Gayle shut the door.

'Would you mind if I take a call from my husband before we leave?' the driver asked and I nodded to her with a small smile.

The window was already open so I leaned out of it. 'Thank you. I'm not gonna refuse your help.'

'Don't worry. And I'll leave when William comes around. Did you hear from him? Do you know where he is?'

'Still with the ex, I'm guessing. He left a note in my room that said *we'll talk later*, but I have no idea.' My eyes slid to my phone, but I knew there was no word from him. My heart squeezed in on itself just a little. Not because I was jealous of him being with his ex-wife – I knew that he really didn't want her back. But she was pregnant and what if . . .

'Don't go there,' Gayle muttered and my gaze snapped to her. 'Anyone can see your emotions play on your face, Charlie. I always tell you. Whatever you're thinking I'm sure it's not that.'

I shook my head, trying to let go of my bad feelings. I forced a smile I wasn't quite feeling. 'I'm not thinking anything. Promise. I'll see you tonight then?'

'Yes. I'll bring food and a bottle of rosé.'

'Perfect.'

The driver finished her call so I looked out the window and waved at Gayle. The car started moving and my gaze snapped to the building, to the 20th floor of Atlas Communications. Not that I could make anything out, but I still gazed up. I didn't feel upset, not really. I actually felt free and happy, but there was just a little tiny place in my heart that was sad to let go.

My phone started ringing as we passed the building so I reached for it.

Nora calling.

I cleared my throat, took a deep breath and let it all out as if I could get rid of all the stress and bad energy clinging to me before I hit the green button. 'Hi Nora!'

'Hey! Did I catch you at a bad time?'

'Oh no. It's good. How are you?'

'I'm good, Charlie. How are you?'

I didn't know her enough to recognize exactly what I was hearing in her voice, but I could tell it wasn't something positive. 'Great. Thank you. How can I help you?'

I bunched up the fabric of my skirt in my hand and waited for her to go on.

'So, okay. I have news, and I'm not sure how you'll take it.'

'Okay,' I said slowly. 'Hit me with it then.'

'So you were gonna be here the last week of this month. That's how we talked, but the situation changed and we kinda need you to be here in forty-eight hours.'

A few seconds passed in silence from both ends.

'New client?' I thought to ask and my voice came out scratchy.

'Exactly. Can't share the name yet until you get here and sign the confidentiality docs, but we really need you to be here right away. It's a big name celebrity and you know how it goes. And I realize we're not giving you any time to prepare for a move across the country, but as soon as you get started with the new client and it calms down a bit, you can go back and handle everything.'

'How long do you think that would take? I know you can't tell me what's happening with the client, but can you give me a rough timeline?'

'It's hard to say because you never know with these things and it depends on how you work – but I'd say you'd be able to head back to NY in a month? Around that time.'

The driver hit the brake a little too hard when the car in front of us suddenly stopped and my box slid forward on the back seat next to me. I grabbed hold of it, pulling it to my lap and clutching it to my chest. Trying to think. Trying to make it work. I had Pepp. I couldn't just jump on a plane with him. There'd be paperwork I'd need to get ready and that meant time. Time, apparently, I suddenly didn't have.

'Do you need some time to think? If you can't make it, Charlie, I completely understand. We'll have to go with someone else for the spot, and I hate doing that because I was looking forward to working with you . . .'

Nora kept talking, but I was still thinking and her voice slowly drifted to the background in my mind.

Work wouldn't be a problem since I'd literally just quit, but Pepp . . . My mind was racing, trying to fit everything together so I wouldn't lose this opportunity. Because if I did, I knew it would take me some time to recover from it. For a quick second I thought about William, but he still hadn't called. What would me leaving so abruptly mean for us? But if he wasn't even around, did he get to be a part of my answer?

And I realized in that moment, among the noisy NYC traffic, that I wasn't going to put someone else before me again. I was done. Not a guy. Not even family in my case. I wanted this and I was going to reach for it. I was done pushing my life back. I knew William was different, he wasn't like Craig or anyone else for that matter, but I needed to do this for myself.

'I can make it,' I announced over her voice. 'I can absolutely make it. No problem.'

She stopped talking, and I was grinning like an idiot.

'You can be here in forty-eight hours?'

I nodded enthusiastically. 'Yes, I'll be there tomorrow actually.'

'Okay! That's good. That's really good, Charlie. We are paying for the ticket since it's so last-minute. We'll book your flight for tomorrow then. That works for you?'

The gears in my mind worked overtime. 'How about very early tomorrow morning? If you can find a flight, can we do that?'

'Done. I'll have it handled. See you tomorrow then. I can't wait.'

I laughed, unable to hold in my excitement. 'Same here. Talk to you soon, Nora.'

We hung up, and I just watched the buildings and people pass by. I didn't hear a single sound; my mind was abuzz.

And it was a new beginning for me. For Pepp and me.

A little part in my heart ached a little, and I put my hand against my chest, surprised to feel it so acutely. I'd wanted to move away and start anew for so long that this hurt that I was feeling was unexpected enough to make me frown.

William, I thought, feeling a new crack form in my heart. What would happen to us now?

William . . .

31

William

16 hours later ...

It was 6 a.m. when I exited the cab and rubbed my temple, only just seeing where I was going. There was hardly any light outside, and I hadn't gotten any sleep at the hospital, which only fuelled my headache after the day I'd had.

Charlie, I thought, as I had done more than a few times ever since I'd left the office. I realized I shouldn't have left the way I did, but I was too frustrated and angry at what happened at the meeting to think clearly. She had nothing to do with it, that much I knew, and she hadn't deserved me snapping at her.

I had left her a note hoping to talk to her at lunch and apologize for letting my anger get in the way, but I hadn't had the time.

I turned around to look at her apartment, trying to decide whether I should knock on her door or not. It was still too early, so I hesitated. I saw her light go on and I let that change my mind. If she had just woken up, I could catch her before she left for work.

Making the decision to go back to my own place, I turned around. I'd take a shower. Change. And then cross the street to knock on her door and maybe take Pepp out for his short morning walk with her. Letting out a long breath, I pushed my hands into my pockets and unwillingly went to my own apartment.

32

William

After getting ready for work and then downing two cups of coffee, I locked my apartment and headed across the street. I knew she couldn't have left for work yet.

I rang her doorbell.

No one answered.

I rang again.

Then again.

And again.

33

Charlie

A few days later . . .

'You sure you're good?' Valerie asked as I tried to get her out the door.

'Yes. For the hundredth time, I'm good. I'm okay and great. You can go.'

She lowered her eyes, but still thankfully moved. 'You're not great. You're just good at hiding that you're not great.'

'Okay.' I grabbed the doorframe and closed it halfway, keeping my body in the opening. 'Still doesn't mean you're gonna babysit me.'

'Maybe I want to stay home. It *is* my home, and I'm a homebody, and again maybe I want to stay home.'

I grinned. 'You said that already. And you're not even close to being a homebody. You already had this weekend away planned a month ago, you're not gonna change it for me. I've been here for four days, so it's not like I just came in the door and you're leaving. I work here now, you'll see me plenty when you come back.'

She hesitated. Her eyes narrowed as she assessed my emotional state.

There had been some crying, for different reasons. Maybe some crying about family. Maybe a little for missing Pepp, and maybe just a little tiny bit of crying for William. But the last one I hadn't done next to Valerie. Those tears had come in private when I had gone to bed and tried to sleep. But I was fine. Completely fine and okay.

'Fine,' she answered after watching me. I have no idea what she saw, but her body visibly relaxed.

'I'll still call from Florida. If this wasn't one of Ed's best friends getting married I'd get out of it. You know I would.'

'I know you would, but you don't have to. I'm spending today looking at houses, and tomorrow I'll head down to the office anyway. We wouldn't have spent time together.'

'I wanted to see the houses with you.'

'You will. I'll send you photos.'

'Valerie!' Her fiancé shouted from the car and we both looked at him. 'We need to leave if we're gonna make our plane.'

Val waved her hand. 'Give me two minutes.'

Turning to me she huffed. 'Fine. I'm leaving then.'

'Have fun.'

'Are you going to call him?'

I didn't need to ask who she was talking about. 'Nope. You know how bad I feel for the way I left, but I didn't have a choice, they would've hired someone else and I'd already quit. I called him before I left. He never returned my call. He didn't even call me *after* he learned I left. What else can I do?'

Valerie winced. 'Are you sure? Maybe he said something to Gayle?'

'If he had, Gayle would've told me. She didn't even mention him, so I'm not going to be the one who asks.'

'Fine, have it your way.'

'No other way I know.'

She started walking backwards. 'If you need anything call me.'

'Okay. Love you! Miss me, please.'

'Already do. Love you back!' She got in the car, pushed her head out the window and sent me a big kiss before Ed started driving away.

I was still smiling when I got inside and closed the door. I rested my back against it and let a breath out.

Pepp. It was all about Pepp. I was this sad because I was missing his little but big face. That first day I'd left, I'd had to leave him with Antonio and Josh. Not only because he was used to them and loved them, but also because Gayle was working and we hadn't set everything up. Thinking of Antonio and Josh, I was already missing them. It had been a hard goodbye for all of us. But they had promised to visit next time they were in LA. After that first day, Gayle had gotten Pepp from them and had been taking care of him the last few days. We FaceTimed every night after Gayle came back from work and as soon as we hung up I'd start to miss him all over again.

I had no idea how my dad had reacted to me leaving so quickly because I'd asked Gayle not to tell me anything related to the office. No gossip on who was saying what about me, or what had happened after I'd stormed off. One way or the other, I didn't care to know. Like I'd told my dad, it wasn't as if I'd never talk to him again, but I needed some time away without any conversations. And it wasn't as if he was calling me all day, every day, and I wasn't answering. He hadn't called. Not at all. But if I knew him at all, I knew he was waiting for me to come crawling back. Which wasn't happening.

As for Pepp, our plan was to get him here with Gayle. She was about to ask for some of her vacation days and jump on a plane with Pepp, whose paperwork was ready.

Only one more week, I thought. I'll be with him in one more week and then I would feel a little better and less homesick. That was the plan. As for William, I was trying my best not to think about him. Sure, I wanted to at least text and ask why . . . why say all the amazing things he had said to me if we were going to crumble at the very first blow? Was he still angry at me? Could I have said something that would have helped things?

I pushed out a breath. This was why I didn't want to talk about William to Valerie and Ed. The moment I started thinking about him sadness would creep up and I didn't know what to do, so I did my best not to. Unfortunately for me, it looked like I was going to do a lot of missing for a long long time.

I walked away from the door, mentally pushing everything that was William out of my head and trying to think of all the things I needed to get done for the day instead. Disappointment got me nowhere before and it wouldn't get me anywhere now.

I had only taken a few steps towards the kitchen when I heard a knock on the door. Thinking Valerie had forgotten something, I rushed back and opened it without checking who was on the other side.

William.

It took my eyes a few seconds to realize who was standing in front of me. My mind blanked. He met my gaze steadily, hands in his pockets, expression unreadable.

Feeling something rise up inside me, I shut the door in his face as quickly as I could. Suddenly I was out of breath and out of words. Suddenly I didn't know what to do with myself.

My mind reeled as I just stood there. The door was the only thing between us.

He didn't knock again straight away, and I didn't know what I should do, let alone how to move.

William was in California?

Then the knock came again. It was a tiny sound, as if he wasn't sure if he should be knocking. I don't think I would've heard it if I were further into the house.

I didn't answer. I didn't know what I could say if I answered. So I waited.

'Charlie.'

When I heard my name, the lowest sound, I made it back to the door and rested my forehead against it. Remembering that just a week ago we were in the same situation, the only difference being we were across the country for this version of it.

I held my breath.

Longing. Deep longing filled my chest. Was he angry at me? Did he still want me? Was I ready to hear any of it?

'I'm sorry I'm here so late. I hoped you wouldn't turn me away.'

That's all he said, yet it hurt my heart so much. Was I going to turn him away? How could he even think that? But maybe he was with his ex again. Maybe they had decided to give it a go.

So whatever he came here to tell me, I would keep my chin up and listen and then say goodbye if that's what he had come here to say. At least this time around we would have that going for us. And then we'd move on. Or try to.

Taking a deep breath and letting it all out, I reached for the door and opened it. He was standing in the exact same spot, in the exact same position.

I made sure I was holding onto the handle so I could stand straight and meet his eyes. I hoped I looked strong and unaffected.

'How can I help you?' I asked and his face fell a little. Then he smiled a sad little smile that I didn't return. Why did it feel like I wanted to cry? I was fine. I'd been fine all week. But he was standing right in front of me.

'I'd like for us to talk.'

'Okay. About?'

He opened his mouth, but then closed it.

I waited. My heart beating in my throat, I waited.

He glanced towards the street, but since I was still standing inside I didn't see what he was looking at.

When his eyes returned to me, the smile on his face was a little more genuine. 'Could you give me a moment, please? There is someone here who'd like to see you.'

Before I could tell him anything, he was walking away. I stood exactly where I was. I didn't even move a muscle. I wasn't sure if I could. Trying to keep a straight face, I waited for him to come back.

If he was here to just apologize and then leave, I wasn't sure if I could keep it together in front of him. And if he was here to apologize *and* bring his wife to meet me? His pregnant wife ... I would just shut the door in their faces and then wait for the earth to open up beneath my feet so I could disappear. If he was here to say he wanted to be with me, I'd drop to the floor and start crying.

I saw William first and then a big, big baby who made me gasp quite audibly.

'Pepp!' I squeaked and slowly dropped to my knees. He swung his head towards me when he heard my voice, his big cheeks flopping with his head. Then he was barking and crying and rushing to my arms. He was strong enough that his weight caused me to fall on my ass even as I wrapped my arms around his already too-big body. He wiggled out of my arms only to run around me and then come back and jump on my shoulders. I noticed tears falling from my cheeks even as I was laughing as he kept bumping his head into mine. It had barely been a week, but I had missed him like crazy.

'Look how big you are, you handsome boy,' I crooned, still laughing as he licked and licked my face while he was whining. 'I missed you too.' I held his big head in my hands and smiled at him as he lolled his big tongue out and smiled back at me. I gave him a big hug and held on tight. 'I missed you so much,' I whispered.

I was still laughing since Pepp was licking my ear and my hair, his body still a wiggling mess in my arms, when I heard William clear his throat.

Still rubbing my hands on Pepp's body, I looked up to meet his gaze. I'd almost forgotten that he was standing there. Almost.

'I think I saw a dog park around the corner. We could take him there if you'd like. He's been in the car since the airport.'

I slowly stood up and brushed off my clothes. Pepp did what he always did since that first day we'd met. He leaned his big body against my leg and gazed up at me as if I were his world. My eyes teared again and I petted his head, watching as he closed his eyes with every swipe of my hand.

I glanced back up at William and nodded.

'I'll get the keys.'

Pepp followed me as I went to the kitchen. For a brief moment I considered maybe changing out of my clothes since I was wearing just comfy leggings and an oversized tee-shirt, but decided against it. Mostly because William was waiting just outside the door and I wouldn't want him to think I was changing to look good for him.

I came back to the open door, put on my shoes and stepped outside. William took a few steps back and handed me Pepp's leash. I put it on the good boy who was just waiting right next to me. I closed the door and we started walking towards the small dog park.

William was walking on my left and Pepp was on my right, looking up at me after every few steps. Quite possibly making sure I wasn't disappearing on him again.

Neither one of us said a word to each other for the few minutes it took us to get to the park. There were no dogs around. We stepped inside the gates and Pepp looked up at me as I took off his leash.

He ran a few steps away, then ran back to me. He did it a few times and made me laugh. When he was sure I was following him and staying in his eyeline, he started to walk off to sniff his new grounds.

I waited, my soul vibrating with hope, but William wasn't speaking.

Having had enough of it, I spoke first. 'Gayle was going to bring him to me next week.'

William cleared his throat. 'I changed her mind.'

'I see.'

'Charlie. Charlie can you look at me?'

I kept my eyes on Pepp. Up until I felt William's finger on my chin. He slowly turned my face to his. When had he gotten so close? We were basically standing on top of each other. He stared into my eyes for a long moment. Why was I so afraid?

'You left,' he said at the end.

'You didn't come,' I replied, in a surprisingly steady voice.

'Did you wait for me at all?'

'I called,' I said softly. 'More than a few times. I don't know what else I could've done. I wanted to stay, but I wasn't sure . . .'

'You could've waited for me. Just a little more.'

'I got scared that it'd end up like the first time I waited for you.' I hadn't even admitted that to myself for the first few days.

He smiled and let go of my chin. 'You're right. I can't argue with that.'

He pushed his hands into his pants again and just waited next to me, both of us watching Pepp run around and come back to me and then run back out again.

A few people walked in and Pepp rushed to greet the newcomers. In just a few seconds it was a pup party.

We watched as he played with the other dogs and timidly said hi to their owners.

We watched as Pepp peed.

'I'd like to go back home,' I said quietly, and I realized there was something in my voice. A little catch. A little something broken. He'd said he wanted to talk, but he wasn't saying anything, and I'd rather go and hide back at Valerie's place and hug Pepp. So he hadn't come to be with me. He'd come to say goodbye. My heart broke.

He nodded and we walked home.

When we made it there, I unlocked the door, opened it. Then I let the good boy rush inside to discover the new place. I stepped in after him and turned back to William. I was thinking I should probably thank him for bringing Pepp to me and just saying goodbye before he could tell me something that would upset me, but he spoke first.

'Can I come in?'

I hesitated, and he noticed it.

'Charlie. We need to talk, and I wasn't going to do it with strangers and dogs running around us. Let me come in. If you don't like what you're hearing you can send me away. You hold all the cards here, not me.'

That raised my hackles. 'I'm not playing a game, William. I never was.'

He pressed his mouth closed, the muscle in his jaw ticking. Then he walked in without waiting for an invitation. When his fingers brushed mine on the doorframe, I pulled my hand back and moved away a few steps, fighting with my body over the tingling sensation his touch had caused. He closed the door and took off his shoes.

I left him alone to go and find Pepp and remember how to breathe. He was walking in circles in the kitchen looking for something. I ignored William's presence as much as I could and went to give my baby some water, which he finished in a second, so I filled it up again. A few moments, a few kisses and another big hug later, he was in the living room already up on Valerie's light grey couch. I winced, thinking how I'd explain the big dog in her house when she came back on Monday. The plan had been me moving out to an Airbnb until I found myself a place and stayed there with Pepp, but I'd thought I'd have at least a few more days to find a place.

I was standing just inside the living room when I felt William coming up behind me.

My nerves were getting to me by having him this close. My heart a jumbled mess inside my chest.

'You're going to avoid looking at me the entire time?' he asked quietly.

Pepp closed his eyes, leaving me alone with William.

I tried my best to steady myself, but I hadn't quite managed it when I finally turned to face William. His eyes travelled every inch of my face as my heartbeat picked up speed. I wanted to cry because not being able to hug him was killing me.

'I missed you,' he said, his eyes trying to catch mine. Not sure what to do with my hands as I clutched one of my elbows to myself. 'Talk to me, please. I'm not used to having you so quiet and it's starting to scare me.'

'Why?' I closed my eyes and took a breath through my nose as I opened them again. 'Never mind. It's okay, William. You don't have to explain anything to me. I understand. We don't even have to do this. Thank you for bringing Pepp, I really appreciate it, but you can leave if you want to. No explanation necessary.'

He tilted his head and watched me. I fidgeted in place under his scrutiny. Wanting him to leave almost as much as I wanted him to stay and kiss me and never let go.

As if he had heard my thoughts, he took two steps towards me, standing right in my face.

'Look at me,' he murmured. 'Charlie, look at me.'

I looked up and stared into his eyes.

'Do you see someone who wants to leave?'

I didn't know. And how should I even know?

He sighed, his body deflating a little. 'I still think of you a hundred times a day, Charlie. Do you remember what you told me once?'

My eyes on him, I waited.

'You said, *I want to find someone who is afraid of losing me.* That's me Charlie. *I am* afraid of losing you right now.' He smiled, a small one that didn't reach his eyes. He looked away. And that's when I realized that William Carter was actually nervous. 'I was afraid of losing you when I stood in front of your door and rang your doorbell for several minutes that morning you left to come here, hoping that you were just sleeping a little too hard. Or maybe that you were making me wait on purpose. Then worried, I went to the office, hoping to see you there, but somehow I knew I wouldn't find you there either. On my way over in the cab, I just knew I wouldn't see you, and it scared the shit out of me that what happened to you six years ago was happening to me this time around.' He paused, licked his lips, eyes searching mine for something. 'So, for what it's worth, Charlie, I'm afraid of losing you. That's not something I want. I hope you know that.'

My lips parted, but no sound came forth. I was surprised that he remembered my words.

After a moment passed, I heard myself ask, 'Why didn't you call me back, William?'

He took another step towards me, and it felt like he was going to reach for me, but decided against it at the last minute. I stood unmoving.

'Can I tell you first what happened after I left the office?'

I nodded.

'I'm assuming you saw my ex?'

I nodded again.

'She's pregnant.'

'I saw.'

'Yeah? Well it shocked the hell out of me.'

He looked away, and I built up the courage to ask what had been on my mind on and off.

'Is it yours then?'

His head snapped back to me, his brows furrowing. 'What?'

'She is pregnant and mayb—'

'No. No, Charlie. No. Is that what you thought?'

'I didn't know what to think. You left without saying anything.'

'It's not mine. It couldn't be mine. We weren't . . . for a long while . . . Doesn't matter. Even when I saw her, I didn't think it was mine.' I moved my gaze away and he reached for my chin, pulling me back to look at him again. Then he let me go, and I felt his loss. 'She is pregnant with her last boyfriend. She was seeing him when we were finalizing our divorce I think. I have no idea. She wanted to talk to me to ask if I'd like to consider starting things back up again. Seeing as I wanted a baby with her, now that she is pregnant she apparently thought maybe I'd like another shot. I told you she was against kids during our marriage and that was one of the biggest reasons we broke up, plus the fact that I couldn't trust her, you remember?'

I dipped my chin.

'She thought now that she is pregnant we could try again. Apparently she broke up with the baby's dad. What do you think I told her?'

'No?' Hope uncurled inside my tattered heart.

The edges of his lips turned up. 'Yeah. I told her no. And that I was seeing somebody. But no, in any case. She was never the one for me. She knows this too, but I'd never seen her as emotional before. I think she is scared to do this alone, but she is afraid to say it out loud. She just saw me as an escape to not to deal with her problems on her own. I got up to leave when I realized the conversation wasn't going anywhere, she started to get agitated and then all of a sudden she was getting cramps.'

I listened silently, taking his words in.

'I had to take her to a hospital and because she has no one in New York I had to stay with her till the morning until one of her friends in Portland could make it to the hospital.'

'She's okay? The baby too?'

'They're fine. Doctors thought it was stress. They explained other stuff, but I wasn't following. She is gonna have to take it easy the next few weeks.'

'You left her there?'

'We don't have anything to say to each other. I'm not the one who will be there for her anymore. I did what I could, the rest is not on me. I have someone else I'd like to be there for.'

I rolled my teeth over my lower lip and his gaze followed the movement.

'I understand,' I muttered. 'You didn't answer your phone. Then it was turned off.'

'My battery died. And at the hospital she was a little . . .' He let out a big sigh. 'Let's just say she couldn't understand how I could turn her away when all I'd wanted to do was have a kid – her words, not mine. I was gonna ask the nurses for a charger, but I was too busy trying to calm Lindsey so she wouldn't risk her baby's health and then it was almost morning.'

I nodded, capable of only doing that. I believed him. I believed everything he was saying.

'What are you thinking?' he asked, tilting his head a little as he tried to catch my gaze.

'I'm not sure,' I responded, truthfully. I couldn't pick just one thing.

'Okay. That's okay. Then the next morning, I go to your house and you aren't there. And I rush to the office to talk to you because I hated how I left things and then Gayle tells me what happened with Kimberly and your dad.'

I let go of the death hold I had on my arm and opened and closed my fingers.

'Long overdue, I guess.'

'You're good?'

I nodded. Again.

'Okay. That's good. I'm sorry for accusing you of working with your sister and sneaking the plan to her. I knew, I knew that wasn't something you'd do, so I don't know what I was thinking. It's not enough, at least not in my eyes, but I'm really sorry for putting you in that position, Charlie. I quit, too.'

That made my gaze jump from the floor back up to him. My eyes big. 'What?'

'You didn't think I'd stay there after I heard how he treated you, did you?' He shook his head. 'I was never gonna stay there after you left anyway, Charlie. I knew it wasn't the place for me. I was always going to follow you. That was the plan, remember?'

I shook my head, taking a step back as if I could run away from his words and what they were doing to my poor heart. 'No. No, that wasn't the plan. The plan was we'd try and see if there was something there until I left and then we'd see where it went.'

He took a step towards me. 'Not my plan, Charlie. I was just going to wait until you caught up with what is between us.'

I took another step back, bumping into a door behind me.

'Does hearing that scare you?'

My brows drew together. 'Why would that scare me?'

He shrugged, stepping up to me. 'You tell me.'

'You don't have to lie to me, William. That wasn't the plan we talked about and we both know it.'

'If I was thrown into a room full of nothing but people, I would always find my way to you. We call to each other, Charlie. Don't you know that? So, yes. I was always going to follow you wherever you go. I knew it the first night I spent sleeping with you in my arms. You're the only one I want. It was the same six years ago, it's the same feeling now. The only difference is I'm smarter now. I wouldn't let you slip through my fingers like that again.'

'William,' I whispered, my voice breaking. 'Don't say things like that to me, please.'

He closed the last inch between us and I had to lift my hand up and place it on his chest so he would . . . so he would let me try and think. He covered my hand with his own and his fingers squeezed mine, his hand warm and familiar.

My head was spinning and my heart . . . my heart was full of hope with his words.

'Would you like more cheese?'

I nodded. I loved cheese. And I loved William.

He pressed his forehead against mine, my body trapped between his and the wall. My eyes closed on their own and he kept speaking.

'My heart is full of you. I wouldn't know what to do with it anymore without you. You can't leave me now. I promise to hold your hand and be there for you and with you for as long as I breathe, Charlie. I want you,' he muttered, a little out of breath even though we were standing motionless. 'I look at you across the room and feel like I'm the luckiest guy for having you look back at me. I'm in love with you. Can't you see it? I want my life to be with you.'

I felt the tears gather behind my eyes, but I tried my best to hold them back. I felt William's hand on my face, gently lifting me up to his gaze. After a few seconds he smiled at something he was seeing. 'I missed you, Charlie.'

Something unravelled inside me and my legs gave out. William didn't let me fall, he picked me up, and I buried my face in the spot between his shoulder and neck, my tears rushing to the surface. I knew he was walking us somewhere, but I didn't have it in me to look or do anything but cry while I was clutching him to me with all the strength I had left.

He gently sat down and arranged me in his lap so I could still keep my face in his neck. He gave me one of the best hugs of my life and drew me to himself. Tight to the point that if he had put on just a little more pressure I'd have felt pain.

'It's okay, baby,' he whispered next to my head. 'I'm here.' He repeated the words over and over again. 'I'm here, Charlie. It's okay. I'm here now. I'm never leaving you again. You will never be alone again. You'll always have me.'

The more he repeated them the tighter I hugged him and the more the tears flowed. 'I'm sorry, William. I'm sorry for leaving like that.'

I don't know how many minutes passed with us holding each other tightly, but I moved my head a little when I felt his warm lips against the skin on my neck.

'I love the way you tilt your head just slightly when I kiss you right here.' He touched the spot he just kissed with the tip of his finger and trailed it down to my collarbone, sending a rush of shivers throughout my entire body. He loosened his arms just slightly, but didn't let me pull myself too far away.

I watched him as he studied me back.

'Do you have anything to say to me?' he asked, his voice a little unsure. I couldn't remember if I ever heard him sound unsure of himself.

I cupped his face in my hands and stared deep into his eyes. 'I'm in love with you, William. And I want you to be mine so badly, I don't know why I was so afraid to say it out loud when you mean so much to me.'

He sighed, his eyes closing. His forehead dropped to my shoulder as he peppered small kisses to my skin.

Then he was staring back. 'I'm already yours. We belong with each other. We both knew it, but it feels good to hear you say it.' He brushed the back of his knuckles on my cheek. 'It's that look in your eyes and your eyes specifically that grabs me by the throat, Charlie. Please, never stop looking at me like this.'

'I hoped you'd come back to me,' I murmured, tears gathering in my eyes again. 'But I wasn't sure if I should even hope because you didn't come. Again. You didn't come. And maybe I overreacted because of that, but I didn't know what else to do.'

'I'm never leaving you again. You'll never have the opportunity to guess. I promise you. I will never find someone like you in a million years. You're all I want.'

'You're in love with me?' I asked, just to make sure and just to hear it again.

He smiled and finally, finally pressed a kiss against my closed lips. I could tell he was smiling. 'I'm so in love with you. So deeply in love with you. I want to give you my whole life, Charlie, if you'll take it.'

I burrowed closer to his body, resting my head next to his.

'You really quit? You won't go back? Your family – do they know? Do you have to go back to New York? Are you going to stay here? *Can you stay here?*'

'I'm staying. I can't let you go for a good while. And I did quit. I paid the amount the contract demanded if I were to quit in the first six months, and left.'

My lips parted, but William stopped me before I could protest.

'Don't even try. I couldn't stay there. Not without you. What I paid doesn't affect me, trust me. My family do know I'm moving back to California. Actually that's why it took me a while to get here. I wanted to go and see them just in case it took me a while to go back. I didn't know how you'd react to seeing me or if you'd take me again. So I went to them with Pepp and then flew in here this morning. I'm staying here. With you.'

I licked my lips and stared at him.

'You're in love with me,' I repeated for the third time.

'Head over heels. And I want us to live together if that's okay with you.'

I smiled. 'You're serious?'

'Why wouldn't I be? I can't get a good night's sleep when you're not sleeping in my arms.'

'I've never lived with a boy before.'

He sighed. 'A man. You're gonna live with a man.' His hands flexed around my waist. 'And good. I'm jealous enough of you as it is. I don't want to imagine you having lived with another guy before. Are you excited?'

I nodded, grinning.

He took me in for a good long while and then it was him asking me, 'You're in love with me too?'

'So utterly in love.' I leaned down and gently kissed his lips, trying to show him just how much. The kiss started slow, just our lips, then I felt the tip of his tongue and we were kissing as if we had been apart for years and this was the first time we were touching each other.

The thirst was unimaginable.

Then I think I moaned and all of a sudden I was under him and his body was over mine. When we stopped, both of us were breathless and his chest was rising and falling even faster than mine. I couldn't remember a single other time I felt the happiness I was feeling in that moment. He brushed my hair away from my face and then moved his hand down our bodies until he was holding my hand, our fingers intertwined.

My heart was drenched in love, there was no other explanation.

'You're the one for me, Charlie. You were always the one, even from the beginning. You're all I need, and you won't ever feel the need to flirt with another guy because you'll have me. I'll banter and argue with you – just to make you happy. Then I'll kiss you senseless and you'll smile at me, just like you're smiling now, and I won't need anything else in life. But we'll never have to *pretend* that we're something because it'll always be *true*. And I promise you, I won't let you die alone while you're choking on your food.' I gasped and he laughed, his fingers flexing around mine and holding tighter. 'It's us from now on. We'll have each other. Always. I won't screw this up, not again. And if by a very thin chance I do, I'll always find my way back to you. In every lifetime. I promise you, I'll make you happy and give you all the cheese. I promise.'

Acknowledgements

Hi. Hello. How was it? Did you enjoy it? It's been a while since we've seen each other, hasn't it? Four years, I believe. That's a very long time. Feels impossible, more than anything else. But here we are. We survived Covid together, lost friendships, gained new ones, went through a break up that hurt us pretty badly, but at least we've had each other. I hope I didn't disappoint you, because that's been a big worry of mine. I hope Charlie and William managed to steal a small piece of your heart. They certainly stole mine. I'm sorry I kept them to myself for as long as I did, but now they are finally ready to keep you company just as they were there for me.

Erin, thank you so much for being with me since the very beginning. I know you must be tired of hearing me talk about my insecurities when it comes to William and Charlie, but thank you so much for always listening to me nonetheless. Hope you're ready for Chloe and Andrew.

Elena, we haven't talked in ages, but I hope you still know how appreciative I am for the time you've given me, Charlie and William. On days where I couldn't find it in me to believe that I'd actually be able to finish their story, your encouragement always kept me going and I'll forever be grateful for this one.

Beth and Shelly, I know how busy you are, but I will never forget how you came to my aid when I needed it the most. Your friendship is one I'll forever be grateful to have. Thank you for being there for me.

Jessica, I'm so happy that you decided to give me a shot and became my agent. It feels so good to know that I have you to hold my hand when I need it. Thank you so much for your guidance. And thank you to everyone at Dijkstra Agency, I feel better knowing I have you guys by my side. Let's hope we'll do beautiful things together.

Molly, I'm so happy to have known and worked with you. And thank you to the entire team at Simon & Schuster UK for giving *Charlie, Love and Clichés* a shot.

But more importantly, thank *you*. My readers. For reading Charlie and William's story. For giving them a shot and for making it to this page. This wouldn't have been my reality without you. I wouldn't have been able to write the stories in my head without your love for my words and your love for me. You have no idea what a difference you guys make. You're definitely the bright sunshine I need in my life and I hope you realize that. I know Charlie is my most vulnerable heroine to date and I love her with all her imperfections, I hope you feel the same way. And I hope you know that you're not alone and that you're the main character in your own story. And if on some days you forget, that's okay. Sometimes I tend to forget too. Thank you for being with me. I will forever cherish your existence.

Don't miss these novels from Ella Maise

Available now...

Simon & Schuster